ALSO BY SHARON GERLACH

Harper & Lyttle Series

Office Politics

The Secret Dreams of Sarah-Jane Quinn

The Devil's Mansion Series

Malakh (novella)

The Wyckham House

Condemned

SHARON GERLACH

BLINK OF AN EYE

RUNNING INK PRESS

A Running Ink Press Novel

Running Ink Press
1419 N Lee St
Spokane WA 99202
www.sharongerlach.com

Acknowledgements

As always, to my wonderful husband, whose belief in my talent is steadfast and unwavering.

To my family, who sacrifices many hours of time spent with me so that I can write.

To my many alpha- and beta-readers and my editor, N. L. Gervasio, who vetted this book and pointed out inconsistencies or plot holes. Any remaining flaws are the fault of yours truly.

And to Cody Tarble, whose long conversations sparked a million possibilities for this post-apocalyptic world and brought to you the truest conclusion of this story.

I have taken gross liberties in many areas of this book: Virology, biology, and genetics – if you're an expert in those fields, please forgive my ignorance and my artistic arrogance in bending reality to my will; the layout of Summit Inn and Summit Pancake House at Snoqualmie Pass in the Cascade Mountains; the hospital in Friday Harbor, San Juan Island; the understructure of the I-90 Vantage Bridge in the Columbia Gorge. Any mistakes or incongruities are my responsibility alone.

Last, but hardly least, a brief section of this book is set on the college campus where I work. I have tweaked the campus to suit my literary needs and made it the epicenter of an apocalyptic event. Likewise, I have decimated my hometown to a burning ruin infested with monsters. I stress again that the artistic arrogance of an author knows no bounds, and I assure all my fellow Spokanites that I have nothing but love for our beautiful city.

July 2154

The end of the world smelled like burning – burning buildings, burning fields. Burning bodies. Smoke hung eternally over the valley, uncontrolled wildfires impregnating the air with an eye-stinging haze and the stench of fire and ash.

This was Mackenzie Bright Runner's world – a world empty of people and full of burning. And monsters.

Today a building blazed a few miles from their settlement and puffed billows of black smoke into the still air. No breeze today; the smoke would hang over the valley, souring clothes and clogging sinuses. And while the Stronghold might know what caught fire, they might never know how it started. Lightning strikes on dry grass were usually the culprit. Sometimes Revenants got into combustible substances that later caught fire, but they couldn't willfully start a blaze themselves. Not enough remained of their logic centers.

One thing she could bet on and be assured she would not have to part with any of her meager personal belongings: it hadn't been started by humans. All the humans in the area lived at the Stronghold. All two thousand thirty-two of them. Well, two thousand thirty-two since her childhood friend Ginny died of cancer.

Civilization ended long before her birth, but the death throes of a planet's population had taken decades and still continued. As she stood where it all began – a college campus eight treacherous miles away from her settlement – she couldn't help but wonder how the world had been before infection wiped out mankind. Couldn't help but wonder if Ginny would still be alive if someone back in the year 2032 had been a little more vigilant and a lot more sensible.

Not satisfied with the meager light from her flashlight, her companion Bon took his own from his pocket and clicked it on. "It's been more than a hundred years since the Upheaval. If he's still alive, by some miracle, what makes you think he's going to help us? Wouldn't he already have if he wanted to?"

Pessimism again. Maybe the heat made him this way; the intensity of the hot summer afternoon held the air in a thick, heavy cloud; even the dust particles disturbed by their passage seemed torpid and reluctant to float. Although, since the day three weeks ago when she first approached him with this insane mission – the day Ginny succumbed to her illness – he had been full of negativity and dire predictions of their imminent and excruciatingly painful deaths at the hands of the most infamous Revenant, the very one they were here to find.

"Legend says he stopped killing as soon as he realized the impact and went into seclusion."

"In the old college building where he used to work?" Bon scoffed. "Where he killed all of his colleagues? For what – sentimental reasons?"

His sarcasm didn't put her off in the slightest. "Legend says he's not like the others, that he's still smart. If he's still smart, he can be reasoned with."

Legend said a lot of things that Bon seemed reluctant to believe, especially about Ren Leonard. And he was likely right: Probably dead ages ago, Leonard was long removed from the devastation his infectious rampage across this campus had brought down upon the entire earth. But the persistence of the legend gave her hope, and she would pursue any hope, however slim, with all she had.

Her boot came down on something that cracked loudly, and she winced. Blown in through the empty frames that once held glass doors, more than a century of autumn leaves and other debris muted the crunch of breaking glass beneath their booted feet but didn't completely disguise it.

"Shouldn't we check to be certain there are no Revenants here before we go any deeper inside?"

She tripped over a rusted metal bar, a remnant from a destroyed desk. The wood had likely been carted off to be burned against the chill of a long-forgotten winter. A solid block in front of her checked her headlong flight to the floor, her impact causing a dull clang inside it.

"Will you be quiet?"

"What does it matter? If there are any inside, they already know we're here. They can smell us. What the hell is this?" She shone her flashlight at the box in front of her. Metal sides, streaked with dust and dirt; open front that might once have held glass; eight rows of widely-spaced rusted metal coils, five to a row.

Bon trekked back to her. "We don't have time for this, Mac. The lights will only last so long. We have to get back to the Stronghold before dark." He looked at the metal box illuminated in her beam. "I think that's what they called a vending machine. I heard one of the elders talking about them."

"What were they for?" She reached inside and twanged one of the coils. It thunked dully, and a puff of rust drifted lazily to the floor of the box.

"Snacks, Louis said. You could get snacks from them. Treats. You know, like cookies and crackers and things. They used to be made by factories and sold in big marketplaces."

Mac marveled at this for a moment before allowing Bon to lead her away. The Stronghold boasted a "marketplace," where all scavenged items were turned in and distributed as needed. As gatherers, she and Bon helped keep the Market full of food, clothes, solar-powered devices, blankets – even livestock, when any could be found or caught. The Stronghold's farm section, a decent distance from the living quarters, housed the livestock: chickens, geese, goats, cows, pigs, and a few sheep. They didn't find animals very often; the Revenants usually made meals of them before the humans even knew they were there.

It was a dangerous job; the gatherers had to venture into dark buildings where any number of Revenants could be hiding. She'd only been scavenging for six months after having been assigned to Bon for training a year and a half ago. The only job more treacherous was that of the hunters, who actively sought the Revenants to dispatch them and decrease their numbers. If the Revenant population could be controlled or eradicated, the survivors of the Upheaval would be able to begin rebuilding the industries that had once made life easier, more comfortable, and longer.

To maximize the light, Bon aimed his beam at the wall so it lit the wide hallway. The reflected light tipped the spikes of his dark hair, making them look like tiny frosted stalagmites jabbing out of his skull. A gloomy cavern ahead signaled an intersecting hallway. He tucked Mac behind him; she didn't protest. Bon had more experience in combat.

They approached cautiously, in combat formation: Bon hunched down against the wall and slightly ahead, the flashlight pointing behind him at the floor, and Mac a few paces behind and a couple of steps from the wall.

Bon started the countdown: three fingers held down near his thigh. Mac opened her mouth to breathe so she wouldn't miss any furtive sounds of a Revenant because of the whistling in her stuffy nose, the remainder of a summer cold that had taken her off gathering duty the last couple of weeks.

Two.

She tightened her grip on her black-bladed machete, which she'd named Black Jack, ready to skewer a charging Revenant when Bon rolled out of the way.

One.

He stabbed his flashlight around the corner into the dark hallway and ducked down.

Silence.

Bon repeated the action: thrusting his flashlight into the hallway and jerking it back. Still nothing. Mac relaxed a little.

"It's safe," Bon whispered over his shoulder.

Mac closed the gap between them as he stepped into the dark intersection and swung his beam down the hallway to see if there might be anything worth scavenging.

A white face loomed out of the darkness. Dark blotches scuttled under the skin's surface in the ebb and flow of a noxious tide. Black irises swam on a sea of bloodshot white, rimmed with an incongruous sky blue.

Bon let out a startled yell and scuttled backward, flinging up his machete in a wild arc. There wasn't time to raise hers; in the split second they were given to react, the Revenant was upon them, moving with exceptional speed. A hand at each of their throats drove them backward into the wall.

"Give me one good reason why I shouldn't eat you."

The Revenant showed signs of cognizance, a modicum of self-control, and a hideous anger management problem.

They had found Ren Leonard.

Bon dropped his machete and the flashlight, which clattered as it fell among the debris of the floor, the beam aimed up at the Revenant.

Splotches of black oozed across its face. Or perhaps it was just that Mackenzie couldn't breathe and the spots were in her vision. She clutched at the hand around her throat but didn't dare claw at it; she hadn't worn her gloves. If her nails broke through its skin, she risked contamination.

"...*please...*" She hit at its fingers, feeling the squish of rotting flesh beneath skin. With the next strike, the flesh firmed. It held no heat; her throat burned from the ice of its touch.

The snarling face pressed closer. Black-and-scarlet eyes bore into hers, their blue rings glowing as though lit from behind. Bon squeaked a protest. The pressure eased on Mackenzie's throat.

"Speak, girl."

She hitched in a breath and broke into a hacking cough. Damn cold. Damn Revenant. She'd never sleep through the night now, not with the coughing and the nightmares that were sure to come.

"I'll give you five minutes before I eat you. You're wasting time."

Bon's blue eyes, slightly bugged as he struggled for air, pleaded with her silently.

"Help." She wheezed, hacked until she choked, and finally gained enough control to spit out a fragment of a sentence. "Came for your help."

Leonard jerked in surprise and drew away, easing his grip on her throat just a fraction more. She sucked in precious air and then wished she hadn't. His rank stench filled the air, thick with rotting flesh and blood. After the first startled seconds, he began to laugh, his breath washing over her face. She gagged at the sickly-sweet stink of decomposition.

He let them go. Mac's feet touched ground but she didn't keep her footing. She crumpled to a heap, wedged between the wall and the vending machine. Bon crashed onto the debris-strewn floor and dragged himself to her, planting himself in front of her, a protective barrier somewhat diminished as his starving lungs dragged air in shuddering gasps.

Leonard's laughter broke off abruptly. "You were foolish to come here. I help no one. You wasted your lives."

Bon threw his arms wide, although neither of them stood a chance if Leonard decided to attack. They'd be slaughtered before they even registered that he'd moved. Mac struggled to see around Bon's head, trying to catch Leonard's gaze again. Finally, she dug the pointed bone of her chin into his trapezius muscle. He let out a squawk and flinched away.

"You could at least listen to us before you kill us. It's hardly fair to slaughter us out of hand. We might be able to come to a mutually beneficial arrangement."

"Beneficial?" Leonard's voice grated like massive stones scraping against one another. It was impossible to tell if it held any emotion, but she thought – prayed – there was a glimmer of interest in its tone. "Beneficial how? What can you give *me*, who has it all – looks, fame, immortality?"

Yep, there was emotion, all right: rancor. Not helpful at all.

"Mercy," she offered quietly.

Bon whipped around, stunned, wary. They hadn't discussed this. In fact, deals with Revenants were extraordinarily unwise and the Stronghold's elders strictly forbade bargaining with them; the creatures' animalistic temperaments made it impossible for them to honor agreements. But they were desperate, getting more desperate every day, and what great reward ever came without great risk?

Leonard loomed closer again. Grey-black lips froze in a twisted snarl, curling back from the pointed, yellow teeth of a meat-eating predator.

Bon trembled against her but stood – or, rather, sat – his ground. Two blotched hands reached down. Filthy nails like eagle talons scraped across her shirt, and then she was yanked to her feet and released.

"You." Leonard pinned her with his ringed eyes. "You interest me. But you"—and Bon was lifted and slammed into the wall once more, his feet dangling several inches from the floor—"have the potential to really piss me off. Keep your mouth shut, eh? And get that damned light out of my face."

Light of any kind bothered the Revenants, made their skin blotch and burn and flooded their permanently dilated eyes with so much light they were literally blinded. Spearing a Revenant with a flashlight beam in a dark place was guaranteed to make it charge in a snapping, snarling frenzy.

Bon scrambled over debris and snatched up the light. The beam hit Ren Leonard full in the eyes once more and then lit the

6

floor, casting his face into shadow.

"Come with me," Leonard growled.

"Where?" Bon demanded immediately, stiff with suspicion.

Leonard loomed over him, glaring, and directed his answer at Mac. "It's not safe to stay too close to the doors for too long. There are Revenants who think a little sunburn is worth a substantial meal – not that you two scrawny chickens are worth the risk of coming in here."

"Risk? What do you mean?" Bon again, pushing his luck. Mac wished he would just shut up. They came here for Ren Leonard's help. Pissing him off wasn't likely to gain it.

Leonard stalked toward Bon, his stride violent and angry. Well, everything pissed off a Revenant, so that wasn't alarming in itself. But Leonard simply passed by Bon and headed deeper into the building. After only a second's hesitation, Mac retrieved Black Jack and followed, snagging Bon by the sleeve and dragging him after her. He didn't resist, but she heard him stealthily retrieve his own machete from the floor. Ren Leonard might not be your typical Revenant, but it was still abject stupidity to let down their guard.

Leonard stopped at the bottom of an iron rack leading upward into muted sunlight. It took Mac a moment to realize it was the skeleton of a staircase. The concrete treads had crumbled away long ago and the iron was infected with a virulent crop of rust, but it looked sturdy enough.

"Will that hold us?" Bon asked dubiously.

"It'll do for the trip up and the trip back down." Leonard shot Bon a look that clearly said, *If you survive long enough to take the trip back down.* To Mac, he said, "I used to paint it with this stuff called Rustoleum. Can't get it now; you people don't make it anymore."

"Whose fault is that?" Bon retorted. Mac closed her eyes. *Shut up, shut up, shut up!*

Leonard neither responded nor killed Bon. He simply started up the clanging stairs, leaving them to follow on their own. Mac elbowed Bon sharply in the ribs.

"What are you doing?" she hissed angrily. "If you keep needling him, he won't help us!"

"What am *I* doing? The question is, what are *you* doing? We came to ask for his help with intelligence. You waltz in and offer him a mercy killing."

7

"Well, he didn't kill me for it, did he? And you can't expect him to help us without offering him something in return."

"Something usually doesn't encompass killing the person helping you."

"Unless it's what they seek."

"Where on earth did you get an idea like that? You can't possibly know what he's seeking. A good meal is more likely, and we just provided him with two."

Mac huffed out an impatient breath. "Can we just go up and talk to him? He didn't kill us, so let's see this through. Stop being so pessimistic."

"In case you hadn't noticed, Mackenzie, there is no optimism left in this world. And walking into the den of a Revenant isn't optimism. It's insanity."

"Yet here you are with me."

He bristled. "I wasn't about to let you walk into this with no defense. What kind of person do you think I am?"

"That," she said firmly, "we can discuss later. But I'd like to remind you that you agreed to do this, and you came here with me instead of turning me in to the elders. Now I'd like to—"

"*I'd* like to get out of this sunlight and hear your insane plan so I can be rid of you that much sooner," Leonard's voice growled down the stairs. "Are you coming up or are you leaving?"

With one last determined look at Bon, Mackenzie clambered up the steps into sunlight, hesitant steps behind her assuring her that Bon followed.

She expected debris and filth. What he offered was a mostly empty room, the floor swept clean, with an aging leather sofa near a window that let in murky sunlight. In a dim, dark corner, she thought she could detect the outline of a chair.

"Nice," she approved. "How do you keep the mice out of the cushions?"

"Mice don't come in here. Sit down and spit it out so you can be on your way."

He held an arm over his eyes and marched through the sunlight to the chair, which creaked under his weight. Mackenzie followed him, squinting. The cushion beside her dipped when Bon sat down, but she couldn't see him. Sunspots blinded her until her eyes adjusted to the darkness below the window, and finally she could see Ren Leonard hunched in his chair, his unblinking stare quite unnerving.

"Well, as I said, we came for help."

"I got that part already." Impatience roughened his voice to a snarl. "I also got the part where you were going to ask me for intelligence, which it's obvious you sorely need."

Bon said coldly, "We meant information, not IQ."

"You could use both, boy. Now shut up and let the girl speak."

Mac cleared her throat nervously. "Things are really bad and getting worse. We're running out of medical supplies, fuel, and—"

Leonard cut in rudely. "And your name is…?"

Mac gaped blankly for a second, derailed by his interruption. "I'm Mackenzie Bright Runner. This is Bonfils Moreau."

Leonard burst into laughter. "Is that right? Well, what do you think of your island now, *docteur*?"

Mac exchanged an apprehensive look with Bon. She didn't know what Leonard was talking about. The Revenant laughed for a few seconds longer, and then he seemed to realize they weren't laughing with him.

"That's a little out of your frame of reference, I guess. It was a movie about a doctor with a lab on an island. He created a bunch of human-animal hybrids and eventually one of them killed him. His name was Moreau."

"Movie?" Bon repeated, puzzled.

"Motion picture. Surely you've seen a motion picture."

Mac suddenly understood. "I remember Gerald talking about them. We don't have electricity, so no one has seen a motion picture for…how long, Bon? Maybe fifty years?"

"Or longer."

"More than fifty years," Leonard murmured speculatively. "Isn't that something? Hollywood would be devastated." A little louder, he said, "Bright Runner? Native American?"

"Once upon a time. There is no America anymore, Mr. Leonard." He was silent, and she ventured timidly, "Didn't you know that?"

"There will always be America, no matter what pansy-ass politician gets elected to the White House. The day they dragged that gutless son-of-a-bitch out on the White House lawn and ate him was a good day for all of humanity. What's left of it."

"You would have ordered the airstrikes?" Bon demanded, a little aggressively.

"Airstrikes and more, boy."

"There were uninfected citizens who would have been killed."

"And now the whole world is killed instead. Yeah, I'd have nuked this place until you could see the glow from outer space. Sacrifice a little corner of the country for the sake of the entire world."

"I'm sure it was hard to think in those terms while it was all happening," Mac said.

"Never hesitate in war, girl. And it was war, no mistake. You said you're running out of fuel. What do you use now?"

She blinked at the sudden change in topic. "Wood for heat, sir. Gasoline is hard to come by and used for the few vehicles we have. And we don't use those often."

"You wander around on foot? You guys really *do* need intelligence. Haven't you heard of bicycles?"

"The cycles are mostly useless now because it's hard to find parts and tires. There are a few left, but the hunters use them."

"Hunters?"

"The hunters scout out areas, clear them of Revenants so the gatherers can retrieve supplies. Sometimes they have to go pretty far afield, so they get the bicycles."

"Hunters and gatherers," Leonard muttered. "We're back in the Middle-fucking-Ages."

Bon snorted. "Worse than the Middle Ages, thanks to you. They didn't have monsters trying to eat them every step of the way."

"Shit for brains," Leonard growled to himself. "I should have eaten you. Wood," he barked at Mackenzie, who jumped. "There's plenty of it now, especially after a century free of clear-cut logging. No danger of running out. No goddamn tree-huggers to protest cutting 'em down. What's the problem?"

"It takes a long time to be able to cut the trees and haul them out of the woods. There are only so many daylight hours. We can't be in the forest after dark; the Revenants come. As it is, we must use one worker as a lookout because sometimes the Revenants will attack in daylight. The sun is not, you know, as bright in the woods as it is outside them."

10

"You came to ask me to be your jolly logger?" Anger boiled up in his tone.

Alarmed, Mac pressed herself back in her seat as far as she could. She itched all over as her body hair tried to stand at attention under her clothes. From the corner of her eye, she saw Bon's hand tighten on his machete.

"No. If you'll let me finish what I was saying before you asked my name...?" She quirked a brow at him. He glowered at her, muttered what sounded like a curse under his breath, and inclined his head.

"As I mentioned, we're running out of gas and oil, not just easy-access wood, as well as food, medical supplies, everything. Our situation is desperate."

"Of course it is. Welcome to the—" He paused. "What century is it?"

"Twenty-second." Bon sneered a little as he answered.

"It's not like we have newspapers anymore, boy. Twenty-second century. I'll be damned. Well, no one said it would be pretty. No one said it would be easy."

"It?"

"The end of the world, Mackenzie Bright Runner. What do you think is happening? The infected have overrun the world. Their numbers more or less stay the same while yours decrease in turn. When there are no more humans, the infected will likely turn on each other."

"Let me guess," Bon cut in, failing to entirely mask his derision. "Until there's only one standing."

"There can be only one, after all," Leonard said and grated out a laugh. Mac didn't understand this reference any more than she understood his reference to Moreau. "No, it would be idiocy to think the world will belong to just one lone Revenant. They will be scattered across the world, but there will only be a handful. A fraction of a fraction of a percent of the world's former population."

Bon pressed his point. "You're talking the end of humanity, not the end of the world. There will still be plant and animal life. The world will go on, just without humans in the equation."

"Oh, fabulous - the damn Zero Populationists are still among the living."

"The what?"

11

"Never mind. Now you've told me your problem. Your circumstances are dire, blah blah blah. Now enlighten me on why I should give a damn."

Bon popped out of his chair. "You ended the world. Now you owe it your help."

"*I* ended the world?"

Mac said, "Surely you know you're called the Father of the Apocalypse." Perhaps he didn't. He'd killed for a solid decade before mastering the compulsion, after all. By then, the media was just a memory.

"Who came up with that gem? No, let me guess. Those fuckers at MSNBC."

Mac didn't know who coined the term. She also didn't know who MSNBC was. It didn't matter.

She said quietly, "You *do* owe the world. You mastered the compulsion to kill and stopped doing it. Now you can help us drag ourselves out of the abyss."

"*OWE!*" Leonard roared, furious. "*I OWE NOTHING!*"

He was upon them in an instant. One hand slammed down on Bon's machete hand, the other on Mac's. Her heart hammered frantically. Oh, Bon was right; it was a mistake coming here.

And now it was too late.

Bon shrank away from the Revenant, scrambling backward as far as his pinned hand would allow, attempting to escape over the back of the sofa. Mackenzie simply closed her eyes, waiting for teeth to find her throat, wondering if dying would hurt any worse than this hopeless existence.

"It didn't start with me, but Father of the Apocalypse, am I?" Her eyes popped open when he leaned in close, his blue-ringed eyes blazing. His foul breath hit her nose like a hammer, a miasma of death she couldn't escape.

He was no longer shouting, but his voiced rumbled angrily from his chest, the growl of a predator deciding whether or not to kill. "Let me tell you about my last day as a human. I graded papers and taught my classes. I went to a faculty meeting and listened to that useless dipwad Jay Fuller bitch about having to teach a class of twenty-five instead of twenty, which would be so much *easier*, as though he were owed a ride on Easy Street.

"Then everyone went home and I stayed to clean the pig sty of a break room. Some weird dude used a rock to break into the building, heard me in the break room, and attacked. I killed him with a carving knife. His blood fell into my eye, and here I am today, listening to you tell me how *I'm* the 'Father of the Apocalypse' and to blame for all the shit in the world and that I *owe*.

"Well, screw you, Mackenzie Bright Runner. Screw you to hell and back. I don't give a damn if you don't have fuel, or if you don't have food, or if you don't have a goddamned Band-Aid. I don't have a *life*, so why the fuck should I care if you're staring down death?"

He withdrew as suddenly as he had attacked, sinking back into his chair. Bon made it over the back of the sofa, where he crouched, trying to pull Mac with him. Too afraid to open her eyes, not daring to believe they were still alive, she sat shaking as silence crept into the room.

A long while later, as Bon inched his way back around the sofa to sit by her, his machete at the ready to fend off another attack, Leonard continued.

"It took me a year to figure out I could control the violence. It took another two to learn what infected me."

"The old news reports say it was a virus that escaped a laboratory."

"Oh, thank you, Hollywood," Leonard muttered in disgust. "Movies and books always blamed a secret lab – private or government, didn't matter – for their end-of-the-world scenarios. The truth of the matter is no lab came up with what hit this old world."

"Are you going to tell us or what?" Bon tried to sound defiant, but the effect was ruined by his shaking voice.

"I may still eat you, scrawny chicken, so watch your tone. It was Mother Nature at her finest."

Three seconds of silence ticked by before Mac could find her voice. "The Revenant Virus is a naturally occurring disease?"

Though much of the texts of the Upheaval period were lost to them, either because they disintegrated over time or were inaccessible because of distance, Mac knew that the Revenant Virus was suspected to be a man-made mutation of two viruses that, for unknown reasons, bonded and caused the mutation of the human genetic code. One virus caused rapid decomposition and the other super-fast healing. You could watch a Revenant literally decompose and heal within a second — that was, if you stayed alive long enough. If you were that close to one, you were in some serious shit.

The mutated virus did more than cause physical disfigurement. It produced an extreme electrical reaction in the amygdala, the almond-shaped part of the temporal lobe that served as the processing center for memories, emotions, and cognitive faculties. At the same time, the virus destroyed the hypothalamus, that great regulator of hunger, thirst, and attachment behaviors. As the hypothalamus failed, hunger consumed the infected and human life lost all value. With the amygdala super-charged with energy, the victim literally possessed no emotional control or decision-making abilities. Hunger and rage became the ruling factors of the mutated genetic code.

"Doesn't really matter now, does it, Mackenzie Bright Runner? Humanity is on the verge of extinction. The factors that brought it there are irrelevant."

"I wouldn't say irrelevant. We need to know what to avoid, what to watch out for in the future."

"There is no future," Bon said. "We have less every year, and this asshole isn't going to help us. We might as well go back to the Stronghold and find some other way."

"You still haven't told me what you want me to do. Not that I'm going to do it. I have to admit, though, it took guts for you to come here, knowing I could just as easily eat you as listen to you."

"You haven't killed humans in a very long time," Mac pointed out. "And if you were going to kill us, you'd have done it by now."

"And how do you know this?"

"Legend."

Leonard rocked forward in his chair, leaning his elbows on his knees and bringing his face out of the darkest shadows. Mackenzie could just see the splotches of black puddle and then vanish beneath his waxy skin.

"Funny thing about legends, Bright Runner. They don't always tell you everything."

"Yeah," Bon interjected. "Like they failed to mention you're a self-serving, sarcastic bastard. Mackenzie, we have to go. We've already stayed too long, and it's going to be nearing dusk when we reach the Stronghold. We're pushing our luck."

Leonard waved an airy hand. "Yes, by all means, abort the mission when you've barely even engaged the target. I can see why you're a gatherer and not a hunter."

Bon stood, anger flattening his mouth. "I'm going, Mac. Are you coming with me, or do I have to figure out some sort of excuse as to why you're not with me when I get back to the Stronghold?"

"Sit down, dipshit," Leonard growled. "You won't get eight steps out the door you came in through. The sun is sinking behind the trees, and the Revenants will be out all over campus, keeping to the shade. You're stuck here for the night."

Ah, hell. Mac slumped in her seat. The Stronghold would be frantic as the sun disappeared, and then they would be resigned. By dawn, they'd assume the worst and would start making plans to break up an experienced gathering team to pair them with novices. The elders didn't let the grass grow under any situation, and sorrow because of any emotional attachment was tempered by logic and necessity. The post-Upheaval world was a harsh one, lacking sentimentality and romanticism.

"You could have told us instead of letting us waste so much of our time!" Bon took an aggressive step toward Leonard, remembered what happened last time, and backed down. He went to the window instead and peered through the grime at the late afternoon sun.

"You came here for a purpose. I assume you didn't think that purpose would be accomplished in a few minutes, conveniently allowing you sufficient time to return home before dark."

Bon lifted a grudging shoulder. Mac simply shook her head.

"And your elders – I expect they understood this as well and won't be alarmed that you don't return today. Won't they assume you found a place to hole up? After all, there was no guarantee that you'd find me here. I'm *not* always here, you know."

Mac couldn't find words. Bon apparently couldn't, either, for he turned back to the window and rubbed his sleeve over it, trying to clean a spot well enough that he could see through it.

"Ah, I see," said Leonard after a moment. "They don't know you came to find me."

"They wouldn't understand," Mac burst out. "They would have forbidden it. We don't make deals with Revenants, even if we could talk to one long enough before it killed us or we killed it. It's been tried in the past, and the Revenants just aren't able to hold to any agreements."

"What makes you think I'm any different?"

"Nothing but legend." Bon ceased his futile attempt to clean a spot on the window; the grime was mostly on the outside, and the window didn't open.

"Well, you've got all night to test your theory." When neither replied, he gestured toward their packs. "I'm sure you brought food and water. Go ahead and eat, and then spit out your your demands so you can get some sleep."

"And what will *you* be eating?" Bon sneered, while Mac wondered if she would be able to eat with Leonard's stench in her nose.

"You, if you continue to be a rude little shit. While you eat, I'll go and discourage any others from coming in here."

Mac wondered if she'd been that transparent, but thought it rude to ask – she didn't want him to consider eating her like he was still considering eating Bon.

"How will you do that?"

"Scare 'em off. They've learned not to come in when I'm here, but the smell of two humans may be more than they can resist. Many won't come in when I'm *not* here, because they know what happens when I come back."

Mac sent him a questioning look, and he elaborated by drawing a blotchy finger across his blotchy throat. Then he rose from his chair and headed toward the iron staircase, where he paused just out of the sunlight. She couldn't see him clearly, but she was sure he was looking at her.

"Legend was wrong, Mackenzie Bright Runner. I'm no fucking martyr, and I'm not a vegetarian. I *do* still kill humans. I'm just more judicious about which ones."

His chilling words paralyzed her. She made a fatal mistake coming to him, putting her faith in legend. Judging from how he reacted when he'd thought they wanted his help logging, he would hear them out, refuse their request, and then kill them. Judiciously, of course.

After a while, she opened her pack, took out some strips of dried meat and a few small plums, and ate her last meal.

"He's going to kill us."

"Eat while he's gone, Bon."

"Why bother? Didn't you hear me? He's going to kill us. He deliberately kept us here until it was too late to leave. He never gave a damn about our mission. We're just two meals that delivered themselves to him."

"I heard Gerald talking about how people used to have food delivered to them. That must've been something, not having to run it to ground and drag it back to the Stronghold before dark."

"Mac, are you listening to me? *He. Is. Going. To. Kill. Us.*"

"Then you should eat, Bon. No one should die on an empty stomach."

He said a vulgar word and turned back to the window. The golden afternoon light gave way to soft blue twilight. Mac loved this time of day, when gold colored the horizon, fading to light blue and then darker blue as you looked higher up. Try as she might, she could never quite discern the lines of demarcation between the colors.

Bon rustled in his pack and then sat beside her, chewing on a strip of dried meat. She reached for his hand, but he yanked it away and tucked it into his armpit, out of her reach. She couldn't blame him. She'd killed them both.

"I've been thinking about the virus," she said after a while.

"What about it?"

"Ren Leonard is different than the other Revenants. I think I know why."

He scoffed. "Are you a scientist now?"

"No, just a thinker."

He let the silence fill the space between them again. She didn't need him to speak to know that he thought her penchant for thinking would be the death of them, and soon.

"He doesn't have as many blotches under the skin as other Revenants do."

"Maybe he just stays out of the sun more."

Sunlight accelerated decomposition in the infected, making it harder for the healing side of the virus to do its work. Once the sun did damage, it was permanent, leaving large black areas of decomposition that never went away.

Early on in the Upheaval, many survivors had tried staking Revenants out in the sunlight. The tactic worked – the Revenants died, almost fully decomposed by the time the sun went down, the damage far beyond what the healing of the virus could fix. But staking came with the nasty side effect of enraging the other Revenants in the pack. The survivors quickly learned that it was better to kill them quickly and from a distance, if possible. Up close and personal – like Bon and she were now – was a very bad idea.

"For what it's worth, I'm sorry."

Bon drew in a deep breath and let it out slowly. It seemed his anger went with it, for his voice was gentle and subdued. "It's not your fault. I agreed to come with you. I knew the risks."

They finished their meal without further discussion. Bon was going to eat all his provisions, but Mac made him save some for morning, just in case they were still alive to want breakfast. The room had fallen into shadows and the moon had yet to make its way to this side of the building. They sat in the darkness until they heard steps on the iron staircase. Bon risked a moment with his flashlight, motioning Mac to keep Black Jack and her flashlight at the ready. They moved behind the sofa, standing on either side of the window to keep from being silhouetted.

The scrape of a step on the dusty tile floor, and then a grating laugh.

"You two are so paranoid."

Leonard. Mac slumped against the wall in relief and then remembered that he was probably going to kill them. "What took you so long?"

"I got my lantern. I keep it up on the roof during the day. It's solar and the storage battery is starting to get a bit finicky, but it works and will last longer than your flashlights. Turn them off."

The lantern flared to blazing light and then dimmed, casting a warm glow around the room. Leonard didn't flinch away from this light as he did sunlight, although he did squint as it flooded his dilated pupils. Mac stowed her flashlight in her pack; Bon tucked his in the waistband of his pants.

"Why do you keep a lantern? I thought Revenants could see in the dark." Bon, challenging again.

"Perhaps I simply don't like the dark. You were about to tell me why you think I'm different than other Revenants."

"The Revenants we come across now don't seem to have retained their higher thinking. They're more animalistic. The decomposition beneath the skin is also more advanced."

"And why do you think that is?"

"It's just speculation, not anything I can prove," Mac said, a blush heating her cheeks. "But it seems that the infection in them is...I don't know...less *pure*, maybe?"

"Pure?" Leonard and Bon said together, incredulous.

The heat in her cheeks became painful. "I said it was just speculation. But maybe it's like the 'flu and mutates. Say you got a dose of the original, or close to the original. And say the virus mutates with every generation. The Revenants you created have created more, and each generation loses what you managed to retain."

"And what happened to the ones I created? If your theory is correct, they'd still be out there somewhere. I haven't seen any sign of it."

"Sometimes we come across one who has more of a grip on itself than most of the others. Perhaps they're not as mutated," Bon mused.

"All right," Leonard growled, more or less agreeably. "Say you're right. It doesn't explain why you came to me for help. I've been hunted for more than a hundred years by your kind; why should I help you?"

"Why not give your life some purpose?" Mac suggested. "You lurk in here in the building where you killed a bunch of your colleagues and students when you could be anywhere else. So it seems to me like you still have a connection to your former self, maybe some guilt over what happened. You can't deny your being infected was the epicenter of the worldwide disaster that followed."

"So you think coming in here blaming me for being infected and starting the end of the world is going to convince me to help you do whatever it is you want me to help you do. You're a piece of work, kid."

"I'm not blaming. You didn't ask to be infected; it's hardly fair

21

of people to lay blame. I'm just trying to illustrate your differences from most other Revenants."

"What does it matter? I'm still infected."

This was getting them nowhere, so Mac abandoned her attempt to explain why she thought he might help them and moved on to *how* he could help them.

"We waste days scouting locations to determine how many infected we'll have to eliminate, then we spend days clearing them. By the time we get the supplies – if there are any left – we're barely, if at all, replacing what we used in the Stronghold in the interim. We're constantly losing ground, making do with less and less."

She turned to the window, peering out through the dust at the deep blue dusk. "Overnight travel is too dangerous; travelers would be walking into an unknown situation. No way to determine how many Revenants are there, whether they would be outnumbered in an attack, whether there's secure shelter. If people don't come back, we lose them, the vehicle and the fuel, and gain nothing."

Behind her, both Ren Leonard and Bon were quiet. Bon's breath rasped in and out, his mouth slightly open as he tried not to suck in the stench of the building through his nose. The stench of Ren Leonard. What must it be like to live for more than a century with no end in sight, knowing your body was in constant shift from dying to healing to dying again, knowing that if you came across those who were everything you once were, they would kill you, holding their noses and grimacing in disgust? Was death a distant hope, unattainable except through horrific accident or horrific murder, a constant prayer for mercy to a God grown deaf to your suffering?

It probably didn't matter to most Revenants. They were either too steeped in killing to have retained any sense of humanity or too mutated to be anything more than animals. But Ren Leonard had held onto something of his *self*, retained more than a scrap of his humanity. She couldn't know what he desired, but in his place, she knew she would be praying for death. For mercy. And would welcome it, no matter if it came suddenly and unexpectedly or came in the form of a seventeen-year-old human offering relief in exchange for the hope of survival.

"People are dying of infections, of injuries. It's a struggle to grow enough plants for food, let alone for medicines. We have herbal guides, but rarely the supplies to make the remedies."

"People are always dying," Leonard said, his gravelly voice a jarring note in the soft velvet of nightfall. And then, knowingly, a bit sardonically, "Ah, I see. You lost someone recently. Inspired you to be noble."

"A childhood friend. Ginny. Cancer took her three weeks ago."

Did she dare tell him that as she lay on her bed after Ginny died, she had cursed him? She stared at the ceiling until it grew too dark to see, then stared unseeing into the darkness, her eyes dry, her heart and mind racing at breakneck pace, and she cursed him, savagely wishing to hunt him down and put him in harness, a small step toward reparation for what his infection-fueled rampage had done to the world.

Her wish became an idea, and she took it to Bon, who promptly refused. So she devised a rudimentary plan and prepared to give him the slip one day soon, after enough time elapsed to make him think she had abandoned the idea.

Bon did not underestimate her, and his instincts were shrewd. On the eve of the day she planned to sneak away, he capitulated with the condition that, being more experienced, he called the shots. And she allowed him to, all the way up to the moment Ren Leonard pinned them to the wall downstairs.

Leonard said, "People die, more are born, and so turns the world."

"I want to them to live, Ren. *I* want to live, not just exist. I want..."

When it became apparent she wasn't going to complete her sentence, he prodded, "You want...?"

"I want to relax. I don't want to always be on guard, expecting a mortal fight around every corner. I want to feel like I'm accomplishing something for my settlement, not just making a futile attempt to stop our constant slide into worse conditions."

"And you think I can help with all this somehow, in exchange for you killing me." His sarcasm was not lost on her.

"Only if you want it."

"And if I don't?"

Of course. She should have expected this. If she had been talking to anyone else, Mac might have been tempted to con her way through this, to talk a circuitous route around the topic and never really touch on it, never promise anything. But Ren Leonard was sharp, and she was certain that he would not be impressed with nonsense. In fact, he was likely to repay bullshit with a swift and painful death.

"I don't have an alternate offer," she admitted, finally turning to look at him.

They regarded each other for a long moment. Were her eyes as strange to him as his were to her? Long under the curse of the Revenant Virus, was he still able to read the heart and soul in a human's eyes? Or did hers, the whites clear of the fiery red blood from burst capillaries and the brown irises ringed in a deep forest green rather than Revenant blue, strike resentment in him at all that had been stolen from him?

Finally he growled, "You suck at negotiating, Bright Runner."

"Why do you think I'm a gatherer?" She left the window and rounded the sofa, perching on the edge of the cushion. "You could help us by scouting out locations, giving us intel on how many Revenants we're going to have to clear, whether there are supplies worth going after. If we know what we're walking into, we can plan our excursions more effectively, bring more supplies home, maybe gain some ground. And if we know where the Revenants are most heavily concentrated, we might be able to take out a large number of them in one fell swoop and make the area a little safer."

"You forget one thing." His rough voice was dangerously quiet. "The Revenants are my people."

A chill walked over Mackenzie's skin. Oh boy. She hadn't considered that he might harbor a strange paternal sense about the Revenants. His reclusion seemed to indicate abhorrence.

"They attack without provocation. We defend ourselves."

He leaned forward again, his hands bridged between his knees. The posture was so human that for a moment Mac was fascinated. He was so different than the Revenants they came across while gathering.

"Consider for a moment, Mackenzie Bright Runner, the scenario I posed earlier."

"The dismal one where the Revenants inherit the world?" she said pointedly.

"That very one. Perhaps young Bonfils Moreau here has the

right idea. Maybe it's time for the humans to pass from existence. If evolution is to be believed, an intelligent, dominant species will eventually rise and will, perhaps, be better deserving of this planet."

A swell of indignation swamped her caution. "Well, you know, the whole of humanity didn't ask for this virus to wipe out civilization. All humans weren't wasteful and selfish and destructive. There were wonderful people, beautiful things, life-saving medicines, technology that delivered heat and emergency help and a hot cup of friggin' coffee when you needed one. Maybe you're so bitter that you think existence is futile, but I'm not."

Leonard sat back in his chair, his impassive expression provoking Mac's anger. She thumped herself in the chest emphatically.

"I'm *not*."

After a moment, he rose, grabbed his chair, and hauled it over to the top of the stair case, where he placed it so that anything attempting to come up the stairs would have to pass him first.

"Sleep. I'll keep watch. And in the morning, I'll make sure the way is clear for you to leave safely."

That was that. A failed mission, wasted time, and tomorrow she and Bon would go back to a desperate existence. She hadn't let herself consider failure when they planned this, so it left a sour taste in her mouth.

She held Ren Leonard's gaze for what seemed an eternity before she leaned her head against the back of the sofa and closed her eyes. The cushion dipped beside her, and Bon's hand covered hers. The scrape of his dry, callused skin on hers was oddly comforting. The hush of the dead world was a bittersweet lullaby, and she fell asleep with the taste of her soul's despairing tears on her tongue.

Mackenzie woke when her dream of suffocating became reality. She bolted awake, but the darkness in the room was so absolute that she was virtually blind. Her fingers scrabbled across the back of the hand over her mouth, but she kept her fingernails brutally short, so all she could manage was to dig the bony tips of each digit into resistant flesh.

A breath whispered past her ear, carrying nearly inaudible words. "Don't. We're in trouble."

She tipped her head back until her lips grazed Bon's ear. "Leonard?"

"Woke me a couple minutes ago. Revenants are in the building."

"Because we are?"

"Yeah."

"Plan?"

"Live through this."

He felt for her hands and pressed Black Jack into them. Not especially promising when she couldn't see. A moment later, cold hands slung her pack onto her shoulder, gripped her elbow, and silently urged her out of her seat. With Bon clutching her other hand, she let Ren Leonard lead her through the darkness.

There was a sense of open space, and from the linear distance they travelled, she suspected they were in a corridor. He must have kept this area free of debris as well, since she didn't trip over anything and their footsteps were nearly silent.

He stopped and moved behind her, guiding her forward. She lost Bon's hand and dug in her heels until Leonard leaned in to whisper, "Doorway," and she understood. They could take no chances of clattering their packs or machetes against the industrial metal door jambs.

Several paces forward, he let go of her with a brief admonition not to move. A minute that seemed to last forever ticked by, and then Bon was bumping gently against her side. There was no telltale snick of a door closing, but when Leonard clicked on the lantern he'd brought along, the door was closed and a rolled-up blanket prevented the light from sneaking under it and into the hallway.

"What—" Mac began, but Leonard held a finger to his lips and came closer to whisper, lisping every S to keep the sound from carrying. She breathed shallow.

"Revenants. They can smell you. I've confused the scent by bringing you here; they won't know which way to go, but they'll most likely end up in the room we came from because that's where your scent is the most concentrated."

"I would think they'd be able to tell we're in this room in full concentration," Mac hissed back.

Leonard smiled tightly. "That hasn't escaped my attention. You two aren't going to like this, but if you want to live, you'll do it."

He pushed the light into Bon's free hand and went to some cabinets across the room. Long ago this had probably been some sort of classroom; the wall opposite the bank of cabinets was gouged and pitted, as though chalkboards or whiteboards had been ripped from their moorings. All furniture had been removed except for another hundred-year-old sofa, remarkably well-preserved.

Leonard rummaged in the cupboard and came back with two ratty blankets, holding one out to each of them. Mac didn't get it at first, but Bon apparently did, for his eyes widened in horror and he shook his head mutely, refusing the blanket.

"Do you want to live, Bonfils?" Leonard asked, his rough voice dangerously quiet. "Do you want young Mackenzie to live? Because if those Revenants come through this door and smell you, they will kill you. And if you're lucky – if you're both lucky – they'll only be the murderous sort. If you're not, you will both be defiled as they start eating you alive."

Mackenzie took her blanket. Bon swallowed hard, still refusing his.

"Have you ever seen a Revenant rape, Bon?" Leonard stepped aside, stopping in front of Mac. The back of one clawed finger brushed her cheek. "They bite the whole time, tearing chunks of flesh from their victims. Then they cram their stinking, rotting flesh into every—"

"Stop," Mac said.

"Stop?" Leonard's hand left her cheek to brush across her

hair. "They like soft, clean hair. You washed yours recently." He leaned in to sniff. Mac gagged. "Herbs and vinegar. Natural enough that it isn't a big signal of your presence, but astringent enough to clean the oil and dirt. They will rip it from your scalp, sometimes with your scalp still attached. And they will eat your flesh while they violate you. As you're dying, you will hear Bon screaming beside you, because everything they do to you, they will be doing to him as well."

Mac quickly drew the blanket around her. Bon didn't, but he looked uncertain instead of belligerent.

"Can you bear to hear Mackenzie scream, Bonfils? Can you bear it, knowing that you can do nothing to stop what's happening, knowing that she could live for hours, and that they will not stop even after she's dead?"

Bon dropped his gaze and unfurled the blanket, sweeping it over his shoulders. His movement disturbed the stifling air, and Mac gagged again.

"Over your heads, too. Leave only your face clear so you can see."

Reluctantly, both covered their heads. Leonard moved toward the door. Mac expected the gagging stench to go with him, but it held. She turned her face into the blanket and inhaled. Bile rose in her throat. The stink came from the blankets.

"What do you do, sleep on these?" she asked, her voice thin and strained as she tried not to vomit.

"Yep. My scent is different than theirs; it disturbs them, frightens them. I try to leave it widespread throughout the campus." He motioned to the corner of the room, where the cabinet and adjacent wall made a shadowy alcove. "Backs to the wall over there. Keep your eyes open, but if any Revenants come in here, half-shut them and watch through your eyelashes. You won't be able to see as clearly, but your eyes won't shine, so they probably won't see you. Keep the blankets on; if they come in, cover everything but your eyes, and they probably won't smell you."

"Probably?" Bon repeated.

"There are no guarantees in battle, Bonfils Moreau."

"I don't like backing myself into a corner," Mac said, eying the alcove apprehensively.

"For the moment, let's hope that it won't matter where you're

29

standing."

They settled in the alcove and turned off the light. Mac didn't hear him leave. Couldn't, in the absolute darkness, see the door open or close. But she knew he was gone. The uneasy sense of security she felt in his presence faded, leaving behind panic at being exposed and unprotected that was only slightly alleviated when Bon adjusted their blankets so he could reach her hand.

Distant sounds reached their hiding places: thudding footsteps over debris, doors slammed open. Once they heard a dull *bong* and Mac wondered if one of them had banged against the vending machine. The clatter of debris signaled they were still downstairs. She hoped they would remain there, that Ren Leonard's scent on the metal stair frame would overpower theirs, make them think that he'd simply brought his dinner upstairs.

But one-hundred-twenty-two years ago, fate proved to possess a cruel streak. Before long, the footsteps thudded on the metal stairs. Mac wedged herself farther into the corner and tightened her grip on Black Jack.

Revenants didn't moan. They didn't shriek or scream unless they were attacking or being attacked. They hissed, reptilian, slithering sounds that might once have been language when their brains were fully functional. Ren Leonard was the exception, but then, he was the exception to most everything Mac knew about Revenants. She didn't understand why he retained so much of his capacity for reasoning. Perhaps the virus hadn't been as destructive to his brain, which would support her theory that his infection was from a more pure source than the Revenants currently rampaging through the building.

Hissing voices approached their door. Passed. Bon clutched her free hand tightly; it would be their only form of communication. Fear thrummed through him, transmitted through their linked hands. Not just fear for his own life but for hers. She was inexperienced, relatively speaking, and had never engaged in a full-out battle with more than one Revenant.

Mac wasn't scared; she was petrified. The risk of contamination was huge even if you didn't get bitten; one stray drop introduced to the bloodstream was all it took. Through the eye, the nose, the mouth, a tiny wound from a sliver or a kitchen knife, it didn't matter. The end result was the same. Dispatching a Revenant was tricky business. Dangerous business.

The hissing conversation passed the door again and faded. Time ticked past; how much, Mac couldn't tell. The darkness of the empty room lay upon them, a shroud of stale, heavy air and cloying stink. They waited. And waited. Should they get out of this alive, what were they to tell the elders about their overnight absence? Could she look them in the eyes and tell them they'd been trapped by Revenants until morning and expect them to not see the lie behind the façade of truth? Negotiating wasn't the only thing she was lousy at.

A commotion came from down the hallway: a roar of rage and thumping on the metal stair frame. Something crashed into a wall. Sibilant hisses turned to snarls of fury.

The hair prickled along her forearms and the back of her neck. The air in the room moved, a light breeze that whispered over her face. Another clatter down the metal staircase. Louder than it should be.

Bon gave her hand two deliberate squeezes and let go. *Be ready. Any second now.* Sweat trickled down her neck, itching as it dried. The blackness was infinite, disorienting, oppressive. She shifted her machete to her other hand, blotted her sweaty palm on her pants, and shifted the weapon back, breathing a mental sigh of relief that she wasn't attacked while she held her defense in her weaker hand.

The seconds dragged by, turning into minutes – too many of them, each taking an eternity. She lived a lifetime in those minutes, and died a swift death at an unmistakable sound from across the room: the snick of the latch as the door closed. She could still feel another presence in the room.

Bon brushed the back of her hand – *Wait…we don't know if it's Leonard or something else…stay ready* – and Mac wondered suddenly how they would be able to fight in the absolute darkness if they were attacked. They would be swinging blindly and hacking each other to bits, while the Revenants were able to see.

She pressed two fingers against the back of Bon's hand and spread them apart. *Split up.* Bon's hand twitched. His fingers closed over her hand and squeezed hard. *Not on your life!* Dammit, he would have to argue. If they didn't split up, they would be slaughtered together.

A whisper floated across the room, a faint hiss that sounded like *Pssst!*

Leonard.

Mackenzie breathed a sigh of relief. She dropped her blanket, snatched up the lantern, and twisted the knob to turn it on as Bon screamed, "NO!"

Mac's relief turned to horror. Bon grabbed her arm and flung her toward the other side of the room, splitting the attention of the two Revenants that were advancing on them through the darkness. She stumbled, crashed into the wall, and nearly lost her grip on Black Jack as she tumbled to the floor. The lantern rolled away, spinning a crazy arc of light around the room.

The Revenant was upon her in an instant, jaws clamping on her shoulder but unable to break through the fabric of her shirt to skin. Mac rolled and gained her feet, bringing the black machete around in a swinging arc. The Revenant dodged and the blade whistled through the air. She let its momentum carry her around and out of the infected's reach as it lunged. It stumbled past her, unable to check its impetus as she whirled away. She brought Black Jack down in a two-handed chop, but before the blade could slice through the Revenant's spinal cord, a heavy body hit her from the side, knocking her clear off her feet.

She landed on the Revenant, who snarled in fury and bucked her off its back just as its fellow pounced. Mac staggered to her feet as the Revenants fell upon each other and wrestled across the floor, snapping and snarling, tearing out chunks of flesh wherever their teeth could find purchase. She lost Black Jack and now watched helplessly as they rolled over it.

Bon pushed against the wall, trying to get to his feet. He looked dazed and his arm hung at an odd angle. Mac kept one eye on the battling Revenants as she hovered a wary distance away from him.

"Are you bitten?"

"No." He gritted his jaw as he tipped against his injured arm. "Here, take my blade. I won't be able to swing it. Watch them."

"What are you—"

With no warning, he slammed his shoulder into the wall. The ball of his joint popped back into the socket with a loud crack. He slid down the wall to the floor, breathing heavily, his face grey in the dim light of the lantern.

The Revenants broke off their fighting, their interest in the humans renewed by Bon's shriek of pain. A third burst into the room as they scrambled to their feet and rushed her. She swung the machete like a baseball bat, following the arc around and dropping to a crouch, ducking under their bodies. Their heads bounced away, leaving blotches on the floor that looked black in the shadows. She spun on the ball of one foot and pistoned herself up from the floor, heaving the blade into the air again to dispatch the remaining Revenant.

A cold hand caught her wrist. "Very admirable, Bright Runner. But you might want to hold off parting me from my head until dawn. You might need my protection again." He pried her fingers off the grip and took possession of the weapon.

"Are they gone?"

Ren Leonard laughed dryly. "In almost every sense of the word."

She nearly collapsed with relief. The adrenaline needed for battle now found no outlet except a violent tremor, and she felt suddenly weak and feverish. Bon, still grey-faced and propped against the wall behind her, gave a pained chuckle.

"Holy shit, Bright Runner. Who taught you a move like that?"

"You did."

Her legs gave up and spilled her onto the floor. She scooted over to him. He draped his good arm around her, and despite his greater height and heavier muscle mass, she managed to hoist him to his feet. Leonard gathered the lantern and the blankets and shepherded them back to his room.

"I'm going lock you in while I get rid of those idiots."

"Lock us in?" Bon repeated, immediately bristling.

"Unless you'd like to take your chances with more of them coming in?" Without waiting for Bon's answer, he slotted a key in the lock on the door, adding, "I'll knock three times when I come back so you know it's me."

Bon collapsed on the sofa, holding his shoulder. Mac realized she'd left her machete in the other room and paced the floor, worrying about it. From the corridor, they could hear the rustle and thump of Ren Leonard removing the bodies of the slain Revenants.

"He still has a key?" Bon said after a while.

"Old habits die hard?" Mac suggested.

33

"A hundred and twenty-two years later?"

"Okay, so he's a little compulsive, maybe."

"That's one word for it."

He didn't say anything for a while. The rustle and thump moved farther away – the first floor, Mac surmised. Leonard was moving the bodies out of the building altogether, from the sounds of it.

"That was an amazing move, Mac."

She waved a hand airily. "I didn't even think about it. Just didn't want to die."

"I don't think I could have pulled that off."

"Sure you could have."

"No," he persisted thoughtfully. "You beheaded two of them, ducked under their bodies, and avoided most of the blood. That was pretty amazing."

Mac shrugged, embarrassed. Say what he would, she knew she wasn't nearly as skilled in battle as he was. It was a lucky strike borne of desperation.

"Do you think he'll change his mind and help us?"

"It's not looking good, Mac. Don't hold your breath."

She dropped onto the sofa beside him. "How much trouble will we be in with the elders?"

"A lot if they ever figure out what we were really up to tonight. We'd better get our story in order before we get back."

"It was my idea; you only came along to keep me from getting myself killed. You can blame it all on me if it comes to it."

He drew in a breath and let it out slowly. His arm snaked around her shoulders. "Never."

Three taps sounded on the door, the key rattled in the lock, and Leonard let himself in. Mac was relieved to see he'd brought their machetes – and that the blades were free of Revenant blood. He held them up in the lantern light, inspecting the razor-sharp edges, and speared Mackenzie with his piercing, blue-ringed gaze.

"Where the hell did you learn to fight like that, Bright Runner?" He sounded troubled rather than impressed.

"Just lucky," Mac said, but she couldn't help a smug grin. She tipped her head back against the sofa cushion and slept.

4

Mac woke sprawled on the sofa with Bon stretched out on the floor beside her. Weak sunlight poured through the grimy window, relieving her of one more worry. If a summer storm rolled in overnight, they would have a harrowing trip home. Revenants were not averse to going outside on an overcast day, but for them a rainstorm was a veritable gift from God. It limited visibility and masked sounds, and made the humans vulnerable in the daytime.

She winced as she pressed her fingers on her bruised shoulder. While Bon slept, she'd chanced the flashlight and peeled back her shirt, revealing the semi-circle of tooth imprints like a purple brand. Since her tendency was to bathe late at night or very early in the morning, she was confident that she could conceal it until the bruise faded enough to be unrecognizable as a bite. Even though her skin hadn't been broken, the elders might insist she be quarantined until it was certain she wasn't going to mutate. Being confined would drive her up a wall.

Bon stirred and stretched. As he sat up, a folded piece of paper fluttered to the floor by his knee. He picked it up.

"What's that? Let me see." Mac tried to snatch it, and he held it out of her reach while he read it. His mouth flattened.

"Well, that's that." He tossed the note to her. "At least I got to see you do that cool move. I think I'm going to keep it to myself, though, or they'll move you to the hunters."

Only a remark like that could have pulled her attention from the note Ren Leonard left in farewell. Bon never indicated he saw her as more than just a green kid he had to train. That considered her a valuable partner he didn't want to lose caused warmth to course through her blood, making her whole body flush.

"Would they really?"

He gave her a sharp look. "Is that what you want?"

"God, no. It's bad enough having to fight them while we're gathering. Seeking them out..." She shuddered. "I don't think I could do that every day and not want to throw myself into the river."

"It's no fun," he agreed absently, rubbing his shoulder. It really should be in a sling; the muscles and tendons would have suffered damage from the dislocation.

Mac forgot all about the note. "Did you used to be a hunter, Bon?"

He squirmed and looked like he regretted speaking. "Yeah," he admitted grudgingly, staring at the ancient tiles, filmed with dust. "For about a year. I was good, too, good enough that they didn't want me to stop."

"Why did you?"

"It does things to a man," he said quietly. "Puts an edge on him. Gathering for the community – well, that allows him to be sympathetic. *Sorry, fella, but I need these things and you're in the way.* He can always tell himself that he wouldn't kill a Revenant unless it stood between him and desperately needed supplies. And usually that's true."

"Like in your case," she guessed shrewdly.

He looked up at her at last, his eyes beseeching, begging for understanding. "I can't see them as enemies that try to kill us, obstacles that prevent us from rebuilding society. I can't look at them without thinking about how much they've lost, too. I began to dread going out."

"So they moved you to gathering."

"I wish it were that simple." She wasn't certain, but his expression looked suspiciously like shame. "I lost it on a mission. It was a bad one, heavy infestation, blind corners, dark rooms, Revenants everywhere. I was too tense, which brought out the asshole in me. My fellow hunters were sick of me, so I was on my own, no one covering me."

Mac fumed, angry for him. "That's not acceptable. They're supposed to cover you no matter what."

He shrugged. "We're only human, Mac. And I honestly did drive them bugshit. I can't blame them. I was attacked by two Revenants, barely fought my way out without getting bitten or otherwise infected. One of the other hunters came up behind me, silently, and tapped me on the shoulder. I nearly beheaded him."

"Jesus. Which one?" There were several hunters who were complete asses; she could see any one of them making such a colossally stupid move.

"Didn't you hear me, Mac? I nearly beheaded him. If I hadn't caught him at an angle, the blade would have gone clean through." His eyes bounced to her, away again. He fiddled with his bootlace.

"After that, they moved me to gathering. The other team members wanted me imprisoned. One of them actually went to the elders and demanded I be executed. But the elders…well, they're not the elders for no reason. They understood what happened, understood their culpability for not moving me when I asked them to."

"Damn right they had culpability!" Mac glowered ferociously. Life was too dangerous to indulge in power plays. Moving Bon from hunters to gatherers should have been as simple and forthright as – well, as it would be now if a hunter asked to be moved.

"That's why they don't hesitate now when someone asks to be moved," she deduced.

"Exactly. Remember when Riemer demanded to be moved to Agriculture? I thought the elders were going to have a stroke. But they did it, because they remembered what happened when they refused to move me."

Riemer had been one of the best hunters: shrewd, instinctive, with an innate ability to strategize. He possessed insanely fast reflexes and a mind to match. The elders nearly cried when he stepped down to tend the cabbage plot. A couple months ago, Mac brought him seeds she scavenged from an urban garden gone wild, and he asked her how it was "out there."

"Dangerous," Mac said without thinking, because the day was intermittently cloudy and she had nearly been cornered in a shady part of the garden by a stealthy Revenant.

Riemer held the small cloth bag of seeds almost reverently as he said, "Then thank you very much for all you risk, Mackenzie." She understood the look on his face now; peace, relief, fear for those who still had to venture beyond the walls of the Stronghold.

"Read that note, Mac, and let's get the hell out of here. If we jog, we might be able to make it back before lunch. I'm sure everyone's worried."

She looked down at the paper and rubbed her fingers across it. It was thin and smooth, quite unlike the paper the Stronghold made. She unfolded it. The first thing she noticed was Ren Leonard's bold, somewhat untidy handwriting, words scrawled in black ink that glinted red when held up to the sunlight. Then the words penetrated her brain.

Because you were brave enough to seek me out and put yourself at my mercy, I've given your proposal careful consideration. I have been convinced for decades that humanity's time on earth is over. What will rise to fill the gap remains to be seen. I fail to see how helping your settlement will make any more difference than pissing in the ocean to raise the water level. Soon, I will lie down in the sunshine for a final nap, because I've known since the beginning what you and your kind refuse to face: existence is futile. Live well whatever life you choose, Mackenzie Bright Runner. Yours Truly, Ren Leonard.

The temptation was strong to crumple the note and leave it lying there on the floor – especially since if she were found with it in the Stronghold, there would be some very uncomfortable questions asked. But to leave it here was to trust that no one else within her lifetime would find their way into Ren Leonard's lair, especially if he were gone as he said he would be. If someone ever saw this and brought news of it to the elders, she would be toast.

Neither could she bring herself to burn it, for who else in the world had placed their lives in the hands of the Father of the Apocalypse and walked away with a polite, personal letter and their innards intact?

So she folded it and stuffed it into her pack, tucking it through a tear in the lining. Even if someone went through her pack, they wouldn't find it. She slung the strap over her shoulder and stood up.

"Let's go. If we set a good enough pace, we might have time to take a dip in the river before going back to the Stronghold."

They crept out of the building as quietly as they had crept into it – perhaps more so, since Mac didn't trip and slam into the ancient vending machine this time. They held their machetes ready to strike, but the area seemed to have been cleared of any Revenants that might think two convenient meals worth the risk.

Bon held out a hand behind him to stop her when they reached the back doors. One pane of glass remained intact after a century, filthy with seasons of winter grime. Cut into the dirt was the message: *Take the bridge. Stay to the middle – Revenants in bridge understructure but too much sunshine to risk attacking. Saves an hour reaching your destination.*

Mac frowned. Bridges were risky – nowhere to run, nowhere

to hide. You had no choice but to stand and fight if you were attacked. But Leonard's advice seemed sound, and in the interest of a cool dip in the river and reaching the Stronghold by noon, she was willing to risk it.

Bon was not as sanguine about the advice, although, standing a safe hundred feet away from the bridge, he was willing to risk the route. "How does he know how long it should take us to get home, and whether the bridge would save us time?"

"I don't know," Mac said, distracted. Was that shadow by the bridge rail moving?

"He would have to know where the Stronghold is to know that taking the bridge might save us time."

"I'm not worried about it, Bon. If he were going to attack the Stronghold, he'd have done so long before now. It's been occupied for over a hundred years." Yes, the shadow definitely moved. Looking from the corner of her eye, she saw the vague form of the Revenant hovering just out of the sunlight. "Revenant at two o'clock."

"I see it. You go first and duck when it rushes you. I'll take it out."

They headed forward, Bon staying several feet behind her. As they approached the bridge, coming close enough that a Revenant would risk sunlight to attack, the form broke from the shadow and bolted toward them, snarling in fury.

Mac ducked as the Revenant came within reach. But instead of sailing over her and meeting the sharp edge of Bon's blade, the infected leapt upon her back, knocking her to the crumbling blacktop. Its weight pinned her hands beneath her. She struggled to free them, and then suddenly the weight lifted as Bon booted it square in the backside.

It scuttled away, regained its balance, and charged him again. Bon used its momentum to his advantage: as it approached, he began moving in the same direction. When it pulled alongside him, he grabbed it by the back of the shirt and the seat of the pants, put some speed into his step, and hurled it over the safety railing. A squelchy thud down below was the only confirmation Mac needed that Revenant was no longer going to be a problem.

"Better run. I think there are more," Bon said, breathing heavily. He massaged his injured shoulder, wincing. "I don't think I can do that again."

She didn't need any further encouragement to break into a run. Two more Revenants popped out of the shadows at the other end of the bridge as they approached, but she and Bon sprinted past them too quickly to be intercepted, and the creatures seemed reluctant to venture farther into the sunlight.

They scavenged their way back to the Stronghold, picking up enough supplies to make it look like they simply had a light day. They would be lectured for venturing too far afield to make it home before sundown, but they wouldn't be the first. The gatherers were all staying out later and bringing home lighter loads. The pickings were becoming scarce. Mac might get off with an easier lecture, as she'd found a cache of steel sewing needles, enough to last the Stronghold's seamstresses for years to come if they were careful. Bon found some jerky, but only two packages, not enough to significantly grow the Stronghold's stores. The plastic package had been vacuum-sealed, and the jerky was still more or less fresh, if one could call one-hundred-twenty-year-old dried meat fresh. They shared it out as their morning meal.

The day remained hot and sunny. They walked down the middle of streets when they could, which allowed faster progress. When the streets were impassable, they edged through yards, machetes ready to cut down any waiting Revenants. There were a few, and Mac couldn't help but notice Bon's grimace of distaste as he dispatched them.

Half a mile from the Stronghold, they found a bare stretch of river bank in the full sun. The bank sloped gently to the water, and a fallen tree created a bathing pool safe from the strongest of the river currents. They stripped off clothes and shoes and splashed into the water with relief. She was sweltering in her pants and long-sleeved shirt; she wished they could travel in shorts and sleeveless shirts, but the probability of being attacked made it impractical and dangerous.

Bon checked out the bite on her shoulder carefully and determined it was just a compression bruise, no broken skin.

"Keep it hidden as long as you can. Otherwise…"

"Quarantine," she agreed glumly. It wouldn't matter if the skin was intact; she'd be tossed in a secure room with an unbreakable lock until she was safely past the incubation period of the Revenant

Virus – which could range from a couple of days to as long as two weeks.

When they cooled down and cleaned up, they sat on the log until they'd mostly dried, then picked their way up it to the shore so they didn't get their feet wet and dirty. Bon pulled on his pants, grabbed his shirt, and then tossed it to her.

"That's yours."

She handed over the shirt she'd been about to put on and picked up the one he'd tossed, pulling it on over a bra that did little to hide the cold river's effect on her body. Mac wasn't bothered; there was little room for self-consciousness when you worked so closely with someone in a job like theirs.

He held her pack while she finished tying her boots, and then slung the strap over her shoulder. They started walking again, a little more slowly since they were so close. They'd reach the Stronghold in about twenty minutes at this pace, provided they experienced no trouble with Revenants.

"I hope they're making stew tonight," he said.

"Chicken pot pie."

"We eat too much chicken. A beef stew would be nice for a change."

"And a raspberry pie."

"If they don't throw us in detention with no lunch or dinner for not making it home last night, that is."

"Don't ruin my daydream, Moreau."

"I hope you lie better than you negotiate."

"We've got our story straight. It'll be fine."

They discussed their cover story over and over on the long walk home, quizzing each other to make sure they remembered details more or less the same. The skill of a good lie, Bon told her, was to not repeat each other word for word. Even tiny contradictions made it more believable, because no one ever possessed the same perspective or saw exactly the same things.

"Do you think he's right?"

"Who, and right about what?" He stopped, adjusted one of his boots, and they started off again.

"That existence is futile?" She didn't name about whom she was speaking; they were too close to the Stronghold and it was possible someone could be close enough to hear.

"No."

"But even you said that maybe it's better if humans become extinct."

"I was having a dark moment."

"No shit, Bon. That was about as dark a moment as one can have."

"Look, Mac." He stopped again, snagging her hand to halt her too. "There are days I feel like giving up, where I just want to pull the covers over my head and forget about gathering, forget about hunting, forget about every damn thing our lives demand of us. Everyone has moments like that, because it's a dark, dangerous world we live in. The elders tell us positive stories about the past so we don't start thinking that living is pointless."

"So why would they be angry about us seeking Ren Leonard's help? What if he'd agreed to it – what then, Bon? How would we have hidden it? The elders would have to agree it's for the benefit of everyone."

He glanced around, his dark eyes taking in the shadows around them, looking for eavesdroppers. When he was satisfied they were truly alone, he said, barely audible, "The elders don't *want* the human race to rediscover what it had once achieved. They have absolute power now. That might change if suddenly we have technology again, or medical services, or supermarkets where we can buy whatever we need."

"Then why do they even tell us about the old days? They should know we would want those things."

"Haven't you ever listened really closely, Mac? They're trying to discourage us from civilized advances. The tales they tell about the old days? They're cautionary tales, warning us about the evils of an advanced society. They want us to live, but they don't want us to be advanced. That's what I think, anyway. I could be wrong."

"They want to keep us primitive, that's what you're saying? That makes no sense. Everyone would benefit from all we've lost in science and medicine alone."

Bon stared at her for a long moment as though debating voicing what was on his mind. At last, he said carefully, "If the Revenants can be backed off enough that we can regain that lost medical and scientific knowledge, not everyone would be content to live within a walled community. People would want to reclaim the world – rightfully so. The Council of Elders would lose power, and what tyrant ever willingly gives up power over the people?"

"Tyrant? You think the council are tyrants?"

Again, he subjected her to a sharp, searching look before he spoke. "When was the last time you ever left the Stronghold walls when you weren't gathering? For that matter, when was the last time you saw *anyone* outside the Stronghold walls who wasn't on a hunting, gathering, or logging team?"

Mac thought long and hard, only able to come up with one meager response. "Just Benny what's-his-name and his brother who handle the tribe of goats. And then they don't leave the area around the Stronghold where the goats are eating the grass."

"Not only that, they're watched by the wall guards."

"Uh, *guards*, Bon. They're supposed to be watching them. You know, *guarding* them? What if Revenants attacked? The wall guards can take them out."

"I'm sure that's the only reason, Mac. I'm sure there's also a reasonable explanation for all the dissenters who seem to go missing, too, and the executions that are held without there having been a trial. And did you get to choose what service you provide to the settlement? No? Me, either. When was the last election to appoint members to the council? How about the new edicts that came down from the Council prohibiting certain clothing and reading material?

"I also heard a rumor that they're quietly gaining support for a law that keeps families in a specific service. If they can pass it into law without much outrage from the citizens, the children of people like Benny Jacobs will be locked into the profession of their parents. Unless, of course, they show promise as hunters or gatherers – or have brute strength that would make them good guards. Then they'll be harvested for those professions. There won't be any picking and choosing. And people will let it happen because it all seems so orderly and simple."

He started walking again. Mac followed silently, chewing over what he'd said. She didn't know if she believed as he did, but she held no doubt that he believed it himself. Maybe she would watch and listen a little more carefully while she was at the Stronghold, see if she began to see things in the same way he did. Certainly something gave him this perspective, and she couldn't deny that often those on the outside of accepted society saw things the clearest.

The Stronghold came into view. Up on the wall, the two east-quadrant guards raised their binoculars to check them out more closely. She dug in her pack and held something out to him.

"Want to give them some sewing needles, too? It might ease the ass-chewing we're going to get."

Bon took them, smiling gratefully. "Thanks, Mackenzie."

She smiled back, bumping his shoulder with hers and making him stagger a step to the side. They passed under an archway that once held letters – the name of the structure that fell off decades ago – and into a wide passageway dimly lit by a shaft of sunlight. A faded mural adorned one wall of the passageway, a few letters still visible:

INL D EMP RE SP RTS ARENA

Without warning, Bon stopped in front of the mural and hugged her. Mac was startled at first, and then she relaxed in his embrace, returning the hug. The metal doors at the end of the passage swung open, and they entered the cool gloom of the Stronghold.

5

Chaos reigned inside, or at least that's how it seemed to Mac. She was engulfed by a group of her friends, who were relieved that she made it back unscathed. In the middle of a bone-cracking hug administered by Zane Allbrook – who was less of a boyfriend than he was just a boy she'd enjoyed kissing a few times out behind the potting shed – she saw Bon melt into a shadowed corner. A couple of guys – Riemer one of them – and a very pretty girl joined him, but she noticed that his return drew much less of a crowd than hers. She'd been his partner for a year-and-a-half. How had she failed to see how cool the folk of the Stronghold were toward him?

The other hunters wanted me imprisoned. One of them actually went to the elders and demanded I be executed.

She guessed that Bon's transgressions had not been so readily forgiven, regardless of the fact that if the elders had acted in the beginning, he never would have been out on a mission with a fractured team to start with.

Gerald, one of the younger elders, snaked his way through the throng around Mac, beaming broadly. "Miss Bright Runner, you have no idea how worried we were. Come, Louis wants to debrief you, and then you can have a long, hot bath and a nap – you look exhausted."

"It wasn't a fun night," Mac agreed. "And we have some things to be taken to the Market."

"What happened, anyway?" Zane elbowed a scrawny boy, who was angling to get another hug from Mac, and edged closer.

"We outstayed our welcome." She shrugged. "Poked around too long, looking for a hidden cache. The exit was in the shadows, and the Revenants were coming out. We thought it was better to hole up for the night and head home at morning light."

"Wasn't Moreau keeping track of the time? He's senior – it's his job."

Now this was new, the edge to Zane's voice. Light on jealousy, heavy on contempt. Or had it been there all along and Mac was just too oblivious to the politics of the Stronghold to register what was said about her partner?

Either way, it made her prickle with irritation, especially when he draped his arm over her shoulders in a clearly possessive manner. She shifted her shoulders, and his arm slid off and fell away.

"He was keeping track," she said coolly. "I was the one who pushed the limits despite his warnings."

"He could have made you leave," Zane persisted.

"I'd like to see him try." Mac started walking, leading Gerald away from Zane. "Shall we grab Bon on the way?"

Gerald hesitated. "I believe Louis would like to question you alone, Miss Bright Runner."

Mac stopped in her tracks and leveled a severe look at him. "If this is a witch hunt to somehow blame Bon for what happened, both you and Louis can forget it. It was my fault."

"Mr. Moreau still shares a portion of the blame."

"Just as the elders share a portion of the blame for him losing it on a mission? Just as his team shares a portion of the blame because they left him on his own with no protection?"

His mouth pursed. "I see Mr. Moreau has told you his side of the tale."

"Only this morning, when he told me to allow him to take the blame for getting trapped on a run."

Gerald looked startled. "Why would he do a thing like that?"

"I guess he didn't want me to be in trouble."

He digested this for a moment. "Either way, Miss Bright Runner, Louis would like to debrief you alone. That's how these things are done, to determine if more training is needed, if reassignment is required, if partnerships need to be reconsidered. To assure you that you're safe to speak without fear of coercion or retribution."

She didn't reply. As she allowed him to lead her deeper into the Stronghold where the elders' offices were located, she sent one last glance at the shadows where Bon all but disappeared and thought she saw him smile regretfully in farewell.

The Stronghold was once a sports arena, where games like soccer, football, and baseball had been played. When Mac was being schooled, Loretta, one of the Stronghold's teachers, told them that the area's largest flea market had also been held here, out in the field that now grew and housed their food supply. Mac couldn't

imagine a market where people brought so many things to be traded or sold that it filled the entire field. Their own market was
spread out between ten of the arena's forty concession stands; the
remaining concession areas were used for storage, offices, or sleeping quarters. Gatherers turned in non-food items to one central
office, who then distributed the goods amongst the ten different
markets. All food items were handed over to the kitchens.

Louis's office was located near the Wool Market. Mac always
enjoyed the journey in the past; the Market staff often lined the
corridors with tables stacked with colorful skeins of yarn, thread,
socks, coats, and blankets. She loved wool: the texture, the warmth,
the versatility. When she retired from gathering, she wanted to
work in either the Wool Market or in wool production, making
blankets.

Today, she barely noticed the goods on the tables. She was
deep inside her head, thinking, worrying, puzzling over the things
Bon told her before they entered the Stronghold and the things
both Zane and Gerald intimated about him. Clearly, he was somewhat ostracized. She had to have been blind to have not seen it before. Blind and self-absorbed.

Gerald stopped at a door just short of the Wool Market and
knocked. The door was flung open and Louis filled the doorway,
smiling jovially and with obvious relief. For him to have summoned
her so quickly, the wall guards must have sent a runner to inform
him of their return. It troubled her that she never before noticed
how intricately and efficiently the elders constructed their network.

"Come in, young Mackenzie. We're so relieved that you're
home safe."

"Yes, well, it was touch-and-go a few times. If it wasn't for
Bo—"

"Please, have a seat," Catherine interrupted, her voice warm to
take the sting out of her interruption.

Mac was taken aback; she expected to be meeting with just
Louis and possibly Gerald, not the entire Council of Elders, all
crammed into Louis's spacious office. All the candles were lit to
make the space bright and inviting, and she was offered a comfortable chair, not the usual wooden ladder-back that made her butt
ache after five minutes. The chair faced Louis's desk, behind which
he retreated, and put the rest of the Council at her back and be-

tween her and the door.

After a second's hesitation – so brief that not all the elders noticed – she moved the chair against the wall near the door, forcing the elders to rearrange themselves. Fleeting annoyance crossed Louis's and Catherine's faces.

"I apologize, but I'm very uncomfortable with my back to the door."

And very uncomfortable being surrounded with her only exit blocked. Maybe Bon's confidence earlier sparked this unusual paranoia, but the atmosphere in the office set her on edge. There was an odd tension thrumming under the pleasantries. Suspicion slowly engulfed her relief to be home.

"Of course," Louis said genially, but Mac didn't miss the look that passed between him and Catherine. "Please, Mackenzie, we would very much like to hear what happened, and then you can be on your way. I'm sure you'd like a good, hot meal and some sleep."

Not only that, she'd dearly love to go find Bon. She wanted to talk about there being only three people to welcome him home.

So she told the story with as few frills as possible, being certain to cast the blame on herself for staying past their time limit. They seemed reluctant to blame her and kept trying to hold Bon responsible but were hard-pressed to find a way around her assertions of his innocence. They were so subtle about it that she doubted she would have noticed before Bon confided in her.

Finally tired of circling around the same subject over and over as they tried to find a way to demonize her partner, Mac said impatiently, "If it wasn't for Bon, I'd be dead." Which was the truth. "If he'd tried to force me to leave, we'd have brawled and probably bought ourselves even more trouble than we ended up with. You can call him in here and grill him if you want, and he'll probably oblige you by telling you that he's to blame, but he's not."

"Why would he take the blame if he's not to blame?" Catherine asked reasonably.

"Maybe he figures you'll blame him anyway. You think I'm clueless, but I haven't failed to notice how he is treated."

Silence filled the room, so pronounced it hurt Mac's head. No doubt some eloquently outraged conversations between the elders happened in that silence. She almost wished she could hear on a psychic level.

She sensed the silent communication was coming to an end and knew they were about to make some sort of proclamation she wouldn't like. Perhaps she should have kept her mouth shut. They would use this opportunity to make it seem like Bon had been working on her, turning her loyalty away from the Stronghold and to him instead. But she understood now Bon's strange smile as she left with Gerald, understood now the unexpected hug he gave her before they walked through the main doors, and understood why he had risked bringing up his experience with the hunters and his suspicion about the elders.

He knew as soon as the sun set on them while they were still in Ren Leonard's lair that the blame would be entirely his and the elders would split them up. His opportunities to educate her to the Stronghold's ways, of which she was blissfully ignorant, had been rapidly vanishing, and their hours together were coming to an end. How many times had they done this to him, meted out their subtle punishment for cutting down a member of his negligent crew even as they assured him that they shared the blame for not moving him sooner?

Gerald shifted closer to the door, then jumped a little as Mac suddenly stood. She barely managed to hold back a wry smile.

"I'm afraid I'm too exhausted to wait any longer. I have supplies to turn in at the Depository, and then I want to grab a quick meal and a long nap. Thank you for your concern for my well-being."

She didn't wait for a dismissal but slipped past Gerald and out the door. Mac was certain she heard Catherine exclaim, "What the hell—?" before the sounds of the Wool Market drowned out the voices in the office behind her.

It didn't take long to unload her haul at the Depository. The attendant was excited over the sewing needles, so Mac made a point of mentioning that Bon found some too, which excited her even more. The Depository attendants never treated Bon any differently than they treated her, and it wasn't until she was walking away that she recognized the attendant as the very pretty girl who greeted Bon when they returned. Girlfriend, maybe? Did he even have a girlfriend? And why would she not know this? They had been partnered long enough that she should know all about his personal life, but now that she really thought about it, it seemed that Bon never

49

confided anything personal before today. Everything was always about staying alive while gathering, but he imparted nothing about himself.

She looked for him in the dining hall but didn't find him. The dining hall held to strict meal times except for hunting or gathering parties who came in after the hall closed. Snacks between meals were bartered for at the food markets throughout the Stronghold. Cook – they were all called Cook for simplicity's sake – fixed her a hot meat pastry she chased with a glass of cool well water.

Bon didn't come in to eat while she was there, which was strange. She hadn't been with the elders for very long, and she was certain they would catch up to each other in the dining hall. She turned her dishes in at the dishwashers' window and went on the hunt for him. Not in any of the common rooms he frequented, nor in the Infirmary. Not in the growing fields, nor in the stables. She checked with his friend at the Depository, who said he hadn't turned in his haul yet. Worry lines had replaced her earlier smile, and Mac found herself reassuring the girl rather than finding any reassurance for herself.

"I'm sure he probably just went to his room for a nap. It's hard to get any sleep when you have to stand watch in a Revenant-infested area for half the night."

But she wasn't so sure herself. The meeting with the elders made her nervous; they wanted something from her, wanted her to say something in particular that would – what? Give them cause to detain him? Incarcerate him indefinitely? Pull him off gathering? Split up their team? But why should they care who teamed with him?

The Council of Elders would lose power, and what tyrant ever willingly gives up power over the people?

The answers lay with Bon. He must have said or done something that made them aware of his criticism. Still, it was ridiculous – no one ever enjoyed a hundred-percent approval. To discredit one's critics was the height of insecurity and immaturity.

Ordinarily, she wouldn't bother him outside gathering duties, but she was worried enough that she headed to his quarters. Everything had tilted off kilter after he told her about his hunting tragedy. Hardly anyone cared if Bonfils Moreau was lost to the Stronghold, and that gave her a very bad feeling.

His door was closed. Mac banged on it with the side of her fist. He didn't answer.

"Bon?" And then louder, "BON! ANSWER THE DOOR!" She slammed her fist on his door over and over, until the commotion drew his neighbors from their rooms. Someone grabbed her arm, drawing her down the corridor and away from Bon's room, hissing at her to be quiet. She was shoved through a door, which banged shut behind her as she whirled around indignantly.

"What do you think you're doing?"

A large hand grabbed the front of her shirt and blazing green eyes glowered at her from an inch away. His breath was cool and minty, as though he'd just chewed a sprig from the garden.

"Riemer?"

"What did you tell them?"

"What are you talking about?"

"You told the elders something about Bon. What was it?"

"Nothing but the truth: we stayed too late to make it home, and it was my fault. Now let me go!" She twisted in his grip, but she was no match against his strength and couldn't break his hold.

"What else did you tell them? They came for him, Mackenzie, and dragged him away at gunpoint!"

Mac stared at him, frightened into speechlessness. Gunpoint? Why would they fear him so much they would take him at gunpoint? Guns were rarely used even against Revenants; ammunition was too scarce.

The eyes staring back burned with suspicion and rage. They bore into hers for a moment longer, and then he released her, spinning away to pace the room, a hand raking through his hair, making it stand up in damp blond spikes.

"I'm sorry I grabbed you."

Mac busied herself with straightening her shirt and regaining her composure. What the hell was Riemer doing here? She'd not realized he was more than a passing acquaintance of Bon's.

"Did they take him to detention? For how long? I don't see how they could even do that – I told the Council that I was the one who didn't watch the time and didn't listen to Bon's warnings. They have no reason to hold him!"

"They arrested him for sedition an hour ago."

Mac flinched away from his words. Sedition was punishable by

51

death. If the Council was kind, they would shoot you in the head. If they were not, they turned you out of the Stronghold at night, leaving you in an area crawling with Revenants and a bullet in both your kneecaps.

Her numb lips struggled to form words. "How...how long until the trial?"

Riemer closed his eyes and turned away from her. "It's too late, Mackenzie. He confessed to protect you."

A buzz traveled down her body, leaving numbness in its wake. Her trembling legs carried her to the nearest seat – Riemer's neatly made bed – and she sank down. Shock anesthetized the worst of the pain, because she knew without him saying the words that she would never see Bonfils Moreau again.

Riemer spoke at last, so softly she barely heard him.

"They've already executed him."

6

It was like fighting her way through an oncoming stampede. Mackenzie elbowed and shoved her way through the throng of people heading the opposite direction, forcing her way inch by inch to Louis's office. She didn't know why there were so many people or where they were going; it wasn't time for dinner and there wasn't a scheduled community gathering.

It didn't matter. Her only goal was to find Louis and assure herself that Riemer's information was inaccurate, because it would be unbearable if it were true. Bon couldn't be dead – it just didn't seem possible. And to be executed for treason to the community was ludicrous; Bon was no more a traitor than she was.

A hundred feet short of her destination, her arm was snagged and she was dragged around. Pain burned through her shoulder from the bite. A furious snarl twisted her mouth, but she bit it back when she saw who grabbed her. Bon's pretty friend from the Depository.

"You're going the wrong way, Mackenzie," she said coolly. Her eyes were frigid blue lakes, chilled to rival a mountain pond in high winter and rimmed with red, and her face was set in a hard smile that seemed more like a grimace. She looked as Mac always imagined a Nordic goddess might: blonde with frosty blue eyes and a haughty cold beauty that was both untouchable and, if the looks she was garnering were anything to go by, highly desirable.

Mac surprised her by pushing her sideways through the crowd to the wall. "Is it true?"

"Shhh!" The icy blue eyes darted wildly around the crowd, searching for listeners.

"Too much noise for anyone to hear us. Is it true?" She gave the captive arm a shake, rattling the hard expression off the girl's face.

"Yes, it's true. Are you satisfied? What did the elders promise you for screwing over Bon?"

Mac pressed closer, pinning the girl against the wall, her teeth bared in a snarl. The blue eyes widened fearfully. The girl was by no means a twig, but Mac had the advantage of intense physical training that had built solid layers of muscle over her otherwise petite frame.

"I'd *never* screw him over. You and I are going to have a nice long chat, because I want to know what the hell is going on."

"We can't. They've called a meeting. We have to go now."

"Not until we settle this."

A firm hand fell on her shoulder. Warm breath bathed her ear, smelling faintly of mint. Riemer had followed her when she'd fled his quarters. For some odd reason, Mac's stomach swooped toward her feet and her heart sped up several beats a minute.

"Yes, Mackenzie: now. They'll be looking for you, and if you're not there, you'll end up just like Bon. Unless they decide to toss you out at night with a couple of bullets in your legs."

He didn't wait for her to answer. He simply took her elbow and steered her into the crowd, calling casually over his shoulder. "Come on, Johanna. We have to go."

Mac tried to free her arm, although she knew it was pointless to try to head back toward Louis's office. Since an assembly was called, none of the elders would be there; they would be in the Hall.

Riemer's voice sounded near her ear again. "We have to sit through this, Mackenzie, and we have to pretend like we didn't know beforehand. You cannot let on that you already know what happened to Bon."

"What difference does it make? You know how the grapevine is here – rumor travels faster than a Revenant chasing an easy meal."

His fingers tightened on her arm, digging in hard. No doubt she'd find bruises there later. "It matters. If you tell anyone that you knew before the assembly, you will jeopardize a very precarious network that took years to put in place."

"What are you—"

"Shhh!" he hissed impatiently. "God, did Bon teach you *nothing* over the two last years?"

Mac bristled, but Riemer propelled her along through the crowd without even sparing her a glance. She glared up at him, but the contained fury in his expression, telegraphed by his tightly clenched jaw and glowering brow, inspired her to keep her mouth shut.

The crowd jostled them from behind. Someone slammed into Mac, tearing her elbow from his grasp. Before she could act on her sudden freedom, warm fingers slid down the back of her arm and twined with hers. She glanced at him in her peripheral vision, and he smirked slightly as though he'd known she might try to bolt. The smirk vanished quickly. The flow of people through the wide corridor bottlenecked at the two sets of double doors leading outside. With only a slight change of posture, he became suddenly watchful and guarded.

Shit just got real.

A quivery sensation in her stomach made her want to hurl. She lived in a world of fear, her daily duties taking her into harm's way nearly every day, but she could not recall ever feeling this trembling nausea. The Revenants might attack her, try to kill her, but not because of who she was. Everything about this —especially Riemer's attitude – told her this was *very* personal, and the danger was lethal. She had one chance to get it right, and she wasn't sure enough of the situation to avoid making a fatal *faux pas.*

Riemer hissed in a breath and gave her hand two hard squeezes. Mac realized she had tightened her grip to the point his fingers turned bright red. She eased off.

"Sorry," she muttered.

He leaned in again. "Whatever you do, don't take his things. Don't take what they offer you as mementos, or you're as good as dead."

"But—"

Now his fingers tightened, grinding the delicate bones of her hand together. "Trust me, Mackenzie."

She looked up. His eyes were intense, earnest, his face close. The scent of mint wafted past her nose as he whispered, and the cacophony of the murmuring crowd faded into the background. They had talked any number of times out in the fields when she brought in seeds to the growers, and he'd always been pleasant and peaceful.

But she couldn't remember his eyes being this green, or his face being so achingly handsome, maybe because he'd always been grimed with planting soil and streaked with sweat, his jaw stubbled with beard if he'd not bothered to shave. As a preteen, she had watched him closely, almost obsessively, not because she coveted him romantically, but because he was different. Not carefree or arrogant, but cautious and observant, wise and respectful of the hazardous world in which they lived even though he couldn't have been more than eighteen at the time. When the elders came to her on her fifteenth birthday and asked her to be Bon Moreau's gathering partner, she readily agreed, because Riemer – or her observance of him, rather – already decided her for a life of dangerous servitude rather than a safer occupation that would keep her within the Stronghold walls. His intense capability was a siren's song, and she was seduced at an early age.

"It's all right to be scared. It's all right to be worried. They won't think anything of you showing those things. But for the love of God, Mackenzie, you can't take anything of his that they offer you, or they will come for you next. Only a co-conspirator would want mementos of a traitor."

She swallowed hard. "I'm in a lot of trouble, aren't I, Riemer?"

He breathed in sharply through his nose. "Yes. But I'm doing my best to get you out of it."

"Why?"

His words seemed to be chosen very carefully. "Because you paid attention. Every time you brought me something, it was always just what I needed. That shows heart, Mackenzie, and hope. I can't let those things die without a fight."

The trembling spread from her rolling stomach to her legs. "Thank you."

"Thank me by staying alive."

The blockage at the door broke free, and people poured through the opening and into the Hall, sweeping Mac and Riemer along with them. The Hall was one end of what had been the sports pitch, with the growing fields surrounding it, and the section of concrete bleachers rising above it were just big enough to hold all of the Stronghold's residents. Not really a Hall at all, but it served the purpose for the warmer months when the Commons would be too hot and uncomfortable if stuffed with people.

They were making their way to a stretch of empty cement bench when an arm inserted itself between them. Mac stopped abruptly, which yanked Riemer backward a step.

"Mackenzie, we don't have time—oh." Riemer's annoyed scowl vanished behind a neutral mask when he saw Zane Allbrook.

"I was going to ask if you wanted to sit with me, Mac, but I see you already made plans." Zane sent a pointed glance at her hand, fingers still laced tightly with Riemer's so they wouldn't get separated.

"Umm...yeah. Sorry." There was no way to indicate to him that it wasn't what he thought. Mac wasn't certain she would have even if she could. Zane was an entertaining diversion, but he was more than a little egotistical and obnoxious. She could overlook this as long as they were kissing and not conversing.

"So," he drawled, leaning against an ancient iron railing, his narrowed gaze sliding to Riemer for a second. "Is this a new development?"

"Fairly new," Riemer confirmed, tugging Mac firmly past Zane. "We have to go get seats. See you later, Allbrook."

Zane bobbed his chin in reply. Mac could feel his gaze drilling into her back as they sidled through the crowd and found Johanna, who was saving a space barely big enough for Riemer. She looked irritated that Mac was still with him.

"Make room," he said as he sat, bumping her with his hip.

Johanna made a face. "Scooch over," she said to the gangly teenagers next to her, and they scooted over to make enough room for Mac.

Riemer pulled her down next to him, keeping hold of her hand as though afraid she would still try to bolt.

"You and Allbrook? Really, Mackenzie, I thought you'd have better taste."

She raised a brow. "I wouldn't have thought you'd given my taste any thought at all."

"Then you really are as oblivious as you seem."

Mac looked at him, surprised. He couldn't mean what it sounded like he meant. Their daily duties brought them into infrequent contact, not enough for her to have made any impression on him at all.

He snorted, amusement replacing the disappointment in his expression. "We had to know what you were all about because you were out gathering with Bon. We needed to know he was safe with you."

"We?"

"Shhh. It's starting," Johanna snapped.

57

Riemer released her hand, but Mac clung to his retreating fingers, suddenly petrified. She could end this day back in her own bed in the gatherers' quarters, or she could end it outside the Stronghold gates, gunshot and waiting to be torn apart by Revenants with no way to defend herself.

"It's okay," he breathed. "Just remember what I told you." He didn't try to withdraw his hand again, a fact that did not escape Johanna's notice or scorn.

Out on the field, the Council of Elders raised their arms to call for silence. The murmuring in the crowd slowly diminished. Louis dragged out an ancient megaphone, amplifying his voice to the farthest bench.

"We have called this assembly today to discuss a very grave matter: sedition."

The crowd gasped. A cold sweat broke out along her brow and spread across her body. Gooseflesh rippled over her flesh. Riemer squeezed her hand. Johanna glared at her from the corner of her eye.

"We will make this short and to the point so you can get back to your activities. One of our own was suspected of sedition. When detained for questioning, Bonfils Moreau confessed to attempting to turn others, including his young gathering partner Mackenzie Bright Runner, against the Council of Elders and, by extension, against the law-abiding people of the Stronghold."

Eyes burned into her from all directions. Angry eyes, accusing eyes, hundreds of judging eyes stabbing her like knives. Riemer clamped down on her fingers, a silent message that was as clear as if he'd shouted it: *Be silent. Don't look around. Just look at Louis.*

"The Law of the Stronghold regarding sedition is very clear: if found guilty, the sentence is death. You may find such a sentence harsh"—all around her, heads shook vehemently; the crowd didn't find the sentence harsh at all—"but our very existence in this post-Upheaval world relies on trust and loyalty. We cannot afford to harbor traitors in our midst."

The crowd cheered. Riemer and Johanna cheered with them. Mac could manage nothing more than a few nods of agreement. Numbness spread from her chest to all parts of her body, a cold, insulating chill. *You can do this, Mac. You* must *do this or they will kill you.*

"In compliance with the law, immediately after his confession, Bonfils Moreau was put to death."

The crowd went insane. Gerald's and Catherine's mouths flattened into grim lines. The rest of the elders, standing sentinel behind the other three, stared impassively at the cheering assembly. Riemer's grip once again ground the bones of her hand together. *Keep it together, Mackenzie. Keep it together.*

Louis's words went through Mac like a sword. Bon really was dead. And Riemer and Johanna thought she was responsible. She thought back to their return home, trying to recall exactly what she had said. *If this is a witch hunt to somehow blame Bon for what happened, both you and Louis can forget it,* she had told Gerald. And then, later, in Louis's office, she had said, *Maybe he figures you'll blame him anyway.*

They were right. It *was* her fault.

"—an offering to acknowledge the bond between the members of a gathering team. Mackenzie Bright Runner, will you please join us on the field?"

"You're on," Riemer murmured.

He squeezed her hand one last time and let go. Johanna muttered, "Finally," but as Mac stood and picked her way out of the aisle on shaking legs, she heard Riemer add, "Please stay alive."

A missing section of railing made the perfect spot for a wooden staircase down to the field from the bleachers. Mac gripped the railing, the sting of a dozen prickly splinters against her palm grounding her to consciousness.

She kept her eyes on Catherine, who waited beside Louis, holding several items. A jacket with TEAM 11 embroidered as a badge on the left breast. What looked like some sort of book constructed of handmade paper. The hat she knitted him this past winter as a birthday gift.

And Bon's machete. He never named it like she named hers, and now she understood why. His inability to see the Revenants as anything other than poor souls who'd been shortchanged by the Revenant Virus made killing them a sometimes necessary but altogether regretful chore.

Her foot thudded onto the last tread, and then she stepped into the grass. She let the insulating chill of grief cloak her, and her trembling ceased. Her legs were as steady as her gaze when she stopped before Catherine. The elder's eyes held a hint of smug challenge.

She thinks I'll take the mementos. She thinks I'm guilty too.

Louis turned slightly so he could see as Catherine held up each item in turn.

"Bonfils Moreau's hunters team jacket!" he shouted into the megaphone.

A grumble halfway up and to the far right of the crowd told her where Team 11 sat.

"A handmade gift, from Bright Runner to Moreau!"

The crowd was silent. Gathering teams were notoriously close, and it wasn't unusual for them to exchange gifts.

"Moreau's defense machete."

An excited murmur swept through the crowd. Of course Mackenzie would take *that*; it had saved her life more than once. What half of a permanently separated gathering team wouldn't want it as a memento?

"And a scrapbook, handmade by Moreau, filled with memories of gathering excursions and holidays and other general observances about his friendship with young Mackenzie Bright Runner."

Mac's eyes flew from book to Catherine's face. Pure smugness replaced the challenge in her expression. They knew Mackenzie wasn't aware of this; it was why they saved it for last. And they knew she would be dying to see what was within the pages. What memories of her had Bon cherished so much that he would build a memory book to honor them?

Her hands itched to take the book, to page through it feverishly, to flagellate herself with every memory that her partner held dear because that partner was gone by Mac's own careless tongue.

"What will you have as a memento, Miss Bright Runner?"

Those were the words Louis spoke, but Mac heard the real ones behind them: *Denounce your partner or forfeit your life.* It didn't matter what was right and what was wrong, what was truth and what was lie. All that mattered was the Council wanted Bon dead and they wouldn't mind making a clean sweep of this particular team, because they could never be sure how deeply his beliefs had affected her.

She returned Catherine's stare, forcibly keeping her own frozen expression in place. Then she turned and looked up into the crowd, seeking Riemer. Her vision narrowed to a pinpoint when she found him. It seemed as though he stood mere inches from her, so close she could see the flecks in his green eyes and the faint freckles across the bridge of his nose.

Please stay alive.

She turned back to Catherine, catching her exchanging a triumphant glance with Louis. With no flash or fanfare, the other elders parted into two groups, revealing a burn barrel concealed behind them, positioned a safe distance from the bean field behind it. Had Riemer not warned her, she would have been utterly puzzled as to why there was a burn barrel on the field. Her eyes closed.

Forgive me.

She wasn't sure for whom she meant it: Bon, or Riemer and Johanna and their mysterious network. Maybe all of them. She opened her eyes, met Catherine's gaze with defiance, and snatched all the items from her hands.

A gasp of shock rose from the crowd. She could feel Johanna's rage and Riemer's sorrow. Catherine's exultancy was almost a physical entity between them. Mac held the elder's gaze with a hard one of her own. *You will not break me.*

She pushed past Catherine, careful not to jostle her, and dumped the items into the burn barrel. She turned back without lingering. Best not to show regret. She could experience regret when she was in the privacy of her own quarters.

As she headed back to the stairs to the bleachers, she paused beside Louis, the megaphone carrying her words to the residents of the Stronghold with the clarity of a bell.

"Burn them."

She didn't know what he replied. The crowd erupted into a deafening cheer as Gerald ignited the burn barrel, and all she saw were Louis's lips moving. She didn't care what he said. Her legs carried her up the stairs, trembling again, lacking the strength to carry her back to her seat.

But her eyes found Riemer's again, and his gaze pulled her to his side as though they were physically connected. She sat down hard beside him. He reached for her hand and held it between both of his, warming it.

People sitting near her patted her on the back, gave her meaningless congratulations. But the only remark that made her smile came from the other side of Riemer.

"Bitch," Johanna muttered.

7

"That was ballsy, Mackenzie. You nearly gave me a heart attack."

"Ballsy?" Johanna fumed. "You were an ice cube. You never really gave a damn about Bon, did you?"

Mac didn't respond. Riemer would back Johanna off before she went too far. For now, Mac was content to sit in Riemer's room, lost in a haze of numb disbelief. She was still alive. The elders let her go, and while they might harbor suspicions, she turned the people of the Stronghold to her favor. They wouldn't have as easy a time vilifying her as they had with Bon.

"Leave her alone, Jo."

"She doesn't even bother to defend herself!"

"Back off, Johanna. She's in shock." Riemer's tone left no room for argument. "We have to start planning how to get her out of here."

"Out of here?" Mac said, looking up.

"And where is she going to go? It's not like there are a dozen different communities she can run to. Smuggle her out, by all means – she'll be dead in a day. Her life for Bon's."

"Jo, you know we have options. And I'd never smuggle her out if I thought she'd end up dead in a day." He started pacing, scrubbing a hand over the stubble on his chin as he thought. "It will take some time. They'll be watching her, so she can't disappear right away. We'll have to wait a while."

"Didn't you hear me?" Jo snapped. "Why should we care if she lives? Bon is dead because of her big fat mouth!"

"What do you mean, out of here?" Mac repeated.

"I care!" Riemer shouted. Johanna fell back a step, startled. "Don't you think we live with enough death? The Council executed Bon; that was a decision they made without the input of or information from Mackenzie Bright Runner. They would have used any excuse; they've been aching to do it since he killed that idiot Goremykin."

"Well, she certainly helped them along, didn't she?"

"Bon was too circumspect," Riemer mused. "He wasn't direct enough to signal the danger of repeating anything he said or of letting the Council know he told her about his hunting team."

"Don't you dare blame this on Bon!" Johanna stabbed a finger at his chest. He knocked it away impatiently.

"We all make mistakes, Jo. Bon wasn't perfect. He made a miscalculation. Mackenzie isn't to blame for that."

"What did you mean by 'out of here?' " Mac repeated again, loudly.

Riemer looked at her blankly as though he'd forgotten she was there. "Out of the Stronghold."

"But everything's all right now. They think I'm not loyal to Bon—"

"You made that pretty obvious," muttered Johanna.

"—so they'll leave me alone."

Riemer knelt in front of her chair. "They will watch every move you make. They will wait for you to make a mistake, just one mistake. And you *will* make it, Mackenzie. You didn't know about his memory book, did you? Eventually, someone will come along and offer to tell you what was in it, and you will accept the offer because you desperately want to know. They will use your sentimentality as proof of your continued loyalty to a traitor of the Stronghold."

"Do *you* know what was in it?"

Johanna snorted. "See? She couldn't make it an hour without asking."

Riemer ignored her. "No. I didn't know about it. Of course, it could have just been a ruse by the Council – I doubt Bon would have been stupid enough to keep anything that would tip them off about how much you meant to him. I *do* know he held you in very high regard. You accepted him with no question despite what happened with Team 11."

"I didn't know he'd been a hunter," Mac said quietly. "What his team did to him was unforgivable. And the Council not moving him from hunting was negligence in the extreme." She looked at Johanna. "You think you know me, where my loyalties lie, what I would do to save my own ass. But you're wrong."

Johanna snorted again.

"One thing you're not wrong about, though, is it *is* my fault he's dead. I didn't know that his telling me about what happened when he was a hunter would be enough for them to accuse him of sedition."

Riemer squeezed her shoulder. Mackenzie winced as his fingers dug into her bruised flesh. His gaze sharpened.

"Are you hurt? Why didn't you say something earlier?"

Before she could stop him, he'd pushed aside the neckline of her shirt to inspect her shoulder. His breath caught in his throat. He stared for a moment, white-faced, and then stood up, backing away several steps.

"Take off your shirt, Mackenzie."

Mac blushed. "No way!"

"Take it off now." His expression hardened. He shoved Johanna toward the door. "Lock it."

There was no escaping this. Burning with embarrassment, she shrugged out of her tee-shirt and clutched it to her chest to shield herself.

"Sweet baby Jesus," Johanna whispered staring wide-eyed at the spreading stain radiating from an uneven circle of tooth impressions.

"Where did you get this?"

"Maybe I got it from rolling around in my bedroll with Bon."

"Bullshit!" Johanna yelled, taking a menacing step toward her.

"Or maybe she just said that to needle you, Jo, because you've been an utter bitch all day. Tone down a little, will you?" Riemer suggested. "Did it break the skin, Mackenzie?"

"If it had, I'd have gone right to quarantine with no argument."

He approached warily. Mac grimaced as he probed the bruise with his fingers.

Satisfied that she wasn't infected, Riemer moved away from her again. Most of the rooms had ventilation windows near the ceiling, but very few quarters had windows for looking outside – and those were all reserved for the elders and others deemed of higher importance. Long ago, someone painted an amazingly realistic mural on one wall. He stared at this as though staring out a window into a forest of mossy green trees, ferns, and dappled shadows. Mac pulled her shirt back on while his attention was diverted.

"What happened?" he asked at last.

"We were attacked during the night. We took evasive action – I'm not even sure how many of them there were – but they found us. One got close enough to bite but couldn't get its teeth through my shirt."

"You didn't report this when you returned. If you'd just one tiny tear in the skin, Mackenzie, you could have been infected."

While the Revenant Virus couldn't be transmitted through saliva, you never knew what a Revenant had been chomping on before it got to you. If it was one of its brethren and there was still blood in its mouth, your chances of being infected soared through the roof.

"I didn't want to be quarantined for a simple bruise. Bon inspected it carefully. If the skin had been torn, he would have tossed me in quarantine. And I would have let him."

"It's not a simple bruise. It's a bite."

"And it's a whole kettle of shit that could boil over," Johanna interjected. The waspish sting vanished from her tone, as though she just now realized how dangerous gathering was.

Riemer stared at his mural, lost in thought. Several minutes passed that seemed to Mac to last for years. He finally murmured, almost to himself, "With Bon taken care of…oh, I see what they're going to do."

"What who is going to do?" Mac demanded.

"Johanna, please leave. I'll see you in the morning at breakfast."

Mac stood up, ready to make her escape with Johanna, as unappealing as that prospect was.

Riemer speared her with a look over his shoulder, his expression unreadable but set with determination. "Mackenzie, you'll be staying here."

Johanna looked indignant. "I don't think the situation calls for such extreme measures."

"It calls for even more extreme measures, but this is all I'll be able to manage on short notice. She has to be taken off the duty roster."

"What are you talking about?" Mac demanded.

"I know that, but…she's only seventeen! What will people say?"

Anger flushed his face. "What do I care about gossip, Jo? That ship has already sailed anyway, thanks to Allbrook. I'm sure he's been spreading far and wide how he saw Mackenzie and me holding hands."

"*What* are you talking about?" Mac yelled.

"We have to set the scene to make that bite look like you got it from a lover. But the only way to do it is to let them see it happen."

She gaped at him, horrified.

He said patiently, "If they see it happen, they will believe—"

"That I'm a whore?" she said acerbically.

"Having sex doesn't make you a whore, Mackenzie. But having that wound will make you dead just as surely as really being infected."

"I'm not going to have sex with you."

He laughed shortly. "I don't believe it will come to that." He looked back at Johanna, who still hesitated by the door. "You can't be here for this. Goodnight."

"I don't think this is necessary," Mac piped up, mortified. By lunchtime tomorrow, the whole Stronghold would believe they'd been intimate.

What do you care what the Stronghold thinks, anyway? They just cheered because the council murdered your partner.

"No one will think twice – they'll assume I was worried when you didn't come back last night, got a little too frisky in my relief when you did return."

Mac's blush deepened until it was painful and itchy.

"That bite will be seen, Mackenzie," Johanna said, surprisingly gentle. "It's going to take weeks for it to fade and to stop paining you. You can't go weeks without being seen in a sleeveless shirt or in the bath. We need to spin this so they think they know how you got it."

"Besides, this gives the elders a chance to search your quarters without you knowing," he said practically as Johanna unlocked the door and opened it. "Meet us tomorrow in the dining hall."

She nodded, sent an unreadable look at Mac, and closed the door as she left. Mac let an awkward silence build between Riemer and her until she could stand it no longer.

"I hope this doesn't cause problems with you and Johanna."

He turned from the door and opened the bottom drawer of a small chest near the bed. After rummaging for a moment, he tossed her a clean tee-shirt that smelled like lemons and turned his back.

"Put it on. At least it's clean."

Mac turned her back to him as well, shucked her shirt and bra, and pulled on his shirt. The shoulder seams hung halfway to her elbows and the neckline kept sliding off to one side, showing an immoderate amount of bare shoulder. Bruised shoulder.

"Okay, you can turn around now."

"Pants and shoes, Mackenzie."

"Riemer—"

"In about five minutes, someone will come in without knocking, unless I've learned absolutely nothing in all the years I've lived here. We have to be convincing."

Resignedly, she kicked off her shoes and began stripping off her pants. "Who's coming in?"

"Johanna and I are not involved."

"That isn't what I asked."

"No, but it's what you were most concerned with."

Mac turned around, tugging at the hem of the tee-shirt to make it cover more of her exposed legs. Riemer's boots lay discarded beside his bed, and he was pulling his shirt over his head.

"What are you doing?"

"Everything I can think of to keep you safe. They ordinarily make a clean sweep of a team – you may have dodged a bullet today, but they're still holding a loaded gun."

With no warning, he crowded her against the cinderblock wall. Taller and packed with muscle, his body seemed to engulf hers. Her hands came up to ward him off and fell squarely on his chest. After the shock of contact with his bare skin, her fingers were quite reluctant to withdraw. They liked the feel of hard muscle beneath smooth, warm skin. Her mind was a blissful blank that couldn't find a single reason why she shouldn't touch him, and a lot.

His breath fanned over her neck as he bent his head to murmur, "Any second now." Booted footsteps echoed down the corridor, approaching fast. When it seemed they would thunder past his door, he added, "I'm sorry about this, Mackenzie."

"About what?" She forgot everything but the intoxicating sensation of his breath wafting over her skin and the brush of his lips against her shoulder.

The door burst open. Four gatherers – the two senior-most

teams – spilled into the room, knocking after the fact. Mac opened her mouth to protest their outrageous rudeness when Riemer's teeth sank into her bruised shoulder and the world went white with pain.

8

"Tell me again why you punched me."

Riemer flinched as the infirmary healer gingerly pressed the puffing flesh under his left eye and sent a scowl at Mackenzie, who was reclining on the bed next to his. But there was amusement in his expression, which made Mac want to sock him again.

"You bit me." She eyed the curtain that could be drawn between their beds – the curtain she regretted telling the healers not to close.

A chuckle came from one of the gatherers who had come to get Mackenzie from Riemer's room. She thought he'd said his name was Will, but she was in so much pain, his words didn't really register. His wavy brown hair constantly fell into his equally brown eyes in a rakish way. One of the healer's young helpers kept giving him sidelong looks, but he never even glanced her way.

"Now you know what happens when you get on your girlfriend's bad side, Riemer."

"I'm not sure I'm going to survive her," Riemer agreed.

Mac clenched her jaw, mostly because another healer was swabbing her wound with what she called alcohol but which Mac was sure was really acid, but also partly because she still couldn't believe that Riemer actually bit her, hard enough to break the skin. And because he seemed entirely unapologetic about it.

Maybe-Will pushed to his feet. "Well, I guess I'd better go see Gerald. The others will have told him what happened. I'll let you know what they're going to do, Mackenzie."

"Do?" she repeated. "Am I going to be detained for this?" Without waiting for his answer, she turned to Riemer with a ferocious snarl. "If I get detained for this, Riemer, you're going to be very sorry."

"Relax," Maybe-Will said. "You won't get detained. *He* might"—he motioned to Riemer—"but you won't. You can't go out with a wound like that, so they'll most likely pull you from rotation for a while, which is lucky for me."

Riemer's humor fled. "Why lucky for you?"

"Because they assigned Juarez and me to new partners." Will grinned. "Mackenzie Bright Runner, thank you very much for the vacation while you heal. I'll come visit while we're off duty."

He winked and took his leave. Riemer glared after him and rose up on one elbow to make sure he was really gone. Not ungently, the healer shoved him prone.

"I'm not so certain I shouldn't keep you overnight in case of concussion. I hear you banged into the wall pretty hard."

"Yeah, I wasn't expecting to be socked in the eye."

"Mmm." She prodded him once more, making him grimace. Mac experienced a savage pleasure seeing his pain, especially since her arm throbbed viciously every time her heart beat. "Yes, overnight for you. Would you like to be separated from Miss Bright Runner, or do you think you two can keep from maiming each other further?"

"We'll be fine, Jan. But I don't need to stay overnight. I feel fine. Barely even a headache." He raised up again, and she pushed him down again.

"You will stay right there all night with the exception of restroom breaks, Eli Riemer, or I will call in one of the guards to make sure you stay put."

Jan glared at him until he gave his reluctant agreement. Mac watched her bustle off. *Eli* Riemer. She couldn't remember ever hearing his full name, although she figured Riemer was his surname. Most of the hunters and gatherers of the Stronghold were referred to by their surnames except with close friends.

"Eli," she repeated after a moment.

"As in Elijah, the prophet in the Holy Book." He stared up at the ceiling, his arms folded beneath his head. He looked relaxed and comfortable and not at all put off by being confined to the infirmary with the girl who slugged him hard enough to give him a black eye and a mild concussion.

"Are you a prophet then?" She grinned at him, rolling onto her side, and gasped with pain. "Dammit."

His peaceful expression faded into guilt. "I'm sorry I bit you so hard."

"I still don't see why you bit me at all."

"We couldn't hide the bruise you got from the Revenant. This way they think they know how you got it."

"Did you mean to break the skin?"

His story to the infirmary was that he hadn't expected Will and crew to barge in when they did. They startled him, and in his surprise he bit down harder than the gentle love bite he meant to bestow. Mackenzie blushed all the way through the story, but managed a cocky shrug when Jan remarked that she'd experienced an eventful two days.

"Yes."

Yeah, she should have socked him again when she had the chance. The startling pain – and the shock of actually being bitten – caused an automatic reaction that was extraordinarily swift and violent. Will grabbed her after she'd punched Riemer the first time, but he lost hold of her when she struggled. She only refrained from springing upon Riemer and pummeling the hell out of every inch of him she could reach because of the apology in his eyes. Well, that and the numbing pain that spread down her arm and the blood that dripped freely off her elbow.

"I had to keep you from going out again."

"Why? It's my job, Riemer."

"That you can't do right now. The bite must have hurt like hell even before I got to it. That would be a serious liability if you were required to fight. It's your right arm – your machete arm. By tomorrow, even without my interference, you would barely have been able to lift your arm above shoulder height. But it would have healed in a couple of weeks. An open wound, however, keeps you off the roster a lot longer – too much risk of contamination."

"That's all good and fine, but your theory makes no sense. I'd have been able to start training with Will sooner without the puncture wounds. The sooner I train, the sooner I can safely go back to gathering."

"I don't want you going back out at all. Ever."

"It's not your choice."

"If you do, there will come a day – and soon – when you won't come back. There will be some grand story to explain your death, and part of it might even be true. They won't trust you now that they know Bon talked to you."

She digested this silently. The healer had given her something to drink for pain, but it only backed off the worst of it. The constant throbbing with the occasional spikes of sharp agony made her

73

headachy and irritable.

"I think you're overly paranoid."

"I'd think what happened to Bon would assure you that I'm probably not paranoid enough."

"Say you're right—"

"I *am* right."

"You think I can't trust Will? That he'll let the Revenants get me, or he'll take me down himself?"

"I didn't say that. I just think you should trust no one."

"Including you?" She arched a brow at him, making the ache in her head turn into a stabbing pain.

"I'm the only one you *can* trust, but I guess I'd say that if I were working against you. So including me." His admission came in a disgruntled tone.

"Why are you so determined to protect me? And just so you know, I'm not entirely convinced that I'm in any danger. Especially not from the elders."

"Have I been wrong yet?"

"I don't know, Elijah," she said wearily. "I'm too tired to think, and in too much pain to make sense out of anything. I just want to sleep."

"For what it's worth, I hope I'm wrong about all of this, but I don't think I am. As for the why of it – well, look around you next time you go outside the Stronghold, Mackenzie Bright Runner. We're an endangered species. Your life is precious."

Mac blinked, trying to dispel to surreal edge his words brought to their conversation. With each blink, it grew harder to open her eyes again. After a time, she heard him whisper, "Sleep well," and at last she saw an end to this long, bizarre day.

Elders Louis and Catherine came for Riemer after breakfast, accompanied by two burly young guards from the Stronghold's security team, just in case Riemer gave them any trouble. Catherine glowered at Mackenzie the whole time, but Louis viewed the whole incident with amusement and the kind of tolerance an uncle might show toward a favored niece: she might step over the line a bit, but it could be ignored to a certain extent.

"Two days detention ought to do the trick, young Eli," Louis pronounced, peering at Mackenzie's wound as the healer – Nanci this time, as Jan went off duty during the night – changed her dressing.

"Two days!"

"You've taken a resourceful gatherer off duty with your antics, Mr. Riemer," Catherine said severely. "If it were up to me, you'd be in detention for a month. But the other field workers would have to cover your duties, and Louis feels we should exercise lenience." She looked highly disapproving of Louis's opinion in the matter.

Riemer looked chagrined. Mac noted that while he *looked* chagrined, the glint in his eye confirmed that he was not embarrassed or regretful in the slightest.

Louis gave them both an indulgent smile, seeming to be highly entertained. "In the future, I'd like to see a lot less physical manifestation of your feelings, Mr. Riemer. In other words, no more marks on Miss Bright Runner."

"It's not Mackenzie's fault," Riemer put in quickly.

"Yes, we know." Catherine's tone suggested she'd like to find a way to blame Mac anyway. "Miss Bright Runner will be taken off duty until healed. When the infirmary releases her to light duty, she can go to work in the fields, gathering seeds or something that doesn't require using her arm or getting dirty."

"And someone will water my cabbages? They're due for a watering today."

"We're well aware of the necessities of your crop, Mr. Riemer," said Catherine coldly. "Shall we? I have more pressing matters to deal with today."

The two guards stepped forward, but Riemer slid off his bed without hesitation or protestation. He paused at the door to send a grin and a wink at Mackenzie, and then Catherine prodded him forward. Mac felt suddenly very alone and uncertain in his absence.

Nanci finished winding a fresh bandage around Mac's wound. "I'll be back with another infusion for the pain. Try not to lift anything or flex the arm too much. No immersion in water until the punctures have sealed."

After she bustled away, Louis perched on the edge of Mac's bed, still looking greatly amused. Mac felt an irrepressible urge to apologize.

"I'm sorry, Louis. I don't mean to be so much trouble lately."

He waved a hand unconcernedly, dismissing her contrition.

"Never mind all of that, Mackenzie. It's a rare person who never finds some sort of mischief. Your Eli will spend a couple of days in the detention room, making soap – he hates doing that – and then he'll be back at your side."

Mac blushed. "He hates making soap?"

"It's not his first time through the detention room," he said with a wry smile.

"Catherine doesn't seem to approve of the sentence."

The smile faded into an oddly reminiscent expression. "I knew your parents well, Mackenzie. Your father was an exceptional hunter, and your mother possessed extraordinary intuition. We watched their accomplishments carefully, very much interested in appointing them to the Council when they retired from hunting."

She knew how that ended. Her parents, along with the other four members of their hunting team, vanished while clearing an area heavily infested with Revenants. Another team was dispatched to investigate. The only evidence of the missing team were bits of torn, bloodstained clothes and a lot of blood.

Mackenzie was three years old at the time. She could barely remember them, just memory flashes of riding on a tall man's shoulders and a dark-haired woman tucking her into bed. Mac grew up in the Foster Parent section with other orphaned children. It hadn't been a bad upbringing; several couples oversaw the children in shifts, and she was well-cared for and loved.

"Catherine and Gerald were appointed to the council in their stead. Catherine has never quite forgotten that she was not our first choice. You're a constant and obvious reminder of that, especially because you resemble your mother more every year."

"She does realize it's not my fault, right?"

His mouth twisted sadly. "I'm afraid that every one of us, the Council of Elders included, has human failings, Mackenzie." He patted her arm and stood up, making his way to the door, where he paused. "I'm very sorry about Bon."

Unease prickled over her skin. "He was a good partner." Not a friend, but a partner. She thought Riemer would have been pleased with her wording. Louis seemed satisfied.

"Yes, he was good. Report to Jonas in the fields when the healers release you. He already knows to expect you soon."

"Thank you, sir."

Louis took his leave. The healer came in with a bitter drink she assured Mac would take away the worst of the pain but would make her very sleepy. She drank it gratefully, and while she waited for it to begin its work, she thought back to the note Ren Leonard had left her, which she kept tucked into the rip in her pack. She'd sewn over it with two loose stitches, which so far had remained unbroken, assuring her that her secret was still safe.

Existence is futile.

Not survival is futile, or living is futile. He saw no purpose in helping the Stronghold but told her to live well whatever life she chose. Because by her own admission, people *existed* at the Stronghold — it was simply about survival, which became more desperate every year. But she had said she wanted to *live*, not just *exist*.

Existence is futile. Live well whatever life you choose.

Two statements whose subtle nuances she missed when she first read his note. He refused to help the Stronghold, but he hadn't refused to help *her*.

She followed this revelation through the tangled thickets of deep contemplation, where slumber found her and swept her away into dark dreams of Revenants and councils and, at long last, more pleasant reveries of Elijah Riemer.

9

Work in the fields was oddly enjoyable. Mackenzie thought she would be bored senseless, but instead she found herself at peace. For most of the last six months, she'd spent five days of the week gathering remnants of a lost civilization to further her settlement's survival. The year-and-a-half before that, she'd spent five of seven days training intensively with Bonfils Moreau, learning to be on guard both physically and mentally at all times.

Now she toiled surrounded by life, and the difference was dramatic. The mental relaxation was the most welcome, although it brought oddly seductive thoughts of Riemer. Her daydreams invited him in even when she tried desperately to keep him out – which was usually when she made some movement that caused her arm to smart with pain and her annoyance to flare.

She'd never been one of those giggling, flirtatious girls who'd gone boy-crazy in her early teens. Her crushes were quiet ones, the objects never being any the wiser, and all faded after a relatively short period. Never before had she allowed her mind to wander down the labyrinthine paths of sexual fantasy, yet over the last few days she'd pulled her thoughts out of more compromising positions than she cared to contemplate.

Elijah appeared after serving his two-day sentence in the detention room. He found her in the seed fields and, smirking slightly, presented her with a rectangle of rosemary-mint soap before heading off to his cabbage patch. She was disappointed when he didn't look back as he left, and then infuriated with herself for even noticing.

The days flew past. Her work-week coincided with his, and he was careful to make sure their weekends were spent together in full view of the rest of their community – especially Will Crawford, her new gathering partner, who seemed nothing but amused by this behavior.

At the end of the first week, she was cleared to do minor weeding, and Jonas allowed her to work with Elijah in the cabbage field. Everyone in the Stronghold seemed to have taken a keen interest in their blooming relationship. Elijah, for his part, did nothing to dispel the misconception – as indeed, it was exactly what he wanted them to think – but maintained a strict policy of minimal physical contact, which only served to add, in the eyes of the Stronghold's population, an element of adorability to their courtship.

Four weeks into Mac's recovery found her decorating tables in the grassy field reserved for outdoor games and playing kids. In years the crops were abundant and the livestock fruitful, the Stronghold threw an end-of-summer celebration, taking advantage of a climate that allowed the warm weather to last through September and often into mid-October. Tables from the dining hall were dragged outside and festooned with bouquets of late-blooming flowers. Two hulking hogs had been roasting on spits for the last two days, the tantalizing aroma of roasting pork driving everyone crazy. A few dozen chickens, three doe, and a heifer gave their lives for the feast as well. Mac and Eli, along with the other field workers, harvested what seemed like an endless supply of beets, beans, peas, summer squash, corn, and various other vegetables. The heady scent of baking bread filled the Stronghold at all hours. Mac had never salivated so much in her entire life.

After dinner, she somehow ended up surrounded by a group of gatherers, drinking cold tea and trying not to think about how much she'd eaten – and trying not to scratch the drying scabs on her arm that itched madly under her shirt sleeve because the punctures hurt like hell when she touched them. Will dominated the conversation with tales of his gathering escapades with Juarez and his training plans for her. Eli sat at another table with a group of field workers and Johanna, whose glacial demeanor toward Mac hadn't thawed in the slightest. He glanced at her frequently, marking her location, but she wasn't sure what to make of the searching looks he sent in Will's direction.

Torches were lit at dusk, and the musicians set up in the courtyard just outside the Commons. The courtyard was paved with flagstones, creating an ideal dance floor, which quickly became crowded with couples. Just as Will nudged her and nodded toward the swaying dancers, Eli extricated her from the group of gatherers with a sardonic smile that made Will grin and led her inside to the Commons. The room seemed oddly bare despite the couples who retreated inside where there was more room.

They weaved through the dancing people to the far side of the crowd near the wall. Elijah surprised her by swinging her around and into his arms, moving in time to the music with a marked lack of self-consciousness. Discomfited, Mac tried several times to make conversation, but he seemed loath to talk. He was a good dancer, leading her through several swing tunes and a lively waltz. The music slowed tempo and a vocalist added a plaintive lament.

"Gypsy music," he murmured in her ear. He'd pulled her effortlessly from the flowing steps of the waltz to the close sway of what had been the modern slow dance at the end of civilization. His cheek was warm, pressed against her temple, and his heart thudded steady and reassuring against her hand, which he held trapped between them.

"I'm surprised they allow it to be played."

"Well, it isn't likely that a band of gypsies will stroll past and coax us into wanton behavior," he replied with amusement.

A good thing, too, for Mackenzie was having trouble enough with her own wanton thoughts. The gypsy lament engulfed her senses, stirring emotions that were dangerous in altogether new ways than the peril she'd experienced so far in her life. The notes rose and fell in patterns that caused her heart to race and tempted reckless behavior. What would he do if she pressed her lips against his throat, traced her tongue along his jawline, worked her way to those wonderfully sensuous lips?

Whoa! She'd gone way far into the danger zone of daydreaming, as evidenced by how she'd tilted her head, bringing her lips within a centimeter of his neck, and how deeply she was breathing in his scent.

"Enjoying yourself, Mackenzie?" he whispered with wicked delight.

Mac blushed furiously and tried to put some space between them. He held her in place, laughing softly. With no warning, he whirled her out of the stream of dancers around them, putting his back to the wall and holding her tightly against him. The laughter had fled his face, leaving behind an intensity that both petrified and thrilled her.

"Mackenzie, I didn't plan on—" He broke off in mid-whisper, movement over her shoulder claiming his attention. His posture shifted suddenly to the tense and watchful warrior that he'd once been, and he plastered a grin on his face with effort.

"What is it?"

"Trouble."

She'd never met the tall dark-skinned man who leaned in from behind her to give Elijah a back-thumping, bone-jarring hug, mashing her between them. She thought he worked in the detention room, and she never had cause to go there. Neither could she hear what the man whispered in his ear, presumably under the pretense of offering congratulations on their budding romance. Nor did she miss the fact that while Eli's grin never wavered as he shook the man's hand enthusiastically, his whole body seemed to be shrieking in alarm.

The man sauntered off. Elijah bent his head to hers, his lips against her ear. "Where did you go with Bon on your last run?"

"What? Why does it matter?"

His arms tightened around her, fingers biting into her ribs. "*Where*, Mackenzie?"

She swallowed over a lump of fear in her throat. "We went to find Ren Leonard."

He sucked in a breath. "Did he leave you a letter?"

"Oh no!" She tried to pull away. She wanted – needed – to see his expression, but he held her tight to him. "They found the note, didn't they?"

"They searched your quarters again. Jesus, Mackenzie, *why didn't you burn it?*"

"I didn't want to. I wanted to remember what he'd said. Elijah, he doesn't—"

"Stop. I don't care about what he said right now. We're in deep shit."

"*I'm* in deep shit, you mean."

He didn't respond for a long moment. Mac was trembling so hard she thought the tremors must be shaking him as well. Or perhaps he was trembling, too. He seemed to have trouble getting enough air.

And then one hand slowly slid around her back, skated over her ribs, and dropped down along her hipbone to plunge deep into her pocket.

"I've put a key in your pocket. There's a house eight blocks south and five blocks west, burned down to the ground. The key is to the shed behind the ruins. There's food and water and other supplies. It's secure."

"Eli—"

"I'll join you as soon as I can. If I'm not there in seven days, leave without me. Take everyth—"

"Leave! Leave where? And how am I going to get out of the Stronghold?"

"You'll get out. Take everything you can carry. I'll catch up to you. Follow the signs."

"*What* signs? What are you talking about?"

"There's a symbol painted inside the shed. Follow that sign west along the old highway. If I can't come myself, I'll send someone."

"How will I know—"

"They'll have a copper disk with the same symbol on it so you'll know to trust them." He set her away from him at last. He still smiled, a mask for anyone who might be watching, but up close the smile was forced and strained.

"This is crazy! I can't leave!" Mac's panic swelled. They found Ren Leonard's note. She would be executed as surely as Bon had been, so why was Eli talking about some stupid shed and following signs? "They'll kill me," she whispered.

"No. *No*," he insisted. "We don't have much time, so listen to me carefully. I won't have time to repeat anything. Two blocks south, there's a house with overgrown holly shrubs. There's a machete hidden in the shrubs. You should be able to dodge any Revenants on the way if you stay alert. Get the machete, and then go directly to the shed. Don't stop and fight unless you have to. I promise I'll be there as soon as I can."

Shrubs? Sheds? What the hell was he talking about? Too many unknowns made her head swim. Fear muted her voice, and her desperate questions log-jammed in her throat. Whatever he planned, she couldn't do. Never had she been beyond the walls of the Stronghold without a partner watching her back.

"Mackenzie! *Trust me*."

She struggled past her panic. "Okay. The machete two blocks south. The shed, eight blocks south and five blocks east."

"*West*," he hissed.

"Yes, west. West. The shed is west. Okay. I can do this." Her fingers curled into his shirt, gripping the fabric as though she could prevent herself from being torn away from him. "I'm scared, Elijah."

He closed his eyes again, and then suddenly he was kissing her, a forceful possession of her mouth that bordered on violence. Mackenzie gave herself over to the brutal invasion. The Council was coming for her. There was no time for tender passion, no time for a sweet first kiss. The air around them shivered with the pagan magic of the gypsy lament. Elijah's lips tasted of mint and limes; his tongue swirled circles of each flavor against hers. The edge of his teeth bit into her lip until she tasted blood.

He broke away, eyes still closed, his breath heaving in and out in time with the frantic beat of his heart. *"Mackenzie,"* he breathed. "I—"

She would never know what he'd been about to say. A tap on her shoulder froze the blood in her veins and made her jolt although she was expecting it. Muscle-bound guards flanked her, each taking an arm firmly, the one on her right careful not to grab her wound. The gypsy lament stopped on a screeching note, and people poured into the Commons, murmuring excitedly. Elijah's face registered shocked outrage.

"What the hell is this?" he thundered, making a futile attempt to reclaim her.

Catherine stepped around the guards. "Mr. Riemer, please restrain yourself." Her voice rose above the muttering crowd, which fell silent under her commanding tone. "Mackenzie Bright Runner, I hold in my hand evidence of your attempted bargain with a Revenant – not just *any* Revenant, but the Father of the Apocalypse himself, Ren Leonard."

The crowd gasped in disbelief. Mac was vaguely aware of Louis threading his way through the crowd, his expression grim and betrayed. She saw Will standing near the doors to the patio, stunned and disbelieving.

"It is a violation of the laws of the Stronghold to bargain with a Revenant. Because you have attempted to enter into a pact with the vermin who brought this plague down upon the earth, your sentence is execu—"

Louis made his way to Catherine's side and now gripped her

arm, cutting off her words. Catherine shoved a paper into his hands. With a sinking heart, Mac recognized the note Ren Leonard left her. It was true; they had found it. There was no mistake, no stopping this.

Louis and Catherine held a vehemently whispered conversation that Mac couldn't make out over the buzzing crowd around her. And then Louis spoke to the crowd, his brutal grip on Catherine's arm ensuring her silence.

"Miss Bright Runner attempted to form a pact with the Revenant Ren Leonard, yes. But this serious betrayal of the Stronghold's laws governing such acts must be weighed against Miss Bright Runner's motives. Leonard's letter to her reveals those motives, which were unselfish and inspired by her love and worry for her community. She sought Leonard's help for the good of the settlement.

"While we cannot excuse this violation of the law, we can exercise mercy in the application of justice. Banishment is the usual sentence for anyone attempting to bargain with Revenants. This sentence shall be lifted if any will stand with Mackenzie Bright Runner."

The crowd erupted into an excited babble. A flash of very real alarm replaced the outrage on Elijah's face. Louis held up a hand for silence. "Elijah Riemer! Will you stand with Miss Bright Runner and plead mercy on her behalf?"

In the blink of an eye, disapproval claimed Riemer's expression, a stony shield that hid his shock. He had no choice – to stand on her behalf would be the same as hanging himself – but to see that disappointment hurt unbearably.

His voice rang out clear and strong. "No."

Arms crossed over his chest, he turned his back. One by one, the other residents of the Stronghold followed suit, until Mackenzie, the two guards, Louis, and Catherine alone stood facing each other. Humiliation burned an acid trail from her stomach through her veins, raising a blush so deep it was painful. Surely her body couldn't withstand it for long, and her molecules would spontaneously disintegrate and she would wink out of existence. That would be good, because she didn't think she could bear walking to the front entrance for the very last time. Without Bon. Without Elijah.

Catherine was unabashedly furious at Louis's interference.

Louis himself looked as though he'd aged a decade in the last few minutes.

"Let the official record show that no one stands with Mackenzie Bright Runner. Miss Bright Runner, you are hereby banished from the Stronghold to make your own way in the world. You will go with only the clothes on your back and the possessions on your person. May God be with you." He turned his back, forcing Catherine to turn away as well.

The crowd parted as the guards elbowed their way through, dragging Mackenzie with them. She didn't struggle, but her feet didn't seem to want to move on their own. The heavy metal doors creaked open, letting in the fragrance of the night. The guards walked her twenty paces outside the doors and released her arms.

"Sit down, please." Shaking, Mac sat on the gravel path leading to the door. "Do not attempt to follow us."

Mac didn't watch them retreat. The crunch of their footsteps on the gravel faded with distance. The doors creaked closed and the bolts slammed home, leaving her alone in a hostile world.

10

When the steel door banged shut, closing Mackenzie on the other side, Elijah Riemer experienced a sensation he had not felt in a number of years: panic. It wasn't supposed to happen this way. She wasn't supposed to be out there alone.

He kept his back turned, like all the other Stronghold residents, until Louis cleared his throat and raised his voice above the low drone of murmured conversation.

"You may all go about your business now. Musicians — please!"

Riemer could see the elder in his mind's eye, urging the ensemble to resume playing. *Not the gypsy lament*, he prayed, because he didn't think he could stand it. The ensemble picked up with a light classical piece — Brahms, he thought, although his heart pounded so hard he could barely hear the music over the beat of his pulse in his ears. It sounded light-hearted and soothing, aimed at taking the dark edge off the evening that Mackenzie's exile caused. Distract the people so they wouldn't realize the horror committed against one of their own.

People flowed around him, some giving him covert looks from the corners of their eyes, others staring openly. He couldn't seem to make himself speak to them or move out of their way. Shock rooted his feet to the floor.

Every action had been thoroughly vetted for flaws, every possible scenario explored, a contingency plan made for every anticipated interference. Mackenzie would need Mark's shed key only if she were being exiled, and that wasn't the plan. The second Mark passed it to him through their handshake, he'd known that their meticulously constructed scheme had somehow collapsed into ruins. How could this have happened?

Johanna stopped beside him. He couldn't see her, but he knew it was her by the irritable vibe she brought with her. And sure enough, a second later she snapped, "Put your eyes back in your head and move along."

Riemer hadn't even noticed the gawker, who now scurried off, chased for a time by Johanna's scowl.

"What do we do now?" she whispered.

"Not here." His paralysis broke. He turned to her, gripped her shoulders, and leaned close to her ear. "Meet me out behind the garden shed in the northwest field. Give it twenty minutes."

"Oh, the shed where Mackenzie used to go necking with Zane Allbrook?"

He ignored her waspish tone. Whatever Mackenzie had done before him didn't matter, and he didn't have time to wallow in jealousy. It was a moot point anyway; she was outside the Stronghold at night, alone and unarmed, without him. Without anyone.

"That's the one. Bring Mark with you."

Without waiting for her agreement, he stalked off toward the patio. People flowed out of his way as though repelled by his grief, clearing his path. He spoke to no one, and no one attempted to speak to him. He would be allowed a period of time to grieve, for even the Council recognized that a loved one being exposed as a traitor to the settlement didn't instantaneously erase your feelings for that person. After that, he would be expected to move on emotionally, eschewing any mementos and spoken memories of Mackenzie like she had never existed.

As if he could ever do that.

His steps took him beyond the reach of the party lanterns, past the cabbage field, behind the shed in the northeast field, and to the corn patch. He counted the rows – twelve – before he headed into the field. The stalks rustled in the breeze, masking his movement. He stopped while he was still close to the back and waited.

Within moments, a breath of a whisper drifted to him from another row. "I'm here."

"What the hell happened?" he hissed. "She was supposed to be arrested, not exiled. This is inexcusable."

"I don't know. I think they might have had a counter plan, just in case."

A chill rippled through him. "That would mean—"

"That I'm found out. Or, at the very least, they suspect me."

Perfect. Just perfect. They'd known they wouldn't be able to do this indefinitely, sneaking out the so-called dissenters under the very noses of the Council. It only needed to hold for another couple of weeks, until the underground pulled out all their agents and loved ones and were on their way to the coast. It was no longer safe for them here. Anyone who disagreed with the Council in the future would have to make their own peace with it or find their own way out.

"Do you understand that she is alone out there? At night. Unarmed. Without me to protect her."

A chuckle floated through the corn. "I think the key words there are 'without me.' "

Completely beside the point, although he couldn't deny the truth of it. When he'd been a hunter, he'd been aware of her scrutiny, mostly because she was unlike the other girls who watched him. For one, she'd been barely twelve and much more solemn than the rest of her age group. For another, her scrutiny hadn't been the flirtatious, hero-worship that was generally aimed at the hunters. Even Laura noticed it.

"She's observing you. Noting your attitude, your demeanor."

He laughed. "And here I thought it was my sexy muscles."

She'd poked her finger into one of the muscles in question, making him squirm. "Although I don't doubt she's noticed your god-like body"—she rolled her eyes—"that's not what she's watching. She's a serious one. They'll make her a hunter."

And the thought made his blood run cold, because little Mackenzie Bright Runner had no one to protest on her behalf. They would take her at fifteen and begin her training, twisting her psyche until killing became as much a part of her as the color of her hair and eyes. He knew, because they had done exactly that to him.

The next three years was a shit-storm of catastrophe. Bon Moreau asked to step down and was refused, and shortly after killed his teammate. Laura was struck in the face with a rusty knife and succumbed to tetanus after a torturous month of excruciating pain. Devastated, Riemer asked to step down from hunting and was assigned to the cabbage field.

By then, he'd put Mackenzie so far to the back of his mind that when she unexpectedly crossed his path one day, he'd been stunned to see not the waiflike preteen he remembered but an intriguing young woman.

And just a few months after that, Bon said to him, "They'll assign her soon."

Riemer followed his gaze to find Mackenzie and a few of her

girlfriends on a blanket in the field, playing with a litter of kittens. There was kindness in her, gentleness. His heart ached to know that it would soon be squeezed out of her. Life was brutal enough in the post-Upheaval world without turning the survivors into savages.

"What are they going to do with you?"

Bon had been cooling his heels since the tragic incident with Team 11 – first in solitary confinement, then in idle freedom, if almost total ostracization could be called freedom. Just recently, he'd been through a couple weeks' worth of meetings with the Council to discuss just where he fit into the community now. Riemer was afraid that they'd decide Bon's place was outside the Stronghold doors – permanently and with a couple of bullets in his legs.

Bon shrugged. "Gathering, Elijah. Some good old-fashioned scavenging to soothe – and possibly save – my soul." He seemed amused by it, but his next words rang with a sour note. "If they can find a partner who will work with me."

Gathering. It wasn't much better than hunting. There was still killing involved, but not as much.

It came to him in a flash, a solution to the puzzle of how to spare Mackenzie Bright Runner the near-inevitable fate of becoming a Stronghold drone, of how to keep her under the underground's watchful eye without being obvious or coming across as creepy.

"Ask for her to be assigned to you."

Bon said, dryly, "That doesn't exactly keep her safe and sound in the Stronghold."

"She won't be safe and sound in the Stronghold anyway. Have you seen the way she moves? Laura was right; they're going to claim her for hunting, unless you claim her as a gathering partner first."

"And what then, Eli? Gathering steals your soul the same as hunting, just slower."

"Maybe we can stop that from happening. As her trainer and mentor, you'll have her trust and her ear. You'll be able to influence her."

And so they orchestrated her life as much as they were able. Bon subtly worked his philosophies into their training, circumspectly showed her the Stronghold government's manipulative, heavy-handed ways. Even through her training, they were planning how to get her out of the Stronghold with him. But the elders separated them as soon as they returned from their overnight sojourn to find Leonard, so that plan had gone terribly wrong, too. One failed plan was unfortunate; two was sabotage.

He closed his eyes. *Oh God, Laura, what have I done? I've as good as killed her.*

To his unseen companion in the corn, he whispered what Johanna asked him only minutes ago: "What do we do now?"

"You'll be arrested in three days and sentenced to execution."

He hissed in a breath. *"Three days!* I'm supposed to be out there with her *right now!"* It was how this whole thing worked: you were arrested and sentenced to execution, and your loved ones were brought to make their peace and say goodbye. The whole lot of you were smuggled out into the cover of the woods by a sympathetic detention guard. As you slipped off to the shed to wait for morning, an equally sympathetic wall guard watched your back for as long as he or she was able.

"That's obviously not going to happen. We have to have reason to arrest you. That will take a few days."

"Okay. You'll arrest me in three days. On what grounds?"

"Publicly defending Mackenzie Bright Runner, a traitor to the community."

"And if there's interference this time? I only have seven days before she leaves without me." *If she even makes it to the shed.*

"We'll have you out before then. You know what you have to do?"

Sure he did: run his mouth. Take his silent grieving to a verbal level. A dangerous course, because in light of the debacle of Bon's extraction and Louis's interference with Mackenzie's escape, he didn't trust that his own would go off without a hitch.

"I won't be able to help with the rest of you."

"We'll manage. The most important thing is to get you to her as fast as we can. This exile feels like a set-up. I don't trust that the rest of the Council will leave her to fate. Three days, Elijah. Make your arrangements."

With what sounded like nothing more than the whisper of a breeze through the corn, his companion was gone. He waited several minutes and then headed back the way he'd come, stopping behind the shed to wait for Johanna and Mark, his face turned toward the dark sky.

The stars were brilliant crystals flung across the velvet black curtain of space. Just three days ago, they had lain in the grass on their backs, staring up at the winking lights millions of miles away, not speaking, not touching, just *being*. Watching her covertly, he'd felt a familiar tug in the vicinity of his heart, something he'd not felt since Laura. Not entirely welcome, but perhaps inevitable.

And oh, what different women they were. Laura, statuesque and commanding, full of confidence, a lethal hunter and a gentle lover, fully immersed in life. And Mackenzie, small and compact, barely reaching his shoulder, just as lethal as Laura but also somehow naïve and uncertain, standing on the periphery of life, observing. Always observing and rarely interacting, especially after her childhood friend died some weeks ago.

The scuff of shoes on grass announced Johanna and Mark's arrival. He looked away from the sky and waited for them to round the building.

With as little finesse as she usually displayed, Johanna demanded, "So what happened?"

"Don't know. We suspect we've been found out. I don't have long to make arrangements." He looked at Mark, whose black skin made him almost invisible in the night. "It's up to you to get them out now. Johanna will be going with me."

In contrast to Mark's near invisibility, Johanna's sudden paleness made her glow.

"We had a plan," she hissed.

"And now we have a new one. I know you're scared, Jo, but things have changed. We can't do anything but change our strategy in response."

"You could let her fend for herself. Or you could send someone else."

"If you know me at all, you know I can't do that. Put on your medallion, keep it under your shirt. Pack smart but light and be ready."

"How long is 'not long'?" Mark asked.

"Three days."

Johanna hissed in a breath.

"Okay," Mark said bracingly. "Three days. A new strategy, you said. Which one?"

"None. We're going to have to wing it from here. We have no idea what they know or how they found out. Or what they plan to do with that knowledge, for that matter. Our best plan is no plan at all."

"Flying blind." Mark drew a deep breath. "All right. I'll get started." He melted away into the night. Johanna shuddered.

"It's creepy how he does that."

"You could do with some lessons in stealth, come to think of it."

"I could do with some lessons in combat," she snapped. "What can you possibly be thinking? We were supposed to go in a group — safety in numbers, you said. I don't know how to fight!"

"Things changed. We adapt our plan or we die, Jo. We go as soon as we possibly can, or they will kill us." He grabbed her hand and squeezed it reassuringly, but her scowl didn't go away. "When you think they have you figured out, do the unexpected."

She stared at the cement wall a couple dozen feet away. "Will they kill us? Do you really think so?"

He dropped her hand. "Remember the group that asked to leave six years ago? Well, they got their wish, not that they're in any position to enjoy it. Carried out in wheelbarrows, one by one over the course of several months, and burned in the street after convenient fatal accidents."

"Maybe they really *were* accidents."

"All dead," he repeated succinctly. "To a man. If the council knows about our sympathetic elder, they know about the rest of us. I don't want to be just another scorch mark in the street, Johanna."

She huffed out a breath, staring off into the dark corn field. "This is insane. Your infatuation with a child is going to get us killed."

Riemer felt a stab of annoyance. Was she really going to do this right now? "She's hardly a child. And that topic is not open for discussion or comment. Now go on back. I'll be in after a while."

He couldn't see her eyes, but he felt the weight of her gaze on him. Felt the weight of her judgment, too, but what answers could he give her when he didn't understand it all himself? The only justification for his panic should be that Mackenzie's life was one for which the underground assumed responsibility. But both he and Johanna knew that wasn't the case.

"Okay," she said softly, the edge disappearing from her tone. "I'll see you in the morning."

When she was gone, he closed his eyes again, trying to calm the swell of panic, the fierce anxiety that made him want to scale the wall and risk a guard's bolt in his back as he made a run for the shed.

A scraping step signaled company. He opened his eyes, following the sound to the top of the wall. The northeast quadrant guard was crouching down. His face, lit by moonlight, held a mocking smile.

"Tough luck about your girlfriend, Riemer. Maybe you should plant a cabbage in her name."

"Piss off, Olson."

"Or maybe *you're* the cabbage. What dumb-ass gets involved with Bon Moreau's partner, of all people? Oh, that'd be you."

Riemer pushed away from the shed wall, stepping into the moonlight. "I'd take ten of her over half of you, ugly. Now get out of my face before I rearrange your features."

Olson's mouth twisted into an ugly snarl. "Think I won't report that, hunter?"

A jab, that, calling him a hunter when he hadn't been for two years now, a reminder that he'd lost his nerve. Well, they could think what they liked. It hadn't been a matter of losing his nerve but of losing his humanity. That he'd chosen to rescue the latter didn't mean he'd lost his instinct for survival or his ability to ensure it. But let them underestimate him.

"Do whatever you want. I couldn't care less. Asshole."

He left Olson fuming on the wall, unable to back up his aggression because he was on duty. As he stalked through the open doors into the Commons, Will Crawford tried to stop him, but Riemer shouldered past him, ignoring the stares, the whispers, the judging. The path to his quarters was unimpeded; people flowed out of his way, repelled by either their respect for him or their discomfort in the face of his distress. Or, of course, by their judgment of the company he'd been keeping. He was finished here, his reputation irreparably damaged; he either got himself out or he'd wind up dead.

He slipped into his room, leaving the gawkers and gossipers in the noisy hall. His back against the door, he slid down it until he was sitting on the floor, finally able to unleash the wild fear inside him that clenched his chest and made his breath come short.

God, keep her safe. I'm on my way. I promise, I'm on my way!

11

Summer nights in a semi-arid desert are cool and breezy. Mackenzie had spent many night hours in the fields, counting the stars scattered like jewels on velvet, the whisper of the air like a silky wrap settling over her skin.

In her first days as a gatherer, she'd calmed her rioting nerves by spending a couple hours watching shooting stars streak across the inky sky. And since Bon's execution, she'd whiled away hours of her sleep-time, staring into the glittering void beyond the earth's atmosphere, questioning a lot of things she'd never before thought to doubt.

Tonight, she didn't linger in the cool dark night, pondering life and the circumstances that shaped her existence. The consequences of those circumstances no doubt lingered in the shadows, picking their way ever closer to tearing out her throat.

As soon as the Stronghold door banged closed behind the guards, she picked herself up out of the gravel, glancing warily around her. The south quadrant wall guards paced the wall, seeming to pay no attention to the lone girl on the front walk as they held their crossbows at the ready, peering into the darkness below them. Mac knew better. If she tried to run back to the front doors, they might zip a bolt into the ground at her feet. If she raised anything toward them that could be construed as a danger to them, they would drop her where she stood, and that would be the sad, sorry end of her very short life.

Live well whatever life you choose.

Time to get moving.

The night was saved from absolute blackness by the waxing moon, three-quarters full. She stepped off the noisy gravel path and into the grass, which was kept short through the judicious application of a tribe of goats and the occasional scythe. Eyes bored into her back as she crossed the crumbling blacktop road and entered the deserted neighborhood beyond. She wondered if Zane Allbrook was on wall duty tonight and what he thought of this whole mess. It would be very awkward if he felt compelled to skewer her with a crossbow bolt after all those hours of indiscriminate kissing behind the potting shed.

But it wasn't Zane Allbrook's kiss that occupied her mind. It wasn't even the prospect of running into Revenants that claimed every ounce of her attention and filled her with black dread. She just realized that Elijah had told her how many blocks away the machete and the shed were, but he had not told her down which street. There were three that butted up to the road that ran the length of the Stronghold's lot.

Use logic, Mac, she could almost hear Bon saying. *Logic dictates they exile you out the front door. Take the closest street.*

Who was she to argue against logic? And Bon never steered her wrong.

She followed the pitted road south, at last feeling the sensation of eyes on her fade as she passed out of sight of the Stronghold. The sensation of being stalked, however, flared in full concentration.

It took half a block to pinpoint where they were: flanking her on her right, keeping to the shadows near the crumbling houses. Mac caught glimpses from the corner of her eye, but she steeled herself to not look around. They would attack if she showed any awareness of them, and there was another treacherous block between her and the house with the holly shrubs and the machete.

Though familiar in daylight, nighttime draped the neighborhood in dark shrouds, and the crumbling houses became sinister ruins limned in silver moonlight.

Mac kept to the middle of the cracked street. It was too easy for a Revenant to hide in the shadow of a house or tree and snag a person as he or she passed by. It also meant that she was going to have to make a dash for the machete and probably fight her way free of Revenants. The rest of the thirteen blocks to the shed would most likely be covered in a sprint. Damn Revenants.

No, not the Revenants. Damn elders. And most of all, damn Catherine. If not for her petty jealousy, Mac would be warm and cozy in the Stronghold, full of good food, heady from good company, and – if her intuition served her right – enjoying the considerable charms of Elijah Riemer in new and exhilarating ways.

Instead, here she was without protection, without shelter, without a clue in hell of where she was heading and what she would find when she arrived. Every hair on her body stood at stiff attention. Anxiety ramped up her nerves until she fervently wished she were anywhere but inside her own skin. If only she'd had more warning, if Elijah had been given more time to prepare her and—

Crash!

Her body was so tense that when she jumped, a sharp jolt shot through her spine and up the back of her head, making her dizzy. She didn't dare look around or break into a run; the Revenants would attack if she did. A surreal sense of vertigo turned her sure-footed stride into a stumbling, uncontrolled gait that aimed her off the street. She stumbled over the curb and fell into prickly shrubbery, landing on something flat and cold and hard. She lay stunned for a second while the world whirled around her and the breeze hissed sibilant love words to the night and something – maybe a tree branch against a house – scraped nearby.

Hissing. Scraping. What did she need to remember about those two sounds?

Revenants.

She plunged her hand into the prickly shrubs as the vertigo gave her one last lurch and then passed. Her fingers closed over a stone. Too small; it would only piss them off. She made a face as her hand squelched through damp, decaying leaves. Gross. Her fingers scrabbled over smooth, hard wood. Nothing important. She continued her frantic journey, something jabbing at the back of her mind. An important detail, overlooked.

Hard, smooth wood didn't happen in nature, except near moving water.

She grabbed the piece of wood but couldn't lift it from the ground. Something moved beneath her. The handle was attached to something she lay upon. The machete. She had fallen into Riemer's holly shrubs.

In one smooth motion, she rolled out of the shrubs and swung the blade in a clean arc. It whistled through the air, the moonlight gleaming off the lethal steel. Her body lowered into a fighting crouch, Mackenzie scanned the immediate area for the enemy.

And found an empty street.

She pivoted on one foot, still lowered into a defensive crouch, but there was no movement. After a moment, she straightened, puzzled. There had been at least three of them, she was certain of it.

No matter. She would undoubtedly pick up more on the way to the shed. Her roll-and-spin pointed her back toward the Stronghold; she pivoted and started in the opposite direction, counting off the blocks and paying wary attention to her peripheral vision.

A Revenant picked up her trail after two blocks. Another found her as she finished the sixth block. She ignored them as best she could, reserving her energy for making a run for it. She would have to outpace them long enough to fit the key into the lock and gain the safety of the shed.

The Revenants kept at a distance, flanking her on either side. That was a problem. She needed them both on one side so she could break and run on the other. Midway down the last block before the turn, they merged their efforts and melted into the shadows on her right.

These houses were even more rundown than those near the Stronghold. Those were kept relatively free of Revenants by hunting parties whose regular rotations cleared the neighborhoods and woods closest to their sanctuary. Without the destructive tendencies of the infected, the structures remained mostly intact, if not somewhat forlorn and dilapidated. By comparison, the roofs of these empty homes had collapsed under snow-weight or because load-bearing walls had been torn out. Debris littered the yards, sidewalks, and streets, making the journey particularly treacherous.

She rounded the corner, turning west, her attention focused on swinging wide to the left and keeping the trailing Revenants on her right, increasing the distance between them – so focused that she didn't see the pack of waiting Revenants until she nearly walked into them.

For a split second, both parties were too startled to react. Just as Mac realized they had not been lying in wait for her, they decided she would serve as an adequate substitute in place of whatever they *had* been waiting for.

Roaring with fury, they charged her, a snarling pack of five infected with murderous tempers. An answering roar came from behind and to her right. She had forgotten the other Revenants, and from the sounds of their fury, they were not from the same pack.

Duck and roll, said the Bon who lived inside her head, the Bon who trained her in combat and cunning. In survival.

She dropped to a crouch and rolled to her left as the first three broke upon her. Their charge was met by the two Revenants tracking her, and they came together with deafening howls of rage.

Mac gained her feet and sprinted west, leaping over rotting boards and tumbled concrete and a fallen sapling. Two Revenants broke from the pack and gave chase. She counted the blocks as she flew past side streets, her pursuers gaining ground every second.

One. Two.

The Revenants shared a sibilant conversation and broke ranks, spreading out to flank her. *Damn.*

Three. Four.

The Revenant to her left gave a hissing growl of pleasure as it closed the gap between them by a foot. It moved behind her again.

Five. The burned-down house would be on this block. She wished Elijah'd had time to tell her what side of the street the shed was on. She raced on, scanning both sides. She leaped over what looked like a vehicle engine and was satisfied to hear the thump and bellow of wrath as the Revenant stumbled over it and slammed into the disintegrating pavement.

And then her heart nearly stopped. The intersecting street was visible in the moonlight, and there were no more houses on this block.

She had come down the wrong street, and there was no time to hunt around for the right one. *Double damn.*

Without pausing, she hurtled through the intersection, following a shining spot of ancient tar that reflected the silver light of the moon. She would keep going forward rather than backtracking. If Elijah Riemer had a secret hideaway, it would be as far from the Stronghold as he could manage. While there was always risk of a hunting or gathering party finding it, there would be less chance of activity around it being seen by the guards who worked the walls.

A stitch jabbed her in the side with every breath. Her thighs and calves burned. The cool air stung her lungs. Behind her, the Revenant recovered his footing and redoubled his efforts.

Another block flashed by. And another. Then, on the left, a dark hulking shadow rose from the ground, a mound of burnt debris silvered by moonlight. And fifty feet behind it, like a grimy white paradise, was the shed.

And hot on her heels were the Revenants, too close for her to unlock it without being torn apart.

She broke left, sprinting toward the charcoal mound of scorched wood. If she managed to get it between her and them, she might lose one or the other when they tried to clamber over the ramshackle remains and tumbled into the basement below. It didn't look as though it could hold the weight of a kitten.

A shriek of challenge drowned out the two hissing Revenants. A third joined the chase. Triple damn with sugar sprinkles on top.

The remains of the house between them now, Mac spun around and dropped into her defensive stance. The third Revenant, bigger and more aggressive than its fellows, plowed into the other two, and they rolled across the ground, snapping and snarling and howling like wolves.

Mac wasted no time. Whoever won, it would only spell trouble for her. She broke for the shed, digging the key from her pocket as she ran. Her hands shook and the key skittered around the hole until finally sliding in purely by accident. She yanked the shackle from the staple of the hasp, threw off the hinged strap, and yanked open the door, throwing a look over her shoulder.

The large Revenant hunkered over the two smaller ones, who lay still and silent beneath him. As though feeling Mac's eyes on it, it straightened, pinning her with a gaze she couldn't see but could feel burning through her. Shrieking, it charged, squelching through the gore of its fellows.

Mac threw the door closed, leaning all her weight on it, feeling around in the dark for something to secure it. She rammed her hand against a metal bar protruding from the wall beside the door and bit back a shriek of pain. With her uninjured hand, she explored the metal bar. It formed a U, and was attached with bolts to the door frame. Not a bar, then, but a bracket. She found another on the opposite side of the door, threaded with a wooden plank. She rammed it through the other bracket just as the Revenant hit the door with the full force of its weight.

The Revenant hammered at the door in a screaming frenzy. Mac shrank away. After several steps, the backs of her knees hit something solid. She gritted her teeth and reached down. A bench, a little dusty but clear. She sat down, feeling through the dark for anything else. Eli had said there was food, water, and other supplies. Hopefully he'd remembered a lantern of some sort.

With a last half-hearted rap against the door, the Revenant fell silent. Mac wasn't tempted in the slightest to look outside. She scooted along the bench, feeling her way to make sure there was nothing that could fall and make noise that would attract the Revenant's attention again. The bench was bare in that direction. She moved the opposite way, finding nothing but a gritty layer of dust. She would have to wait until daylight to explore her surroundings. The thought held little appeal.

She got up and pressed her ear to the wall, listening for sounds outside. The night was still and quiet. The breeze whispered through vents at the peak of the ceiling, but otherwise the shed seemed solid and warm. She turned to grope her way back to the bench and clanged her head on a metal object suspended from the ceiling. Wincing, she reached up. A lantern. What idiot hung a lantern where no one could find it in the dark until they'd concussed themselves on it?

The roof slanted down on the bench side at the back of the shed. The lantern hung at the front. It took Mac some tricky maneuvering on her tiptoes to free the handle from its hook. A round cylinder was attached to the handle. She searched its circumference for a latch, relying on her fingers to be her eyes, and found none. Screw-top, then. One side of the container was rough. She thought she knew what it was: a waterproof container for matches, although where he'd found matches… They were a rare commodity these days. The Stronghold relied on flint and strikers, ferrocerium rods, or the magnesium firestarters one of the gathering teams brought back a couple years ago.

She fumbled for the fuel valve, opened it all the way, then unscrewed the top from the match container and shook one out, striking it against the rough side of the cylinder. The lantern blazed to life when she held the flame close to the holes at the bottom of the glass, and now she could see it was a dark lantern, with shields to cover the light, powered with a rare bottle of propane. She dialed down the valve, dimming the brightness, and held the lantern aloft, surveying her shelter.

The shed wasn't large, perhaps ten feet by six feet with a mortared, flagstone floor. The bench ran the length, deep enough to sleep without constantly falling off and long enough to fit two people if they didn't mind their legs tangling. Just above her on the wall hung two backpacks, mashed flat and zipped to keep out insects. The wall opposite was decked out with shelves, which were stocked with all manner of supplies. She would go through those tomorrow and plan out her rations. For now, all she wanted was to sleep.

There were no pillows – it would be hell trying to keep mice and bugs out of them – so she took down both backpacks and folded them over. Settling the lantern on the stone floor with the match container still secured to the handle, she turned off the propane to squelch the flame and stretched out on the bench.

She fell asleep thinking about Elijah's eyes and dreamed of Ren Leonard. *The truth of the matter is, no lab came up with what hit this old world.*

And she woke in the morning, considering those words for the first time since leaving Leonard's lair, and wondered if something worse than Revenants waited in the world outside.

12

Riemer woke to the smell of hay and puppy breath. He opened one eye, staring directly into the face of a retriever pup Mackenzie and Bon had brought back to the Stronghold a couple of months ago. Since the dogs were usually kenneled at night, he guessed that he'd slept through the morning bell.

He opened the other eye, and the puppy took this as an invitation to swipe its tongue from his chin to his forehead.

"Yuck! Where'd you come from, mutt?"

"You looked like you needed company last night. You slept through breakfast. I smuggled you out a breakfast sandwich. They're pretty good – made from croissants left over from the feast last night."

The middle-aged man who lounged on a nearby hay bale produced both a croissant wrapped in a cloth napkin and a dog whistle. He puffed on the whistle and the puppy scrambled off Riemer's makeshift bed, settling at the trainer's feet. With the dog contained, he offered the sandwich to Riemer, who took it and began wolfing down ham, egg, and cheese on flaky pastry. It was still warm, which meant he hadn't missed breakfast by much.

The noise in the hallway outside his room was deafening last night, especially to a man planning his escape from a desperately dangerous situation. So during a lull, he'd crept out of his room with his blanket and begged the use of a few bales of hay in the dog kennels, a cozy niche in a corner of the livestock section. Justin, the dog trainer, wasn't part of the underground, but he *was* a friend. He'd helped arrange the bales into a serviceable bed and apparently loosed the puppy as a sleeping companion sometime after Riemer fell asleep.

"You're welcome to hang out here today, Elijah. I don't think they expect you in the fields – I saw Jonas watering your cabbages after breakfast."

"Idiot. They're not due to be watered until tomorrow."

"That's hardly your biggest concern right now."

Riemer grunted in agreement. He stuffed the last bite of sandwich into his mouth, saving back a bit of egg, which he slipped to the puppy, ignoring Justin's disapproving frown. Truth be told, he was looking forward to working in the field today. His work was mostly solitary, giving him time to think, and he needed to be visible. People must see his displeasure, must hear his disgruntled muttering, must witness his defense of Mackenzie. He'd start slow and build steam over the next two days, until finally they came to arrest him.

"Thanks for the sandwich and the bed. I've got to get to work." Snagging his blanket off the bales, he made for the door.

"Hmm."

"What?"

"Just wondering if you're trying to get yourself killed."

"What's that supposed to mean?"

"You've got a look about you. I've seen that look on many a man's face right before they fly in the face of authority. Son, you might want to rethink your angst before it costs you a knife across the throat."

Riemer stopped, unease rippling over him. The older man still lounged casually on his hay bale, feeding the puppy pieces of his own croissant sandwich.

"Is there something you want to tell me?"

Justin's mouth quirked. "Yeah, just one thing. Be careful. Aside from liking you myself, my dogs like you. I'd hate to trust their care to someone else when I'm sick or on an extended break."

Still Riemer hesitated. "Is that all?"

"Nothing else to say. Except maybe take my warning seriously."

Troubled, Riemer made his way back to his quarters, where he left his blanket and traded his clothes for clean ones. He visited the washroom to clean his teeth and wash his face, and was startled to see the dark circles under his eyes. Sleep had claimed him quickly last night, but worry had troubled his dreams and robbed his slumber of any rest.

A quick visit to the kitchens secured him another two croissant sandwiches, and then he headed out to the field, where he found Jonas pouring water into the irrigation pipes in the cabbage plot.

"That shouldn't be done until tomorrow," he said, taking the bucket from the field.

The field supervisor shrugged. "I wasn't expecting you to be here, and I have other things to do tomorrow."

"Why wouldn't you expect me here?"

"Well, you know, the thing with Mackenzie and all." Jonas seemed to be having trouble meeting Riemer's gaze. He looked everywhere but in his eyes. "The elders figured you'd need a few days."

"Oh, so the council is going to tell me how to grieve, too?" Riemer didn't have to feign anger. He was so angry over the disastrous derailment of his carefully laid plan, he could barely see straight.

"No, Eli, they just figured—"

"I don't care what they figured. They can mind their own business for a change."

Jonas looked around nervously and lowered his voice. "I know you're upset, Elijah, but you don't want to anger the council."

"And why exactly is that, Jonas? Because they might exile me, too? Or arrest me? Is that how it is now, they try to shut up anyone who disagrees with their exalted decisions?" That was exactly how it was, but he'd never stated it so baldly to anyone outside the underground.

"Aahhh," said Jonas, his eyes wide. "I don't really think—"

"Nobody does, and that's the point, isn't it? If they'd done more themselves to improve our situation – before Mackenzie's best friend died – maybe she wouldn't have felt like she had to do something herself. And instead of thanking her for trying, they throw her out the door at night."

Truly alarmed now, Jonas backed away, his hands held up in a placating gesture. "Okay. All right. I'll just leave you alone. Ah…let me know if you…er…need anything."

The field supervisor hurried away, sending one last apprehensive glance over his shoulder. Middle-aged and mousy, small in stature and gentle in demeanor, Jonas obviously was uncomfortable in the company of a deeply disgruntled, highly trained killer and would be slow to report it – which was exactly why Riemer chose him to be the first to hear his long list of criticisms. His campaign of bellyaching had to be carefully orchestrated. It must start a buzz along the grapevine but not too quickly. It could not reach the ears of those militant in their support of the Council of Elders or he'd be arrested too soon and not by the right people.

For the next two nights, he sacrificed sleep to strategize on who would be the next, most effective person to complain to. And complain he did, to the other field hands and the pickers, to the cooks and to the laundry attendants. Once to a healer and at length to a huddle of three very discomfited teachers in the dining hall.

On the day he was to be arrested, he sat alone in a corner of the dining hall, the rest of the residents too afraid of his increasing vocal remonstrance against the council to risk being seen socializing with him. Judging by the many whispered conversations and covert looks, he had done his job well. He wondered when they would come for him. If everything went correctly, the two guards who had escorted Mackenzie out the doors on her night of exile would be the ones to haul him off, Mark would be the guard in the detention cell who would take custody of him, and he would finally know the identity of the sympathetic elder. To date, he or she was simply a whispered voice in a dark cornfield, too many rows away to see. He thought it was one of the women, or possibly one of the younger councilmen like Gerald, judging from the voice's higher timbre.

He glanced up from his breakfast in time to see Johanna in the doorway of the dining hall, her gaze methodically searching each table for him. When she spotted him, she weaved her way through the tables, ignoring the whispered and stares that followed her.

She scooted onto the bench across the table from him, leaning forward to speak. "My medallion is missing."

Dismayed, he laid his fork down beside his plate. "I told you to keep it on."

"I did. The cord broke last night while I was sleeping. I found the medallion on the floor by my bed when I woke up in the middle of the night. I laid it on my bedside table to fix today. When I got up this morning, it was gone."

He picked up his fork and began eating again, aware that they were being avidly watched by many in the room.

"Is it vital that we have the medallions?"

He shrugged to make the watchers think he wasn't interested in what she was saying. "It's our identification. We have the medallions, we get help along the way. Otherwise, we're on our own. So yes, it's very vital. " He couldn't believe she had lost hers. If they were separated along the way, only the one with a medallion would receive help from the underground.

She leaned forward across the table as though pleading with him. "What do I do? Do we have time to make another?"

"No. Take mine. We'll be together, so one should do. I can't risk it being removed from me when they arrest me, so I buried it in a small pouch in the cabbage patch. Mark was going to bring it to me when I'm taken to the detention center."

"Am I to guess exactly where or should I just dig up the whole field?" she asked acerbically.

"The first cabbage in the northwest corner of the plot."

"Okay. Oh, and Zane Allbrook is looking for you."

His annoyance increased. "What the hell does he want?"

She smirked. "I don't know. But ten-to-one it's about Mac-kenzie."

"Don't you have somewhere to be?" he asked pointedly.

Still smirking, she swung off the bench and stalked out of the room. Many eyes followed her, but where they once held covetous desire, they now held suspicion. She was marked as surely as he was now. Her haughty posture indicated she didn't care about their judgment, but he knew she was a bundle of jittery nerves and hurt feelings.

He worked at weeding the cabbage plot, starting at the corner where Johanna had dug up the medallion to hide her excavation. It was mildly vexing to look up just minutes after the kitchen rang the lunch bell to see not the team of guards he was expecting but Zane Allbrook, striding purposefully through the fields toward him.

Riemer dropped his hoe and went to meet him, putting some distance between himself and the wall guards, who gathered close to where he was working so they could maximize every opportunity to goad him. As Allbrook came closer, Riemer stopped.

"Look angry and push me," he said in a low voice.

"What?"

"We're being watched. Look angry and push me."

So Allbrook did. As he stumbled backward, Riemer rather thought the other man got entirely too much satisfaction out of that push.

Riemer held his hands up peaceably. "What do you want?"

"I don't know if it means anything, but I saw two teams of hunters slip into the Stronghold neighborhood early this morning. Very early, right at shift change, so everyone was pretty distracted. I don't know if anyone else saw."

Allbrook worked a six-hour shift starting at midnight. Right at shift change would have been six in the morning. Riemer's stomach rolled. "Routine clearing?"

"Just done a week ago. Not due for another three weeks." Routine clearing of the neighborhood surrounding the Stronghold was only done on a monthly basis. It took that long for other Revenants to realize the area was free of rivals and start to move in.

Damn. Was the council just being thorough, or had his vocal condemnation caused this? Jesus, what a mess this had turned into. "Two teams, you said?"

"Yeah."

"What teams?"

"You know what teams, Riemer," Allbrook said evenly. "The worst ones to be looking for her, because they *will* find her."

Mackenzie was a skilled fighter, but while she might be able to take out a hunter or two by herself, she would not be able to triumph over two full teams. Especially not two full teams comprised of the most ruthless, brutal people he'd ever seen. It was long suspected by the underground that these two teams were responsible for the demise of many of the hunters and gatherers supposedly lost to Revenants. Criticism was increasingly being met with force.

Riemer narrowed his eyes. "And why are you telling me this? Just to rub it in that I can't help her? I don't get the feeling that you care whether she and I are separated."

"This is about Mackenzie not dying."

"I notice you didn't stand with her to keep her from being exiled."

"I notice you didn't, either," Allbrook replied, a bit angrily. "How about we not play this game, okay? You and I both know if we'd stood with her, we'd be dead, too."

"That damn near borders on sedition, Allbrook."

"You ought to know. You're not a stupid man, so all your complaining must have a point. I don't know what you're planning, but you'd better do it soon. They won't stop looking for her, and she can only avoid them for so long." Zane grabbed him by the front of the shirt and brought them nose-to-nose. "They will kill her if they catch her. I'd rather she be alive and with you than dead and lost to both of us."

He let go and marched away, not looking back. Riemer went back to his plot, anxiety coiling in his gut.

The sun marched across the sky. The bell for afternoon break rang. Riemer drank a couple cups of water from the well and ate four plums Jonas left by his work gloves. Ordinarily this exchange would have been accompanied by conversation, but these days found the citizens of the Stronghold avoiding him as much as they had avoided Bon Moreau the last few years. He expected Johanna to visit him in the field on their breaks, but she never did.

When the dinner bell rang, he went to the dining hall because he was hungry. Since everything was served buffet style, he didn't worry about being shorted on rations, but he *did* worry they would take him before he had a chance to eat. He didn't have to bother saving a seat for Johanna, because no one wanted to sit with him. But still Johanna didn't come.

He lingered over a cup of chamomile tea, watching the tables closely to time his departure for the right moment. They would want to make a show of taking him when the Commons was full, not during dinner when there would be almost no one to watch. A public arrest made a secret execution that much more believable.

When the dining hall was mostly empty, he took his dishes to the dishwasher window and headed for the Commons. He wondered if he would have time to find Johanna before they took him, and while he was wondering, his upper arms were seized from behind and two burly guards pressed in close.

"Hey!"

An excited whisper rippled through the crowd. As he tried to shrug off their hands, two more guards circled around the front of him. Riemer raised his gaze. His heart sank.

They were not the guards he was expecting.

He stopped struggling. "What are you doing?" His voice was calm, but inside a clawing panic was trying to free itself in the form of a scream of frustration. What the *hell* had gone wrong this time and how was he supposed to fix it when he was in the custody of unknown factors?

The guard in front of him on the left said, "Elijah Riemer, you're being detained on suspicion of sedition."

"Sedition? Don't be ridiculous. I've done nothing to incite a rebellion. I've just bitched about an action of the Council of Elders

111

that I disagreed with."

"That counts as sedition," the guard in front of him on the right informed him, a bit sardonically.

"So no one can disagree anymore? This is unacceptable."

"You shall be detained in seclusion until the Council of Elders has time to review your case. And then you shall be executed."

Riemer blinked. "I think you meant 'and then you'll get a trial.'"

"I said what I meant."

"But what if I'm found to be innocent?"

"In that unlikely event, you shall be honored."

"Oh, well, that's all right, then."

"*Posthumously* honored."

Or maybe not so all right. From their demeanor, he rather thought they were not friendly to his position. Which meant he was in serious trouble. What the hell had happened to the guards friendly to their cause?

They dragged him away, pushing and prodding even though he wasn't struggling. The crowd grew louder behind them. Some people even cheered. Whispers followed him. Eyes slanted looks at him as he passed. They passed through the doors to the detention room, at which were posted four guards armed with pistols, and none of them the people he expected. They shoved him into a dark room with no windows, hard enough he staggered and fell, landing on something soft that emitted a yell of pain. The door clanged shut.

"Johanna?"

"Oh, thank God!" Her hand groped in the darkness, her fingers stabbing him first in the chest and then feeling their way down his arm to his hand. She twined their fingers together. "They kept telling me they were going to execute you as soon as they arrested you."

He squeezed her hand. "What happened, Jo? I was supposed to be arrested, then you were supposed to be brought to see me, and we were supposed to be on our way to Mackenzie by nightfall. Where the hell is Mark?"

"I don't know. They took me after you went out to the fields this morning – they were very quiet about it. Said the elders wanted to talk to me about Bon – well, it wasn't the first time, was it? We kept things secret, but I think they somehow knew we were involved. They got me to Louis's office and arrested me there. I don't think anyone even knows."

"They know we're leaving," he said softly. "Somehow, they know."

She said, with her customary sarcastic bite, "*I* know how they know. We've been betrayed, Elijah."

13

Riemer lost track of time in the darkness of their cell. The only light came from beneath the steel door and reached just a few meager inches into the room. It wasn't a large room by any standards – just enough that both he and Johanna could stretch out to sleep without being too much in each other's way or in the path of the door, which opened twice a day: once to give them food, and once to give them water.

The first time the door opened after Riemer had been brought in, he was able to see Johanna, and his blood had not stopped boiling since. The right side of her pace was puffy, her eye blackening underneath and swelling shut. Warner – the guard who brought their water – closed the door before Riemer could react.

He found her by feel, examining the wound by touch "Did they hit you with the butt of a gun or their fists?"

She touched his cheek gently. "Don't worry about it, Elijah. I'm tougher than I look."

"Butt of gun or fists?" he repeated.

Her answer was impatient. "Fist. Just one. And what does it matter? It'll go away."

"Was he facing you or was he on your right? Did he sucker-punch you from the side?"

"Eli—"

"Jo, just answer."

"He was facing me." Her chin lifted, dislodging his fingers from her face. A trace of pride crept into her voice. "I didn't fall down, and I didn't cry."

"It was Warner, wasn't it?"

For a moment he thought she wouldn't answer, and then her incredulous reply: "How the hell did you know that?"

"He's the only left-hander I know of in the guards. Anyone else hitting you while facing you would have blackened your other eye. He's going to pay for that."

"For hitting me in the right eye instead of the left?"

He ignored her sarcasm. "For hitting you at all."

She was silent for a while. "How did you know he was left-handed? How do you remember all of this stuff about people?"

"It's my job."

"Your job is growing cabbages, Eli."

"My job is keeping the people I care about alive."

There had been two armed guards behind Warner when he had opened the door. They kept their hands on their firearms but didn't exhibit any suspicion that he would give them trouble. He expected they would be with Warner again, demonstrating the same carelessness as before.

The second time the door opened, Riemer was ready, standing just out of the reach of the light. The guards behind Warner seemed more interested in caressing the butts of their guns than they were in drawing them. Warner carried a tray of food, and as he leaned down to set it on the floor, Riemer caught him with an up-percut to the jaw that sent him sprawling on the floor in a splatter of mashed potatoes and gravy.

The guards drew on him. Riemer put his hands up. Warner scrambled to his feet, but he seemed loath to venture away from the small circle of light into the dark recesses of the room.

Riemer looked past Warner to the other two. He didn't know their names, but then, he'd never been in this part of the detention room before. He'd been just troublesome enough to gain a working knowledge of the layout and the dedication of the guards.

"If he comes one step closer, I will kill him. And then you'll have to decide if you're going to kill me or help me."

While one guard covered Riemer, the other inched forward far enough to reach in and snag Warner by the sleeve, tugging him backward.

Riemer put out a hand to stop the door from closing once Warner was out of the room. The guards' guns both aimed at his heart. He reached behind him and dragged Johanna into the light, turning her bruised eye to the light. "If you don't hit girls, I don't hit you."

The other two exchanged a glance. Riemer let go of the door. It banged shut, Warner's force behind it, and they were left alone in the dark again.

"What good did that do? Now he's going to be three times as mean."

"He won't be guarding us at all now."

She huffed out a breath, which made him smile. Politics were an abstract concept to her. "That makes no sense."

"The other two will tell their supervisor that I hit Warner because he hit you. Because he's abusing detainees, he will be removed from guard duty. The other two will harbor a small amount of sympathy toward us – or toward you, at least. Me, they will respect because I defended you."

There was a scrape and a rustle, and her voice sounded from nearer the floor. "That's a whole lot of supposition."

"Sure it is. But I bet I'm right."

"You're very confident. Maybe overly so. In case you hadn't noticed, Elijah, we're in jail. We aren't getting out of here. It's been...three days, I think. I'm not entirely sure. Mackenzie probably left the city today."

"I'm not confident. I just know people. And yes, if she followed my instructions, she left the city today. We should have no problem catching up."

"Elijah," she gritted out through clenched teeth. "We aren't going anywhere. We. Are. Locked. Up."

"Yeah, we are."

She didn't respond. Riemer felt his way over to her and sat down beside her.

"That was our dinner Warner splattered all over the floor."

"Don't be sullen. It was a crappy dinner. The gravy smelled awful."

"Elijah."

"Johanna, someone from the underground will get us out of here. Or someone here will make a mistake and we'll take advantage of it. Or someone here, not of the underground, will look the other way while we escape because this doesn't sit right with them. Those are the three ways this can play out."

"I wanted those potatoes. And the crappy gravy."

"Be glad we have the water. I waited until dinner to confront Warner for a reason. The water is more important."

She hmmphed. He could hear her teeth grinding together. "You are a maddening man."

He smiled again even though she couldn't see it. Despite his outwardly sanguine attitude, he was experiencing panic himself.

There was absolutely nothing to signal the underground would come to free them; he had made it up to ease her fear. He knew as well as he knew his own name that they would have to fight their way out of here, and they would most likely die in the attempt.

If they weren't executed first.

He made her drink half the water, and then she dozed, leaning against his shoulder. He had just set the empty bucket aside when footsteps sounded outside the door. He nudged Johanna awake, and they stood up as a key rattled in the lock. Maybe he'd been wrong and the underground wasn't completely compromised. There was still a chance a version of their original plan could be pulled off.

The door opened. The lamps in the corridor were dimmed, so all he could see was a silhouette of a tall man carrying a bundle. Blankets, finally.

"Catch." The man tossed them unceremoniously into the room. Riemer reached out to catch them before they landed on the floor and were soiled by the potatoes and gravy. His hand struck something solid and sticky that thudded to the floor a second later.

Before Riemer could get his hands up again, something hit him in the chest. He scrambled to catch it, just managing to snag it before it hit the floor. A flashlight. He flicked it on and aimed it at the shadow in the doorway.

"Mark?" He scrambled for a reason for Mark to be there that didn't involve betrayal, but his mind kept throwing up a memory from Mackenzie's exile: Mark leaning around her, shaking his hand, pressing the shed key into it, already knowing that she would be exiled rather than sentenced to execution. Mark had all but shouted his duplicity, but Elijah, too focused on playing his role convincingly – and, truthfully, too distracted by his unexpected physical and emotional reaction to holding Mackenzie in his arms – had failed to see the truth behind it. And if Mark had tipped his hand that night, so had their mystery elder.

"Think carefully on your choices from here on out, Elijah. Your decisions affect more lives than just your own." Mark closed the door.

Riemer swung the flashlight around to the bundle on the floor, hoping there were enough blankets to give them some relief from the cold, hard cement floor. He sank to his knees in despair. Johanna gasped, clapping her hands over her mouth, and dropped to her knees beside him, crying silently. When he rolled the bundle over, a thick, braided cable of dark hair spilled onto the floor as the woman's head lolled to the side. Blood formed an apron of crimson over her chest and shoulders – blood from the deep cut across her throat.

"Catherine?" Johanna said, astonished. "Catherine's the elder helping the underground?"

"I should have known when she was so furious with Louis for exiling Mackenzie. I should have known a lot of things that I missed because of…" He trailed off.

At length, he swept his hand over Catherine's lifeless eyes, closing the lids even though he knew they would just pop open again. Grabbing Johanna's arm, he pulled her away from Catherine's body, aiming the flashlight at the wall so they could see each other but Catherine was thrown into shadow. He gave her clothing a cursory examination and her eye a closer one.

"What size shoe do you wear?"

"Seven. Why? We going shopping?" Her sarcasm was ruined by a hiccupping sob.

"Try on Catherine's boots."

"What?" She smacked him in the chest. "Jesus, Riemer!"

"You won't make it two miles in the shoes you're wearing."

"First, I didn't plan on being arrested or I'd have dressed appropriately for travel. Second, I can't believe I have to remind you yet again that we are in jail and escape seems highly unlikely."

"Try the boots. They're quality and if they fit, you'll need them."

"Elijah."

"What do you want me to do, Jo?" he shouted. "Just give up? All we can do is be ready to act on any opening they give us. If we just let them lead us to the execution trees, we will die there."

"And we may die there anyway, even if we try to fight our way out."

"That doesn't mean we don't try, Jo. We have to be ready for every contingency. Try on the damn boots."

She moved away from him, crossing her arms over her chest and frowning. "Fine. But I'm not taking them off her."

Riemer did, as gently as he could. He didn't know how long

Catherine had been dead. Not long judging from her still-warm skin and pliant body. There were a couple of blood spatters on the boots, but nothing glaringly obvious or grotesque. He hoped Johanna wouldn't notice.

She took them with a moue of distaste, shucked her own shoes, and pulled them on, tying the laces. After pacing the small cell a few times, she dropped back down to the floor, sitting cross-legged beside him.

"They fit."

"Okay. Now listen to me closely."

Listen to what? A half-baked plan that involved no real planning? Their opportunities were unknown and depended on the unpredictable actions of their captors. He couldn't even tell her what to expect.

"They're going to come for us soon to take us to the execution trees."

She flinched. The execution trees were just outside a service door on the forest side of the arena. The detention center had been located here because of numerous storerooms that now served as cells and the close proximity of the woods. Those sentenced to death were secured to the trees (usually naked, to preserve much-needed clothing for other Stronghold residents) and their throats cut. The bodies were left for the Revenants to ravage after dark. There was no fanfare or ceremony. No one came to watch the executions; the elders who long ago set up the Stronghold's governmental structure had deemed it unproductive, which was a stroke of luck for Riemer's underground. Since the executions were done in relative privacy, it made for a system that could be corrupted for the underground's cause.

"We have to fight, Jo," he said desperately. "We fight or we die. We may die anyway, but we will *certainly* die if we don't. Be ready. Take any opportunity to get free, even if it means killing someone trying to stop you."

"I can't *kill* someone!"

"Jo, these people are going to kill us. If you have to kill them first to free yourself, that's self-defense. You *must* do it, or you'll die."

"What about you?"

"Don't worry about me. If you can get free, run. Head west

and find the old highway."

She grabbed the front of his shirt, practically crawling into his lap. "I've never been out of the Stronghold, Eli. I've only seen the maps in passing. *I don't know where to go!*"

He wanted to tell her he'd catch up, but he'd told Mackenzie the same thing, and it didn't look like it was a promise he would be able to keep. "Just...head west. You know the points of the compass. You'll find the old highway."

"Maybe you're wrong. Maybe they won't come for us tonight."

"They will."

"How do you know?"

"If they moved on Catherine, they don't need her for information anymore. If they let me know my contact in the council is dead and my contact in the guards is a traitor, they don't need me anymore, either."

She backed away a few inches. "Do you mean..."

He nodded grimly. "They have Mackenzie."

She shrank back down, curling into his lap, tucking herself under his chin. "I'm sorry," she whispered.

Riemer couldn't find the words to respond. He held onto her fiercely, his heart a cold knot of disbelief that stubbornly still beat in his chest for no reason he could fathom. Survival instinct. He would live, or attempt to, even if he lost everything he'd been living for.

Oh, Mackenzie, I'm sorry. You trusted me, and I'm just so damn sorry that I'm all you had to rely on.

A while later, he heard them outside the door again. A key slotted into the lock. He pushed Johanna off his lap and stood up, reaching down to help her to her feet. He didn't need to tell her to be ready; awareness thrummed through the very air of the cell. His heart tried to gallop out of control as adrenaline pumped through his blood. He took several deep, steadying breaths to calm his panic. They'd have one shot at this. They either escaped or died.

Mark called, "We're coming in, Riemer. You try anything, we'll shoot you dead. Do you understand?"

"Yeah, I understand." Understanding wasn't the same as obeying.

The key turned. The lock tumbled. The sound echoed in his head, a portentous bell that signaled his impending death. Keeping

Johanna behind him, he clenched the flashlight in his hand and dug deep inside himself for the things he had locked away after Laura's death: his lethal cunning, his lightning-fast reactions, his unflinching brutality. The settlement had claimed his fate when he was young and trained him to be a ruthless killer, because they lived in a ruthless world.

Tonight, they would see what a mistake that had been.

The door burst open, an explosion of movement spilled into the cell. They'd brought reinforcements; they remembered his reputation as a hunter. Not well enough, however. As they swarmed the cell, he didn't waste words or seconds. He raised the flashlight and struck, and struck again, and again.

Bodies fell in his wake. He dragged Johanna over them. He struck to the left, to the right, straight ahead, clearing the way, only to have more guards fill the gaps. A hand grabbed him from behind, dark against the tan fabric of his work shirt. He brought the flashlight down with all his strength, cracking it against Mark's arm just above the wrist. Mark howled in pain as the bone snapped. Riemer slammed the flashlight into his face, and the howling stopped.

Johanna screamed as two guards seized her and dragged her through the throng of their fellows. A red haze descended over his vision. A killing haze. He struck. He struck again. The flashlight cracked into pieces and he used the jagged shards as shivs, carving his way toward her captors.

Three bodies hit him from behind. More fell on him as he went down under their weight. His face was mashed into the cement floor. His arms were twisted up behind his back and secured with an ancient but undeniably effective pair of handcuffs. Two guards on either side of him hoisted him up by his arms, setting him on his feet. The red haze obscured his vision, distorting faces and voices until the two dozen guards became fifty twisted demons. Bellowing with rage, he summoned the bulk of his strength and spun around, dragging his jailors off their feet. He charged forward, plowing into the guard gripping Johanna's right arm, knocking him to the ground. He turned to the guard on her left and found himself staring down the barrel of a gun.

"One more move, Elijah Riemer, and I will shoot you through the head."

The red killing haze fled in the face of cold reality. "You'd love that, wouldn't you, Olson."

"Let's get moving."

His arms were gripped again. He didn't bother to look to see who escorted him. They were rough and unsympathetic, so it didn't matter who they were. All that mattered was *what* they were: enemies.

The outside door slammed open. The cool air hit Riemer, soothing his rage, quenching the fire of violence and cruelty. The tops of the wall were lit at intervals with burn barrels, enough for him to see a solitary guard at the top of the wall, crossbow aimed at him. Southeast quadrant, night shift – that would be Allbrook up there. *Ah, Allbrook, you'll have your revenge on me for stealing your girl after all.*

Johanna cried out in pain as she was shoved against a tree. Numb himself, he barely noticed the scratch of pine bark against his back. The guards circled the trees, winding rope around them, pinning their arms down. Olson paused before Riemer and patted his cheek, a nasty sneer curving his mouth. The guards retreated into the Stronghold, leaving one of their fellows with the dirty deed of slitting their throats.

While Johanna cried, and prayed, Riemer found himself thinking of an old poem he'd read, of how the world ends with a whimper. Wrong.

It was more like the hiss of a crossbow bolt.

14

The hunters were thorough.

Mackenzie was paranoid.

The end result of this combination was that Mac held the precarious upper hand.

She'd heard them coming three days ago, mounting a dwelling-to-dwelling search that encompassed the block on either side of her shed. The presence of hunters confused her at first. Generally, they only kept the blocks nearest the Stronghold cleared of Revenants and took care of any packs as they came upon them when venturing farther afield.

Curious, she slipped out of the shed just before dawn one morning and hid herself in a house they had already cleared on the block they were currently searching. She didn't have to wait long for them to arrive – they must have left the Stronghold at sunrise – but it took half the day for her to hear anything of use.

Two of the six-man group was dispatched around to the back of the house next door to keep watch while the other four searched the house. This was mostly standard procedure, except usually the team split into two groups of three: one to clear the interior, and the other to circle the house regularly so no Revenants would creep up unnoticed.

These fellows made their circuit three times before either spoke.

"This is a fool's errand." He spoke low, so the rest of the team in the house couldn't hear. Mac, secreted in the house next door and listening from her horizontal position under a broken window, heard him clearly as they paused between the dwellings.

"How so?"

"Sending us searching for a girl who was probably dead ten minutes after she was put out on the street."

"No evidence of that. We've looked. No blood, no hair, no clothes. The elders think she's alive and hiding somewhere."

"They're worried about one girl who doesn't even come up to my shoulder? What's she gonna do – launch an attack on the

Stronghold singlehandedly?"

"She could ambush the hunters or gatherers who come out in this area," his companion pointed out. Mac made a face. As if she would bother.

"Bright Runner, ambush people?" The first guy snorted. "This doesn't sit right with me. Exiling her is one thing. But for us to hunt her down and—"

The second guy shushed him as the rest of their team came out the front door. They completed their circuit and moved on to the next house. Mac lay on the grimy floor beneath the window, waiting for sunset to take them out of the neighborhood and back to the Stronghold, mulling over what they'd said.

The elders wanted them to hunt her down and – what? Warn her off? Maybe give her a good thumping so she knew they were serious? Kill her? A chill prickled over her skin. She hadn't forgotten that Catherine very nearly sentenced her to execution, *would* have if Louis hadn't intervened and exiled her instead. It wasn't farfetched to think Catherine might have secretly sent a team to make sure Mackenzie didn't survive.

Damn you, Catherine, you vindictive bitch.

It was well after sundown when Mac made it back to the shed, but she didn't encounter any Revenants. In fact, the Revenants were much less of a problem than she had anticipated. A couple of nights she awakened, certain one was poking around outside, but it hadn't tried to attack the shed. After a while it moved off, and she went back to sleep.

The day after she'd stalked the hunters, Mac packed all the supplies she could fit into the two backpacks, threw dust over everything in the shed to confuse her trail, and relocated a block south and two blocks west, in a small house that somehow escaped the ravages of time and destructive creatures. She returned to the shed only once to leave a coded message for Eli on the wall, cleverly worked into the secret symbol he told her to look for – a sun with a crescent moon etched into the right edge – to let him know where she'd gone.

She didn't feel as secure in the small house. Too many rooms. Her slumber was fitful; it would be quite easy for someone to sneak in through a window while she slept. She confined herself to a room with boarded-up windows, and that was the only room in which she allowed herself to use the dark lantern. The only advantage to the house over the shed was, against all odds, the porcelain commode was intact so she didn't have to risk going outside to relieve herself. Although it no longer flushed – the days of sewer systems were long gone – it served her purpose for her short stay.

Tomorrow would be the eighth day since she had been ousted from the Stronghold. If Elijah didn't show up by morning, she would pack what supplies remained and start walking west, looking for the sun-and-moon symbol to guide her. She hoped she would pass close enough to the river to bathe; she didn't want to risk venturing that far away while the hunters were searching for her, and she was starting to smell pretty ripe.

Mac expected the night to drag past, but the hours sprinted toward dawn. She woke several times during the night, certain someone called her name, disappointed to find she'd only been dreaming. When the sun rose, she filled one backpack with the remaining food and stuffed the empty one inside. A few handfuls of fine dirt collected from just outside the back door and scattered over the floors masked her footprints. Leaving the back door locked to slow down the hunters – or even deter their investigating this place at all – she worked her way toward a bedroom at the back of the house, where she would climb through the window – which she'd spent the last two nights opening and closing to dislodge dirt until it was mostly silent. From there she could dust the last of her footprints and close the window from the outside, supplement her food stock by picking a couple dozen apples from the tree out back, and then make her way out of the neighborhoods before the hunting team descended on the area again.

The plan held her in good stead until she reached to open the window and saw someone moving in the back yard. She froze. The grime on both sides of the glass made it almost impossible for the intruder to see her as long as she stood still.

The house stood on a concrete slab with no basement or cellar, easily accessible to the intruder, who was male and tall, if she could judge his height compared to the small, wild apple tree by which he stood. He was peering up into the tree, and then – damn him anyway! – he began picking apples, examining them for worm holes. He tossed a couple aside as he steadily filled an empty pack he carried with him.

127

Mac fumed silently. Now she was going to have to climb the tree to get any for herself. The intruder stopped picking when he filled the pack. He zipped it closed and slung it over his shoulder, then leaned against the tree as though waiting for someone.

Perfect. Just perfect. She would be stuck here for another day if he didn't leave soon; every minute counted when traveling long distances on foot. She needed enough time to make it to shelter before dark.

And just who was this idiot, anyway? Gatherers and hunters didn't travel alone, and they never separated. It was the most important rule of survival. To her knowledge, there were no people living in the area except those in the Stronghold.

Moving slowly, she bent toward the window, trying to line up less grimy patches on both sides of the window so she could see more clearly. He came into focus. Mac straightened abruptly. What the hell was *he* doing here?

He glanced sharply at the window as though he'd seen her movement. She stared at him hard, willing him away. After a moment, he reached into his pocket and dangled something from his fingers, swinging it back and forth. Sunlight glinted off a round disk. The moron – what if the hunters were nearby and saw the flash of metal?

She bent to the window again to see what he held and sucked in a breath. A leather cord was twined around his fingers, and from it swung a copper disk. Mac eased the window open and climbed out, dropping her pack at her feet. She stood on it to throw dirt over the last of her footprints, and closed the window.

"It's about time. I was beginning to wonder if I was going to have to come in to get you."

"Why are you here, Crawford?"

He held up the leather cord, dangling the disk in her face so she could see the sun-and-moon symbol engraved on one smooth side.

"I've been sent."

"I wasn't expecting *you*."

Will took a moment to answer. "He couldn't come, Mackenzie."

Her heart plummeted. Elijah wasn't coming? Did he really expect her to leave the city without him?

128

"How did you find me?"

"You left a message in the shed, inside this symbol." He gave the copper disk a flick. "Obviously, I decoded it. I also obliterated it before that team of hunters found it – they're only a few houses away from your shed."

That gave Mac pause. The hunters were closer than she'd thought. She hoped they'd be able to slip out of the neighborhood without being seen.

"Why are they looking for me?"

He looked surprised. "You know for sure they're looking for you?"

"I stalked them, heard two of them talking."

His surprise turned to admiration. "You're one ballsy girl, Bright Runner. Time's our enemy though, so we'd better get a move on so we can cover some distance and find shelter before nightfall. Too much talking here and the hunters might hear us."

"Maybe we should wait for nightfall. They'll go back to the Stronghold and we can slip out of the neighborhood."

"You think they can't clear two or three blocks in a day? They'll find us before nightfall. We should go now while we have the advantage. We are not skilled enough to take out six killers."

She couldn't argue his point, so she grabbed her pack, dusted it off, and slung it over her shoulder.

"Just the one pack? I thought there'd be more supplies."

"I've been living on them for a week, Will. Even rationing, I had to eat enough to stay healthy. The other pack is folded up inside, in case we come across a cache of food somewhere. Like my apples you were stealing."

"I wasn't stealing them; I was securing them for both of us. If we go through the woods, there's a footbridge across the river. Then we can follow the road past the burned-down college to the old highway."

Mac just gaped at him. Nothing he'd said made any sense.

"Haven't you ever studied the maps?"

She shook her head. "Just the areas Bon and I were assigned for gathering. We hadn't expanded yet – he didn't want to push me too fast."

He didn't seem pleased by this revelation, but he didn't waste words on it. He tugged on her pack, urging her into motion. "Let's go."

The little house sat only a couple of blocks from the woods. They should be able to make it out of the neighborhood and to the footbridge without the hunters seeing them. While very visible on the road should the hunting team happen upon their street, it would be tragically stupid to wade through the tall grasses in the yards; their path would be easily tracked and the movement of the grass might attract attention.

Mac unstrapped the machete from her backpack. Will unstrapped his own, and she felt a moment's regret that he hadn't been able to bring Black Jack to her. They crept around the side of the house.

"Don't run. Walk carefully. Be sure to lift your feet and not scuff. Sound carries a long way."

She rolled her eyes. Did he think she'd never been out of the Stronghold before? He looked chagrined and peered around the corner to check the street. He recoiled immediately, taking three huge strides backward and plowing into Mac, knocking her off her feet. She landed hard on her backside, the shock traveling through her body and making her teeth clack together, barely missing her tongue.

For a long moment, they were all silent: Mac, Will, and the hunter who was edging around the corner as Will leaned around it to check their clearance. Mac recognized him – his name was Pearson – but she'd never had any reason to hang out with him.

Will held up his hands, placating. "Just let us go, Wayne. We're not going to cause any trouble. We're leaving the area."

"Do you have any idea how many people are out here looking for her?" Pearson hissed, motioning to Mackenzie with his blade. "What the hell are you doing in the middle of it, Crawford?"

"Apparently I'm in the middle of it to protect her."

"You're not going to be enough. There are two hunting teams after her."

"Two?" Mac piped up, getting to her feet. She brushed off her backside, keeping a wary eye on Wayne Pearson.

"You're damn lucky they're working east of here or you'd be dead by now."

"You're here. Somehow I don't find myself to be all that safe."

Pearson huffed out a breath, his expression clearly wondering how he ended up in this position. "This doesn't sit well with me," he muttered.

Mac allowed herself a little hope; he'd been the one she heard while she'd stalked the hunters.

"Give us ten minutes," Will pleaded. "Just ten. We'll be far enough away they won't catch us."

"Why should I help you?" Pearson challenged, his chest puffing out.

Oh great – male posturing. Mac didn't have time for this. "Because this doesn't sit well with you," she reminded him, careful to keep her tone neutral. "Why aren't you with the rest of the hunters?"

"A few of us were sent down the side streets, looking for signs you'd been around."

"They want you to kill me, don't they? The elders, I mean."

Pearson's face shuttered. "My first duty is to the Stronghold," he said coolly.

Mac tightened her grip on her machete, preparing to fight. She didn't want to cut him down, but neither could she allow him to call the rest of the hunters. They wouldn't stand a chance against twelve killers.

"Then we're at an impasse," Will replied. His own fingers tightened on his weapon.

"I said my first duty is to the *Stronghold*," Pearson repeated, every word succinct. "Not to the elders."

And what the hell did *that* mean?

"Go through the back yards and stick close to the houses. You'll be seen if you go out on the streets. Check around corners before you dash from yard to yard; I'm not the only one in the area. You have ten minutes before I call the others to this house."

Will didn't waste any time. He nodded his thanks at Pearson and spun around. "Come on, Mackenzie."

"Thank you, Wayne."

"Go!"

She backed away two steps and then hurried after Will, who was waiting for her around the back of the house next door.

15

Following Pearson's advice, they stayed close to the houses where the wild grasses weren't as tall, maneuvering carefully over fallen debris from the houses.

Pearson went back around the front of the house as Mac slipped around the back. She and Will made it through four back yards – almost to the end of the block – when they heard another hunter call out.

"Hey, Pearson, whatcha got there? Find something?"

Will swore violently under his breath.

"Should we hide?" Mac whispered.

"We'll never make it out of here. If they see any clue that you've been here, they'll search all day, camp out all night, and start in again tomorrow. We'd have to chance Revenants in the dead of night, and even then we might not make it. They'd post a night watch."

Pearson's reply came to them clearly. "Looks like someone might've been here recently. Could just be a Revenant scrounging."

"Not enough damage to the house," his fellow said.

"I think we can get in through the front."

"I'll go around back and see if there's a broken window."

There was nothing Pearson could have done to stop him without giving away his own betrayal.

"We can't hide," Will hissed. "He's going to call all the hunters over here to search the area once he sees the apples all over the yard. Our best bet is to keep running, and maybe we can make it across the river. They won't want to chance the woods."

"Do *we*?" Mac wondered out loud.

"No choice now. It's our best hope of surviving. He's going to see us any time now."

They made it through another yard. One more house and they'd clear the block.

"Hey, there's an apple tree back here!" the other hunter called. "Looks like some have been picked recently!"

And two seconds later: "There she is! She's running west!"

Will put on a burst of speed. Mac followed suit, but his stride was longer and his stamina greater. He pulled ahead and was soon sprinting across the street into the cracked driveway of a house on the edge of the woods.

Pounding footsteps on her right brought her up short in the back yard of the last house on the last block to freedom. Pearson and his fellow hunter rounded the corner from the street, too close for her to dash across without having to fight her way past them. There was no way she could beat two hunters.

"Give it up, Bright Runner. You're not gonna make it across that street."

Mac recognized him but wasn't sure of his name. She'd always avoided the hunters if she could; most of them swaggered through life as though being a lethal hunter afforded them status as elite members of society.

"And your justification for hunting me down like a common Revenant is…?"

"You're a traitor to the Stronghold. They should have cut you down like the criminal you are right there in the Commons."

"And my crime?" Mac's pulse roared in her ears, and she frantically tried to calm her heart. She couldn't afford an overdose of adrenaline right now; rather than lending her strength, it would weaken her motor skills and reaction time.

"Your partner was a murderer. Your boyfriend lost his nerve, leaving his team one man short so he could go off and plant vegetables. Did Riemer ever tell you they lost two men the day after he resigned?"

"They shouldn't have gone out a man short. That wasn't his fault, and it certainly isn't mine."

"The company a person keeps says a lot about that person's character, don't you think? And then there's *you*, trying to make deals with the Revenant who destroyed civilization."

"As long as man remains civilized," she said reasonably, "civilization is not destroyed. While you're here acting like a barbarian, it doesn't stand a chance."

The idiot was obviously relying on Pearson to keep an eye on Will and prevent him from interfering. Pearson was studiously ignoring the fact that Will was lowering his pack to the ground, moving cautiously and quietly. Mac ignored Will, too, not wanting to draw any attention to what he might be up to.

"Congratulations. You win the Philosopher of the Year award. Now accept the inevitable. Throw down your weapon, drop your gear, and kneel on the ground, your head down so the back of your neck is exposed. I'll make it quick."

Mac barked out a laugh. "If you think I'm going to do that, you win the Idiot of the Year award."

Will launched himself over the curb. Pearson shouted a warning to his companion a second too late for him to be able to defend himself. The men tumbled onto the fissured street, swinging fists and hurling curses. Over the cacophony of their struggle, Mac heard pounding feet coming toward them. More hunters.

"Let's go!" she screamed at Will, leaping into the street. She yanked on his arm, but he pulled away and cracked his fist on the hunter's jaw just as the hunter grabbed Mac's ankle and pulled her down.

Pearson jumped into the fray, landing his own blows. He managed to extricate them from his companion's clutches while making it look as though he was trying to subdue them, even taking Will's roundhouse blow without dodging.

Will staggered to his feet, delivering a powerful kick to the hunter's abdomen with his booted foot. The hunter released Mac, along with all the breath in his lungs. Will hauled her to her feet, dragging her across the street.

Five hunters sprinted around the corner of the last house. Will didn't bother retrieving his own pack. He forced Mac to keep pace with him, leaning down as they passed the pack to grab his machete. Her feet missed the pavement several times as he towed her along, the hunters only yards behind them.

They raced at a breakneck pace through the narrow copse of pines between the last houses and the remains of a road. They widened the gap when the ground sloped suddenly downward and the hunters paused to gain surer footing. Mac and Will plunged down the slope, skidding on their heels and backsides, rolling onto a wide, flat expanse where another road had once been.

"How…much…farther?" Mac panted. Her chest heaved. Her lungs were reluctant bellows, dragging in air and gasping it out with difficulty. If she ran much longer, she'd probably throw up and faint.

"One more slope."

He leaped over a fallen tree. Mac followed suit, catching her foot on a treacherous branch. The sudden change in her trajectory wrenched him around. She hit him square in the chest, and they tumbled down the next fifty feet of the slope before fetching up against another tree.

The upside of their free fall was they gained a good lead. The downside was everything hurt, and they were both bleeding in several places. When Mac climbed to her feet, she was dismayed to find her ankle screamed in unbearable pain every time she put weight on it.

"I'm done, Will. I can't run."

He cast a look up the slope, judging how much time they could spare, and knelt beside her, yanking up her pants leg. A thick sliver of wood stuck into her flesh just above the ankle.

"Grab onto the tree." He nodded toward the tree they'd hit. She braced herself against it. He grasped the splinter and yanked it out. Mac's world tilted precariously. She thought she must have fainted on her feet, because the next thing she knew, Will's arm was around her and he was whispering frantically in her ear.

"Don't you dare faint, Mackenzie. Come on. We've gotta go."

She was vaguely aware of movement, a jostling that made her want to vomit. Pain spiked through the wound in her ankle. A roaring clouded her hearing. She was going to faint despite knowing it would seal her fate. But her vision grew steadily clearer and the cold chill that enveloped her body vanished by degrees. A cool breeze washed over her face, bringing her fully to her senses, yet the roaring remained.

They had reached the river and the footbridge.

Mac wasn't encouraged. The pedestrian suspension bridge had fallen into disrepair since the Upheaval. It was constructed entirely of stout wooden beams thicker than Will's thigh, the only metal the rusting cables by which it hung and the bolts that connected the cables to the railings and the treads to the supporting beams below. Several treads were missing, leaving petrifying gaps through which the whitecaps of the raging river seemed only inches away.

"Mackenzie!" Will yelled desperately.

Mac jumped. She'd stopped dead in her tracks while she stared at the bridge in horror. The crack of branches and rattle of stones on the slope galvanized her. She followed Will out onto the bridge, and when both her ankle and the first beam of the bridge held her weight, she pelted after him as fast as they dared.

The bridge swayed with their weight and the wind, the cables creaking ominously and raining flakes of rust on them. *Hold, please hold!* She leaped over a gap and nearly lost her footing. Will caught her hand and yanked her forward. Three strides later, he hit a rotting beam and his foot punched through, sending him sprawling on the treads. The beam beneath his left side cracked and fell away. He screamed as his head and shoulders slipped through the hole, his right arm flailing to find something to grab onto. Mac threw herself on him before he tumbled through the gap, pinning him to the sturdier board on his right.

A thump traveled through the bridge. Mac spared a glance behind her. Three hunters made the bridge, hopping over the missing treads. Four more were skidding down the slope beyond them. She freed Will's foot and he rolled away from the broken tread, white-faced. The sight of the hunters picking their way steadily toward them got him to his feet.

More treads splintered beneath them, but their weight came down for only a second before lifting again. At last, they gained the bank on the opposite shore. Will didn't look behind him as he sprinted up an incline and into the woods.

Halfway up the slope, Mac's ankle sent stabbing pains through her leg and foot. She limped after Will, casting fearful glances over her shoulder, but the hunters gave up the chase. Will waited on a path at the top of the slope, just around a bend to the left.

"Are they coming?"

"I don't think so. I can't hear them, anyway."

"We'd best not wait around to find out. This way."

He started off on the narrow path, no wider than a deer trail. Mac followed, the vise around her heart squeezing tighter with every step that took her farther from her home.

They spent the night in a stone maintenance shed that had once held equipment to service the now overgrown state park. Mac had brought along a rudimentary medical kit that had been in the shed, and they took turns treating each other's wounds, which necessitated undressing to an embarrassing degree. To his credit and despite all his previous flirtations, Will was all business as he smeared yarrow cream over her abrasions. The puncture above her ankle from the splinter still oozed blood; he used a precious bit of their water to clean it, smeared it with ointment, and covered it with a thick cloth pad he tied on with string.

Afterwards, they shared strips of dried beef from an ancient tin. The beef was fairly fresh; Mac wondered when Elijah stocked the shed, and why. Had he planned on leaving the Stronghold himself? Perhaps her crashing into his life postponed, or even ruined, his own escape.

Beside her, his head pillowed on the rolled-up spare pack, Will's breathing was deep and even, but she didn't think he slept. They didn't have to keep watch; the maintenance shed's high windows were too small for anyone but a young child to crawl through, and the double doors could be barred from the inside

"This place seems pretty solid. We could wait for Eli here."

Will's voice was sharp as he said, "We leave in the morning."

"But—"

"Mackenzie, I was sent with two objectives: to find you and to follow this." He flashed the copper medallion at her.

"Follow it where? Do you know where we're going?"

"No. I guess we'll both find out when we get there."

"And Riemer – he's coming soon, right?"

"Go to sleep, 'Kenz. We have a long, difficult journey ahead of us."

Mac was afraid to push for an answer she wasn't sure she wanted to hear. It could be that Elijah wasn't coming because he didn't want to. Perhaps, in the week they'd been apart, he'd realized how glad he was to have her out of his hair. That kiss had probably been a momentary impulse.

"Good night, Will," she said quietly.

The hush of the forest around them lulled her closer to sleep. Just as she was about to drift off, he said, "Riemer lost his girlfriend to lockjaw three years ago. She was cut in the face with a rusty knife while they were hunting. A few weeks later, she was dead. A pretty nasty death, I hear."

Mac remembered hearing something about the young woman, but she hadn't realized Riemer was romantically involved with her.

"I'd never seen him with another girl since Laura died. Not

until you."

A flush of pleasure heated her body. "It's not like that."

"You're blind if you really believe that. I saw him kiss you." He reached for her hand, curled his fingers around hers and squeezed reassuringly. "If he were able to come, nothing would stop him. Now go to sleep."

She did. With slumber came a confusing tangle of Revenant packs, hunters, the cozy shed, and Elijah in the cabbage field, showing her a copper disk engraved with an image she couldn't see clearly. *Go west*, he kept saying, but her dream-self didn't know which direction was west. When she turned to ask him to clarify, he vanished and no one knew where he had gone.

Morning found her grainy-eyed and irritable and just a little disquieted, because during her night of uneasy dreams, she realized that Will had not actually said that Elijah was coming.

Will reorganized their packs, distributing the supplies between them, while Mac slathered her wounds with more yarrow cream. He submitted to her first aid ministrations while they waited for the sun to fall upon their shed, ensuring no Revenants would be lying in wait outside.

He unbarred the door, easing it open slowly, checking outside for any immediate danger. Mac tried to edge around him, but he put out an arm to stop her, suddenly tense and watchful, his eyes scanning the woods around them with the keen attention that made him one of the top gatherers.

"What is it?" she whispered.

Satisfied there was no lurking threat, Will shoved the door open wide, his eyes on something just over the threshold. Mac stared for a moment, then lifted her gaze to his.

"Pearson?"

"I doubt it. No way could he get away from them long enough."

They stared for a moment longer at the pack full of apples that Will had abandoned on the other side of the river, which had seemed to appear outside their door as though by magic. Then, without another word, he strapped it to his back, and they began their long walk west.

16

"Do you think it's safe?"

Crouched low behind a tall field of wild wheat, Mac strained her eyes to see the house. The sun-and-moon figure was painted on the side in fresh white paint that seemed to glow in the dark, an inviting icon that indicated safety and refuge.

They followed the symbol out of the ruined city and across the farmlands, once even finding it painted on the side of an old motor home parked at the edge of the road on flat, crumbling tires. The motor home's kitchen cupboards was packed with dusty military pouch meals and they were ecstatic to find several seven-gallon containers of potable water stored in a closet. They spent a grateful two days there, resting and eating and enjoying being out of the wind. Mac was most reluctant to leave, but every delay meant they risked reaching the mountain pass after snowfall. Mac wasn't so certain they needed to go through the pass – wherever the symbol was leading them could very well be on this side of the Cascade Mountains – but Will, ever practical and prepared, insisted.

Will held the field glasses to his eyes, scanning the rolling prairie for both shelter and threat. The house in question, half a mile or so away, offered potential safety, but it could just as likely hold danger. A week ago, they'd come across what appeared to be an abandoned dwelling only to find a pack of Revenants waiting inside, driven in by the increasingly cold weather. A hair-raising fight brought them terrifyingly close to being killed.

"It seems abandoned," he said uncertainly. There was a shadow of suspicion on his face, however.

"We could just camp here," she suggested. To their left a short distance away huddled a cluster of small boulders, deposited eons ago by glaciers that had carved the landscape. It provided a more than serviceable windbreak, and they could probably risk a fire to keep warm since they no longer slept anywhere without keeping watch. The fire would keep away the Revenants – they despised the brightness of the flames and avoided them – but Revenants weren't the only dangers out on the road.

"It'll be a cold night," he cautioned. He didn't seem thrilled with the prospect.

"We can't keep walking; it's almost dark. We could end up in the middle of a Revenant nest without even realizing it."

Mac took the field glasses from him, keeping the edge of her hand over the top to keep the lenses from reflecting light and giving away their presence. The old farmhouse was weathered to the bare siding, some of which hung off the structure like peeling skin. A rusted hulk of a truck was parked close to the house, its windows free of glass. The wild grasses, long unattended, grew taller than the sagging front porch. A short distance from the house lay an orchard, the trees a wild tangle of overgrown limbs and dusty red apples.

The sight of the apples made her mouth water. The fruit they'd brought with them was just a memory now, and they had yet to come across another stash. The last orchard they happened upon two days ago was half-burned down; the other half offered a meager supply of deformed, wormy fruit.

She gave him back the field glasses and crouched behind a scrub of sagebrush. A hundred feet behind them lay the tattered ribbon of the old highway. Decades of harsh winters had dug their fingers into the blacktop, prying loose huge chunks and crumbling the edges. Still, it was easier to walk on it than it was to walk along its edges, which were overgrown with sagebrush and wild wheat and, along one memorable stretch, a trailing mat of peas.

Mac stuffed herself and then suffered terrible gas pains for the rest of the day and into the night. They camped under the sheltering boughs of a hemlock, and unable to sleep, Mac kept first watch. Even so, it had taken Will a long time to fall asleep, as he kept snickering each time she broke wind. He didn't tease her too mercilessly, though, because they both were craving the green vegetables that were becoming harder to find as the summer waned and the nights – and days – grew colder.

Will lowered the field glasses and hunkered down beside her, his troubled expression fairly shouting his unease. All Mac saw was a decrepit house and an untended orchard, packed with nutritious apples. If they weren't filled with worms or bitten by frost, that was.

"I know you want to stop for the day, but…I don't know. I

142

just don't feel right about this. I feel like we're being watched."

"We've felt that way the whole journey," she reminded him. Already her feet were protesting carrying her farther than the giant boulders she'd mentioned to him.

"I know. This is worse. "

"Revenants?"

"Could be. They're starting to migrate inside as it gets colder."

"Do you think they'll leave us alone if we camp out here?"

"Probably. They won't want to come out in the cold."

During the first winter of the Upheaval, it became apparent that the infected could not survive freezing temperatures. Efforts were made to capitalize on this, and groups of Revenants in majorly infected areas had been rounded up and dumped by cargo plane in the Arctic Circle and on the Antarctic continent. It worked beautifully for a time; after the infected succumbed to the subzero temperatures, teams would return to burn the bodies.

But then several planes and their crews went missing, and all attempts at relocation to a hostile environment ceased. Two years later, air travel was all but impossible. Likewise, all hope was abandoned that the Revenants would migrate south as temperatures dipped when, instead, they hibernated indoors.

"But if it's not Revenants watching us, 'Kenz, we could have trouble on our hands."

Mac was smart enough to know that not all who lived in this post-Upheaval world considered life precious and sacrosanct. But it had been decades since roving bands of marauders ravaged settlements of survivors. Once gasoline became harder to find and keeping vehicles in operating condition was nearly impossible, pillaging gangs ceased to be threats. One generally only worried about coming across ruffians when traveling, and no one did that anymore.

"The symbol is painted on the house."

"It could be a ruse."

Will pondered the problem for a couple more minutes, and finally shook his head. "The sun's going down. Let's camp at the boulders. If there's something or someone in that house watching us, they've already seen us. We'll just have to be on our guard. But I'm not going to risk going in there and being trapped."

"No sleeping tonight, huh?" Mac made a face. It wasn't the first time Will insisted they pass by a shelter bearing the sun-and-moon icon. Sometimes, he said, he just had a feeling that a place wasn't safe, and he'd learned long ago to trust his gut.

"We don't dare. Let's head over there and then gather some wood before we lose all the light."

They'd skipped sleeping on this trip several times when Will's hackles were up. As they gathered fallen branches around a small copse of trees nearby, she predicted tomorrow would be a day of sleep-deprived headaches, grainy eyes, and irritability.

"Hey, 'Kenz, look at this."

Will crouched at the edge of the copse, studying the ground. No, not the ground, Mac realized as she joined him, but at a line of stumps leading in a fairly straight line into the distance.

"Windbreak for the farm?"

"Undoubtedly. What bothers me is the stumps should all be rotting by now if they had been chopped years ago. Some are barely showing any weathering, maybe a season, possibly two at most."

"So someone's living in the house."

"If they are, they're keeping a low profile. If they're trying to keep their presence hidden, they won't chance a fire and they'll have as cold a night as we will." He seemed to relish this thought.

"Maybe they're just scared. After all, they don't know that *we* aren't a threat."

"True. I'm not going to take any chances, though." Her disappointment must have shown on her face, for he added, "I'm supposed to keep you safe. It's why I was sent. I can't do that if I'm not cautious."

"I know. I'm just tired and cold. And tomorrow you're going to be a real crab-ass and I'm not looking forward to it."

He grinned. "Suck it up, Bright Runner. I promised you protection, not a sunny disposition."

They made three more trips to the copse until they gathered enough to burn through the night if they were frugal. Mac added a pile of tumbleweeds to serve as kindling, and they settled for the night in the scant protection offered by the semi-circle of boulders.

Their days walking were spent in conversation, but their nights – even the nights when they both stayed awake on watch – were mostly silent so they could hear any unusual sounds. They built a small fire at the open end of the semi-circle, which would keep at bay any Revenants or curious animals, and wrapped up in their blankets to stay warm. Every fifteen minutes, they took turns peering over the boulders with the field glasses, scanning the area for imminent attacks. The night song of coyotes in the distance lulled Mackenzie toward sleep; she shifted into an uncomfortable position to fend off drowsiness and broke the no-talking rule.

"Why didn't he come? The real reason, I mean."

Will didn't answer for a long moment. He was draped over a boulder and staring through the field glasses for any sign of movement in the house, and when he was finally satisfied that there was no change in that direction, he lowered himself to the ground beside her, pulling his blanket over his shoulders. His expression in the flickering firelight was guarded.

"It's not as easy as you think to get out of the Stronghold, especially if you aren't a hunter or gatherer."

"He'd have found a way. If he told me he would come as soon as he could, then he knew how to get out."

"He also told you if he couldn't come, he'd send someone. And here I am."

"That doesn't answer my question. Was he being watched? Was he detained?"

He broke a tumbleweed into small pieces, feeding them into the fire and making it flare. "Everyone is watched, all the time. Either by the elders, their spies, or by Riemer's underground."

"*Riemer's* underground?" Mac repeated sharply. "So he's the leader? Is that why he's not here?"

"I doubt he's the leader, but I don't think there are very many people between him and who's in charge. To be able to get people out of the Stronghold – like he got you out – he would need help from an elder."

"He didn't get me out. I was exiled."

Will looked amused. "Sure you were."

"I saw his face when he found out about the note Ren Leonard left me."

"Do you think he didn't know about that note already? As soon as you came under his scrutiny, he would have searched your quarters thoroughly so he knew what he was dealing with and what he could use to get you away. He probably started making plans for you as soon as Bon was taken."

Mac couldn't argue his logic. On the day Bon died, Elijah himself said he needed to start planning how to get her out of the Stronghold. He also said they would have to wait awhile, because the Council would be watching her. But she wanted to find fault with this line of reasoning, because if she acknowledged its likelihood, she must accept that he was too important to the underground to leave the Stronghold.

"Look at the events of that night, 'Kenz. All evening, he sat apart from you with his friends, but he knew where you were every second. And then, just half an hour before Catherine came in with that note, he suddenly takes you inside. It smacks of planning."

"He'd have told me, prepared me." But would he? Elijah Riemer did what Elijah Riemer thought was best. The whole four weeks she'd been under his wing, he controlled everything, including making sure she did not go out gathering again. Something niggled at the back of her mind about that, but Will spoke before she could put her finger on it.

"I'm not saying that you were unimportant to him personally, Mackenzie."

"No, you're just saying that the underground is more important than I am." She shrugged, swallowing past a lump in her throat. Really, it was silly to get so upset over losing someone you'd spent less than a month with, someone with whom you weren't even romantically involved. "I understand that. But it brings up another question."

"It does?"

"Are you not important to the underground?"

He broke another tumbleweed into twigs, tossing them by handfuls into the fire. "I'm not part of the underground," he admitted grudgingly. "It was just easier for me to get out of the Stronghold."

"And he trusted you enough to tell you all this?"

"We had a conversation after you were exiled, Riemer and me. I knew enough and guessed the rest from his behavior after you were put out the doors that night. He was too purposeful. Two days after you left the Stronghold, a gathering team was attacked and one of them killed. I was partnered with the remaining member. Riemer gave me the medallion and told me where to find you. I managed to conveniently vanish on an excursion."

He slanted a somewhat crooked smile at her. Mac didn't smile back. Nothing was as simple as she assumed. And nothing he said tonight gave her any hope that Elijah would be catching up to them.

She held out her hand. "Give me the field glasses. It's my turn."

"I'll do it. Why don't you go ahead and get a little sleep? I don't mind keeping watch by myself."

"I'm fine." But she dropped her hand, allowing him to take her watch.

"I'm sorry, 'Kenz," he said quietly.

She shrugged. "I'll live."

He looked away as though uncomfortable with her distress. After a moment, he shrugged off his blanket and straightened slowly, leaning on the boulders to stay as low as possible, and raised the field glasses to his eyes.

Without warning, he gave a shout and dropped the glasses, staggering backward. Mac sprang to her feet, instantly alert, her hand gripping her ever-present machete. The blanket dropped from her shoulders and puddled at her feet.

A dark form hurtled over the boulder, landing on Will and driving him backward into the rock behind them. She raised the machete and swung as the intruder turned toward her. The blade whistled through the air, and the figure ducked.

Another dark form charged into the shelter, jumping over the fire. Will, dazed from his impact with the rock, peeled himself off the ground and flung himself against the new intruder's legs. They merged into the darkness of the ground, a writhing shadow of curses and primal war cries.

Mac followed her blade around, spinning down into her fighting crouch. The intruder sprang before she quite completed her spin. One hand snaked around her wrist, squeezing until she dropped the blade. The other fell in a swinging arc, the fist cracking against her jaw. Her face exploded in blazing white pain, and she tumbled into darkness.

17

Tick. Tick. Tick.

The sound drew Mackenzie out of the cocooning comfort of darkness. Her jaw throbbed, making her whole face ache, and her whole body was numb with cold. Her eyes opened to a room as devoid of light as it had been with them closed.

Tick. Tick.

Something was wrong with the clock. She'd been telling Bon for two months now that she thought it was dying, and they needed to be on the lookout for a new one while they were out gathering. The *tick* was slipping into a *snick* sound, probably as the gears wore down.

T-sssnick. T-sssnick. T-sssnick.

One day soon, it was going to fail and she would be late for gathering, and they would get docked their dessert at supper. And if it was cherry pie that night, she was going to be really angry.

She reached for the clock. Her arm wouldn't move. Oh, that was right – she'd been bitten by that Revenant at Ren Leonard's college. And considering the absolute darkness, she now realized that they were still at the college and Leonard was getting rid of the Revenants they had killed. The *t-sssnick* sound she was hearing must be him dragging the bodies down the metal frame of the old staircase.

"Bon, I can't move my arm."

Her voice was muffled, her mouth stiff and dry, her words unintelligible. A glimmer of light appeared at the foot of the sofa where she made her bed. She tried to raise her head, but a band closed off her airway.

Whispers floated across the room, and soft laughter, and the steady *t-sssnick t-sssnick t-sssnick*. Metal on metal, that's what it was. She'd heard it before, but she couldn't place it. It was nothing good. Nothing to do with Revenants was ever good.

"*...nice and muscled...no fat though...*"

"*...probably gamey...but young, so it should still be tender...*"

The light moved from her feet. The darkness brightened

slightly, but still she couldn't see. She blinked, her lashes brushing along something in front of her eyes. Fingers scrabbled through her hair, and the blindfold was lifted. She stared up into a gaunt, grimy face. Unwashed and starving, but not a Revenant. A human.

"Where is this?" is what she said, but it came out *Weh ifff thffff?*

A grin split the face, showing rotting teeth. A wheezing laugh washed the smell of decaying meat over her face. Mac gagged – and then realized she really was gagged. A cloth was tied around her head, cutting into her cheeks, tasting of sour water and old blood. The figure stepped away from her. She rolled her head to the right to ease up the pressure on her throat.

The gag muffled her scream. Laid out on a long, blood-soaked counter, the body was stripped of skin. And legs. And arms. She fought back a wave of nausea, knowing she would choke on her own vomit if she threw up. Another thin, grubby man stood on the other side of the counter facing her, his clothes stained maroon. He ran the sharp edge of a carving knife over a whetstone over and over. *T* as he set the knife to the stone; *sssnick* as he drew the blade over the rough surface. As Mac watched, he bent to the body and sliced a long strip of meat from the chest.

Oh dear God, don't let that be Will!

She turned her head away. The band around her throat tightened, a thick edge cutting into her throat, so she turned farther to her left, not wanting to watch as they carved up whomever was on the counter. Someone else lay on the floor in the shadows, hands and feet tied, face turned away from the light. She stared, willing him to move, to show his face, to be Will Crawford.

Each *t-sssnick* was followed by the wet squelch of raw meat being carved. Mac appended her prayer to include *I hope they kill me before they start slicing me up.*

Indistinct thuds behind her preceded the scent of smoke and firewood. Warm air currents teased her chilled face and danced away, and then back as the wood caught and crackled in the flames. She fought the lethargy of near-hypothermia, throwing herself against her bonds. Being burnt alive hadn't been on her agenda, either.

Footsteps thudded across the floor. Mackenzie didn't turn her head even when they stopped beside her and someone bumped the table. She closed her eyes and waited to die. Wet, cold metal pressed against her cheek: the flat of a bloody blade.

"Pretty girlie, tender girlie," he crooned in her ear. "Carve you up, make some tender steaks. But not before we've had our fun."

Mac opened her eyes, boring her gaze into the spine of the person on the floor. Was that a subtle shift of shoulders or a trick of the firelight? *Wake up! Wake up, damn you!*

The strap over her throat tightened, and then loosened and fell away completely, clattering into the floor. A belt, maybe. She tucked the information away in her brain; if she managed to free herself, it might come in handy as a weapon.

Cold, bony fingers gripped her chin, forcing her head back around. The bloody knife came to rest at the base of her throat while the grubby fingers of his other hand scrabbled with the buttons of her jacket.

He bumped the table again as he peeled back the flaps of her jacket and leaned over her. The table swayed to the left on rickety legs, and the man teetered off balance. Seizing her chance, she slammed her forehead against the side of his head. He roared with pain and fell onto the table. The legs collapsed and the table slammed to the floor.

The impact jarred every joint in her body. The table top broke in half. Her assailant landed on her, stealing half her breath, his head bouncing off the hardwood floor as he rolled away from her. He lay still, blood trickling from a scalp wound. Her bindings were so tightly cinched that she could only move the leather straps by fractions of an inch toward the shattered ends of the ruined table.

The repulsive butcher across the room saw he was in imminent danger of losing his livestock, and he abandoned his current grisly project. Lantern light glimmered over the bloody blade of his carving knife as he advanced cautiously, his eyes darting from her to the still figure in the shadows only a couple feet from her.

The leather strap pinning her arms caught on a jagged splinter of wood. *Damn, damn, damn!* Her lungs hitched and spasmed on a breath. Panic sped her heart as he crept closer. Still pinned securely to the broken table top, she could not roll over, could not raise her arms or legs to defend herself. If she couldn't free herself, she was dead.

And then he loomed over her, baring rotting teeth in a snarl. A hideous clarity stole over her senses, sharpening each to painful

151

starkness. The air carried warm currents from the fire, rich with the scent of burning apple wood. The current swirled away, replaced by a cold chill that smelled of death and decay. Every smear of blood on the steel blade shone in three-dimensional wonder, swirls and drops and splotches of crimson shimmering in the firelight. Next to her, the fallen cannibal snored heavily, still unconscious, and between his grunts and snorts she could hear the steady, even breath of the body on the floor. Her clothes lay heavy, almost painfully, on her skin, which prickled as every hair struggled to erect itself, soundlessly screaming RUN, a command she was powerless to obey.

His battle cry shattered the air in the same second he raised the knife and fell upon her.

And then he was gone, yanked into the gloom behind him as though the shadows had grown hands and claimed him. Mac blinked in shock, raising her head, but he was nowhere to be seen in the limited circle of light the fire provided

Her assailant groaned, coming to consciousness. His hand twitched across the shattered remains of the table. The body beside her erupted, a motion blur of pale skin and dark clothing. Her attacker gurgled deep in his throat. Blood pulsed from around the jagged, broken table leg driven into his neck. Will, attached to the end, lurched to his feet, staggered a few steps, and fell. The firelight glinted off the droplets of blood splattered across his face as he rolled into a ball, clutching his head.

"Other one?" he ground out between clenched teeth.

"I don't know. He just…vanished."

"God, my head!" he groaned. "There are two of you."

A sharp crack followed by a thud echoed in the house, coming from the darkened hallway. Mac yanked the leather strap against the splinter of wood, which still refused to give way. She cast a glance at the hallway, then at Will, who was slowly rolling onto his knees.

"Get these damn things off me, Will!"

He crawled to her, a drunken course that brought him closer to her feet than to her hands, where he'd been aiming. He fumbled with the strap. The hallway was silent now, a silence that made her heart race and her mind work overtime to produce any number of nightmarish images, each packed with malevolent, rotting, scrabbling monsters.

The bindings fell away, freeing her feet. Will rolled a few feet away and threw up. Mac pushed her feet against the tabletop, trying to wriggle upwards and free her arms, but the strap was cinched too tightly.

"Sitting duck here!"

Will waved a hand at her impatient hiss, drew in a shuddering breath, and scooted to her, moving slowly. A few minutes of fumbling and her arms were free. She tried to push herself upright, but her limbs felt dead.

"Oh, God, Will – I think they paralyzed me!"

"Bindings were too tight, deadened the nerves. The feeling will come back in a few minutes."

"We don't *have* a few minutes. There's something in that hallway."

"If it was going to attack, it would have by now. Especially if it's a Revenant." He collapsed onto his side, breathing heavily. "I think my skull is split open."

Mac turned her head to look at him. Blood bathed one side and the back of his head, an alarming amount of blood. Scalp wounds bled a lot, but still...if his skull was cracked, there was nothing they could do about it but pray that his brain didn't swell enough to kill him.

Feeling returned to her arms slowly, starting with a prickling in her fingertips. The prickling grew by degrees to the lazy flutter of a butterfly, then the drone of bees, then the stinging buzz of a swarm of hornets. She shook them to speed recovery. When the pain passed, she sat up, keeping a wary eye on the shadowy hallway. She couldn't tell if she really saw movement in the darkness or if her eyes were playing tricks.

"Let's get out of here. This place gives me the creeps."

"And go where?" Will hunched over, rocking on his knees. "I won't make it a hundred feet out the door, 'Kenz."

"We could stay the night in that old truck parked by the house."

"That thing probably hasn't run in a hundred years or more."

"I said stay in it, not drive it."

"If it doesn't move, it's too close to this freakshow of a house."

"Our only other options are try to make it back to our camp

or stay here inside the house."

He groaned. Mac pushed to her feet, swaying precariously before regaining her equilibrium. She pulled at his huddled form until he raised his head from where he'd tucked it between his knees, and propped her shoulder under his arm, using her legs to lift him to his feet. He staggered, falling against her and nearly taking them both back to the floor.

"Head's spinning."

No doubt, if she could judge by their meandering course to the front door. She reached out to turn the knob. Will slithered out of her grasp and sprawled on the floor, unconscious. Mac stared down at him blankly. It had taken the last of her reserves to get him off the floor; she didn't have the energy to even consider a solution.

An arm hooked around her neck from behind, choking off her air. She clawed at it, feeling her fingers sink deep into spongy flesh. The next instant, the flesh was firm.

The world went black. Her last thought as she fell was *Revenant.*

She was dead.

18

Surely she was in heaven, because she was warm, truly warm, for the first time since they'd left the motor home two weeks ago. Mackenzie sighed and stretched. Her leg nudged a warm body beside her, and she froze. So Will had died, too. That was unfortunate. But he'd been clocked in the head hard enough to concuss him, and that was bound to have caused some brain swelling. With medical aid unavailable — and primitive when it could be found — it was not surprising when even a simple blow to the head resulted in death.

She opened her eyes to unexpected darkness, dimly lit from somewhere behind her. Wouldn't heaven be bright and cheerful? Maybe she'd gone the other way instead. She'd tried to live a good life, to follow the teachings of the Holy Book, but her report card on her behavior was, of course, subjective at best.

The rumble of machinery beneath her was a discordant note in her utopic state. Heaven wouldn't need machines, surely. But it rocked and swayed her makeshift bed, lulling her back toward slumber. She closed her eyes and shifted closer to Will.

The machine lurched and bounced and shuddered to a stop.

"Shit!"

The imprecation, uttered in a gravelly voice, brought Mac from under her blanket and into a defensive crouch in a split second. Her head banged against something overhead, making her wince.

"Settle down, Bright Runner. You're going to concuss yourself, and then what a pair you two would make. The addled leading the comatose."

"*Leonard?*" Ren Leonard turned in his seat and gave her a two fingered salute. "What the *hell* are you doing here?"

"I would have thought the more important question is 'where the hell am I?' but I've ceased to be surprised by your reactions."

Where turned out to be the back of some sort of utility vehicle, possibly new at the time of the Upheaval. What she could see in the dim glow of the instrument lights told her the automobile had been cared for over the decades. Heat poured out of ceiling vents above her despite the fact that his window was open several inches. No wonder she hadn't smelled him; he was venting his stench.

"How'd you get a vehicle?"

"I requisitioned it from your dubious friends back at the farmhouse."

"They were no friends of mine." Mac made a face. "But you still haven't answered the most important question. What are you doing here?"

"I've been keeping an eye on you since you left my building."

"Why?" She couldn't fathom any reason she'd warrant his continued interest.

He stared out the window into the night for a long moment. "Let's just say I didn't trust that Stronghold of yours. We hit something; I'd better get out and see what it is. By the way, you run like a girl."

The door opened, flooding the car with light and cold air. Will didn't even stir. In the brief moment of light, his face glowed waxy white under a turban of makeshift bandage – a shirt, maybe? The door thunked closed. Alone in the dark again, Mackenzie shifted into a more comfortable sprawl, contemplating this turn of events. If he was here, he must have been watching her for some time or he would have missed her expulsion from the Stronghold. And if he'd seen *that*, then he must have been aware of the hunters searching for her before Will and she escaped the city.

By the way, you run like a girl.

They hadn't run since the Revenant-occupied house a week ago, and before that, since they'd sprinted into the forest after escaping the hunters. She wondered if he'd followed them home the day Bon died. If so, and if he'd been watching her since she'd gone to solicit his help, then he must have holed in up one of the houses near the Stronghold. Those were cleared regularly by a special team of hunters overseen by Catherine, who handpicked the most brutal, efficient killers from the most experienced teams. Only an exceptionally clever being could avoid them for so long.

The door opened. The dome light made Leonard flinch as he climbed back in. Blotches of dark color scuttled under his skin. He pulled the door closed, cutting off the light.

"We hit a giant pothole. Damage isn't as bad as it seemed when we hit. I won't be able to push us out until closer to dawn when you can help."

"I can help now."

"No, it's safer if you stay in the car. No telling what's out there in the dark." He locked his door and scooted onto the passenger side, leaning against the door and stretching his legs along the bench seat. His bloodshot eyes glittered in the dim light.

"Won't we run out of fuel if we leave the car running all night?"

"I'll shut it off periodically."

She pulled her knees up to her chin and circled her arms around them, staring out the window into the night. There wasn't much to see; the sky had been clear most of the day, but a cloud bank rolled in as dusk fell, obscuring the stars and the moon.

"You're the one who choked me."

"I'm the one who saved you."

"By choking me?"

"I figured if I surprised you after what you'd just been through, you might have a heart attack or try to find a way to part me from my head."

Mac chuckled. "Maybe so. I don't have my machete, anyway. I lost it at our camp when we were taken."

"I gathered all your stuff. It's in the back seat." He motioned at the void of dark space between them. "Our friends the cannibals didn't seem too interested in your possessions, though no doubt they'd have gone and scavenged it all in the morning."

"They were more interested in my liver."

"And your flanks. Maybe some breast meat." He barked out a laugh. "The situations you find yourself in, Mackenzie Bright Runner."

She bristled. "I didn't *try* to get myself filleted. Who expects to run into cannibals out in the middle of the farmland?"

Leonard was silent for a long while. When he spoke, his voice was a grating whisper. "It's a brutal world now. The pillagers are mostly gone – can't get around very well without vehicles and it's pretty risky to camp out. But there are threats everywhere – settlements borne of and ruled by violence and oppression. Cannibals." He waved a hand in the general direction of the farmhouse. "Revenants aren't the only hazard out there. Maybe not even the worst one."

"How can men be worse than Revenants?"

"Revenants kill because the virus destroyed most of their brains. Man kills for power. Or pleasure." He studied his hands in the instrument lights. "When my brain settled down and I discovered I was still able to think, I found my sympathy for mankind was in short supply."

"You said you learned what infected you. What was it?"

Leonard dropped his hands back into his lap. She thought for a long moment that he was going to ignore her question. Then he let out a breath.

"You ever hear of vampires?"

"You were bitten by a vampire." She couldn't hide her skepticism.

"Am I telling this story or are you?" he snapped. She flinched and held up a placatory hand. "I'm not talking about vampires like Dracula. Ah...you do know who Dracula is, don't you?"

"There were several copies of the book in the Stronghold," Mac said, a bit dryly.

"They were dubbed vampires because they craved protein like crazy, but they couldn't process anything but liquids. Blood is the most plentiful protein, so it's what they went after first. The origins of the condition are unknown; epidemiologists thought some sort of viral infection caused a permanent genetic recoding. It's a very rare condition that when crossed with a flesh-eating disease...you get Revenants. Ever wonder why we're called that? Know what the word means?"

"Ghost?" she ventured.

"A person who returns after dying. A spirit. The flesh-eating virus speeds us toward decay"—he held up a hand to the light, showing her the pooling black pockets of decomposition under his skin—"and the vampire mutation heals us. We're always caught between living and dying."

"How'd you learn this?"

"I broke into the right places." His mouth twisted in a semblance of a smile – a very sarcastic smile. "I had a lot of time on my hands. I've been all over the country. Made the mistake of going to Detroit – it's no better post-apocalyptic than it was before the Upheaval. Eventually, I found my way into certain government labs—"

Mac held up a hand to stop him. "Wait. I don't know much about the world before the Upheaval, but I rather doubt they'd leave an important lab full of infectious diseases so accessible you could just walk in."

"They didn't, but I knew the way in. And it's not as though they had time to lock up nice and tight once the shit hit the fan. The details were all there, printed and scattered across the floor of a lab where someone dropped it. I'd do the same thing – print out all the data on the weirdest shit in the database. And I certainly qualified as weird shit.

"At any rate, I wasn't the first to try to steal classified documents. Or maybe they were just trying to preserve the data before they lost electricity, not stealing it. Who the hell could they have sold it to? There was no one left to buy black market information."

He chuckled. His gaze shifted, moving to the reflection of the instrument lights on the driver's window.

"How did the lab get information about you?"

Leonard slanted her a look from the corner of his eye. "I wasn't always roaming free and killing people. You know how some people are naturally immune to certain diseases, like measles or mumps?"

"You were immune to the vampire virus?"

"Do I *look* like I was immune to the virus?" He scowled. "Some people are immune, and some people show a high resistance, while others fall victim to illness every time they turn around.

"The classified reports said I had a super-high resistance to both mutations. It took a long time for the bonded virus – the Revenant Virus – to have any effect on my genetic code, and once it did, I went crazy for a time. When the craziness passed, I found I was still capable of higher thinking and emotional control, although I have to admit my temper's a bit hotter than it used to be. The Revenant Virus hadn't destroyed my hypothalamus."

Mac thought back to their conversation in his lair at the old college campus. "So it's not that you were infected by a purer strain, but that you had a higher resistance."

"That's what makes some of us different, a super-high resistance just short of immunity that allowed us to retain our higher thinking. I'm sure there are others out there like me, who have chosen not to kill if they can help it. And others have let anger and hatred bitter their blood, and they vent their despair over what they've lost on the uninfected."

His head swiveled around, his gaze now so intense she shrank back. "It's true that I killed my coworkers and many of the students on campus. I escaped the hospital while they were waiting for the CDC to take me away. So yeah, maybe I sparked the spread of the virus. I was loose and killing people for a good nine days before they captured me. After that, I was quarantined by the CDC in a secret installation deep underground somewhere in Wyoming for several years."

"CDC?"

"Center for Disease Control. They handled pandemics, and this was the mother of all pandemics."

Mac chewed her lip. She understood the words he spoke, but they made no sense. Her frame of reference was so far removed from his experiences. More than a century lay between the end of his human existence and her birth; during that span, civilization fell and from its ruins rose a brutal fight for survival. Not life, really, not to Mac. For her, life meant contentment and joy and abundance, and this world held none of that.

"Will you tell me about what happened after you were attacked?"

He didn't answer for a long time, just stared at her with those discomfiting, unwavering eyes. After a long, uncomfortable minute, he turned back to the window.

"Go to sleep, Bright Runner. It's been a long day, and this is no story for the dark."

"But—"

"Sleep well."

Surprisingly, she did.

19

It rained during the night, leaving the pitted road wet and muddy but cleansing the air, if only temporarily, of the acrid stink of burning fields and forests. Mackenzie huddled in her jacket, glowering at the grey day. The land was shrouded in fog, reducing visibility to a hundred feet or less, which caused no end of uneasiness, although she expected Ren Leonard would hear any sneak attacks by wandering Revenants before she did. He didn't seem concerned.

In fact, she didn't think he noticed anything beyond the front tires that were wedged into the mother of all potholes. He'd said many rude words since dawn pulled him out of the car to assess their dilemma, all uttered in that inhuman, gravelly voice that made her nervous. The fog flattened their voices and gave back an eerie echo.

"Can we get it out of there?"

"We can," he admitted gruffly, "though it's going to be a bitch of a job. Would be nice if Sleeping Beauty in there wasn't comatose."

"It's hardly his fault." He didn't reply. "Do you think his brain is swelling? How would I be able to tell? Is there anything I can do for him if it does?"

"Pray." Hands on his hips, he heaved a sigh and headed for the back of the vehicle. He came back with a jack. "Look around for some flat pieces of wood."

She eyed the fog-covered countryside. "Uh..."

He flipped his hood off his head, listening. "Nothing for miles, except maybe some jackrabbits and a coyote or two."

"Well, that's good to know," she said, a bit impatiently. "But if I get lost in the fog, I won't be able to find my way back. I can already see from here that there aren't any flat boards nearby."

His brow lowered. Mac backed away several steps. No matter his tenacious hold on his humanity, he was still a Revenant, and his temper was short-fused by his own admission.

Silently, he slotted the jack into the bumper and started pumping the lever When he was satisfied it was stable, he motioned her over.

"Jack it up until the tires are clear of the hole. I'll look for the boards."

"What if—"

"*I* won't get lost." And with no more than a cursory glance, he disappeared into the fog.

She cast an apprehensive look into the back of the vehicle – which Leonard kept referring to as a "truck" even though it was all enclosed. Will's breathing had been steady and deep this morning, and his color better than last night, but he still didn't regain consciousness. He probably would when it was least convenient and would freak out when he saw Ren Leonard. Hopefully she would have time to keep him from skewering the Revenant. Or to keep Leonard from having to kill him.

She pumped the lever of the jack until the tires rose out of the hole, and then gave a few more pumps for good measure. While she waited, she checked on Will. Leonard shut off the vehicle's engine during the night to conserve their fuel. She awakened warm and cozy under her blankets and breathing cold air. Before she'd climbed out of the car to relieve herself and help get the tires unstuck, she'd pulled Will's blanket most of the way over his face so his body heat would warm his breathing air. The last thing he needed on top of a concussion was pneumonia or worse.

But Will was warm – warmer than Mackenzie was at this juncture – and snoring lightly, although not as bad as last night. She climbed back out of the car, closing the door quickly to preserve what little heat there was. Leonard still hadn't returned, so she sat on a small rock at the side of the ruined roadway, her machete close at hand, and examined her fingernails. Normally kept brutally short with the use of small scissors, they had grown longer and were chipped and crusted with dirt from use. She longed for a bath – she really couldn't judge Leonard's Revenant stink when she hardly smelled like a flower garden herself.

A clatter of stones was her only warning that she was no longer alone. She swept up the machete and slid into a defensive crouch. Fog was her least favorite environment in which to fight; it dampened sound while at the same time echoing it, making it impossible to tell from which direction it came.

162

The fog chuckled around her. "You're so paranoid, Bright Runner."

Ren Leonard appeared, the mist and his long, flapping duster giving the appearance that he was materializing from thin air. And then he passed her rock, carrying four wide, splintery boards on his shoulder. Paint clung to them in tenacious, flaking streaks.

"If I wasn't paranoid, I'd be dead."

"Not by my hand. Come on, give me a hand." He laid the boards on the ground and crouched by the front tires. Mac crouched beside him. "Take one of the boards and lay it over the hole so the tires can go over."

"Just one? Why did you bring four boards?"

"In case they break. They're a hundred and some-odd years old; I'm amazed they didn't disintegrate when I picked them up."

She took a board and scooted around him, laying it over the pothole under the tire. "Where'd you find them?"

"There's a farmhouse not far from here. I found them in the barn. If they hadn't been painted, they would have been mulch long ago."

He moved the extra boards aside and stood up, lowering the jack and setting the tires down. The boards creaked ominously but held the weight of the car.

"Let's give it a whirl."

He got in the car and fired the engine. Although he left the car door open, Mac felt very alone. If something came at her through the fog, would he be able to get out of the vehicle in time to help?

The car rolled slowly over the boards and thumped to the tattered pavement on the other side of the pothole. The right tire barely cleared the hole when the board cracked and broke into several pieces.

Leonard stopped the car and got out, stooping down to peer at the board. "Good thing I brought extras."

He examined the board on the left and discarded it, deciding it wouldn't hold the weight of the vehicle a second time. Mac took one of the extra boards and laid it over the right side of the hole while he placed the other under the left. She backed away from the car again, glancing around nervously. Leonard slanted her a wry smile as he got behind the wheel.

"There's nothing out there." He cocked his head and listened.

"Well, maybe a coyote or a dog, but it's not close and it's heading away from us."

The car rolled forward again. The boards held, cracking only slightly. She reckoned it was fortunate they didn't have a convoy of vehicles; the ground to either side of the highway sloped down several feet and then back up again, creating drainage ditches. There would have been no way to go around.

She climbed in the back with Will, ducking under her blanket, and was surprised when Leonard shifted the car out of gear and moved to the passenger seat, stretching his legs across the seat.

"Aren't we going?"

"I'd be an idiot to drive over a bad road in fog like this. But I feel better knowing that if we *have* to go, we can."

A smart strategy, actually. If the fog didn't burn off, she supposed she could pilot the vehicle while Leonard scouted ahead to make sure there were no dangers.

She laid her head against the back of the seat in front of her, watching Will sleep. He'd rolled onto his side since she last checked him, which she took as a good sign.

"Have you ever driven a car, Bright Runner?" Leonard asked abruptly.

Mac moved her gaze from Will to Leonard.

"Just a tractor at the Stronghold."

"I might have to give you a crash course. If the sun comes out, I won't be able to see well enough to drive."

She hesitated. "Is it hard?"

"Not really."

He stared out the window at the fog pressing in on the car. Heat poured out of the car's vents, warming the air and making Mac drowsy. To hold sleep at bay, she asked, "What have you been doing since the Upheaval? I find it hard to believe you just sat around reading novels and brooding."

"You're right. I didn't. Well, I *have* been reading, but very few novels. Books on solar power and electricity." He slanted her a sidelong look. "And biology and genetics. Teaching myself to be a goddamn scientist."

"Why? You've already said you have no desire to help humans."

"Not the particular batch of humans left in my city."

She couldn't argue with that. While there were some great people in the Stronghold, it was governed by some heavy-handed power grabbers.

"Will you tell me more about what happened to you after you were infected?"

He speared her with a sharp look. The rings around his irises were a vibrant blue in the daylight. All Revenants had the blue ring; the virus rapidly degraded the pigmentation in the stroma, causing a loss of original color, but no one could explain why the bright blue pigment appeared in just the outer circle. Gerald read many of the science books previous generations of gatherers brought back to the Stronghold, but there was nothing like it explained in them. She wondered what color Ren Leonard's eyes were before he'd been infected.

"What color were your eyes before the Revenant Virus changed them?" she blurted and then blushed so deeply that her skin hurt. She hadn't meant to ask.

"Brown. Shit brown." And he laughed his gravelly laugh that held no humor. "The beginning of the end of the world is where I came into the story. I'm hardly the first one that was infected, but the blame was laid at my door. Isn't that special."

Remembering how angry he'd gotten when she mentioned he was called the Father of the Apocalypse, Mackenzie remained silent. He would either continue or he wouldn't. Will shifted beside her, drawing her attention away from the Revenant, but he didn't awaken. Maybe he would by degrees and realize the Revenant in their presence was their unlikely ally.

"I was cleaning the break room on a Friday evening after everyone went home. We all took turns, and it was mine. Luck of the fucking draw, that – it could just as easily have been Jay Dipwad Fuller if the goddamn asshole who attacked me waited another week to break into the building."

The young man – barely more than a boy, Leonard said – used a rock to break the glass from the outside door after staring at it stupidly for several minutes. His backpack hung off his shoulder, one strap broken.

The break room door didn't lock, and it was the only entrance to the room. Leonard, moving as quietly as he could manage, groped in a drawer for anything he could use as a defensive weapon.

"I found a can opener. Plastic forks, knives, and spoons. Giant plastic serving spoons. Plastic salad tongs – every fucking thing was plastic." His humorless laugh grated out again.

The drawer beneath it yielded more useful treasures: a couple of paring knives, a vegetable peeler, three steak knives, and a medium-length carving knife usually employed to cut birthday cakes.

And that, of course, lay under all the other knives.

One by one, Leonard lifted out the other knives, setting them silently on the counter, until he reached his prize. Clutching it in his hand, he moved cautiously to the closed break room door, thinking he could brace it shut if the freak tried to open it.

The sleeve of his sweater caught on the point of a steak knife. The handle of the knife dragged two other knives off the counter. They hit the floor with a deafening clatter. *Shit!*

"He opened the door then," Leonard said quietly. "I knew just from the way he was standing, the odd way he moved, that the kid was just...*wrong.*"

But it was too late to run, too late to hide, and too late to call campus security – the phone hung on the wall just inside the door, within reach of the strange intruder.

Leonard fell back on his professional, I'm-a-college-employee-and-entitled-to-be-here demeanor he used with students who overstepped their boundaries. He'd honed the tone to perfection over his forty-two years; with a name like Clarence Leonard, bullies just lined up to give a figurative or literal beating. His don't-give-me-shit-asshole tone had made most of them think twice since the fourth grade. It didn't hurt that he was broad-shouldered, built like a fireplug, and had served in the Marine Corps for eight years before he became a teacher.

"You can't be in the building. We're closed."

The kid didn't answer. His head lifted slightly, and he seemed to be sniffing the air.

Leonard gripped the knife tighter. "Look, man, you gotta go. You can't...be..."

The intruder stepped into the light, and he got a good, clear look for the first time. Words vanished. His mind scrambled for an explanation in a suddenly blank landscape.

The kid wore a cadaver's face, the skin stretched taut and thin over his bones. Where there *was* skin: infection had eaten through his left cheek from the corner of his nose, across his cheekbone, to just under his eye. Another raw, red patch spread from his hairline over his right eye.

The young man didn't blink. He didn't speak. He didn't breathe. He just...stared. The hand that reached toward Leonard was a bloody, pus-filled mass of infection.

Without warning, the kid lunged forward, snarling like a wildcat. Without thought, Leonard raised the knife and plunged it into the kid's eye.

Blood spurted. The young man fell forward against Leonard. Time slowed as they tumbled to the threadbare, stained carpet, Leonard on his back with the odd kid – now the dead kid – draped over him like a noxious blanket. In the surreal moment that followed, red drops of blood fell through the air between them: perfect, glossy beads of crimson.

He blinked.

And one round, red bead plunked into his eye.

"With one blink of an eye, I was screwed. I threw him off me, threw up in the garbage can, called the police, and threw up again. The kid's body was taken to the morgue; I was taken to the hospital. Nothing they could do, they said, just keep doing blood tests every couple of weeks to determine I'd been infected with HIV and—"

"What's HIV?" Mac interrupted.

He struggled for words for a moment, then said, "Jesus. They finally found a cure for AIDS. All they had to do was wipe out ninety-nine percent of the population." He sighed. "HIV is – was – a disorder of the immune system. The virus replicated itself using certain cells in the body, destroying those cells. It replicated so fast it overwhelmed the immune system.

"It's really not unlike the Revenant Virus, except most HIV suffers developed full-blown AIDS – auto-immune deficiency syndrome – and died. Those infected with the Revenant Virus simply mutated, most of them after their brains were permanently fried. Anyway, I never had a chance to go for my first HIV test. The medical examiner didn't know what to make of the kid's infection – it was like nothing she'd seen before – so I was detained at the hospital while experts were called in. A week of testing gave them no answers.

"I started spiking a fever and the color of my eyes started to change around the outside of the iris. Finally realizing they were out of their element, they called the CDC. I escaped around then, but they rounded me up and whisked me away to the CDC's facility in Atlanta, Georgia. Within a couple days of arriving, I was med-evac'd to the installation in Wyoming, out of my mind. I remember very little of it – mostly just my head hurting like it was going to explode. Most of what I know was told to me by the epidemiologists at the CDC after my first reactions to the virus settled down."

Mac thought about this for a minute. "Why didn't they take you to Wyoming first? It's closer."

"I see they at least taught you geography at your Stronghold. Yes, Wyoming is closer. But they didn't realize at first what they were dealing with. When the virus reached my hypothalamus, they knew they couldn't adequately control me, so they tranquilized me and shipped me off to the more secure facility in Wyoming."

Where, by his reckoning, he stayed for the next two or three years. By then society had fallen, but the scientists – epidemiologists, virologists, scientists of all kinds, secure in the self-contained compound – were still working on finding a cure. He gave them blood, they tested cures, and every month they came closer to halting the virus's destructive path through the brain.

And then someone got careless. A door was left unlocked or left open for a fraction of a second too long, and the facility was overrun with Revenants. During the ensuing chaos, the Revenants accidentally freed him.

"I didn't argue. There was no point in staying after the Revenants killed all the humans. I was tired of being locked in a suite of rooms underground. Tired of waiting for results that never came. I wanted a Big Mac something fierce." He laughed at his own stupidity. "I didn't realize McDonald's was gone. Everything was gone. Every*one* was gone."

Mac didn't know what McDonald's or a Big Mac were, but she understood losing everything you knew, your very way of life, every person you knew. She had cried herself to sleep the first few nights of her exile, and then again – albeit quietly – after she and Will left the city.

"I didn't know what else to do, so I made my way back home.

But no one was left. My ex-wife was dead. My girlfriend and my close friends had vanished." He fell silent for a moment and then barked out a laugh. "It was probably Jay Fuller who told everyone I was the Father of the Apocalypse, the fucker."

Mackenzie said, "You swear a lot."

"Maybe you don't swear enough." He looked out the window again and reached into his pocket, taking out a pair of dark glasses. "The fog's lifting. I can drive for a while with these, then we'll talk about your on-the-job training."

Beside her, Will groaned, grimaced in his sleep, and rolled into his back. Leonard gave him a dispassionate glance.

"And we'll discuss what to do about him."

"What do you mean, what to do about him?"

He stared at her for a long, uncomfortable moment, then shrugged and scooted behind the steering wheel.

"I'd just like to make sure my head stays on my shoulders where it belongs," he said blithely.

It sounded like a lie, but Mackenzie didn't feel like challenging it. The car rolled forward again, taking her farther from her home — farther from Elijah — and ever-closer to her unknown destination.

20

The sun just started its slow descent behind the hills when three unpleasant events occurred.

The front tires fell into a massive ditch where the blacktop had completely washed away, cleverly hidden by a slight rise just before it. Ren Leonard swore loudly, cursing everything from flash floods to the progeny of some fornicating female dog, using many words of whose meanings Mackenzie wasn't quite certain. He climbed out to assess the severity of the situation and almost immediately leaned back in to shut off the engine, cocking his head toward the open road ahead of them.

The fog returned with sunset, settling in thick puddles at the lowest points of the road, clearly carrying the muffled shouts of men calling out to each other over the rumble of vehicle engines.

Ren came around to the back of the vehicle and opened one of the barn-style doors. Mac had been riding in back with Will so she could subdue him if he freaked out when he saw the Revenant with them. She climbed out, shrugging into her coat.

"Who are they?"

"Could just be harmless nomads."

"But you don't think so."

He shrugged. "There's not much looting left to be done, not many people left to terrorize. It's doubtful they're marauders." Yet he looked uneasy.

So she kept her question simple: "What do you suggest we do?"

"I have to disappear."

Her breath caught on a sudden swell of panic. Sure, she wasn't exactly comfortable in his presence – experience had taught her never to trust a Revenant – but she couldn't deny that he had saved their lives, as well as saved them days of walking.

She drew in a steadying breath. "All right. We're going with you. Can you carry Will?"

"Mackenzie, you can't come with me." She stared at him blankly. "They are coming down this road, and they will see this car. It's in too good of shape to have been abandoned here very long ago. They will touch the hood and feel that the engine is still warm. And then they will start combing the area for you."

"But they don't know who we are. And why would they bother, anyway?"

"The greatest commodity right now is human life – to either grow their numbers or provide amusement – or food. If they see me, they will not hesitate to kill me, and then I won't be able to keep you from being their amusement."

"Maybe they're friendly."

"Maybe. Even if they are, their friendliness won't extend to the Father of the Apocalypse." He sneered the words. "I can get a fair distance away before they get here and then move back toward you after nightfall."

"I might have become someone's amusement by then," she replied sardonically.

"What else do you suggest – that we all get caught, they kill me, and then do whatever they want to you? They're an unknown quantity, and I'm not willing to trust my head to their potential civility."

"But you're willing to trust mine to it."

"They're not going to—"

"How do you know? You just said—"

"—have time to rape you before I come to get you. The sun is—"

"—that human life is a commodity for amusement—"

"—going down; it will be dusk by the time they reach us and—"

"—and that they're an unknown quantity."

He stopped speaking. She crossed her arms over her chest, glaring at him.

As though to prove out the ancient theory that bad things always happen in threes, Will came to sudden life in the back of the truck, exploding from under his blankets and out the back of the vehicle so rapidly and furiously that Leonard sprinted backward to avoid his ferociously slashing machete.

"Get the hell away from her, Revenant!"

"Whoa, dude!"

"Will, stop!" Crouching low, Mac tried to wade in below the

172

arc of the blade and neutralize him, but Will's attack was too violent for her to risk it.

"You ungrateful little bastard!" Leonard bellowed indignantly.

"Stop it, both of you!"

"Keep clear of this, 'Kenz," Will snapped, not taking his eyes from Leonard. Leonard, for his part, kept sending apprehensive looks toward the approaching convoy.

"We don't have time for this, shithead. I saved your ass back at the House of Cannibals, but if you kill me now, there's going to be no one to save you from whatever's coming down that road."

"Just make this easy on us all. Kneel down, and I promise I'll make it quick."

Leonard growled in frustration. In a blur of motion too fast for Mackenzie to follow, he pinned Will to the back of the truck and wrested the blade from his hand.

"Run, Mackenzie!" Will shouted, grabbing hold of the front of Leonard's duster. "I'll hold him off as long as I can!"

Leonard laughed sarcastically. "You'll hold me off, will you? Here, Bright Runner." He thrust the machete behind him, blade down, holding it out in her general direction. "Can you keep him contained while I get hidden?"

"I'll do my best." She took the machete. Will was goggling at her in shock, but they didn't have time to deal with his hysterics. "If you don't come back and I get raped, I will hunt you down and stake you out in the sun myself."

"You people sure know how to say thank you," Leonard growled.

He broke Will's hold on his coat and shoved him to the ground. With barely a glance spared for Mackenzie, he jogged off into the gathering dusk. Will scrambled up from the ground and sprinted after him. Mackenzie hooked her foot around his ankle and sent him sprawling back into the dirt.

"What the *hell*, Mackenzie?" He raised his chin from the dirt, looking for Leonard, who had already vanished from sight.

"He's helping us."

"Revenants don't help humans. You've got to grow up. You can't be this naïve and expect to survive." He pushed himself up with his arms. Mac used the toe of her boot to shove him back down. He grunted and swore as his chin smacked into the dirt again.

"I am not naïve," she said coldly. "And that is not just any Revenant."

"They're all just Revenants. Vermin. Every one of them."

"That vermin saved our lives."

"Can I get up now, or are you fixing to bash my head in with a rock?"

"Don't tempt me." She reached down a hand. He stared at it in silent contemplation, then accepted her help. "I knew we should have waited for Riemer."

"You think Riemer wouldn't have tried to hack off the head of a Revenant that came anywhere near you?"

"Not that Revenant. Riemer would have understood the situation."

"So a Revenant just comes along and – what? Kills the people trying to kill us? Why do you think that is, Mackenzie? So he can eat us himself, that's why."

He raked a hand through his hair, which stood up in greasy spikes. Lord, they needed baths. And why was she thinking about baths when Ren Leonard was on the run from the unknown people who came closer with every second, and when she was arguing with Will about not killing the one person who might be able to guarantee they lived long enough to discover where Elijah had sent them?

She said quietly, "Because Riemer knew Ren Leonard wanted to help me."

Will froze. Understanding replaced the anger in his eyes, but he didn't look any more pleased. "Ren Leonard?" he repeated incredulously. "Oh, *great*."

She held up her hands, placating. "It's all right. If he were going to kill us, he would have already. Now, let's just deal with these people, and then we can get on our way. Although…" She frowned. "Maybe we should go back to the motor home and wait for Riemer to catch up."

He turned to the west, his hand over his eyes to block the last of the sun, watching the approaching vehicles. "He's not coming."

"He wouldn't have said he was coming if he didn't plan on actually doing it."

He sighed. "We've been over this. If he could come, he would have. Since I'm here, that means he couldn't. Now drop it. We have more important things to worry about. There are four trucks, and I think there's a guy with a rifle hanging out the window of one."

Will retrieved her machete and traded it for his. They leaned against the truck and watched the other vehicles come closer.

"How's your head?" she asked grudgingly.

"Hurts," he said simply. "You could have left me there. Thanks for not doing that."

She grunted. The vehicles reached the other side of the wash-out and stopped. The man with the rifle slid back into the cab of the truck, and a moment later both doors opened. The men who climbed out wore heavy coats and sturdy pants that likely bore the brand name Dickies or maybe Carhartt, companies long gone but whose products endured four-hundred-eight seasons later, with-standing even moths and other insects. The citizens of the Strong-hold passed many articles of both brands' clothing down through the generations.

They approached with their hands up, indicating they were not aggressive. She and Will exchanged a look, and then he moved to the edge of the wash-out.

One of the men cupped his hands around his mouth and called out, "Hello there!" Will raised his hand in greeting. "Got car trouble?"

Will glanced back where Mackenzie waited by the back of the truck, huddled in her coat and trying to not look like a girl. "Yeah!" he hollered back.

"May we come over and have a look?"

Will hesitated only a second. "Depends on whether you plan on killing us when you get over here. Because we don't plan on dying."

The men exchanged a look and burst out laughing. "Friend, you've got some powerful paranoia."

"Hang on." Will strode back to Mackenzie and leaned close so their voices wouldn't carry. "What do you think?"

She gazed at the men over his shoulder, and the vehicles behind them. More men poked their heads out open windows, and some even climbed out of their trucks and were watching the meet-up.

"I think we don't have much of a choice. We're here, they're here, and whatever's going to happen can't be stopped now."

"And you say you're not naïve."

"Will, they have guns. We have machetes. They have"—she broke off to do a cursory count—"a dozen or more men. There's just the two of us and a Revenant who doesn't dare show his face or he'll be killed on the spot. Tell me how that's a choice."

He drew in a deep breath and huffed it out. "Be on your guard."

"I always am."

"Not always." He walked back to the edge of the wash-out. "All right, come on over."

The men scrambled down the banks of the wash-out, picked their way through the debris at the bottom, and clambered up the other side. Mac wished the truck could make it to the other side as easily, but although it wasn't deep, it was too deep for the vehicle. They'd go ass-end over tea-kettle just on the journey down.

The man who had spoken for his party stuck out his hand. Will shook it.

"Ed Weaver – Weaver's my name, not my profession," he clarified, although they hadn't asked. "We're from a village northwest of here, near a city that was called Wenatchee."

"What do you call it now?" Will asked.

Weaver shrugged. "Wenatchee."

His companion stepped forward and shook Will's hand. "Rob Bowers."

"I'm Will Crawford. That's Mackenzie Bright Runner by the truck."

"Bright Runner, huh? Nice to know some Native blood made it through the Upheaval. The Wanapum seemed to have all vanished in the early days; they lived downriver from Wenatchee. Some men from our village made a trek down there a few years after everything went to hell, but there was no sign of life."

Mac watched the men warily for covert signals – deliberate looks, hand signals, strange blinks of their eyes – but they seemed legitimately friendly and helpful. Of course, they didn't have to worry about two malnourished travelers armed only with machetes, not when their party outnumbered them seven-to-one and carried rifles.

"Well," Weaver said heartily. "Let's take a look at your ride."

He bent to examine the front tires with Will, but Rob Bowers hung back looking over the vehicle. After his first initial smile of greeting for Mackenzie, his easy demeanor slipped away by degrees. As he circled around the back of the truck, he frowned, and the next look he gave her was cold and forbidding. Uh-oh. Trouble.

Weaver nudged Will, and they both stood up. "We won't be able to push it out — have to stand in the ditch and won't be able to get enough leverage. But maybe with all of us, we can pull it back from the edge. Not sure how you're going to continue west, though, unless you want to stick around a couple days while we build a land bridge over the chasm."

Bowers said, "Ed, we've got a problem."

Mackenzie straightened and edged casually around the back fender of the truck. Bowers turned so he faced her, suspicion stamped on his face.

"Oh, what's that?" Weaver asked without much interest.

"This truck is Claudio Montoya's."

Weaver froze. "Bullshit."

"No bullshit," Bowers insisted. He backed away from Mackenzie a couple of steps and leveled his rifle at her. "Drop the blade, girl."

21

Mackenzie held her ground.

"Understand my position, Mr. Bowers. I'm the only woman here. Your party is armed and outnumbers us. Now you're becoming aggressive and asking me to disarm myself. Would *you* disarm yourself in my position?"

"How do you know this is Montoya's truck?" Weaver interrupted.

"The plate number."

"What's a plate?" Mackenzie asked.

"License plate. It's how they identified vehicles before the Upheaval." Bowers' suspicion deepened. "Where you been all your life, girl?"

"My name is Mackenzie, or just Mac. Not 'girl.' And we didn't have vehicles at my settlement. Just a couple of tractors."

"No wonder you drove into a ditch," Weaver said. "Let's just dial it down a little, Rob. Hear what they have to say."

"Have to say about what?" Will challenged. He skirted around Ed Weaver and joined Mac, pulling her a little farther away from Rob Bowers. "We found this truck at a farmhouse where we were almost eaten by some cannibals. And now you're saying it belongs to your guy Montoya, which makes me wonder if we're your next meal. I told you we didn't plan on dying."

The men exchanged the look Mac had been expecting, but it was neither shifty nor suspicious. It was knowing and apprehensive.

"Cannibals?" Weaver said carefully.

"Well, we have to assume they were cannibals," she amended. "Will was knocked unconscious and I was tied to a table. They were carving meat off what remained of a human body."

"How many were there?" Bowers asked sharply.

"Just one body that I saw."

"Not the body. The cannibals."

"Oh. Two, as far as I know. If there were others, they didn't show themselves."

Ed's shoulders slumped. "Sounds like the men we're after," he said dejectedly. "Montoya...damn, he was a good man."

Bowers gaped at him incredulously. "You're just going to buy what they say wholesale?"

"Who would make up stuff like that?" Weaver asked reasonably.

Bowers rounded on Mac. She backed away a step, crowding Will. "Describe the house."

"Look, buddy," Will began angrily.

"Describe it!"

"Just a farmhouse!" He blinked at her raised voice. "No paint left on it, the siding's starting to fall off. There's an old truck parked next to it and an orchard a little way behind it. There used to be a windbreak, but someone's been chopping down the trees."

"Montoya," Weaver said. "His wife died of infection several years ago, and he wanted to go off somewhere and live by himself. We gave him a vehicle and wished him luck. He came back to the village to visit a few times a year during good weather."

"You said you're after these men," Will said. "You know who they are?"

"Over the last year, some of our people have gone missing. We've found evidence that they were killed by cannibals." Bowers glared at them mutinously. "How do we know you're not part of their party?"

Weaver snorted. "Look at them, Bowers. They haven't eaten a decent meal in weeks."

"We don't even know they were at the right farmhouse."

"There is a symbol painted on the side of it – a sun and moon," Will said. "This symbol." He pulled the leather cord with its copper medallion from his pants pocket and swung it in front of Bowers' face.

Bowers stopped its swing and examined it. "It's the right farmhouse," he admitted grudgingly. "That doesn't mean I'm convinced you didn't kill Montoya."

Mac sighed in exasperation. So did Weaver. "We don't even know that Montoya's dead. Rob's sister was Claudio's wife. When she died, Claudio went ... a little off. Rob's been worried about him for months when he didn't show up after the spring thaw. Guess we know why."

"The guy we saw is recently dead. If anything stopped Claudio from coming, it was the road being washed out." Will pocketed the copper charm. "Well, it looks like we're stuck here for the night. You think the truck is stable enough for us to sleep in it?"

Weaver shrugged. "I wouldn't risk it. You're likely to end up at the bottom of the wash-out, upside down. If you've got outdoor gear, you're welcome to pitch it over with us. We can offer a hot meal and a bath – both of which you look like you could use – and a good night's sleep; we have more than enough men to keep watch through the night."

Mackenzie moved to grab her gear, but Will snagged her arm, not budging. "We'll make do here."

"Will," Mac hissed.

"Suit yourself," Weaver said, holding his gaze. "You're both a little worse for wear, and we're offering to help you out. We're just across the wash-out if you change your mind."

She wrenched her arm from Will's grasp. "I'm hungry and I want a bath and a good night's sleep. Please, Will. Besides, they know about the symbol; they must be part of the underground."

"All right, all right. We'll go." And he added under his breath, "Riemer would have my head."

Her knees went weak with relief. She hugged him. Surprised, at first he stood awkwardly without touching her, then he put an arm around her and hugged her back. Weariness dragged at her body; even though she slept last night, she had done so in fits and starts, surfacing into wakefulness to escape nightmares of cannibals and Revenants. And the promise of a good meal already made her salivate.

They gathered their gear, closed up the truck, and followed the men through the wash-out and to the convoy, which was made up of four vehicles of varying types and condition. Weaver briefly explained the situation while Bowers shot them mistrustful looks. No one else seemed particularly suspicious of the story, which set Mackenzie a little more at ease. She didn't want to have to sleep with one eye open, worrying about misplaced vengeance.

The men arranged the trucks in a loose circle, gathered stones for a fire pit, and started a fire with wood they had brought with them. In short order, they were eating the hot meal promised to them while pots of water for a bath heated on hot stones at the edge of the fire.

181

After their dinner of beans and sausage, the men erected a mostly private bathing enclosure using rope and sheets. A young man about Elijah's age brought a bar of soap and the hot water, pouring it into a basin and then tempering it with a bucket of cold.

It was only a sponge bath, but it felt like heaven to sluice all the grime and oils off her body. Despite her time on the road with Will, she felt a little self-conscious stripping naked with him just few away, equally naked, but he seemed to care more about getting clean than he did about inspecting her goods. He rinsed her hair for her and they dried off with the scratchy wool towels their hosts provided. Mac rummaged in her pack for clothes; it had been so long since they were able to do their laundry that she settled for clean-ish clothes.

Will helped the men clear away the makeshift bath while Mackenzie ran a comb through her hair. She'd found it in the motor home they'd stayed in weeks ago; there had been several of them, so she didn't feel guilty pocketing the sturdiest of the package. By that time, her hair reached past her shoulders and she was having a hell of a time keeping the tangles out.

"Why are you traveling through land that doesn't have any refuge?"

She looked up in surprise. Was this a trick question, perhaps to vet drifters from the refugees the underground was helping?

The man who spoke was the one who'd brought the soap and water. She thought his name was Rico, but she was having trouble keeping them all straight. The trucks circled the central camp with a men perched on top of each, able to see over the glow of the small campfire and each watching in different directions. He was crouched on top of the truck closest to her.

"Nowhere else to go."

"Huh." He stared at her for an uncomfortable moment, then scanned the dark terrain around them. In the distance, coyotes began a song to the night. Mac liked their howling chorus, as long as the pack stayed far away.

"You came from somewhere," he persisted. He stared hard in the direction of the howling pack until satisfied they were keeping their distance. "They generally won't bother humans; prey is plentiful out here. We rehabbed one that broke its leg last winter, and it still tends to come sniffing for a treat now and then. But she's not getting as close anymore as she used to. She'll soon forget us."

"There were a few packs that roamed through the city," she said. "One that stayed very close to our settlement, we think because we guarded it against Revenants so well and they felt safer."

His eyes swept the dark land again. She wondered how much he could really see in the moonlight.

As though reading her mind, he said, "The four of us use night vision goggles. We found them in an army surplus store on one of our trips into Wenatchee. We should have grabbed more, but we were lucky to make it out of there with our lives. Too dangerous to go back.

"Our village is outside of Wenatchee, in an old smelter. Close to the river and some orchards. Your settlement – it was in a city?"

"It was called Spokane in its day."

"What do you call it now?"

"Ruined," she said bluntly. "Some survivors holed up in a sports arena, where eventually all the small settlements moved for safety. Turned out to be a good idea. With some modifications for heat and sleeping quarters, it was an ideal location. A huge outdoor area where we have our gardens and stables and some gathering areas for picnics and outdoor games. Tall, defensible walls. Impenetrable metal doors."

"Sounds nice and safe – and not exactly like you had nowhere to go."

Mac fidgeted. She'd never had to explain to anyone why she'd been exiled from her settlement, for the simple reason that they hadn't run across any living humans other than the cannibals they'd just escaped. And if he were part of the underground, wouldn't Will's flashing the medallion at him be all the information he needed about why they were on their own in the middle of nowhere?

"I was exiled."

He leaned closer, bringing his face into the fire's glow. "Exiled?" he repeated incredulously. "You can't be more than sixteen and you're no bigger than a minute. How could they justify exiling you?"

"I'm almost eighteen. But I associated with someone our elders forbade contact with. Hence…exile."

He drew back into the shadows again. "Mankind never learns. They always must make someone an outcast."

"Rico, less talk and more keeping watch," his fellow advised without rancor.

Rico did another sweep of the area, and then pointed to a truck on the opposite side of the circle from his. "They've set you guys up in a tent in the bed of that truck."

"I can help keep watch," Will said from behind her. She jumped in surprise. He was frowning as he came around to stand beside her. "No offense to any of you, but I'd feel better seeing to Mackenzie's safety myself."

"I'm cool with that. I'm sorry I don't have any night vision goggles to offer you." He tipped his head at Mac in farewell. "I don't know if you're brave or stupid, but I'm impressed nonetheless."

Mac blushed, glad Rico couldn't see it in the firelight.

"Oh, before I forget…" Will dug in his pocket and held out the medallion. Rico snagged it by the chain and tilted it to catch the moonlight. "What can you tell me about that symbol?"

Rico shrugged and handed it back. "It's painted on the side of Montoya's house. We don't know why. Claudio kept it freshly painted every year; I think he liked it. We've seen it on a few places here and there, all on the old freeway, but not on anything up in our neck of the woods."

"Thanks." Will pocketed the copper disk and took her elbow, steering her toward the truck they'd been assigned. She was surprised when he climbed up into the tent with her.

"I thought you were going to keep watch."

"I am. They can keep watch over camp. I'm going to keep watch over you."

"You can't possibly think—"

He lowered his voice to a whisper. "I *can* possibly think it. And if you think I'm going to sleep while we're surrounded by men we don't know, you're insane. I promised Riemer I'd keep you safe. These men aren't part of the underground; for all we know, they've disrupted the whole set up. I'm not willing to trust our throats to them."

She rolled her eyes but didn't continue the argument. She shed her boots just inside the tent and crawled under the blankets. Will sat atop them, propped against the cab of the truck. The covers warmed with their combined body heat, and she was just relaxing into her usual pre-sleep daydreams when Will spoke again.

"You shouldn't have told them so much about the Strong-hold."

"It's not like they're going to go there."

"Maybe they will. They seem to have sound vehicles and fuel."

"And even if they did, it doesn't mean they'd go with evil in-tentions. Maybe they'd just want to join forces. Safety in numbers, you know."

He was silent for a while. Mac drifted back into her day-dreams. At last, he said, "The Stronghold can only support so many people. They can't keep increasing the population. If they did, it wouldn't be long until they were sacrificing space needed for farm-ing or storage or heat to give way to living quarters. It's a delicate balance, Mackenzie."

She rolled over to face him, although it was too dark in the tent to see him. "Did you ever think that maybe the elders don't want the population to grow because they might not be able to control a larger group like they control people now? Or that they *want* to keep us from recapturing the technology and medical knowledge we lost in the Upheaval?"

He snorted. "That's Bon Moreau talking."

"Maybe Bon was right."

"And you wonder why you were exiled," he muttered. "Bon was a dissenter. Eventually, he would have started a rebellion against the elders and everything would have fallen into chaos. The level of civilization the settlement was able to achieve would be set back a hundred years."

She sighed and rolled so her back was to him again. It made her anxious and defensive when someone spoke harshly about Bon. Will was wrong about him. Bon never would have started a rebel-lion; he simply didn't swallow everything he was force-fed

Her voice, although pitched soft, seemed to ring loudly. "Did you ever stop to think that maybe, because Bon was on the outside of everything, he saw things the clearest and truest?"

After a long pause, Will said quietly but with finality, "Go to sleep, 'Kenz."

Tired though she was, her mind kept circling around the reve-lation this conversation brought. Will and she held entirely different viewpoints about the Stronghold and the governing system the long-ago elders adopted. And if they didn't agree about the possible corruption of the Council – well then, why had Will helped her escape the assassination team?

22

The next morning after a breakfast of more beans and sausage, most of the men climbed down into the washout and back up the other side. With ropes hooked to the truck's hitch, they managed to pull it away from the chasm. The truck safely on level ground, everyone but Weaver, Bowers, and Will returned to the camp.

Mackenzie, drying the breakfast dishes that Rico was washing, watched with some trepidation as the three climbed into the truck and headed back toward the farmhouse. Her disquiet came from the fact that Bowers insisted that Will leave his machete at the camp, apparently still not trusting their story.

A new apprehension made itself known as the morning crept toward the noon hour. With their leaders and her companion away, several of the other men seemed to have a little less self-control and fewer manners. At first, she laughed away their innuendos, but their persistence finally tried her tolerance. Rico frowned a lot and stuck close to her, taking her with him even when he was just getting something out of his truck.

On one such errand, Mac asked him quietly, "Am I in danger?"

Rico sent a disparaging look at his companions. "I don't think they'd dare – Ed would be very displeased if they tried anything."

"But Ed's not here right now."

"Exactly. Keep your machete on you. I think it will be all right – they aren't bad men, just a little unruly sometimes – but it's better to be armed and give them pause to think than to take a chance that they might act without thinking." He slanted her a sardonic smile, but she noticed that he looked uneasy.

Because Weaver and Bowers knew the road better than Ren Leonard did, their trip would likely take less time than it had taken her party to travel the same distance. Still, they wouldn't return until after dark. She tried not to think about this too much as the day wore on. She washed her and Will's clothes, hanging them to dry on a line Rico strung near the campfire for this purpose. She made dinner with him and another man who seemed irritated by their companions' behavior, and as the sun sank below the horizon, she made sure she was with one or the other of them at all times.

The other fellow – Nick or Mick, she hadn't quite figured out which – moved her to another truck, this one with a canopy over the bed that blocked much of the chill and the danger. Rico assured her that it was safe for her to sleep, but slumber was a long time coming, and when it did, it was filled with ferocious Revenants and grinning cannibals. She was strapped to the table again and the cannibal was slowly creeping up her body, the bloody butcher knife in his hand leaving dark smears on her blanket. A bloodstained hand closed over her mouth, cutting off her scream.

Mackenzie bolted out of sleep to a hand over her mouth and a heavy body next to hers, an arm pinning hers to her sides. Warm breath washed over her face, scented faintly like mint and reminding her of Elijah.

A voice rasped in her ear: "Don't scream."

Since his hand covered her mouth, she couldn't if she wanted to. But then it moved away and he made no more aggressive moves toward her. She gulped in the chilly night air.

"It's me – Rico. There's a Revenant near camp. We're moving out."

"Just one? It can hardly be a threat against twelve men," she whispered back.

"Taking no chances. This one is pretty wily."

Leonard. It must be. And good Lord, what was he going to think when the party moved camp in the middle of the night, taking her with them?

"What about Will? And Weaver and Bowers?"

"They just got back. Weaver spotted the Revenant as they were coming out of the washout. They're in Bowers' truck."

The engine rumbled to life. Around them, the other trucks' engines started. Rico released her as the vehicle lurched forward. A suffocating fear clenched her throat closed and squeezed her heart; she had only Rico's word that Will had returned. What if they'd abandoned him and were now heading back to their settlement, with her as the spoils? Or maybe they killed him and she was now at the mercy of a band of murderers. If they were willing to murder, violating her wouldn't make them turn a hair.

Rico's hand fumbled in the dark, scrabbling over hers and then squeezing firmly. She jumped and bolted to the corner of the bed, away from him.

"Mackenzie, trust me. Will is safe and in the other truck. I'm not lying to you. Take a deep breath; you're hyperventilating."

She was. Her breath was coming in short, frantic gasps and she was getting lightheaded. A few deep breaths put her right and calmed some of her anxiety.

Of course, he would claim innocence even if he were being deceitful, but there was nothing she could do about it now. The vehicles were bouncing their way down the pitted road, taking them God knew where, and she was powerless to stop it. If she tried to jump from the truck, Rico would stop her. And if she managed to get away from him, she risked them coming after her and finding the Revenant with her.

So she didn't try, but she did stay pressed into the corner, crouched into her standard defensive posture.

The truck swayed down the road. The minutes crawled by. Mac's legs began to fatigue and she abandoned her crouch to sit cross-legged in her corner. Rico tried twice to engage her in conversation but gave up when she offered brief, terse responses. She wondered where her clothes had gone; they'd still been on the line when she'd gone to bed, drying by the fire that was kept burning all night. Will would be pissed if she'd lost him his underwear; they'd managed to find a couple of packs in his size in a small general store in one of the towns they'd passed through. They'd had to cut down three Revenants to get them.

And then she thought of Eli and what he'd say if he knew how easily she'd been manipulated into this situation. *I just think you should trust no one.* If he'd managed to follow their trail, how many more days would their travel by vehicle put them ahead of him? Her heart ached at the thought of the growing distance between them.

She took refuge in her memories of him – four short weeks of memories – and put aside the niggling suspicion that she was obsessing and needed to put him behind her.

Mackenzie, I didn't plan on—

Plan on what? Becoming involved with her? Adding her to his already considerable list of things to worry about? Her falling for him so spectacularly in such a short amount of time? Maybe he had been trying to tell her he wasn't interested in a relationship with her, and sending Will instead of coming himself was his way of ensuring she got the message.

"You said you were exiled," Rico said. "You could come live in our settlement. There's plenty to go around and we're relatively safe – as safe as anyone can be in this world, anyway. You'd be welcome."

Mackenzie said nothing. No doubt men outnumbered women in his settlement, and even a malnourished, grubby teenager seemed a viable prospect for a man looking to warm his bed and continue his bloodline.

"I know this world has taught people not to trust. It's not just the Revenants you have to watch out for. But we're good people, Mackenzie, and we'd take care of you and treat you well. You wouldn't be any man's property or slave. No harm would come to you. I'm just offering you a place to be safe."

She could feel Rico's gaze on her, steady and reassuring. But she wasn't reassured. His nervousness around the other men when Weaver and Bowers left camp with Will told her that she might not necessarily be as safe as he claimed. How long until one of them tired of her waiting on a man who might never come for her and finally just took what he wanted?

"Just think about, that's all I'm asking. It's dangerous out here. No one should have to go it alone. Every life is sacred."

His words – in fact, his very demeanor around her, protective and dependable – reminded her of Elijah Riemer. Mackenzie turned her face away, glad for the darkness that hid her misery.

The clatter and sway of the truck as it bounced over the ruined highway lulled Mac to sleep. So when the motion ceased and silence fell, it was as though a rooster crowed directly in her ear.

She shot awake and immediately moved to strike her usual defensive crouch, only to find herself tangled in something heavy and warm.

"What the *hell?*" she swore violently, ripping at the unseen covering.

"Relax, it's just my coat." Rico's voice was sardonic. "You were shivering in your sleep."

Mac went still. It took a moment to dial down her alarm, and when at last she subdued it, she grumbled a thank you that made him snort in amusement.

"Why are we stopping?"

"Checking out a farmhouse. The road through here isn't the greatest; we don't want to break an axle and get stranded in the dark. If the house is clear and can be secured, we'll stop for the night."

"Why not backtrack a ways and make camp by the road? It's insanity to clear a house in the dark, especially when it's cold out. There are bound to be Revenants in it."

Rico shrugged, a movement she just barely caught by the light of a stray moonbeam. "I don't know, Mackenzie. Bowers is insisting. He doesn't want to sleep with his legs all cramped up tonight."

He didn't sound sarcastic, but neither did he sound like he was defending Bowers' decision. He was simply following orders, like a good soldier – right to his death, if Mac's instincts served her right. When he opened the back hatch of the canopy and lowered the gate, she made no move to join the gang of men gathering behind the vehicle.

"Come on, girl," Bowers growled. "You shared our food and protection. The least you can do is lend a hand."

"Offering me food and protection does not mean I need to commit suicide for you. Where's Will?"

"Right here." He shouldered his way through the throng. His machete was already unsheathed, ready for battle. His expression, however, was worried. She crawled to the open hatch and grabbed a handful of his jacket, yanking him closer.

"Are they crazy? It's base stupidity to clear a house in the dark. We're going to get slaughtered."

"I guess it's a fifty-fifty shot," he said reluctantly. "They *have* helped us out."

She shook her head, stunned that he wasn't putting up a protest. Will Crawford was one of the best gatherers the Stronghold had ever known, and the reason he kept coming home from gathering missions was because he was extraordinarily careful.

"Got your blade?"

"Yeah, I've got it," she grumbled. "If we die, I'm going to resurrect us both just so I can kill you again."

He smiled, looking more like the Will she was familiar with: cocksure and untroubled by danger. She dragged her bag from the back and stowed it on the tailgate in case she needed to grab it and run, though God knew it might be the last thing she did if a Revenant was chasing her. The night was cold but not frigid, so she shrugged out of her jacket and left it with her bag; she would fight better without it.

The Wenatchee men whispered amongst themselves as they checked each other's weapons and devised a strategy.

Mac's only strategy she'd learned from Bonfils Moreau, drilled into her head during their months of training: *Stay alive. Do whatever it takes to stay alive.* She flexed her shoulders and adjusted her grip on her machete, wishing for the thousandth time that she held Black Jack in her hand.

As she followed the men toward the derelict farmhouse, she saw Elijah in her memory, his eyes as green as a summer cornfield as she stood to face Bon's executioners, murmuring *Please stay alive* as she walked alone to her fate.

I'll try, she promised silently, but she already felt like a dead girl walking.

She pulled even with Rico. "Please stay alive."

He flashed a tight smile. "It's not my night to die, Mackenzie Bright Runner."

The men split into three groups: one to take the front door, one to take the back, and the other to wait as reinforcement once the first two groups gained entrance to the house. Sexist or not, Weaver put her in the last group, and Will quelled her protest with a frown and a slight shake of his head. He wanted her out of it even as he waded in on the front lines. Well, she supposed it wasn't altogether stupid; if something happened to him, there was still Ren Leonard to watch out for her, although she rather doubted the wisdom of leaving her safety in the hands of a Revenant, regardless of how in control of his faculties he appeared to be.

She hung back from her group, standing absolutely still, head cocked, listening for any suspect movement. The only sounds were the night breeze, rustling through the wild alfalfa fields and the muted whispers of her companions.

The night felt wrong.

It was nothing she could put her finger on, just a discordant tone in an otherwise peaceful scene, like a splash of muddy brown in a jewel-toned painting. Her skin itched as all the hairs on her body tried to stand on end. A swell of panic rose in her throat and propelled the words out of her mouth:

"Call them back. Now."

"No need to be nervous," Nick-or-Mick soothed her. "The house is abandoned. We just need to roust any nesting Revenants. It'll be over soon."

She faced the old house, her chest heaving, her eyes crawling over it, seeking the source of her anxiety. The paint had peeled off most of the wooden lap siding, leaving pale streaks of white like phantoms. Surprisingly, the siding hadn't begun to fall off. Mac supposed that the winters were milder down in the river gorge. Still, something was off, something small, something so ordinary it would be easy to overlook.

The first group was on the porch now, stepping carefully, quietly, so skillfully she only knew they were moving by watching their feet touch the floorboards in the moonlight. A few of the boards glowed as though they repelled dirt. Strangely, the sight of them made her pulse race.

Weaver reached for the doorknob with one hand, the other counting down silently.

THREE!

Mac's heart hammered in her chest. *Come on, come on, what's wrong? Why can't you pinpoint it?*

TWO!

Something simple, easily disregarded. She gazed hard at the porch, at the ghostly white boards. Her pulse thudded in her ears. She drew in a deep breath, dragging in oxygen and the sweet scent of sawdust.

Sawdust.

The pale boards – pale, because they were new.

Revenants didn't build.

ONE!

Mac shoved Nick-or-Mick out of the way, sprinting toward the porch as Weaver's hand turned on the knob.

"STOP!" she screamed.

He shoved the door open.

Bedlam exploded into the night. Screaming war cries rent the air. Shadows spilled from the door onto the porch, mingling with the panicked men. Blood flowed black in the darkness; whose, she couldn't tell. She vaulted over a fallen body, swinging her blade, and cleaved the head from a dark figure bearing down on Will with an axe, following the blade down to the porch in a roll that saved her own head from being claimed. As she spun smoothly into her crouch, Will skewered her assailant through the gut, driving him backward and pinning him to the wall, where he barked questions.

"Who are you? How many are you? Why did you attack us?"

A body stumbled out the door, tripped over Mac's victim, and sprawled on the boards at her feet. A shaft of moonlight bathed his bloody face. Rob Bowers. One eye was out, hanging on his cheekbone. A black stain spread across his abdomen.

"*Run, girl!*" he gasped. "*It's…the cannibals…run!*"

Behind them, an unearthly howl of rage shattered the night, rising above the cacophony of battle. Bowers screamed. Mac cringed and ducked just in time to avoid being knocked in the head as a flapping figure soared over them. Booted feet slammed onto the porch, shaking the boards, and the dark figure vanished into the house.

The screaming started in earnest. Three men – the remainder of the backdoor group – jammed in the doorway, all trying to exit at the same time. One broke free and the others followed, racing toward the trucks.

"*Revenant! It's a Revenant! We gotta go!*"

Will yanked his blade from the man he had skewered, who died without answering his demands. He spun around and grabbed the collar of Mackenzie's shirt as the truck engines rumbled to life.

"Let's go."

"We can't leave Bowers. He's injured."

Will looked down dispassionately. "He's dead. Let's *go*."

He didn't wait for her compliance, simply dragged her toward the trucks, which were already pulling away from the house. She gained her feet and sprinted after the truck with her pack. The tailgate was still down and the canopy hatch still open. Rico was sprawled in the back, propped against the cab, a dark stain soaking his shirt. He held one hand over the opposite shoulder to staunch the flow of blood.

"*RICO!*" she screamed and kicked up her pace a notch.

"*MACKENZIE! STOP THE TRUCK! STOP! STOP!*" He banged on the cab, but the driver paid him no heed, instead goosing the accelerator so the truck shot farther out of her reach.

Rico kicked out with his leg. A dark object fell out and smacked the gravel. *"I'm sorry, Mackenzie!"* He yelled something else, something about the bridge, but the vehicle put too much distance between them for her to hear his words clearly.

She watched the trucks bounce away, leaving them behind, alone with the dead, the remaining cannibals … and a Revenant.

23

Mackenzie stopped running, bending almost in half and bracing her hands on her knees, dragging in desperate gasps of air. Angry tears blurred the trucks' taillights as they receded in the distance and then completely faded from sight. Great, just great. One pack down – all of Will's stuff and the food – their clean clothes gone, and stranded miles from their original path. In the dark.

Will passed her, using precious energy from his flashlight to locate her pack and her coat in the road. He swung it to his shoulder, clicked off the light, and strode back to her. His face, dimly lit by the moon, held what she interpreted as an accusatory grimness as he watched her slip on her jacket.

"We can't stay here. Let's get moving."

"We can't travel at night, Will. We're just asking to be attacked."

"We can't stay here, either. There's a Revenant a hundred yards away, and no telling if any of the cannibals survived."

"The Revenant's probably Leonard."

"Maybe. Even if it is, he's in a bloodlust, and I'm not trusting my innards to a Revenant in a bloodlust. Let's go."

When she didn't move on her own, he took her arm and started walking. She let him drag her for a moment, and then realizing he wasn't to be swayed, she lifted her feet and tromped after him. Guilt weighed her steps, making her slow and clumsy. They wouldn't be walking through the nighttime desert if she hadn't insisted they throw in with these men. She thought he was passing silent judgment although he said nothing, and with every step she withered.

You've got to grow up. You can't be this naïve and expect to survive.

He was right. She *was* naïve. She expected the best of people even though she knew the desperate lives carved out by the survivors of the Revenant Virus brought out the very worst in many.

"I'm sorry," she said at length. They had walked for nearly half an hour, during which Will was utterly silent. "This is my fault. I shouldn't have insisted we throw in with them."

Will didn't respond right away. When he did, his voice was

quiet and regretful. "No, you were right. We were safer with them, until they decided to pull out and head north."

Until they'd decided to stop at a random dwelling for the night. She wondered how many times the men passed that house on previous travels, how many times they'd just missed being a cannibal's next meal.

"Is that what direction we came? I was in the back of a truck and couldn't get my bearings."

"Yeah. They were good men, 'Kenz. You didn't steer us wrong."

"They left us here." She didn't want to tell him about her uneasiness while he'd been absent, that she feared the men weren't as good as they'd professed to be. There was nothing he could do about it now, and expending his energy on anger was pointless and wasteful.

"I would have left us, too. You stop, you run the risk of being overrun by Revenants or worse."

"What's worse than Revenants?" she muttered.

"The uninfected who prey upon their own kind." He bumped her shoulder with his. "Have you slept at all tonight?"

"Yeah, for a while before we broke camp. And a little while we were moving."

"Good thing. We have ahead of us another night of walking rather than sleeping."

"We've done it before."

But somehow, before, it hadn't seemed as disheartening. She hadn't realized how much she enjoyed riding instead of walking, how exhausted she had been before Ren Leonard rescued them at the farmhouse.

"I wonder if Leonard will be able to find us now."

"We're probably better off without him, 'Kenz. He's a Revenant, after all, and unpredictable."

He was probably right. It didn't stop her from wishing the Revenant was with them, however. Somehow she felt safer, even though she knew, deep inside, that he was a danger to them.

"Do you think we're going to have to cross mountains?"

She knew there was a range this way; she remembered it from the maps of the state Loretta had shown them when she'd still been schooling. Mountains brought dicey weather; one day it could be warm and beautiful; the next, it could snow up to your hips.

"Dunno. I have no idea where Riemer was sending us. He just gave me the medallion and said to follow the symbol."

A bloody hard job it had been so far, too. Sometimes the symbol wasn't obvious. Often it was faded, weathered by time and the elements. Other times, it was a long journey between sightings.

"I wonder who set up the Underground. It must have been in place for a long time to have reached this far across the state."

"Not necessarily. All it would take is some detailed planning and a few people to slip out of the Stronghold and not come back. They set up the route as they travel it, trusting that the people left behind won't be found out."

"But wouldn't they need to have known where they were going?"

He shrugged, barely visible in the darkness. "Not so much. You just go your way, paint your symbol, and find a safe, decent spot to settle. Me, I'd choose farmland like this, where the closest houses are a hell of a long way away."

"What about islands?" Mac remembered enough about the maps to know the coast was dotted with them.

"I can't imagine sending anyone on his own all the way across the state and through cities to the islands. There are lots of cities on the coast, all jammed together with the big one they called Seattle. Easier to settle in the farmlands, get some sheep or goats, if the Revenants haven't eaten them all, start farming. You'd be set."

"Yeah," she agreed absently, silently thinking that an island would be better. Perfect defense, surrounded on all sides by water. Clear the territory of all Revenants and never have to worry about being attacked, even at night.

Mac's legs began to ache, soon followed by her back. She thought that Will might be carrying the pack longer on his turns than he allowed on her turns. And then eventually he stopped passing it to her at all, confirming her suspicions of his latent chivalry.

Her feet sent stabbing pains through her ankles and calves with every step, but she didn't ask him to stop, although he did allow them frequent rests, if only for a few minutes. Her stomach growled, but their food had been in Will's pack; she guessed it would be a while before they saw another meal. They still possessed her canteen though, so at least they could stay hydrated, as long as they could find water.

The moon traveled around them. Mackenzie sank into a fog of introspection, her best defense against the pain racking in her legs but also a dangerous one. Will, though, somehow seemed able to remain aware of their surroundings and keep plugging on despite her dragging pace. Perhaps the two days of rest — if being unconscious could be called resting — made all the difference. They didn't speak, simply trudged through the night down the abandoned road of a lost civilization.

They'd been good roadbuilders, she couldn't deny; even if the asphalt had crumbled into gravel, the roadbeds were still solid and well defined, although a few more seasons would fill in the drainage ditches to either side. Even now she could see the buildup at the edges of the road.

She stopped walking and looked around. She could see a lot of things, mostly sagebrush and rolling, open country, all dimly lit with grey predawn light.

"It's almost dawn," she said.

Will, several steps ahead of her, stopped. "Yeah. Let's keep going until it's full-on daylight. Then we can find somewhere to lay out in the sunshine and rest."

"How far do you think we've walked tonight?"

"A lot of miles. Maybe fifteen, twenty? Though we did slow down there for a couple of hours. I don't know for sure how far north they took us, so I don't really know how far we have to go until we reach the main road."

They started walking again. Will pressed his hand against the backpack strap to keep it from rubbing. Daylight crept across the land, but it was weak and filtered through a generous cloud covering. They would see rain before afternoon, unless she was much mistaken. When the sun blazed through a large break in the clouds, he stopped and let the pack slide to the ground. Still pressing his hand to his shoulder, he eased himself down on the ground and sighed.

"Let's rest for a while here. The sun feels nice."

Mackenzie herself couldn't discern much difference between sunny or cloudy; it was cold, period. Walking meant staying warm; sitting meant letting the chill get a bone-deep grip that would be hard to shake before nightfall. But she folded herself onto the ground next to him, because it meant easing the ache in her legs.

"Did you wrench your shoulder in the attack?"

He grimaced. "No."

"Backpack rubbing a raw spot? I can carry it, you know. It won't hurt me."

"It's fine."

"Maybe I should take a look at it. Though I'm not sure what we can do for it – the first aid kit was in your pack." She reached for his hand to pry it off his shoulder, and he jerked out of her reach.

"It's no big deal."

"Fine, whatever." She abandoned the effort and snagged the strap of the pack to rummage through and see if there was a scrap of food they may have missed in the dark. She was tugging on the zip pull when she noticed the red smears on her fingers. Blood.

"Eeew! Someone bled on our pack. Maybe Rico – it looked like he'd been injured."

She bent closer to the pack to examine the strap. Her heart hammered into her throat, blocking her air. The strap hadn't been smeared or splattered with blood; it was saturated.

"Will, there's a lot of blood on this. I don't think—"

She looked at him – *really* looked – for the first time since dawn. His face was grey, his mouth stretched into a tight grimace of pain. Blood spilled from between his fingers. She jumped up and backed away.

"You're bitten."

"No."

"The Revenant—"

"I'm not bitten, Mackenzie," he snapped impatiently. "I got skewered with a butcher knife in that goddamn house."

"And you're just now mentioning it? Oh wait – you *didn't* mention it. You just bled all over everything and thought I wouldn't notice?" Her voice rose an octave, threaded with panic. She hated that she heard it, hated even more that *he* heard it. If he'd been bitten, or if he slowly bled out, she would be alone in this unfamiliar wasteland.

"The strap of the pack was pressure-sealing the wound. I thought it would be closed up and crusted over by now."

But it wasn't. It had continued to bleed, soaking into the backpack strap. A lot of blood. Enough to turn his face that sickly hue and sap his strength. How much longer would he be able to travel before blood loss, hunger, and fatigue dropped him? And then what would she do? She couldn't carry him, and she couldn't leave him.

"Take off your jacket and your shirt."

"And freeze?" He lifted a sardonic brow.

"Just do it."

Her hand twitched toward her blade. He didn't miss the movement. Slowly he unzipped his jacket and peeled it off, grimacing. The left side of his thermal shirt, a lucky find in the same store they'd found new underclothes and outerwear, was crimson from collar to ribs. Somehow he managed to extricate his wounded arm without uttering a single sound of pain, but his face turned waxy and sweat dotted his forehead.

He'd been skewered, all right – a clean entry, leaving only a deep, thin, vertical wound that pulsed blood with each beat of his heart. Mac stared at it, a huge swell of dismay clogging her throat, threatening to turn into panic. *Calm down, Mac. You can deal with this. You had first aid training in case something like this ever happened to your partner.*

And Will was her partner, regardless of the fact they'd never actually gone on gathering missions together. What they'd been through the past six weeks made them partners more swiftly and surely than training or daily shared duties ever could have.

She knelt at the pack and rummaged through until she found a clean pair of socks. She had hoped to change into these later today, but it was more important to bind his wound. Reluctantly, she pulled the cinch cord from the hood of her jacket, certain she would regret it later when the rain and wind came. But she didn't have anything else to tie on the dressing.

"Give me the canteen." She held out her hand.

He gripped it tighter. "No, we need the water to drink."

"I need a little to clean your wound. I won't use much."

He regarded her outstretched hand and then her determined expression and finally passed the canteen to her. She worked quickly and efficiently, as Bon had taught her. The last vestige of color drained from Will's face as she tied the sock securely over the wound. It was pretty shoddy as far as field dressings went, but the sock was absorbent and the cinch cord, crisscrossed over the wound to apply pressure and hopefully stop the bleeding, was sturdy and not likely to break with repeated tying.

"Rest for a little bit, and then we'll need to go. We have to find shelter soon – it's going to storm and I don't like being the tallest thing out here on the plain."

He didn't answer. He leaned against a large rock, face tipped up to the weak rays of the sun peeking between huge black storm clouds. While he rested, she emptied the pack, took note of their inventory, and shared out two stale strips of beef jerky she found in a forgotten package underneath her clothes. She had two more clean pairs of socks, thanks to her laundering efforts while they camped with the Wenatchee men. With no idea of how far the next town was or how overrun with Revenants it might be, she decided to save them for Will's wound, just in case.

She took a sip from the canteen and allowed him several, then strapped both it and the pack over her shoulders.

"We should go. It's getting colder; it will rain anytime now."

Will opened his eyes and sat up, looking up at the sky. The blue patches had vanished, and the day was darkening. She thought for a second that he was simply going to ease back down against his rock and refuse to move, but then he reached up for her hand. She tugged him up from the ground. He stared at her for a long moment.

"If I don't make it, Mackenzie, keep going west. Just follow the road. Eventually you'll come to large cities. Try to skirt them, even if it means you add days of travel to go around them. You won't be able to fight your way through a city alone, and it looks like we've lost Leonard for good."

"You'll make it," she said, her tone sharp. "We'll find a place to hole up and get some medical supplies. I can stitch the wound."

"There's a good chance this will get infected, 'Kenz, and you know it. You won't be able to save me from a bad infection."

"Watch me."

She turned and started walking, expecting him to follow, surprised when he did so without further argument. Not that it meant he believed her. It just meant he was picking his battles.

Mac set a steady pace somewhere between a stroll and a purposeful walk; she didn't want Will's heart to pump too hard and pulse out more blood, but they had to keep moving to find shelter. After about an hour, they passed the burned hulk of a farmhouse. A moderate distance from it – far enough away to have escaped burning – lurked a decrepit barn. She dismissed it as a possibility of shelter. For one, it looked about to fall over and she doubted it kept out much more rain than it let in. For another, she didn't have the energy – and neither did Will – to fight off any sheltering Revenants.

Another half-hour later, they rounded a curve in the road, and what looked from a distance like a natural crevice in the terrain resolved itself into an irrigation canal. The water level was fairly low, but there was enough to drink away their thirst and fill the canteen. The first drops of rain splattered them while she filled the canteen, icy on her already cold skin. The only shelter available was under the road where it passed over the canal.

"We'll get wet and freeze to death, Mackenzie," Will protested half-heartedly.

"We'll get wet and freeze to death if we stay out in the rain. We have at least a fighting chance to stay dry under the road – the water in the canal is pretty low. We can sit on the bank under the middle of the road."

"Yeah, until the canal floods from the rainwater and we drown."

But he followed her along the edge of the canal under the road, grunting in pain as he crawled up the bank away from the water. He sighed in relief when he sank down beside her.

The rain began in earnest, draping each side of the raised highway with curtains of water. Above them, the wind whistled past, but it lost most of its momentum before it reached their perch.

"Go ahead and sleep," Will said after a loud thunderclap jolted him out of a semi-stupor. "I'll keep watch – it's pretty noisy and if we both sleep, we won't hear if something is creeping up on us."

"I'm not tired," she said, although even the marrow of her bones ached. "You're wounded. Sleep while you can."

He did. Mac sat with her machete in her hands, alternating her gaze to each side of the road. She doubted that anything would be moving about the countryside during this ferocious deluge, but Bon always said it was better to be prepared rather than to be caught unaware. Being caught unaware was likely the last thing you were liable to do in this brutal world.

It rained steadily through the night. Will dozed for a couple of hours, and then she changed his dressing and caught a couple hours of sleep herself. They traded off and on like that until dawn, although Mackenzie didn't sleep much after the first couple of hours, instead lying with her back to Will and staring at the rain with despondency. She had loved the rain since she was a child, even when she was caught in a downpour while gathering; there was the promise of a hot meal and a warm bed waiting for her at the end of the day.

Not now. No warm meal – an omission her stomach was loudly protesting as hunger gnawed a hollow spot in the pit of her belly – and no warm bed, not for the foreseeable future. Just more walking and shivering and huddling under scanty shelter, waiting for the rain to pass. Her last stormy day had been spent in Elijah's quarters, the door chastely left open while she lounged on his bed and read and he folded his laundry and generally tidied up. She dozed for a while and woke with the scent of rosemary and mint teasing her nose. The source wasn't hard to find: he had finished his tasks and dozed himself, sitting on the floor by the bed, scrunched down so his head rested on the corner of the pillow adjacent to her.

And then Johanna burst in, her impatient snort waking him, her admonishments that he was neglecting their plans ushering him out the door. Mackenzie hadn't minded much; she knew he would be back, and she felt secure in the knowledge that he planned to keep her safe and that plan included his direct involvement.

Now she huddled on the mostly dry bank under a ruined roadway, shielded by a fragile curtain of frigid rain, and she wondered, when he sent her out alone to trek hundreds of miles away from home, just what the hell Elijah Riemer had been thinking.

24

The rain abated by dawn to a drizzle that fell somewhere between an inconvenience and a damned annoyance. Mackenzie still
hadn't decided which it was when Will shouldered the pack and
declared it was time to head out.

She let him carry it only because it compressed his wound.
She'd found a small cluster of yarrow, drenched from the downpour but otherwise untouched by the cooling weather, chewed the
leaves, and pressed them to the wound, trapping them beneath a
clean sock. Hopefully, the yarrow would stop the bleeding soon, if
the wound wasn't deeper than they thought. After drinking roughly
their weight in water from the canal and refilling the canteen, they
scrambled out from under the road, climbed the embankment, and
resumed their weary walk.

Mac carried both machetes, crisscrossed on her back, the handle of his pointing toward him so he could easily grab it. Not that
she thought he could fight worth a damn today, not with that
wound. He could barely lift his arm, and even now walked with his
hand tucked into the strap of the backpack to ease the throbbing.

They didn't take many breaks. With no food, there was little
reason to stop, and resting only brought their weariness and hunger
to the forefront of their minds. Walking kept their bodies warm as
the wind grew steadily stronger and chillier as the hours ground
toward noon. Around mid-morning, Will halted their travel long
enough for them to fill their bellies with water to ease the ache and
nausea of their empty stomachs, and he refilled the canteen by
holding it under a dripping tree branch. Mackenzie shivered as the
cold gale buffeted her, and even her weariness didn't dampen her
relief when they started walking again.

An hour later, they came to a small pond surrounded by cattails. Shooing away a pair of quacking ducks, Mac dug out as many
as she could with a pointed shard of slate. The roots could be
cooked like potatoes if they could find wood dry enough to start a
fire. She washed off as much dirt as possible before stowing them
in the bottom of the pack, a layer of soiled clothes between them

and her few remaining laundered items.

Leaving the ducks squawking indignantly in her wake, she clambered out of the reeds and back to the road and Will. She judged it was just past the noon hour (taking a cue from the increased rumbling in her stomach) when the road veered closer to the edge of the river gorge. The river sounded a long way down, but Will judged the footing too precarious and the wind too strong to look.

"We'll be able to see it when we get to the bridge," he said, and then added under his breath, "If the bridge is still there."

It was … in a manner of speaking.

The iron girders, brownish-red and flaking from a rash of rust, had withstood the decades since the Upheaval. The concrete road had not. Worn away from both above and below, chunks of roadway had crumbled and fallen through into the river below, leaving gaping holes like ravenous mouths waiting to swallow those foolish enough to attempt crossing. She stared at the treacherous journey ahead, dismayed at the thought of performing a half-mile balancing act on the girders over a river far below. A very deep, powerful river.

Will cast a look at the sky, trying to judge the time. "I think we have enough time for a half-hour rest before we tackle that. I'm not—"

"Will."

"—sure how long it is – maybe a half a mile, a little less – so the distance isn't too formidable, but—"

"It's what we have to cross that's formidable," she interrupted. "Have you thought about what happens if one of us falls off? There's going to be no rescue from that river. It's a long way down."

"Looks like the water level is low – see there, on the gorge walls? You can see the different marks where the water was higher, probably during spring run-off."

"Will, did you not hear me? *It's a long way down.* There won't be anything to rescue – from this high up, it'd be like hitting hard ground when we hit the water. We'd be fish food."

His mouth quirked. "Well, thank you for your optimism, salmon bait. Sit down for a few minutes, and let's talk about this without the hysteria."

"I'm not hysterical. I'm just being practical." *And scared. I'm very, very scared of walking across that bridge.*

Will unshouldered the pack and eased himself down to the soggy ground, sweeping crumbles of old asphalt road out from under his more tender areas. He unzipped his jacket and peeled back his shirt, lifting the bloodstained sock away from his wound.

"The yarrow did the trick; it's not bleeding anymore." He pressed the pad down and zipped his jacket back up.

"It will probably still seep. We need to get to the water so we can wash all the socks; the biggest problem now is infection."

"No reaching *that* water," he said reasonably.

True enough. The water was an unreachable distance down, accessible only by climbing down the basalt cliff. Judging from the old water level marks on the cliff across the river, it had never been accessible from this area anyway.

"There's a town across the bridge. Maybe we can find a way to the water – or *some* water – over there."

"Not much of a town," he surmised, squinting through the mist at the huddle of buildings on the other shore, his hand flattening his hair so the wind couldn't blow it into his eyes. No, not much, but they didn't need a huge metropolis. They just needed a hand pump to bring water up from a well, and they were most likely to find one in a small town. Big cities were dangerous anyway, with shade and shadows and gangs of voracious Revenants.

"Maybe we can find wood, too. Have a fire. Cook some cattail roots."

His glance was sympathetic. "You're pretty hungry."

"I'd eat them raw if it came down to it, but they're much better cooked."

"Maybe we can find some late dandelions, too. They might be a little bitter this late in the season, but a salad would go well with the cattails."

"You're pretty hungry yourself."

He grimaced. "Hungry enough to eat a Revenant."

They looked at each other and said together, "Not!"

They drank more water. Will picked a broad leaf from a wild plant and made a funnel to catch more rain water in the canteen, using his body to shelter it from the gale.

"Leaflets three, let it be," Will said now and chuckled. "When

209

Juarez and I were first partnered together, I picked a leaf from a
shrub to funnel water into the canteen and he wasn't paying attention to what I was picking. Poison ivy. By the time we got to the
river to wash off the oils from the plant, my lips had swollen twice
their normal size. My hands were blistering. By the time we got
back to the Stronghold, I was hurtin' for certain."

She laughed at that. "Hurtin' for certain?"

He grinned. "I read it in a book."

"Fiction, I'm betting."

"Oh yeah. You won't find much slang in textbooks. I thought
Juarez was going to strangle me. We'd walked five miles to gather
in a new area, and we'd barely started when we had to leave because
the blisters got so bad and I'd contaminated our canteen. He was
going to make me do a full shift anyway, but he backed off when I
reminded him that I was the one watching his back, and I was less
likely to be doing so if I was scratching like fury."

"He sounds like a charmer." She wasn't familiar with Juarez,
herself. While the gatherers frequently assembled together for brief-
ings and training, there were a couple hundred of them, and she
hadn't had cause to rub elbows with a senior team. And now that
she thought back on it, none of them sought out Bon and her.
Funny how she'd never made much note of the settlement's avoid-
ance of her partner.

"He was a hard-ass," Will agreed and added thoughtfully, "He
wasn't very nice sometimes, but I sure learned a lot from him."

Mac stared at the bridge, wondering if she'd be as afraid of
crossing it if she were with Bon. Her heart gave a painful lurch of
fierce longing. He'd been the closest thing she had to a best friend.
Because of her gathering duties and intense training schedule, most
of her childhood friends were relegated to the fringes of her life,
still there to welcome her home and available for fun when she was
off-duty.

But no one inspired the same level of trust she had placed in
her partner, not until Elijah Riemer. And although they relied
heavily upon each other for survival, she had not formed the same
kind of bond with Will. She reserved a little corner of mistrust, because Eli told her to trust no one.

"Bon wasn't a bad guy. He loved the Stronghold. He just
didn't think they wanted things to get better," she blurted. She

turned her burning face away from him. She hadn't meant to speak at all, nor to do it so vehemently from her heart.

Will was quiet for several minutes. "I'd just started gathering when Bon killed his teammate."

"Really?" She turned back, surprised. She judged him to be about the same age as Bon. Considering it now, though, she recalled that hunters went through two years of training before they were added to a team. Bon had been a gatherer for a couple of years before being paired with Mackenzie, and then there had been his own year of training for that.

"He was older than he looked," Will said, watching her closely. "Twenty-four, almost twenty-five when he died. After the incident, he said he'd been hunting on his own because he'd pissed off the team, and his partner came up behind him. No one will ever know if that's the truth."

"It is."

"How would you know, 'Kenz? You were – what, all of ten when it happened?"

"Twelve. Bon told me that's what happened. That's how I know it's the truth."

He digested this silently, his gaze never wavering from -hers. "All right. But it's not the story the others gave."

"Really? And how would they know, since they weren't right there when it happened?"

"They *were* there, according to their version of events. And they said Bon just lost it. He was pissed at everyone, was bugging the hell out of everyone. And Duke Goremykin – that was the dead guy's name—"

"Duke?" she repeated. "What the hell kind of name is that?"

"I don't know. A nickname, maybe. That doesn't matter. Duke needled Bon one too many times, and whack! Bon sliced and diced him."

Mac felt sick. She could imagine that scenario all too easily, not because she wanted to but because it was just as likely as Bon's version. But she trusted Bon, and more importantly, *Riemer* trusted Bon and had held him in high esteem. Riemer would not have been an easy man to fool.

"Well, if they were all pissed at him and then he killed one of them, I can see them constructing a story like that. But Elijah believed Bon, and I trust Elijah."

"We aren't likely to confirm either version now."

"He will come," she said with confidence.

Will turned away from her without speaking, as he always did these days when she mentioned Riemer. Dread nibbled at a corner of her mind. *What if he's...* She brought the thought to a screeching halt and shoved it deep, so deep that maybe even her subconscious wouldn't be able to find it.

"Let's get across that bridge and find some shelter."

The bridge was even more formidable closer up. Mac's dismay morphed into outright alarm at the chaotic landscape of crumbled concrete and rusting reinforcement bars, with glimpses of iron framework nearly two feet below the disintegrating deck.

Will stretched out an experimental foot and pushed on a bent end of rebar. It broke off with a puff of russet dust and a dull crack. His eyes traveled from the deck to the arch, hopping from column to column.

"You're right. There's too much distance between them," he said finally. "We won't have anything to hold onto, and the wind is worse closer to the river."

Mac chewed the inside of her cheek. The bridge, mangled by time and the elements, made her stomach swoop. "It's what – fifteen, twenty feet between them? Could we cross in the middle? That way if we fell, we'd have a better chance of landing on part of the bridge rather than falling into the river."

He raised a brow. "Unless you fell where there's no roadway anymore – which seems to be most of it. You really want to chance it?"

She shuddered. "Not really."

"Let's look underneath. Maybe there's a maintenance walkway."

"Somehow the thought gives me no comfort."

Will flashed her a tight grin, obviously not finding the idea much more palatable than crossing the ruined deck.

They picked their way carefully down the abutment. Will made her hang back while he ventured closer to the edge of the cliff, peering under the bridge for access. He looked for a long time. Once, he climbed up under and grabbed something, giving it a hearty shake and her a near heart attack. When he came back, his face was grim.

"There's passage underneath."

"Better than above?"

"Hard to say. Problem is, while it looks fairly passable and still sturdy enough, I can't say we'd be able to get out from underneath on the other side. If I had the field glasses..." He trailed off. The field glasses were lost with his pack.

"A lot of debris to cross?" She could see from here the crumbled blocks of cement deck that had fallen through the superstructure, streaked red-brown from rusting reinforcement bars. The steel grating forming the catwalk held, though, and that seemed to bode well.

"A fair amount. It's just a catwalk, and I think there are some missing pieces of railing." He wiped his hands on his pants. Flakes of red-brown floated to the ground. "I'll leave it up to you, 'Kenz. If you want to cross up top, we will."

She studied him closely. Sweat beaded up on his face, his skin grey from exhaustion and hunger and blood loss. If he lost his balance on the catwalk, he'd probably be all right, provided he didn't stumble where there was no railing. On the other hand, if they made it across and then found they couldn't exit the catwalk on the other side, they'd have to backtrack and cross the deck anyway.

"Let's try the catwalk," she said, thinking of the look of dread on his face as he had studied the distance between the columns up top. "If we have to backtrack, so be it. But we'll never know until we try it."

He breathed out a sigh of relief and gave her the first genuine smile she'd seen since they'd met the men from Wenatchee. Her own relief was tempered with the worry that Ren Leonard might have a hard time tracking them if they went under the bridge rather than over it.

"The approach has been damaged, so it looks like it will be a bit of a challenge to get onto the catwalk. I'll climb up first, and you can pass the pack to me. Then you come up, and I can help you. It will be easier if neither of us are wrestling with our gear."

She shouldered the pack and followed him to the edge of the cliff, holding her breath as he scrabbled back up the bank under the bridge. A section of the concrete deck had fallen through and damaged the access point. Will picked his way over it, placing each step carefully and testing for firm ground before rocking his full weight onto his foot. When he steadied himself, he motioned to her.

"Come on up."

She followed the path he'd taken, digging the sides of her shoes into the embankment for traction. He leaned over the railing and grabbed the pack as she swung it up, wincing as it hit his wounded shoulder.

"You all right?"

"Fine. Just get up here so I can breathe easier for a couple of minutes."

She hoisted her leg over a rusted piece of mangled railing, found a sure footing, and heaved herself up. It was a small matter to pick her way over the debris; she was lighter than Will, shorter and more compact, and the heap seemed solid enough. Beyond the debris a narrow walkway about four feet wide, made of metal mesh and flanked on either side with handrails, ran the length of the westbound lanes. There was no access under the eastbound lanes; she wondered what had happened to it.

She was almost over the blockage when several smaller chunks of concrete shifted beneath her, spilling her toward the hip-height railing. Her heart leapt into her throat, cutting off her air so that she couldn't even scream as she hit the railing...

...and toppled over.

25

The world spun crazily. Once seeming impossibly far away, the river now loomed before her, inches away, a wild, raging beast with a voracious appetite just inches from her face, keen on wrapping its icy arms around her and dragging her into the fatal embrace of its turbulent current.

Her fingers caught solid metal and held. Her cheek crashed against something hard and cold. Her shoulders jolted and her arms screamed agony all the way to her fingertips. Her first instinct was to relax, ease the strain, stop the stretching of muscles and tendons that was causing pain to shriek through her nerve endings, but something stopped her – perhaps Will, who was screaming over and over: *"Don't let go, Mackenzie! Whatever you do, don't you fucking dare let go!"*

Vibrations roared through her arms. The world shook. Her fingers slipped a fraction of an inch, and then another. Metal clanged beside her ear, deafening in the echoing underworld of the bridge. The hood of her jacket snagged on something. Her weight hung on the top of the zipper, closing her airway to a pinhole, and then freed suddenly. She closed her eyes against sickening vertigo as she rolled and spun, and then she was falling, spinning…

…and crashed onto the deck of the catwalk, sending a ringing shudder through its length. Another thump brought her eyes open – Jesus! The catwalk was collapsing! – to find Will sprawled beside her, his face an altogether unhealthy greenish-white, his hands still clutching the hood of her jacket by which he had hauled her back over the railing.

Mackenzie sat up slowly and opened her eyes. The world still spun in its treacherous vertigo dance. She chanced a look below and closed her eyes again as everything tilted.

"Jesus. I'm alive." Her faintness was now borne of relief. She began to laugh and cry at the same time. "I'm alive. I'm alive."

She said it over and over again until Will scooted closer and wrapped his arms around her, and then the laughter faded and she simply cried. He was shaking, his hand smoothing her hair convulsively, his embrace so tight she felt both unbelievably secure and unbearably stifled.

But she didn't make him let go. She didn't think he could. Didn't know if she wanted him to. For this brief moment in their hellish lives, she felt comfortable, safe, and absolutely joyful to be alive. He deserved to be borne along on this tide of elation, for he was the reason she was slouched on this catwalk, alive, and not floating away in the current below, leaking her innards from a dozen impact-sprung holes in her body.

So they sat for minutes…or hours…or days…cheek to cheek, their tears mingling and dripping from their chins, and at last she felt the bond between them, maybe not as strong as she had felt with Elijah or Bon, but there, at least. At the very least.

With one last, shuddering breath, Will tightened his embrace and then let her go. "We've got to get moving, 'Kenz. We need to find shelter before nightfall."

He uncoiled from the catwalk and hoisted her up with his uninjured arm. The platform suffered no visible damage from the violent activity, but she was reluctant to move, nevertheless. She forced herself to plod after him, though, not wanting to be left behind in the gloom.

A couple hundred feet convinced her that the decision to travel the catwalk instead of the upper deck might have been premature. The path was littered with debris that lurked in the shadows, jubilantly twisting their ankles and skidding their footsteps. One heart-stopping stretch of thirty feet or more became a balancing act on a three-foot wide metal mesh plank with no hand rails. Mac got safely to the other side behind Will and stood panting, clutching the hand rails, while Will vomited over the railing into the river far below. His face grew greyer by the minute, or perhaps it was just the reflected light from the dismal day. The treacherous journey was taking its toll on him, regardless, and her near-fall had done his injury no favors.

The wind gusted, knocking them off balance. Several times, they were forced to stop and wait for a lull so they could climb over a pile of fallen roadway. Once they waited twenty minutes on opposite sides of huge jagged block until the wind died down enough that she could scramble over. She hadn't dared breathe until she was safely on the other side, for there was nothing – literally nothing – she could hold onto except the crumbling concrete should the wind pick up again.

Not long after, the rain came in sheets, a deluge of frigid water that would have drenched them in seconds had they been up top. As it was, the wind was happy to fling handfuls of icy drops under the bridge with gleeful abandon at the most inopportune times. The catwalk became slick and perilous. A ten-foot stretch with no railing took fifteen minutes to cross. They shimmied their way on their bellies, clinging to the sides of the mesh platform as the wind blasted over their backs and threw glacial rain down the necks of their jackets.

They found temporary respite on the leeward side of a hunk of roadway that had settled vertically. Will leaned his head back against the crumbling concrete, water running in rivulets down his face, breathing raggedly.

"I could punch Riemer in the mouth right about now."

Mac chuckled weakly, surprised that he brought up Elijah. Generally, he avoided all mention of him. "If we make it to wherever it is we're going, you may get the chance yet."

He grunted noncommittally. "I'd sleep here if I wasn't petrified of rolling off the side and into the river."

"Me too."

He swiped a hand over his forehead, diverting the tracks of rainwater away from his eyes. He cast a glance up the catwalk toward the opposite bank, which was invisible in the gloom. It seemed an unbearable distance away. When he turned back, he stared down at the river, its powerful current sweeping toward destinations they would never see. The Revenant Virus had stolen more than just the humanity of the infected; it had stolen most of everything from the uninfected too, travel and safety among them. With those two things compromised, everyone felt the pinch of being confined: fewer resources, dwindling prospects, fading hope.

"Why are you doing this, Mackenzie?" Will asked unexpectedly.

"Doing what?"

"Traveling across the state, following a sign you can only hope hasn't been replicated by people with ill intentions, heading to an unknown destination."

"Well," she said slowly, thinking the cannibals must have hit

217

him over the head harder than she'd thought. "I was exiled. Leaving the area seemed like a good idea, especially with the council sending two teams of hunters to execute me."

"Those are just circumstances." He waved a hand wearily, dismissing her answer. "I mean *why*? The *why* that made you question the elders, that made you seek out Ren Leonard, that made you really listen to what Bon Moreau had to say about it all. There must be something you want, very badly, to have made you risk everything like this."

She drew in a breath and opened her mouth. Just as quickly closed it. What *did* she want? A husband, children, a home. Maybe some goats. A dog that didn't get eaten if it escaped the confines of safety.

But those were just things, just like her exile and near-execution were just circumstances. What she wanted, in her deepest, most desperate heart, was what had led her to Ren Leonard in the first place.

"I want to *live*."

"You were living at the Stronghold."

"I was *existing*. We were all existing. Every day things became more hopeless, and people just refused to see it. The Stronghold started out with over five thousand residents. We were down to two thousand when I left. The Revenants picked us off, illness took more, and our numbers dwindled every year. That's not even surviving, Will."

He looked back at the river, watching the distant current for a long time before asking, "And if Riemer never comes, Mackenzie? What then?"

While her heart refused to believe Elijah would never come, her mind was a practical entity. "Then I'll live without him." Grudgingly and reluctantly at first, but she wasn't walking across the state to a hopefully better life just to waste it by pining away over an absent man.

Whatever Will was thinking seemed to have him conflicted, but he didn't share it with her. Their whole journey together had been punctuated with his thoughtful silences. She assumed he was worrying about what lay ahead and planning out maneuvers for all possible scenarios, but now she wondered if it had more to do with his own desires for his future.

"What about you, Will?" she prodded. "Will you stay wherever we end up, or will you return to the Stronghold?"

She thought he wasn't going to answer, because he didn't for so long. And then he said reluctantly, "It depends."

"On what?"

"A number of things. Come on, the wind's let up a little. Let's see if we can get the rest of the way across before it picks up again."

The wind buffeted them with less force than before, which should have eased their way, except that while most of the rain drained through the platform, drops clung to the holes of the mesh and made their feet slip. They climbed more piles of crumbling concrete road and rusting rebar. Rain poured onto them from the gaps in the deck above, drenching them.

The gloom deepened as they drew closer to the abutment on the other side. Will peered down at the water below, where pools of water rippled between large boulders, and sent her a tight grin over his shoulder.

"Well, the good news is we won't be swept away by the current if we fall. The bad news is we still won't be in any position to appreciate not drowning as we'll be splattered on those big rocks."

"I'm comforted," she said irascibly. She'd just been doused by an unavoidable stream of icy water from above that carried bits of blacktop in it. She was certain her scalp must be bleeding in a dozen or more spots.

"Almost there, I think. We just have to get around this and then find a way off the catwalk and onto the bank."

Ahead, a tumble of concrete blocked their path, one finger of fallen roadway pointing like an accusatory finger at the deck above them. It was tall enough that she was certain they could climb through to the deck if they wanted.

"Maybe we should just climb up and out onto the deck. We can't be any wetter than we are now, so staying down here is not much of an advantage, especially since we don't know if we can get onto the bank."

"If you want. I don't know that we're close enough that topside won't be more dangerous."

"You just said we're almost there."

"Figuratively speaking. We're closer to that side than we are to

219

where we started."

Mac snorted. She'd learned with Bon that "almost there" meant all sorts of things to a man except what a woman wanted it to mean: almost there.

Will began climbing the debris. A few pieces shifted under his feet as he propelled himself upward, favoring his injured arm, but it seemed sturdy enough overall. When he was close to the top, he motioned for her to start her ascent. He swung a leg over the slab at the top, pivoted on his belly, and swung the other leg over. He rested on the slab, looking up through the gap in the upper deck. If he stood, he would be halfway out of the understructure and easily able to climb topside. She wished he would at least stand up to see how treacherous the deck was at their present location, but instead he watched her to make sure she was climbing with no difficulty, a hand pressed to his shoulder. He had to have torn it open rescuing her when she'd gone over the railing. All this climbing up and down had probably torn it even more.

Mac found sturdy hand- and footholds and climbed. Chunks teetered but held. Assured that she was safe enough, Will descended the other side. For a while, all she heard was the scrape and clatter of debris falling, dislodged by their climb. When she was nearing the peak, a thump and clang told her he'd reached the catwalk on the other side.

"The path is clear from what I can see, but it's pretty dark."

"Maybe you should climb back up and we can go topside." She was almost there; two more steps up and she would be able to touch the top slab.

"I'd like to see if we can make it off the catwalk first. There aren't many more gaps in the deck, so we won't get as wet. And we know now that we don't have to go all the way ba—*aaack! Sonofabitch!*"

"Will?" She climbed frantically, displacing fragments of concrete that clattered down the slope of the scree, masking the sounds she thought she'd heard: hissing, growling, snarling.

Revenants.

"Bastards!" Will screamed.

Debris rattled and the catwalk clanged. A Revenant howled. Mackenzie's fingers reached the top slab and she pulled herself up, her feet scrabbling for traction. Unable to retreat because of the close proximity of his assailants, Will was hurling jagged lumps of concrete at the three Revenants bearing down on him. While it held them at bay, it wasn't enough to topple them off and into the river.

She wouldn't be able to reach him in time with his blade, which she still carried strapped to her back with hers, so she reached down by her thigh and grabbed a small hunk of concrete with rusted rebar sticking out of it. She took a second to aim at the Revenant closest to Will, then flung it. It sailed end over end through the air and whacked the Revenant in the face, the rebar stabbing through its eye. The concrete fell away, and blood gouted from the wound.

The Revenant shrieked, clawing at its face even as the impact set it off balance and it staggered back against the railing. The railing gave way with a squeal, rusted bolts unable to withstand the weight of the frenzied creature. Railing and Revenant tumbled off the catwalk, the latter screaming and clawing at its eye as it plummeted out of sight.

Will was pelting the remaining two with anything he could grab from behind him, which was not enough to halt their advance. One lunged around him and began climbing the scree toward Mackenzie. Will booted the other in the chest, sending it hurtling through the gap in the rail and off the catwalk, its shriek echoing under the bridge as it fell toward the river.

Mac reached behind her for her machete, ready to part the Revenant's head from its body. Will flung himself onto it, his feet clawing for purchase on the loose pieces of concrete near the bottom of the pile.

"Go up, Mackenzie! Up! UP! CLIMB OUT, DAMMIT!"

And then she heard clomping footsteps on the catwalk, furious snarling, roars of challenge. Reinforcements.

She abandoned her quest for her blade and climbed onto the top slab, one eye on the Revenant that climbed ever closer despite Will riding its back. Fat drops of rain stung her head and shoulders as she rose into the hole. Not as tall as Will, she jumped to give herself the leverage needed to pull herself out. Her foot sought traction on a wet girder under the concrete, slipped off, and she tumbled back toward the slab. Purely by accident, her boot caught the Revenant in the face. Will rolled off its back as it skidded several feet back down the scree, then climbed for all he was worth, wriggling upward and kicking out behind him to keep the Revenant from climbing back up.

Mackenzie jumped again; her foot slipped again. This time she held onto the edge of the deck, flailing for a foothold. The battle cry of the oncoming horde approached with startling swiftness. Will shouted something at her that she couldn't hear, and then her legs were grabbed from below. She screamed, trying to kick free.

"Stop it! It's me! Go! *GO GO GO!*" He pushed her feet and she used the pressure to piston herself out of the hole, rolling over jagged shards of concrete that ripped at her flesh through her clothes. He dragged himself out of the hole, kicking downward into it several times before scooting away on his backside, stopping beside her to grab her jacket and roll her onto her back.

"Up, Mackenzie! They're coming! *They're coming!*"

She tottered to her feet. He tried, but his arm wouldn't support his weight and he fell onto his knees. A nightmare crawled halfway out of the hole, its waxy face pooling black puddles under its skin as daylight struck its flesh. She grabbed Will's good arm and dragged him to his feet as the Revenant pulled itself out of the hole and stood on the deck, squinting in the light.

Will said in tones of fascinated disgust, "What the *hell?*"

26

Its eyes were slitted, though she couldn't tell whether from the light or from a strange mutation. The daylight threw iridescent rainbows off its skin, as though it were covered in fish-like scales.

She took an involuntary step back, knocking a small piece of concrete with her boot. Its head whipped toward the sound and it hissed like a snake. Its tongue lapped the air as though tasting it. It froze, its focus locked on them. She glanced at Will, who returned the glance with apprehension. This was a mutation the likes of which she'd never seen.

He motioned to her to start backing away and took her hand. She did so, looking behind her to keep from kicking more debris or falling into potholes while Will kept his eyes on the mutant, allowing her to lead him. The Revenant followed, undulating toward them like a sidewinder. Behind it, one of its fellows poked its head out of the hole in the deck.

Will whispered, "Blade."

She pulled his blade from its bindings on her back and pressed it into the hand she'd been holding. The rustling made the Revenant hiss as she drew her own machete.

"We can't let them all come up out of that hole."

"Right. On three, I'll make noise that distracts it, and you lop off its head."

"Me?"

"Not sure I can swing the blade one-handed with enough accuracy to kill it." He paused, fixing her with a level gaze. "You're going to have to dispatch them all, one by one, as they come out of the hole, until they either give up or they're all dead."

She drew in a shaky breath.

"Can you do it?"

She was exhausted, starving, and freezing, but if she didn't do it, she'd also be dead. "Yeah."

He looked relieved. "Ready? Okay. One…two…*three!*"

He shouted the last word, dodging to the right and kicking a shard of concrete at it. The Revenant shrieked and bolted toward him, running blind in the light. Will dropped to his knees and Mac darted in, swinging her blade in an arc that was less smooth and graceful than normal but which was still brutally efficient. The mutant's head bounced across the deck and over the edge.

"The hole," Will gasped, clutching his shoulder as he staggered toward the gap in the deck.

Mac edged her way between potholes filled with crumbled concrete and rainwater. The Revenant in the hole had been trying to lift itself out when they dispatched its companion. Now it scrabbled to get back down below the deck. Its way was clogged with the rest of its pack. Will dropped his blade and grabbed it by the hair. Mac swung her blade, parting head from body. The body dropped onto the pack crowded around the hole, and they hissed and snarled.

Will stood over the hole, looking down at them dispassionately, and then he flung the severed head onto their snarling faces.

As a unit, the snakelike Revenants retreated into the darkness under the deck.

Will said, "Let's go. Now."

He bent and retrieved his blade. Mac followed him, weaving around potholes and gaps in the deck in case Revenants were waiting in the darkness below.

But none popped up, even when they gained the land bridge. Will set a brisk pace up the ruined highway. His face was the alarming hue of spoiled cottage cheese, but he didn't slow down, not even to veer off toward the town.

"Will, aren't we going to stop?"

"We can't stop there now. The rest of the pack is riled up – they'll wait until dark and then look for us in the town."

"Well, we have a better chance of defending ourselves if we're in a house. Out on the road, we're pretty well screwed."

"There's bound to be a house somewhere along the road that isn't in a town. And I doubt they'd come several miles to seek us out."

Mac bit back a sarcastic response. She wanted nothing more than to get off her feet and out of the rain and find a way to cook her cattail roots, not walk an undetermined distance to find a house that may or may not exist away from the Revenant pack at the bridge.

You've got to grow up.

And maybe part of growing up was going hungry and taking more weary steps when you didn't think you could go on, because the alternative was paying a steep price for momentary respite.

"All right," she agreed grudgingly. "But you should know I'm on the brink of collapse, and you're three steps closer to that state of being than I am."

He gave her a mocking sidelong look, but his lips twitched. And then he turned inward, lapsing into one of his morose silences where he seemed to be struggling with some internal conflict. She trudged beside him, their strides eating up the miles, her thoughts eating up the hours.

Sunset came, a lusterless event that brought colder temperatures and no relief from the rain. Old windmills dotted the skyline, a few of them missing their blades. And then, like a mirage, a cluster of small buildings rose out of the night. Will stopped.

"That's not a house." Lacking windows and possessing two doors at either end, the cinderblock structure appeared to be more of a utility building.

"I bet this was a place for travelers. I think they called them leisure stops or something like that. They had washrooms and snacks and coffee."

"I'd like some coffee," Mac said darkly, though she doubted it was in the foreseeable future.

"No lie. Come on, let's go see if we can hole up here for the night. If there's a way to barricade the doors, we might be able to get a good night's sleep."

Will stumbled with fatigue as they circled the buildings, blades at the ready, and made sure the area was clear. She made him open the doors to each side of the building and spear the darkness with the waning beam of their flashlight. Nothing snarled out of the darkness.

"Light up the room. I'll go in first," she whispered. He obliged. Mac edged cautiously around the edge of the doorway and into the room, her blade aloft and ready to strike.

The room was empty, although it showed signs of having been used after the Upheaval. The metal walls of one stall had collapsed and leaned heavily on the neighboring section. All of the toilets were full of dried, crumbling excrement that emitted a faint but

225

pungent odor like a past season's fertilizer.

"A latrine," Will said. Mac wrinkled her nose.

The left-hand room was likewise empty, only this room appeared to have been used as living quarters. Two rough bed frames made from two-by-sixes and plywood lined walls stripped of sinks and hot-air hand dryers. The commodes, likewise, had been stripped from their moorings and the plumbing capped. A small shelving unit housed pots and pans, plates and tableware, all covered with cobwebs and dust and the sandy soil of the desert. Two tattered wingback chairs, stuffing sprung and leaking from several tears, occupied the space in front of the shelves, a small table with a smoke-darkened oil lamp stuffed between them.

But the most striking part of the room was the message scrawled on the wall in black paint:

MAISIE DEAD
WALKING TO COAST TO FIND AN ISLAND
JAMES FRALEY ~ 2046

"Think he made it?"

Will shrugged, wincing as he did. "Probably not. Well, maybe. Who knows?" he added when he saw her flinch. "But it was the early days of the Upheaval, and the Revenants were probably still pretty thick. The coast was pretty much one big city – and cities are deadly."

He looked longingly at one of the beds. Mac sidled around him and closed the door, glimpsing an iron bar in the corner behind it. She threaded it through metal brackets that the long-dead-regardless-of-how James Fraley most likely installed to reinforce security.

Will had lain down while she was seeing to their safety. She prodded his foot as she passed him, jostling him out of the semi-doze he managed to achieve in the few minutes she left him alone.

"We should probably see to that shoulder," she said solemnly.

"Leave it for morning."

"I don't think—"

"I don't think I can stand to stay awake for the time it would take, 'Kenz. Let it be for now. In the morning we can try to find a water source, and then you can have at it to your heart's content."

He closed his eyes.

"All right. But if you die of infection, I'm carving 'Too Tired to Live' on your gravestone."

He chuckled. Seconds later he was snoring.

Mac dug out a semi-clean fleece shirt that she folded and tucked under his head. She hesitated before taking off his boots, but the small building had only tiny transom windows that could be opened to vent hot air in the summer months, barely big enough for a toddler to crawl through. No one would be able to launch a sneak attack while they slept. So she loosened the laces and slipped them from his feet, dismayed to see that his feet were bleeding from broken blisters. Another thing that would have to wait until morning. But maybe, when he stopped long enough to fully appreciate their precarious health, he would see the benefit in resting here for a few days.

She shed her own boots, made a pillow of the fleece pants that matched the shirt under Will's head, and climbed tentatively onto the platform bed frame, clicking off the flashlight. What kind of mattresses had James Fraley and his beloved Maisie enjoyed, and to where they had gone?

Speaking of gone... They had traveled at least thirty miles since losing Ren Leonard. Revenant senses were heightened compared to the uninfected, but with the rain and the distance and traveling under the bridge, their trail was most likely cold.

She hoped that if at long last he took his nap in the sun on the next clear day, he was truly ready, but the thought gave her a pang. Selfishness, that's all it was. Pure selfishness. She spent their time together with an undercurrent of apprehension but also with a relative sense of safety. She had much to fear from him and his volatile temper, but she had much to fear from the world around her as well. He had been a radar for danger, alleviating the larger threats so that she didn't have to be constantly on her guard.

Mackenzie closed her eyes and sent the wish his way – *Live well whatever life you choose, Ren Leonard* – and when she next opened them, sunlight streamed through the transom windows and the gaping door of the restroom. She sat up, blinking against the light, her eyes falling on the bed next to her.

Will was gone.

Mackenzie bolted off the bed. Halfway to the door, her feet

tangled on her pack and she sprawled prone on the dirty cement floor. Something was burning, and only now she realized the rain damped down the ever-present smell of fire and ash. Buildings and fields were always on fire in the Stronghold's city, often even during the wet winter months, and she had a split second to marvel at how fast she had grown accustomed to fresh air since they entered the farmlands.

Panic swamped her wonderment. Will was gone. His boots were gone. Her pack had been discarded near the door. She pushed herself to her feet. Took a step. Sprawled on the floor, feet tangled in the straps of her pack. She kicked one foot free, rolled onto her back and used her free foot to push the strap off the other. Dread bloomed in her chest, filling the space her lungs needed to expand. She couldn't draw a breath.

She rolled back onto her knees, shoving herself up from the floor even before she completely turned over, running even before she was completely upright. Bouncing off something warm and solid. Not some*thing*, some*one*. She reeled backward from the impact, arms windmilling to keep her balance, and she landed smartly on her backside.

Will drew in a deep breath. "'Kenz," he said with weary patience, and then he shook his head, swallowing whatever words had been on his tongue. "I found wood, and there was a big pot and some flint on the shelves. I started a fire to get some water boiling."

Blood bloomed on the left side of his shirt – fresh blood. He'd broken open the barely sealed edges of his wound, probably while gathering the wood. Her dread evaporated, and her lungs drew in air.

"You thought I left you."

She nodded.

"I hunted up wood dry enough to burn, spent an hour getting it to burn so I could heat water to cook your cattails in, and you're in here thinking I left you."

"Yeah," Mac agreed faintly.

"Goddammit, Mackenzie."

He bent and retrieved her pack from the floor, then walked away without another word, limping slightly.

Mac groaned. Great. Silent-and-thoughtful was a mood she could deal with, but silent-and-sulky was not. She brushed dirt and debris off her socks and pulled on her boots. Best just to get it over with – her apology, that was. Perhaps if she offered it quickly, it would ward off his bad mood.

He wasn't visible at first glance, so for a moment she thought he really *had* left her this time. But then she rounded the smaller building – maybe that's where they once offered coffee and snacks – and saw him at an old-fashioned hand pump. He had shed his bloody shirt and was rinsing it under the water. The water stopped, and he pumped the handle again. With every flex of his muscles, his wound gaped open and spilled a thin rivulet of blood down his chest.

"Here, let me do that." She held out her hand for the shirt.

"I've got it." He wrung water from the shirt and held it up to the sun, inspecting the stain. "That's as good as it gets."

"We should eat, and then we should boil some clean water to wash our clothes in. We're going to need fresh socks to cover your injury."

"The clothes would need time to dry." She shrugged. "Which means you want to stay here for a couple of days." She simply looked at him silently. "And that means we'll be even farther behind reaching the mountain pass before snow flies."

"We won't reach it if you get an infection, either."

Expressionless, he stared at his stained shirt, then looked at the fire and then around the surrounding landscape and finally up at the sky. He didn't need to tell her what he was doing; she knew him well enough by now to know that he was concerned about fuel for the fire and the clear weather holding out.

"Three days," he said. "Counting today. We'd better get busy."

He led her around to leeward side of the smaller outbuilding, where he'd built a fire in a knee-high steel drum perforated with holes. He'd rigged a grate from discarded metal rods he'd found by the drum. The pot of water sat atop the rods, emitting a fine cloud of steam.

"Where'd you find this?"

"Just sitting here. I figured this must be where they used it. It's kind of rusty, but I think it will hold for a few days. Just don't cut yourself on it."

Yeah, a good dose of tetanus would make even their Revenant troubles pale in comparison.

She left him tending the fire and went scavenging for a sharp-edged rock to use to cut up the cattails, already salivating.

Mackenzie hadn't thought Will's face could get any greener, yet as she sponged away the crusted blood and pus from the beginning of infection, he'd gone a delicate shade that reminded her of mold.

The long-departed James Fraley left behind an ancient first aid kit that included, of all things, a suture kit, all sealed in a heavy-duty plastic bag with a zipper closure. She expected the plastic bag to crumble when she touched it, like so many of them did, but this one was made of durable material.

The crown jewel of the kit turned out to be a small printed handbook of basic first aid, with several pages of handwritten instructions for more serious injuries. Following Fraley's neat but cramped penmanship while also keeping a wary eye on Will, lest he topple over in a faint, was testing every ounce of patience Mac possessed.

"Is that...the last...one?" Will asked through gritted teeth.

"No. I should do probably"—she consulted the instructions—"three more."

"Christ."

"I'm sorry. I'm going as fast as I can."

"It's okay."

It didn't seem okay as she threaded the curved needle through his skin and he broke out in a sweat. She tugged the suture filament, and his eyes rolled up in his head. He spilled sideways. Malnourished and exhausted as she was, she had only enough strength to ease him into a prone position on the platform bed. Well, if she worked quickly, she would be able to finish the last two sutures while he was unconscious, which would be better for them both. She couldn't stand to see how much the wound pained him, especially while she fiddled with it.

She tied off the knot and was cutting the filament when he stirred. His eyes fluttered open. They were the color of root beer when the sun hit them.

"All done."

"Great." He closed his eyes again. Some color was leeching back into his face. He started to sit up, but she planted a hand in his chest and pinned him down.

"Stay there for a while. The cattails shouldn't take too long to cook. We can eat and then start on the rest of our wounds."

"'Kenz..."

"We both have blisters on our feet that are bleeding and oozing. We can't risk infection. Once we've eaten. I'll start some fresh water boiling and wash all the socks."

"How will they dry?" he asked practically.

"I thought we could bring in the metal fire drum once the flames have died down. The embers will keep us warm, and we can hang the socks over the edge. They should be dry by morning."

"Or scorched."

"Ye of little faith."

His eyes opened. The hopelessness in them stole her smile.

"Faith in what, Mackenzie? We're in a desperate spot. We were better off running from the hunters back home than we are out here on our own. No food, limited fuel for heat, no shelter most of the time, no idea where we're going or when – *if* – we'll ever get there."

"We'll get there."

"I'm not long on faith right now, 'Kenz. No offense."

"None taken. Rest a while. I'll tend to things."

She draped his jacket over him and pulled the door mostly closed to minimize the drafts. He didn't call her back, and a while later she heard him snoring softly.

Did he think she didn't have her own doubts, that as she cut cattail roots with a sharp hunk of basalt she didn't wonder if Elijah Riemer hadn't been one step short of insane by sending her out of the city? Come to that, did he think she *wanted* to eat cattail roots as her first meal in two days?

If she lost faith, she would have no reason to continue to take one step after another. She had to believe in Elijah; she had to believe that there was something better than what the Stronghold was offering. That belief was what caused this mess, and if she lost faith – well, then, it would have all been for nothing. There would be no reason not to just lie down and wait for death, and it wouldn't matter in what form it came: hunger, thirst, or exposure. Cannibal or Revenant.

She dropped the roots into the water, which was sending up a promising cloud of steam. As they sank below the surface, she sorted through the small pile of sticks and tumbleweeds they gathered for fuel and tried to estimate how long it would last. Probably the day – she must wash their socks; there was no getting around that, and she would need fresh water for that. The water came out the pump at a frigid temperature and it would take a good amount of wood to heat it to a temperature adequate for sterilizing.

After checking on Will, who was sprawled on his bed and snoring steadily – she searched the area for more fuel, gathering a respectable pile of pine branches from a tree a small distance away. A few more tumbleweeds would ensure kindling – no shortage of those things. She didn't even have to look far; clumps of them clogged the inverted corners of a windbreak wall.

She let Will sleep until the cattail roots were ready and then she shook him awake. They ate in silence, sucking the starch from the fibers of the roots. It wasn't the tastiest of meals – a bit like potato but stringier, with a greener taste. But it was hot and it was nourishing, and that's what mattered most. She gathered enough that they could have another large meal tomorrow. After that – well, they'd be hungry for a while until they happened upon another pond or a town.

Will slept again while she heated clean water to wash the socks. She added their undergarments to the load, both thankful to be out of them and self-conscious at the lack of them under her clothes. And he slept through her wrestling the metal drum full of hot coals into their room, waking only when she was hanging their garments over its edges and onto a makeshift clothesline she'd strung close to it.

"Where'd you get the rope?"

"It was in the room next door. There was another metal drum like this, but it looked kind of disgusting."

"I would have helped get that in here." He jerked his thumb at the fire pit.

"And that's why I let you sleep. I didn't stitch you up only to make you break all the sutures by hauling this around. It wasn't heavy."

He sat up. His color was better, although it could be a trick of light. The day was waning, and the afternoon sun cast a flattering golden hue over everything.

"Any more of those roots left?"

She hesitated. "Enough for a big meal tomorrow. Or a couple of smaller ones between now and when we leave."

"Let's go for smaller. Keep the belly from grumbling longer."

She shrugged. "I'll heat more water. We might find some more cattails along the way."

"Not until we're out of the desert, I'd wager." He hesitated, then plowed on in the determined way she associated with men talking to women whom they thought were being deliberately un-reasonable.

"Mackenzie...I think we're going to have a really hard time of it if we keep going further."

"It hasn't been hard up to now?"

"I mean it's going to get harder. Bad weather. Lack of food and water. Lack of shelter – in case you hadn't noticed, we're in a kind of desert wasteland. We're going to be coming to bigger towns and cities, which means confrontations with Revenants are a lot more likely."

"I'm aware of all of this." Even though she struggled to keep the bite out of her tone, his expression told her he'd heard it loud and clear.

"We'll be approaching the mountains soon," he continued quietly. "It will get colder. Rain, sleet, and snow. God knows what the roadways are like, or if there is anywhere we can shelter where we can find food and water and fuel for heat."

"If we follow the symbol—"

He interrupted. "Yeah, about that. What if we miss one, 'Kenz? We could end up freezing or starving to death because we were too tired or it was dark or the weather was bad and we didn't see it."

She digested this silently. All true, everything he'd said. They were taking a huge risk, following a symbol across a land barren of civilization.

Have faith, Mackenzie. Eli had his reasons for sending you this way. And he knew it would be a hard journey. So it stands to reason he knew you could survive it.

With a remarkable calm she didn't feel, she said evenly, "I sense you have a different idea about where we should go from here."

He drew in a steadying breath. "Yeah, I do. I think we should stop at the next city, close enough that we can go in to scavenge and stock up for the winter, but not so close that Revenants are a big problem. We could winter over and continue in the spring."

"And what if Riemer's on his way? If he passes us and we never show up wherever the symbol is leading us, what then? He'll think I'm dead, Will. I can't do that to him."

"Mackenzie, we've been through this. He's not coming. He couldn't get away."

"Maybe he managed to get away after you left. You don't know – you weren't there."

He held up a hand, his eyes rolling heavenward. "I'm not going to argue about this right now. It's not the most important thing, although I will say that Riemer wouldn't exactly be thrilled if you got yourself killed trying to travel through the mountains in winter."

She bit her tongue on the waspish words that wanted to tumble from her mouth. No good would come of it; it would just be wasted breath. "Let me sleep on it. I'll get us some water and bring in some fuel for the fire before it gets dark."

His mouth opened, but she slipped out the door before he could reply. At the hand pump, she filled their canteen and the pot, set them just inside the door, and then gathered some sticks and tumbleweeds from her stash to keep the embers from dying.

The coals took off the worst of the chill in the room by the time she slid the iron bar into place, securing their sanctuary for the night. She tossed in a tumbleweed and a couple of sticks. The fire flared for a moment, making her wet socks steam, and then died back. She put the grate in place over the open top and set the pot on it to heat.

Will was quiet as he cut cattail roots, but she caught him sending her frequent speculative looks, which she ignored as she tended to her blistered feet with the crushed leaves of a sheltered clump of yarrow she'd found behind the windbreak wall. When he finished with the roots and cleaned his hands, he took the yarrow as silently as she offered it.

It was only after they ate and were lying down to sleep that she finally spoke.

"I promise I'll think about it. Goodnight, Will."

"Goodnight, obstinate female."

She cracked a faint smile, and he closed his eyes, seeming to fall asleep remarkably fast.

Slumber was a long time coming for Mackenzie, however. With no pressure and no distractions, she was finally able to consider his point.

He was right, of course. The way was dangerous, the weather treacherous, starvation imminent. And yet...

And yet, there was Elijah, who sent her out of the city in September, knowing she might not make it to the mountains — if indeed that was their destination — before snowfall.

Please stay alive.

Not just while she denounced memorabilia of Bon Moreau, but always.

Your life is precious.

And he wouldn't risk a precious life unless he was sure that life would prevail.

I'm sorry, Will. Over obstacles, through dangerous weather, in spite of starvation, she would press on. With or without him.

27

Mackenzie lifted her foot and took another step in spite of the invisible weight that tried to drag it back to the ground. The weight had a name – exhaustion – and it was every bit as inexorable as gravity.

A gust of wind threw sleet into her face. Will turned away from the wind, but he didn't stop walking, although their pace was that of a half-dead snail. The skin around his eyes, the only visible part of this face through the ski mask, was chapped and raw. She was afraid to finally find a mirror, because she was sure hers was just as bad. They'd tried to find ski goggles, but they'd been chased out of the winter sports store by a pack of Revenants hiding in the fitting rooms. There were too many to fight, and they hadn't possessed the strength for it anyway. As it was, they'd been lucky to escape into the daylight with heavy coats, gloves, boots, and face masks.

"There has to be shelter soon." The howling wind stole her words and flung them off the mountain. Maybe she hadn't even spoken. Perhaps it was in her head. She likely had no voice anyway; the biting cold scorched her throat and it seemed they hadn't spoken in days.

They'd left their desert shelter ten days ago, the last seven of which nearly convinced Mac that Will was right about wintering over and crossing the mountains in spring. The higher the elevation, the worse the road became, until finally it went completely to hell, washed out by floods. It was not much more than a very wide deer trail, rough and pitted from spring run-off, pebbled with rocks and debris from the woods. They spent the last three nights huddled under the broad branches of mountain hemlocks at the side of the road, too afraid of hypothermia to sleep. The day before yesterday, they passed a huge lake, and the wind blowing across it was so mind-numbingly frigid Mackenzie nearly just sat down and waited to die.

Will snagged her sleeve and tugged her along beside him, though where he'd found the energy was a mystery. Their last meal was the inner bark of a white pine tree that luckily had been shorn from the top by the wind, splintering the outer layer of bark. With a rock and most of their remaining reserves of strength and vigor, they were able to peel off enough of the inner bark to stop their stomachs from grumbling. That was been yesterday. Or maybe the day before. She wasn't certain; the days all bled together, full of cold, biting air and sleet and pain and hunger and bone-deep weariness.

The mountain rose by degrees — sometimes steep degrees, sometimes a gradual incline that seemed to last an eternity. The muscles in her calves and thighs screamed with each step. Her feet, thankfully, were so numb she could no longer feel the broken blisters and rubbed-raw flesh.

The road curved. It flattened for a stretch and then rose again. Curved again. Rose again. Mackenzie trudged along, half a pace behind Will. She was going to die on this road. Her body would be picked clean by the crows and the eagles and the hawks, perhaps by the wolves they'd heard singing in the night. Her bones would be washed into the mountain ravine by spring run-off, and no one would ever know what happened to her.

It sounded like a fine thing just about now.

They rounded yet another curve. Will stopped abruptly, and Mac ran into him, knocking him to his knees in the mud.

"Shelter," he said.

She stared, unable to comprehend what she was seeing. The hotel huddled before a white-frosted mountain, with a portico supported by stone pillars and a metal roof that was red by design or by rust. Scrawled in black paint on its white clapboard siding, the sun-and-moon symbol beckoned like a long-lost, treasured friend.

Relief flooded through her, almost immediately followed by panic. She couldn't move her feet another inch. She was going to die within sight of sanctuary.

Will laboriously pushed himself to his feet, swayed, and staggered back to her. "Come on, 'Kenz," he said gently.

Well, she supposed he meant to sound gentle; his voice rasped harshly out of his raw throat. He tugged her sleeve, propelling her forward, and her feet somehow received the signal her brain was sending even though her brain wasn't quite certain her feet were still there.

The last fifty yards to the hotel were the most agonizing. Shelter, warmth and hopefully food were close – so close! – but they were tired and moving so slowly that it took nearly fifteen minutes to get there. She expected the doors to be locked, and she wasn't disappointed. A quick search around the door frame yielded a nail on which hung the key to survival.

They spilled into the lobby, closing the door and locking it behind them. Out of the howling wind for the first time in days, the silence of the building seemed unnatural. For a long moment, they simply stared around the room, unable to quite believe they were out of the storm. A stone fireplace opposite the reception desk was flanked by two hand-crafted sofas with thick cushions, either relatively new or remarkably preserved. Firewood was stacked from floor to ceiling in one corner, and a plain silver tin on the raised hearth promised "MATCHES." A recessed compartment in the wall by a set of stairs looked like it had once held shelves and glass doors. Both were long gone, and the alcove was packed with all manner of books.

"We died," Mackenzie said faintly. "We died and this is heaven."

"Nope," Will disagreed. "When we thaw out, we're going to believe we've arrived in hell."

He wasn't wrong. Pooling their meager physical resources, they somehow they got a fire started. They each claimed a sofa, sitting as close to the hearth as they could, soaking in the heat. Warming skin began to prickle and burn. Nerve endings shrieked pain as they thawed. The heat burned the chapped skin around her eyes.

She closed her eyes, too exhausted to fight the pain. Let it come; it meant she was alive. Her stomach grumbled but it was a distant complaint, one she didn't have the energy to address. Something hot pressed against her hand, and she opened her eyes to find Will looming over her, pushing a mug into her hand.

Hunger thinned his body and sharpened his features, and exhaustion pulled his face into lines of weariness, but he smiled a genuine smile.

"Coffee," he said.

Ambrosia, he meant. She breathed in the exotic aroma and savored her first sip. Coffee was a rarity; it didn't grow well in their climate, and often the crops failed. They could sometimes find it around the city in cans at the old supermarkets, old and stale but still coffee.

"I fell asleep," she said. Will had the fire roaring, and heat poured into the room, bringing the temperature to a comfortable level. She must have been out for a couple of hours. She cast a glance at the wood pile, wondering how long it would last them even with careful rationing.

"Yeah, for a while. I did too. When I woke up, I started poking around. Made sure the rooms on the main floor were clear – lucky break, that. We were both asleep at the same time; if someone or something were here, we could have been ambushed."

She made a face. "We were so tired, I don't think either one of us could have stayed awake. We should make sure the rest of the hotel is cleared before we get too comfortable. And I hope you found more wood."

"A whole room full of it. I kid you not – the whole room is packed with it. You can barely open the door." He grinned, tucking himself carefully into the corner of his sofa, cradling his mug of coffee. "And – you're going to like this – the kitchen is stocked."

"With what?"

"Well, food, obviously. A lot of those military meals like we found in that motor home. Canned vegetables and fruit. Dried meat."

She made a face. "Hundred-and-twenty year old meat. Tasty."

"Seems fresh. This place is kept stocked for people like us, 'Kenz."

"What kind of people are we?"

He considered this for a long time before replying. "Refugees."

They finished their coffee in silence and then ate until the worst of their hunger pangs subsided. Mackenzie could have eaten her weight in military pouch meals, but Will only allowed them two, saying it was better to go slow so they didn't vomit everything back up.

Fortified by hot food, heat, and rest, they explored the hotel, lighting their way with a pair of propane lanterns, taking note of provisions and vulnerable areas. There didn't seem to be many – if any – of the latter on the main level. The upper floor, which overlooked the lobby and was bordered by a knotted-pine balcony and accessible by a set of stairs on a wall adjacent to the reception desk, was filled with gloomy shadows. A wooden plaque nailed to the wall at the foot of the staircase cautioned them in woodburned letters:

REVENANT-FREE AS
OF MID-SEPTEMBER.
PLEASE USE CAUTION
IF ARRIVING AFTER
SEPTEMBER OR IF
FRONT DOOR WAS NOT
SECURED WHEN
YOU ARRIVED.

Will brushed his finger over the sun-and-moon symbol, the same one they had followed into the mountains. Instead of being reassured by it, he looked annoyed. A pang of guilt sent a twinge through her heart. She couldn't blame his animosity toward this symbol of the underground. They had starved, froze, walked their feet raw, and had been ambushed by cannibals – twice – while allowing this symbol to lead them ever farther from everything familiar and trusted. Exiled as she was, Mac had little choice but to leave the immediate area – she doubted that the Council would ever abandon their mission to kill her as long as she was in the city. But she wouldn't have gone as far if not for this symbol. And Will – well, he hadn't needed to leave at all. Through Mac's own naiveté, Will had been dragged from his home and half-killed trying to see her to safety. And it was not lost on her that they were lucky to have made it to the hotel. If not for finding it when they did, they would probably be lying dead right now in the sleet and freezing mountain air.

A window at the end of the hallway let in enough dull, grey light to reflect off the doors lining the walls on both sides of the long corridor.

"Look at all the rooms," Will whispered, stopping by the balcony. He seemed entranced. Mac stopped alongside him, a glance at his face telling her it wasn't awe he was experiencing, but despondency. There must be at least sixty rooms on this level.

"We could each take a side. It only takes a minute to make sure they're clear."

"It only takes a minute to die when you run into a Revenant," he said sharply. "We stay together."

The rooms were mostly identical. The only things crouching in the dark corners were miscellaneous pieces of furniture left behind in long-ago purges, possibly burned for warmth in those first desperate years of the Upheaval. The bedsteads were free of mattresses and bedding, most likely carted off the mountain to more livable climates. It would be an uncomfortable winter with no blankets, but with enough wood, they could keep the fire going and stay reasonably warm as long as they didn't sleep far from the fireplace.

It took three hours to check the upstairs and assure themselves it remained Revenant-free. By that time, the nausea of hunger made Mac desperate to complete their task and fill her belly again. When he finally declared they were alone in the hotel and the building was secure, the nausea gave way to a gnawing hollowness. He allowed her two more pouch entrees and a dessert, followed by a pot of green tea, a huge canister of which he'd found in the well-stocked kitchen. They sweetened it with honey that was just starting to crystallize in the jar and sat sipping it near the warmth of the fire.

"We're going to have to figure out how to ration the supplies," Will said after a long, comfortable silence. They were both enjoying the safety and sense of well-being that had become a rarity in their lives since leaving the Stronghold.

There was a second room full of wood, across the hallway from the first one Will found. The room next to it was filled with clothing. Mac nearly cried in relief and would have been content to dive right into the neat stacks of clothes but for Will's insistence that they eat and rest first.

Down a short hallway on the other side of the lobby were roomy conference rooms with fireplaces. In the largest of these, they found the missing mattresses, up on end and packed between the walls like large, cushy books. In one of the smaller ones, bedding was stuffed into thick plastic sheaths and, in some cases, oiled sailcloth bags and stacked neatly along one wall. Mac explored the plastic, expecting to find it brittle and surprised that it was not.

"When do you think the weather will clear up enough for us to risk traveling? April?"

He shrugged. "Maybe even May. We're stuck here for at least the next six months, 'Kenz. We should take inventory tomorrow, watch how much wood we use over the next couple of days and then calculate how much we have in stock so we can adjust how much we use."

"We can always chop some if we think we're going to run low. There was an axe and a splitting wedge in one of the wood rooms. And one of those big hammers."

"Sledge hammer. And that is a maul, not an axe."

"Don't they do the same thing?"

"Nope." He flashed her a grin. "My father was on the wood crew. The heads on splitting mauls are shaped differently than those on faller's axes."

This was the first time Will mentioned one of his parents. She assumed he was orphaned, like her, because so many of the Stronghold's children were.

"Does he still work the wood crew?" She asked it casually so she wouldn't sound like she was probing.

He shook his head, sipped his tea, breathed in the clean, soothing aroma. She thought he wasn't going to answer, but then he offered her a twisted smile. "No. The Revenants got him in the woods one day. Overcast day, the crew stayed too long. A pack crept up on them and attacked. He held them at bay while the others escaped. All that was ever found of him was a scrap of material from his shirt and a couple of bones."

"I'm sorry," she whispered.

"Yeah, me too."

"And your mom?"

His smile was genuine this time. "Works in the wool room. Spinner. She always smells like lanolin and dye."

"You left her to come with me."

"Yes."

An indescribable sorrow filled her as she thought of the rough mountain road, the desert with its sparse shelter and random cannibals, the ruined bridge with the snakelike Revenants. There was no going back; he was stuck here, the journey too perilous to survive alone.

"I'm sorry."

"Your need was greater." He struggled to his feet, tired muscles visibly protesting. "I'll get us some clean clothes, then maybe we can heat some water and wash up, go to sleep clean."

And she could check his sutures and their raw, blistered feet. Maybe somewhere in all these rooms of supplies, they would find a first aid kit. She had brought along James Fraley's kit, but it was limited and old. What they needed now were salves created within the last couple of months, not something from twelve decades ago.

When he returned with clean clothes, he rummaged in the kitchen until he found a pot, and set to heating water over the fire. She went down the hall to choose bedding. It seemed that whole sets of bedding were packaged together, so she took two in colors she liked and dropped one at the end of each sofa.

"Did you find a first aid kit in the kitchen, by any chance?"

He was using a metal poker to fish around in the fire and barely glanced up. "No, but I only took a quick look around for food."

"What are you doing?"

"Those rocks in the bottom of the fireplace – the ones I built the fire on top of? I think they were for setting pots of water on. I'm trying to get them out from under the wood."

"Where'd you get the water?" Working plumbing was unheard of. At the Stronghold, their water was drawn from wells, and for large quantities, there was a hand-pump like the one at the leisure stop.

"Rain barrel on the kitchen patio. We're going to have to figure out the water situation."

"It would have been nice if they'd left some detailed instructions," Mac said. "Like where the first aid kit is, how we get water, who they are and where they're leading us."

Will gave her a sharp look. "That's too convenient to even hope for."

"I know. I'll be back in a few minutes."

She was, carrying a large plastic tote packed with jars full of herbs and salves and creams and ointment, all carefully labeled in neat handwriting. She set it on her sofa, meeting Will's wide-eyed stare with one of her own.

"Who the hell *are* these people?"

BLINK OF AN EYE

28

The snow began in earnest in early November after some preliminary flurries, as though the mountain performed a few test runs before getting down to business. It was a strange feeling, watching the snow pile higher and higher every day, like being entombed. Will assured her that there were bound to be a couple of melts during the winter, but she thought he looked a bit worried himself.

Will's knife wound healed with only a thin silver scar left behind as evidence. Mackenzie cut out the sutures several days after they arrived at the hotel, and he worked the muscles slowly back into shape. Their feet healed quickly once they were no longer subjecting the torn, raw tissue to further abuse.

The kitchen had once been part of a pancake house attached to the hotel via the lobby. Cleared out of all tables and chairs except a couple of ragged, patched restaurant booths, the dining area served as storage for yet more wood. The kitchen itself was remarkably free of clutter. The pantry overflowed with canned goods, and boxes of military pouch meals lined a couple of walls, stacked in rows four deep. Just out the back door of the kitchen, a hand pump brought up cool, sweet water from a well. Across the ruined highway and a short way into the woods was a creek in case the hand pump failed.

A thorough inventory of the kitchen pantry's contents assured them they wouldn't starve, even without careful rationing. Mackenzie insisted on drawing up a plan that would ration their provisions while still keeping them adequately nourished. They would need to take food when they left in the spring, and she didn't trust that they would find any on their way down the other side of the mountains. Neither did she want to leave the hotel with no resources in case someone else needed its sanctuary before it could be restocked. *If* it could be restocked.

They limited themselves to four pairs of clothes – sleepwear, two outfits they alternated throughout the week, and another outfit to wear while they were waiting for the others to dry after laundering. Between meals and clean-up and tending the fireplace, they read and told stories and practiced training maneuvers once they'd rested and healed.

She thought Will's strange, pensive moods would end once they reached shelter and regularly filled their bellies, but as November bled slowly into December, his brooding silences sometimes stretched for days. Thanksgiving was celebrated with two pouches each of chicken and noodles in gravy and a blueberry turnover. Midway through their meal, Will set down his pouch, started to say something, and then just as suddenly started eating again, studiously avoiding her gaze.

December brought several howling snowstorms, and it was with difficulty that Will, donning snowshoes he'd found in the clothes room, found a suitable specimen for a Christmas tree. It was only after he'd succeeded in chopping it down and dragging it back to the hotel that it occurred to them that they didn't have a tree stand. Annoyed, he tied a length of rope around the trunk, took a picture off the wall, and hooked the rope on the empty nail. Her gaze alternating between the tree, which swayed precariously on the nail, and Will's scowling face, Mac wisely did not remind him that they also had no Christmas ornaments.

Midway through the night, the tree slipped its moorings and crashed onto his sofa, jabbing prickly limbs into his ribs and leaving behind sticky sap. Bleeding from several scrapes and cursing violently, he stuffed it unceremoniously into a far corner of the lobby and became taciturn and grouchy for several days preceding the holiday.

On Christmas day, he was still quiet and thoughtful but seemed to have made peace with whatever bothered him. Using an old recipe book she found on the bookshelves and some of the few pantry staples on hand, she tried her hand at making a cake that didn't require eggs or milk and baked it in the heat from the fire. Aside from being gooey in the center and a little charred on the edges, it was delicious, and they gorged themselves until all that remained were the crumbs in the baking pan.

Will found a battered copy of Charles Dickens' *A Christmas Carol*, and they took turns reading out loud throughout the day as the other went about chores. Dinner was beef ravioli followed by apple turnovers, both eaten out of pouches. Try as she might, she couldn't help but think of the Christmas feast that would be laid out in the Stronghold, the concrete corridors filled with the smell of baking rolls and roasting turkey. As the afternoon waned, Mackenzie curled up under a blanket next to Will on his sofa while he read out loud, her eyes closed, her mind creating the scene from the words he read.

"Are there no…" Will trailed off. She waited, and when he didn't continue, she opened her eyes to find him staring fixedly at the page.

"Will? Are you all right?"

He didn't answer. He didn't even appear to have heard her. His fingers clenched around the edges of the book, rumpling the pages.

"Will?" she tried again, this time tentatively. He speared her with a blazing look from which she barely managed not to recoil.

"Why don't we just stay here, 'Kenz? In the spring, when your underground people come to check on the hotel, we could convince them to let us stay on as caretakers."

She drew in a deep breath. "I don't know, Will. Those pouch meals – there isn't an endless supply to keep us going forever, you know. Those will run out some day."

"We could get some goats and chickens and stable them in another part of the hotel. It could work. We'd have warm shelter, plenty of wood for fuel, no Revenant problems in the winter…"

Mackenzie was silent for a long time, her mind racing. A tempting thought, to see the end of this hellish journey and find safe haven. But how long until they drove each other crazy, until they craved the company of others, until they went stark raving mad in this white-and-green wilderness? And what of Elijah if—*when*—he finally caught up with them? Would he be so eager to co-habitate with Will Crawford, whom he viewed with a modicum of suspicion?

"I really want to know what's at the end of the line, Will. Where the symbol is leading us, I mean. And living in the mountains…I don't know. It's awful cold. And I think I heard an avalanche the other day – what happens if one comes down on the hotel?"

He stared at her without speaking for so long that she became uneasy, as though he were evaluating not just her words, but *her*.

"And when we find out where this all leads"—he gestured to

the sign on the wall that bore the symbol of the underground—
"what then? We just…integrate with whatever society they've created? What if we don't like their way of doing things?"

"Well," she said slowly. "I didn't exactly like the way the
Stronghold did some things. We aren't going to get our every desire, Will, but we can at least hope for something better than what
we left."

"It wasn't that bad."

"It was oppressive. I didn't realize it until we got out from under the Council just how controlling they were, right down to what
you could criticize."

"That's Bon talking again."

"Well, you've been the one with me for months now, Will, and
I'm still saying the same things. It's not Bon's words; Bon just
opened my eyes."

He shrugged off her comment, neither agreeing nor disagree-
ing. "And when we get there – will I still be with you or will you
just run off into your Shangri-La and forget about me?"

"Is that what you think of me?" At first she thought the crackling fire stole her words, she had spoken so quietly, but then he
shook his head. "We're friends, Will. We'll always be friends."

"Maybe that's not what I want."

She flinched. His words struck a blow as surely and solidly as if
they possessed fists of their own. "Wow. Okay. I guess I just
thought—"

He pushed her against the back of the sofa and kissed her, his
hand against her chest pinning her in place. Mac's mind went blank
with shock. What the *hell* did he think he was doing?

She shoved a hand against his chest, trying to wedge him away
from her. Even after their arduous journey and his injury, he was
formidably strong. She turned her head and lifted her chin, breaking the contact of their lips. Will pressed his to her throat, breathing
raggedly against her skin.

"Mackenzie," he whispered, but in her mind she heard Elijah
Riemer breathing her name after his heart-stopping kiss, saw Elijah
Riemer's eyes, wide and green as a spring meadow, tasted mint and
lime from Elijah Riemer's lips.

She wrenched away from Will. "No. *No.*"

He caught her arm and tried to pull her back into his embrace.

"Why not, Mackenzie? There's just the two of us here, no one to object."

"*I* object! Will, you don't understand!"

"What's to understand? What more is there? There's just you and me and *this*." He snaked his arm around her waist and dragged her against him, pressing her close.

Oh, lord… "This" was quite evident, mashed against him pelvis-to-pelvis as she was. How had this happened? Why hadn't she noticed it? Seeing him as her traveling companion and protector, and eventually as her friend and partner, had she missed the telltale signs of a growing attraction on his part, subconsciously dismissing it because she didn't feel the same way?

She closed her eyes, took a steadying breath, and said, "I want to be with Elijah Riemer."

"You only think you do. *I'm* the one who's here, the one who walked two hundred miles with you, protected you, took care of you, for *months*. He was only there for a few weeks."

"On Riemer's orders."

He scoffed. "You think I came because Riemer told me to? I came because I *wanted* to."

She opened her eyes, tried again. "I'm waiting for him to catch up."

"You'll be waiting a long time."

"I'm a patient girl. I don't care if it takes five years, he will find me, and I will be waiting."

He let go of her, spinning off the sofa, raking a hand through his hair as he paced. Finally, he rounded on her, his internal struggle reaching breaking point. She shrank into the corner of the sofa, wishing she'd chosen to sit on her own couch, closer to her machete just in case his behavior needed to be corrected with a show of force.

"He's not coming."

"He is. Or he will. Eventually."

"He's. Not. Coming."

"Will, just stop. I don't want to talk about this anymore. You obviou—"

"Riemer is dead, Mackenzie!"

He'd ripped out her lungs. He must have, because she couldn't breathe. Her heart stuttered and then thudded wildly, trying to escape the airless confines of her chest.

Through numb lips, she whispered, "What did you just say?"

"Elijah Riemer is dead. Why do you think *I'm* here? The only reason for him to not be with you right now is because he *can't* be. Ever."

Her tongue struggled to form words her brain forgot how to say. "You're...you're lying. Why? Why would you... how could you say... you're just..."

"They came for him three days after you were exiled and arrested him. I don't know why – I think they were watching him, somehow knew he was preparing to leave. The day before I came to get you, they announced his execution to the Stronghold. They didn't tell us why, just that he'd committed crimes against the settlement."

Just like Bon, oh Jesus, just like they had done with Bon, no public trial, just a murder in a back room of the jail, with no more thought to it than they gave to butchering a hog.

She slid to the floor, desperate to move but no longer able to control her limbs. Her nerve endings buzzed, her mind disconnected from her body, and she huddled before the fire, not feeling its warmth, not feeling anything but the ice that flooded her veins.

"You didn't tell me," she whispered. "You let me think...all this time..."

Will's tone gentled, lowering several decibels. "I knew you wouldn't leave the city if I told you they'd killed him. So I...I just let you believe...until we were far enough away... I made a promise to keep you safe!"

"A promise," she repeated dully.

A promise. Big deal. Who cared? Elijah made a promise, too – what was it he'd said? *I promise I'll be there as soon as I can. I promise!* Then he kissed her so hard he'd drawn blood, and the salty copper taste had still been with her when she'd found sleep in the dubious safety of the shed. The cut his teeth opened in the soft lining of her lip was still healing long after he'd died.

"When I found you at that house...if I'd told you...you would have gone back to the Stronghold, wouldn't you?"

"Yes."

"To avenge him."

"Yes."

"Now you see why I said nothing? They'd have slaughtered you, Mackenzie!"

She came to her feet snarling, and hit him in the chest, driving him backward. "Slaughtered me like they slaughtered him, you mean? How could you not tell me? You had no right to keep that from me! You had no right to decide for me whether I lived or died!"

"I promised him! It was his only request after he was arrested. He asked to see me, asked me to see you safely to your destination."

She hit him again. "Yeah? And did he tell you where that *is*, pray tell? Because I sure don't know where the hell I'm going or why!"

With one final shove, she turned her back to him, burying her face in her hands. Her eyes stung, but she couldn't bring the tears. They hung just behind her eyes, salty curtains of pain that clouded her vision but refused to fall and bring catharsis.

Elijah is dead. Oh God, it couldn't be possible. What was she going to do now?

Her hands fell away from her face. "I'm going back."

"What!" He grabbed her sleeve. "Are you crazy? We can't just go waltzing back across hundreds of miles! That's suicide, Mackenzie!"

She yanked away. "No one asked you to come."

He threw his hands in the air in frustration. "Oh, by all means, go by yourself, because you can handle snake Revenants and cannibals and every other fucking thing we've encountered all by yourself, eh?"

"I'll get back to the Stronghold or die trying."

He was silent for so long that she thought he'd given up the argument, or perhaps he'd fallen down dead of an exasperation-induced stroke. Or from guilt. She found a vicious satisfaction in that last thought.

Then he said softly, "I see. A suicide mission. And for what, Mackenzie? The man died buying your freedom. He risked everything to get you out of there before they came for you and executed you, and you're going to repay him by wasting your life on a senseless act of vengeance – an act you probably won't live to see completed."

"It's none of your business. You lost the right to have any say in what I do the second you lied to me about him."

"Oh, that's perfect. You'd have been dead weeks ago if not for me."

"Is that what this is about? You feel I owe you something because you've kept me alive?" Mackenzie had no word for the emotion surging inside her, a mixture of anger and betrayal and disgust that left a slimy film across her soul. A wave of nausea brought a cold sweat all over her body.

His tone was flat and emotionless. "No. You don't owe me anything. I just thought that maybe, after all we've been through together..."

He trailed off, staring at her silently for so long that the urge to run and hide became too strong to repress. She sidestepped him, moving toward her sofa and her weapon. Will backed away from her.

"It appears I was mistaken. I'll be in the dining room, if you need me for anything." The last was said with an ironic twist to his mouth, underscoring his silent subtext: *but we both know that you don't need me at all.*

She watched him go, his spine held straight and stiff by wounded pride, his movements made with an economy of energy, his footfalls the silent tread of a hunter. When he vanished into the dining room, she sank down on the raised hearth as close to the fire as she dared in an effort to drive away the chill.

Elijah Riemer was dead, and Will wanted to take his place, not that Eli really *had* a place. Four weeks wasn't enough time to explore the possibility of a real relationship.

And with that in mind, why was she so resistant to having that real relationship with Will? She didn't find him repulsive; he was certainly attractive and his personality pleasant and even-tempered, his brooding notwithstanding. And maybe, under different circumstances, before Elijah...

Before Elijah what? Secluded her from the rest of the Stronghold so he could more easily smuggle her out of the Council's reach? Before he turned her loose in the wide, dangerous world to fend for herself or die trying? Before he died and left her drifting in the wind, relying on a man he hadn't quite trusted?

There it was: Elijah Riemer's legacy to her, the reason she

could never, in his permanent absence, involve herself with Will Crawford on a romantic level: Eli hadn't trusted him. And so Mackenzie couldn't completely trust Will, either. Damned if she did, damned if she didn't, and damned if she could find a graceful way out of this situation.

Moving from the hearth to her sofa, she curled into a ball, hugging her knees to her chest like a shield. Maybe if she made herself as small a target as possible, the grief would sail right past her. But her body ached as though she had been beaten, and grief swamped her heart with suffocating blackness.

Merry Christmas, Mac. Here's your broken heart, the gift that keeps on giving for a lifetime.

As the hours crawled and the hotel became dark and brooding, Mackenzie wept.

29

Winter limped toward spring, crippled by Mackenzie's sorrow and Will's disillusionment. While on the road, she kept track of the days with pebbles, selecting a new one from the ground each morning and stowing in her pack. She kept to the routine after arriving at the hotel, but where before she chose small pieces of quartz or granite, now she selected drab grey and nearly black stones that reflected her emotional state, picked from a sheltered patch of ground covered with a thin layer of snow.

By the count of her stones, it was March 13. Some of the days were downright warm lately, and from a distance came the worrisome roar of avalanches. So far, none came down the slope of the mountain behind them, but that didn't mean none would.

Also by the count of her stones, it had been six days since Will last spoke to her, and then it had only been to inform her he found another box of blueberry turnover pouches.

At first, after the disaster of Christmas, he asked after her well-being, his demeanor polite but distant. The distance grew over the weeks until, sometime in mid-February, he stopped communicating, at first for only a day or two, then three or four, and now a week or more. As the weather warmed and the snow melted, she began to worry that he would slip off on his own when the elements were hospitable enough to survive.

She began studying the huge framed map on the wall in the dining room of the restaurant, committing the land to memory as best she could, because getting off the mountain by herself would be tricky enough, but getting through the enormous Revenant-packed city called Seattle on the other side would be impossible. She needed to remember the routes around it.

Will disappeared into the depths of the hotel for long periods of time. Sometimes she saw him poking his head into rooms and then closing the door behind him; sometimes she heard him clattering around in the upstairs corridor where they rarely ventured. And sometimes she swore she heard movement down one of the long halls of rooms when Will was right beside her.

In early April, she decided to draw the route around Seattle with pen and paper. It would be rudimentary at best, but with some judicious notes, she should be able to pinpoint the route by landmarks or, if she were lucky, signage that had withstood the elements and the passage of time.

"Going somewhere?" Will drawled behind her. Although Mac kept herself on alert as always so she wouldn't jump when he spoke or approached, she couldn't help the sudden tensing of her spine and shoulders.

"I think we should avoid that city – it's huge. We'd be killed for certain. If we take these routes around it, we still have to go through some small towns, but we'd stand a better chance of surviving any Revenants we meet."

Not that he would be going with her. She didn't need confirmation of the obvious; everything he did these days shrieked of his intention to separate from her. But sometimes it paid to be prudent, and perhaps his behavior of late was a direct result of believing she no longer wanted him to travel with her. He could be distancing himself because he thought she didn't want him around any longer.

"That adds a lot of miles."

Very noncommittal. Not exactly encouraging.

"Yes, but safer miles. The traveling will be faster because we won't have to fight every inch of the way. Plus, we need to go north anyway."

"Why?"

"The islands are north. There's bound to be boats to get to them."

"The islands? Why the islands?"

"That's where I would settle. Surrounded by ocean, it would be a rare thing for a Revenant to make it across the water. I bet that's where they are. The underground, I mean."

He stared at the map silently. His breath drew in and blew out, a steady susurration in the stillness of the room. She glanced at his profile, held expressionless as he examined the route. More than fearing him, she missed him. Missed his company, his friendship.

"Are you ever going to speak to me again?" she blurted.

He turned to look at her, still silent. His eyes travelled over her face in a leisurely but thorough inspection. Did he see what she saw when she looked in a mirror these days: brown, almond-shaped eyes, swimming with anxiety and underscored with purple shadows? A face paler than it should be, given they had food and shelter, water and warmth? Her near-black hair, always pulled away from her face and secured in a braid or a ponytail these days, accentuated her wan complexion. Worry and sorrow robbed any evidence of restored health from her face.

"I'll cut your hair, if you want," he offered quietly, seeing her fiddle unconsciously with her braid.

Some of the tension left her. Maybe everything would be all right.

They sat on the hearth so he could sweep the cut hair into the flames. The snick of the scissors seemed loud even over the crackling fire. He worked without speaking for a long time.

"I used to braid my mom's hair." His fingers threaded through her damp locks, separating it into sections. A steady tug on her scalp told her he was braiding. "She liked long hair but it got in her way. Not very practical or safe while spinning wool."

"I'm sorry I didn't know her."

His fingers paused, then continued with perhaps a bit more force than previously. He tied off the braid with a thick hank of yarn and rested his hands on her shoulders.

"I'm sorry I didn't tell you about Riemer. I thought it was the right move, but I see now it was a bad decision."

"It's okay. I shouldn't have been so angry with you. You were only trying to protect me."

His breath stirred against her neck as he leaned in closer. "Is there no chance that you...that we could..."

Mackenzie closed her eyes, thankful that he couldn't see her expression. "I value our friendship, Will, but..." He sighed heavily. "I'm sorry."

"I am, too."

He moved away. Mac turned, but he didn't look at her as he cleaned up.

She expected the silence to fall between them again, and was surprised when, after dinner, he said, "I don't want to alarm you, but over the last few weeks, I think I've heard something moving elsewhere in the hotel."

"Oh, thank God," she exclaimed, and he raised a questioning

brow. "I thought it was just me hearing things. Do you think it could be a raccoon or two?"

"I've been checking all the rooms." He looked a little self-conscious now. "That's what I've been doing the last few weeks. But I haven't seen any sign of animals. Could just be snow sliding off the roof, squirrels on the roof, whatever. Probably nothing."

Mackenzie's sleep was sporadic for several nights afterward, but the odd sounds ceased – almost as though by talking about it, they banished whatever was making the noise. So her mind turned to planning the departure from the hotel, and although her main plan was for them to travel together, a prudent part of her mind constructed Plan B: her departure alone, because she still wasn't completely sure that Will wouldn't leave without her. Despite his seeming acceptance of her rejection, he hadn't resumed their previous camaraderie. Silence fell between them again, laden with emotional undercurrents and words held carefully in check.

Although he was not speaking to her, Will had taken to watching her. Often she would be going about her laundry or cleaning the lobby and tidying their messes, when she would suddenly have the sensation of being observed. She would turn around to find him leaning in a doorway, or sprawled on his sofa, his flat, cold eyes following her. A couple of times, he observed her from the balcony railing of the second floor. And a few times lately, she felt his gaze but hadn't been able to find him. Unease was a constant companion that prickled along her scalp. Anxiety chased away slumber and knotted her chest so that she lay awake late into each night, struggling to breathe and afraid to sleep. During the day, she exercised her muscles to stay toned and in walking shape. In fighting shape, because she knew, deep inside, that she would be making the rest of the journey alone.

The first week of May brought warm daytime temperatures and a nasty cold. Will succumbed first, and by virtue of her insistence of taking care of him through the worst of it, Mackenzie sealed her fate.

"I'm sorry," he said with a glimmer of ruefulness in his eyes the morning she woke with crusted nostrils and incessant sneezing.

She waved away his apology and accepted the cup of green tea with thyme that he'd made for her. The next day, the sneezing passed and she felt rather well, so she assumed she had escaped the worst. The third day brought sinuses so congested that her face was puffy and a deep, rattling in her chest when she coughed. Her green tea infusions began to taste more strongly of thyme. On the fourth day, they began to taste of thyme-laced spinach, and she thought her sense of taste had gone haywire until Will confessed that he'd found dried nettle leaves in the first aid kit and decided nettle infusion, loaded with minerals, would be more beneficial than green tea.

On the fifth day, she woke with her symptoms unabated and a headache behind her eyes. She huddled over a bowl of hot water, a rough towel over her head to trap the steam, but nothing cleared the congestion, even when she used aromatic oils such as eucalyptus and rosemary. Resigning herself to a few days of abject misery, she rubbed some eucalyptus oil under her nose and into her chest and collapsed on her sofa by the fire with the hot cup of nettle infusion Will made for her, a hot wet cloth over her face.

Her slumber was filled with disjointed, surreal dreams featuring the hotel with long corridors that never ended, with thumps and sliding footsteps and the rattle of plastic MRE pouches all around her, and a stone-faced Will who was dressed in charcoal grey and carrying a fully loaded pack to the door. She tried to call out, to reach out a hand to snag his attention, but he simply passed by her sofa and scattered the logs in the fireplace. At last she was dragged into dreamless sleep by exhaustion, and she didn't wake until darkness embraced the hotel. Her skin was clammy, and she felt hot and achy with fever.

"I think I have the 'flu." She pulled the wet cloth off her face. It was cold and made her shiver, but she didn't have the strength to toss it aside.

Will, sitting upright on his sofa, his hands clasped between his knees, said, "Funny how we're stuck in the same place, just the two of us, and I got a cold, but you got the 'flu. That's what I call providential."

"Providential for whom?" Mac croaked, her sarcasm lost to the phlegm clogging her throat.

He shrugged. "For me. Sit up, Mackenzie. It's only fair that I explain some things before we begin."

A chill walked over her skin. Belatedly, the fine hairs on the back of her neck stiffened. *Danger!* Those hairs fairly shouted, but her foggy mind was several steps behind.

"Begin what?"

"Sit up."

Her heart quickened. The hairs shot upright all over her body, taking up the alert. *Danger! Danger!* She sat up slowly. Her head shrieked pain and took up a thumping rhythm inside her skull. Will was a blur on the sofa across from her. The cloth she held was still wet, so she dragged it across her eyes to clear them, one at a time so she could keep him within sight. He was dressed in dark grey, just as he had been in her dream. The fire was banked so that the flames were low and the glow of the coals barely lit his face. She wondered if she would find a loaded pack by the front doors. Not fever-dreams, then, but semi-wakefulness that had inserted itself into her dream-state.

"That's better. If you'd like to take the time for a hot cup of tea, you can. I owe you that much."

"And after that?" Her voice cracked on the last word as she choked on phlegm, triggering her cough. She felt it breaking loose but nothing would come up. It rattled around, making her cough more. When at last she gained control, Will rose to his feet. He held something out to her.

"Take your blade. You'll need it."

"For what?"

"Defense."

Her body went cold, a bone-deep chill borne of dread. She could barely force out her words. "Defense against what, exactly?"

"Me."

Somewhere in the back of her mind, she must have known all along, in the things she'd said that he'd ignored, in the things he didn't say but should have. And, of course, in the things he'd said to which she'd assigned her own meaning.

You think I came because Riemer told me to?

No. Not anymore. He had been sent, but not by Elijah Riemer.

"Why?"

"Take your weapon."

No, that was a trick. He was holding it out to her, blade first. If she took it that way, he'd whip it backward and slice open her hand, possibly severing her fingers. Her heart hammered in her chest. She tried to think past its thundering beat.

You'd have been dead weeks ago if not for me.

But how *many* weeks ago, precisely? Had he come on this journey to make sure her life saw an end, or was his decision to kill her a recent one, prompted by her rejection, an "if I can't have you, no one will" scenario?

"Mackenzie," he said impatiently. "Take your blade."

Her mind hurtled her back in time. She was standing by the grimy window of the long-abandoned house, watching Will pick apples from the tree. Nonchalantly, carefree, as though he wasn't worried about the twelve hunters in the neighborhood who were searching for her. And Wayne Pearson...Pearson, who said his first duty was to the Stronghold. The Stronghold that, to a man, turned its back on her and allowed her to be exiled, seeing her as a threat to their safety. And sure, he'd said it didn't sit well with him, but many a man performed his duty with reluctance in his heart but no hesitation in his actions.

"How did you get past the hunters, Will?"

He laughed, a sharp sound full of derision. "I can't believe it took you this long to figure it out."

"Just tell me."

"They were never a threat to me. I had a mission. My mission changed theirs. As soon as I came on the scene, they were hunting to find you for me, not to kill you for Louis. You, on the other hand – well, you presented a threat to *everyone*. Going to Ren Leonard for help – Jesus, Mackenzie, you might as well have just thrown yourself into the river. You couldn't expect them to exile you and just trust you wouldn't return with a pack of Revenants to tear down the walls."

"An unfounded fear, made ridiculous by the assumption that Ren Leonard could command a pack of Revenants."

As she spoke, Mackenzie's eyes crawled around the room, looking for weapons. No way would he hand over her machete; he wasn't stupid enough to give her any advantage. Eluding him for any length of time would be difficult, because God knew what waited for her in the empty hotel rooms. *I think I've heard something moving elsewhere in the hotel. I've been checking all the rooms.* Checking them, or booby-trapping them so that when it came to the final confrontation, she would either lose in face-to-face combat or through the trickery he'd devised in all her possible hiding places?

"It's best not to take chances. You were a loose thread."

"If your mission to kill me overrode theirs, why am I still alive?"

The room held nothing she could use as a weapon. She would have to flee instead of fight. If she could make her way to the kitchen, there would be plenty of knives. But knives were a close-combat skill of a different nature than the machete. Where she could swing a machete and lop off a head, she would have to get kissing-close to kill him with a knife.

"My mission was to find the end of the line for the underground and to dismantle the route. You remained alive to watch my back as long as I deemed it necessary."

"You're never going to make it through the city without me."

"I'm not going through the city. I've come far enough to disrupt the trail. I'm going to burn this hotel to the ground, backtrack our steps, and obliterate any sign of the underground on my way back to the Stronghold. And by the time I get there, they should have been able to ferret out any remaining subversives."

"Why? Why not just let people go if they want to? If people don't like the way things are done, they can just go somewhere else and do things the way they want to."

"You understand nothing about survival. Your subversives threaten the very way of life at the Stronghold. So we get rid of them, lose one or two people, no big deal. Anyone thinking of rebelling gets the message: don't do it or you'll be gone. Our way of life stays safe and secure.

"But let you go? What would happen if even a quarter of the people decided they wanted a different way of life and just up and left? Sure, there are fewer mouths to feed, fewer people to keep warm. But there are also fewer people to do the work, fewer to ensure survival."

"Fewer to find a way to regain the knowledge and technology lost in the Upheaval?" she added quietly.

"Knowledge and technology," Will scoffed. "We don't need those things. What good did they bring the world? We don't need your kind dragging us back into the age of distraction and greed."

"Both would have saved Ginny Miller's life."

"Nature chooses who survives. She didn't make the cut."

His callous indifference burned through her. As though it had happened yesterday, she saw in her memory the day of Ginny's death, how she had breezed through the infirmary doors to find her friend too quiet and too still, her eyes open and unblinking. She could still feel the weight of the healer's arm around her, guiding her out of the infirmary and murmuring soothing words Mackenzie could not to this day remember. And then came the numb walk through the Commons on autopilot, and she had been unable to stop her forward motion or break out of the disbelieving haze that engulfed her even when Elijah Riemer tugged on her arm and asked her a question that she could not now recall. Ginny's death sparked all the events that had brought her here to this hotel. This killing place.

Only one question remained. Mac voiced it with reluctance, knowing her time for delaying had run out.

"And your big seduction scene...what was that all about? Distraction? Not wanting to waste an opportunity?"

"No. That was your one chance for survival. I'd have turned my back on my mission if you'd agreed to stay with me."

Mac laughed bitterly. "Yeah? But for how long, Will? Until you tired of me? Then——" She drew a finger across her throat.

"That's about the size of it," he agreed. "Now get on your feet and take your blade."

She stared at him without flinching but made no move to get up. Subtly, millimeter by tiny millimeter, she moved her bare feet into position.

And it came to her, the information of vital importance that she had forgotten, what the niggling at the back of her consciousness had been trying to remind her of.

I don't want you going back out. If you go back out, there will come a day — and soon — when you won't come back. There will be some grand story to explain your death, and part of it might even be true.

Elijah suspected that whomever the Council paired her with would be her potential executioner. He didn't trust Will Crawford from the start.

But she did. She had forgotten his caution, and she placed her safety — indeed, her very life — in Will's hands from the moment he showed up at her hiding place. And now here she sat, no weapon to hand, nowhere to run, and every hiding place a potential trap.

Slowly, she raised her head and met the gaze of her executioner.

30

"Get up," Will snarled. He abandoned all pretense of giving her the blade and hurled it behind him across the darkened lobby. It clattered somewhere near the reception desk. It didn't matter; she'd never be able to find it. What little element of surprise she was able to gain would have to be spent eluding him.

Mac lowered her gaze again, staring at her hands. Almost ready. She adjusted her feet. To the casual observer, it would appear as though she were fidgeting. But she had to get the balls of her feet into position to carry her weight. Another fraction of an inch. And another. And at last, she was ready.

"GET ON YOUR FUCKI—"

She launched herself from the sofa while he was in mid-bellow, a trick Bon taught her that she thought strange at the time, since Revenants didn't hunch over when they yelled. People did, however, and Will was no exception. Her shoulder planted into his midriff, and she plowed him off his feet and into his sofa with all the force she could muster.

They slammed into the back of the sofa, sending it skidding. The legs caught on a loose floorboard, and their momentum carried it over backward, spilling them onto the floor in a tangle of limbs.

Will recovered with dismaying speed, gaining his feet and lunging at her. She threw herself into his legs, toppling him back to the floor. Her right hook connected with his chin and spun his head to the side. She scrambled to her feet. He hooked a hand around her ankle and jerked her off balance. She spun in mid-air so that she landed with full velocity onto his rib cage. His shout of pain was rendered to a wheeze as his diaphragm took a direct hit.

Mackenzie rolled off him, pushed to her feet, and sprinted for the stairs. In the room below, only dimly illuminated from the fire, Will was getting to his feet, cursing and groaning. The darkness played tricks on her perception and she missed a step. She landed in an ungainly sprawl and banged her chin on a tread.

She got to her feet and started her climb again, this time more slowly even though the rustle of clothes and muttered imprecations told her he was coming up behind her.

The curse of this hotel was the layout: long, simple halls and no nooks or crannies. It was also a blessing, as she was navigating in absolute darkness. She felt her way along the wall, trying doorknobs as she went, painfully aware that she could no longer hear Will behind her. The doors were all locked. She blew out a silent breath of frustration and watched, horrified, as the white vapor drifted away from her like a phantom.

The blackness of the corridor was her refuge from a killer, and her betrayer was the very breath of her body. If Will was behind her in the hallway, he could mark her location with every breath she took.

She pulled her shirt over her mouth and nose to mask the vapor. Predictably, the tickle in her throat burst into vibrant life, aggravated by the cold air and her flight up the stairs. She swallowed convulsively to soothe it and crept farther down the hall, resisting the urge to move to the opposite side of the corridor. He would expect that.

The night watched with dispassionate eyes – God's or Will's, she couldn't tell – as door after door, she closed her hand around cold metal, turning, seeking entry, finding each locked. After the first fourteen, one turned easily, noiselessly.

About to push it open, she paused at the last second. Why would all the doors be locked but this one? It had to be a trap. She eased it silently back to resting position and let go, feeling her way to the next doorway. Locked. As were the next four. Then one that turned. The five after it were locked, the next unlocked, and the last four locked.

Mac pressed herself into the corner at the end of the hallway, shivering, tucking her hands into her armpits for warmth and wishing she could do the same with her feet. Although daytime temperatures were nearly pleasant now, nighttime temperatures still hovered just above freezing, enough to make her bare feet ache with cold. The rest of her seemed to burn from within, the achy, cold-edged heat of fever.

If she could get to the clothes storeroom, she could outfit herself with winter gear and slip out of the hotel. The woods across the old highway could shelter her long enough to put some distance between Will and her, and there should be enough moonlight to navigate by.

She felt along the end wall where the window should be and found it covered with a heavy blanket. If she moved it, she would give away her location. Too late, she realized she had boxed herself into a dead-end.

Unless… If memory served her right, there were emergency stairs at this end of the corridor that led down to the outside, with a separate door that led into the restaurant – if he hadn't found a way to rig the door so it wouldn't open. Oh, he'd been a busy boy while they'd been avoiding each other. If she could make it to the kitchen, she could get a knife.

Oh, but that was a trap, too. She'd been sick for days, and he'd had plenty of opportunity to remove all weapons and hide them. If she were to find her way to the wood rooms, she bet she would find the splitting mauls missing. He'd probably even removed the splitting wedges.

Take that scenario even farther into paranoia, Mackenzie, and assume he's moved all the clothes to another room, as well. He's had time to set this up while you slept through your cold, time to move all your assets, hide all your weapons, turn everything to his advantage. You know what your only option is.

Somehow, with no weapon, caught in the grip of fever and illness, outmuscled and outmaneuvered, she would have to kill him.

The tickle started again. She swallowed and flexed her throat to back it off, but it was persistent. She would cough soon, whether or not she wanted to. The desire was strong to simply lie down in the corridor, curled into the corner, and let happen what would happen. Elijah was dead; she could join him this night if she so chose. What came in the afterlife could only be better than this difficult existence without him.

But he would never accept her giving up. She didn't think she could accept it herself. If she died, she wasn't going to do it lying down. She would not make this easy for Will, and she would take him with her if she could. *Move, you've got to move. There is nothing to help you in this barren hallway.*

She forced her legs to move, to carry her step by halting step across the corridor, forced her arm to raise and feel along the wall for the staircase door. Every step, she expected to run into him as he searched for her in the darkness, equally blind. Her chest ached with the effort of suppressing her cough.

Her hand touched cold, smooth metal: a fire door. She brushed her hand down it until she found the push handle. *God, don't let the door squeak or squeal. Give me one damn break on this otherwise completely shitty night.*

The push bar depressed silently. The door swung open on equally silent hinges. Mackenzie raised her foot to step into the stairwell, and as she brought it down, the phantom Bon Moreau in her head shrieked a belated warning.

TRAP!

Stabbing agony from a dozen points screamed through her sole. Her teeth clenched on her screech of pain, and it curled through her whole body as a wave of dizzying nausea. Liquid warmth suffused the bottom of her foot, giving a second of relief until she realized what it was. Blood. *Her* blood. He'd scattered the stairwell landing with broken shards of glass.

With the first shock of pain, she'd let go of the door. She frantically grabbed for it and missed. It shut with a telltale click that sounded like a gunshot in the silence of the hotel. With her location pinpointed as surely as if she'd lit a signal lantern and hobbled by the glass embedded in her sole, she was surely dead.

She brushed her injured foot across the landing, sweeping fragments of dishes and glassware out of her way, then limped to the first stair, feeling her way carefully so she didn't tumble down them. Easing herself down, she examined the bottom of her foot with her fingers, brushing away clinging slivers of porcelain and glass. There were several punctures with fragments sticking into her flesh. She pulled out all but two, hot tears coursing down her cheeks, her whimpers muffled against her shoulder. Most of her weight had come down on the remaining pieces and lodged them too deep into her heel to be fished out with just her fingers.

Will Crawford, you fucking asshole!

What now? The door had snicked shut so loudly the dead had to have heard it. The crunch of glass and pottery beneath her foot echoed like cannon-fire in the stairwell. He knew where she was as surely as her name was Mackenzie Bright Runner. Two choices lay before him that she could see: follow her into the stairwell or race through the hotel to try to waylay her at the stairwell exit in the restaurant.

If their roles were reversed, she would not expect him to risk his bare feet to the glass again, so she would intercept him as he exited the stairs into the restaurant. With the delay to remove what shards he could from his flesh, she would reach the restaurant exit first and simply wait. He'd be an easy kill, trusting that she was waiting in the corridor above.

Which meant she must go back into Stygian blackness she had just escaped, make her way down the stairs to the lobby, and find her discarded machete or some other weapon. Maybe she could hide in the wood room and cave his head in with a piece of pine.

Jesus. Bile rose in her throat at the thought of bludgeoning him with a hunk of firewood. This was Will — the same Will who walked countless miles with her, the same Will who huddled on the catwalk under the bridge and cried with her, the same Will who pulled her past the frigid lake and through the sleet and wind to shelter.

The same Will who, if he could not possess her, would follow through on his mission to kill her and dismantle the underground. Yeah, with that in mind, she didn't think she'd have any problem staving in his skull.

She pulled her shirt back over her mouth and nose and got to her feet, bearing her weight on the ball of her injured foot, and tip-toed back through the narrow trail she'd made. She'd missed a few pieces in her sweep, which found the tender flesh of both feet, but she was able to remove those pieces and they didn't seem to have cut deeply.

With one hand cocked to punch, she used the other to open the stairwell door as quietly as possible. Her fist punched through the opening. *Ha! Take that!* But no one was there. She crept out into the corridor, easing the door closed, and lurched down the hallway as fast as she dared, her fingers skating against the wall to her right for balance. She counted the doorways as she went.

Twenty-nine, twenty-eight, twenty-seven, twenty-six, twenty-five, twenty-four

The fragments of glass in her foot moved with every step, cutting deeper into her flesh. Sticky blood coated the bottom of her foot, too much to be blotted away by the carpet.

Twenty-three, twenty-two, twenty-one, twenty, nineteen, eighteen

By now he would have reached the restaurant and would be waiting for her to come out the stairwell exit. Or would he venture into the stairwell, hoping to catch her off-guard on the stairs where she thought she was relatively safe?

Seventeen, sixteen, fifteen, fourteen, thirteen, twelve

How long would she have to wait in the wood room before he thought to check it? And in the dark, would she be able to aim accurately enough to bash his face in when he first opened the door? She couldn't lie to herself about her physical condition. He would overpower her in direct combat.

Eleven, ten, nine, eight, seven, six

Of all the times she could use Ren Leonard's help, right now was the most urgent, topped only by the scuffle with the cannibals.

She'd expected to have more visibility the closer she got to the staircase; the corridor overlooked the lobby below and the firelight should be reflecting off the walls. He must have banked the fire after she fled, for she saw no flickering or glowing embers.

Five, four, three, two —

CRASH!

There was no warning, no sense that he was even there until they collided. Her forehead hit his chin and he swore violently. They tumbled to the floor. Smarting pain burned across her cheek as the threadbare carpet erased her skin. She rolled to her hands and knees and scrambled for the stairs. Will snatched at her, his hand catching and twisting into the folds of her loose sweatshirt. He dragged her backward, trying to force her body beneath his.

Mac snarled in frustration and jabbed her elbow backwards, catching him in the face. He howled in pain, his grip loosening. Warm blood splattered on the back of her neck; she'd broken his nose.

She slithered out from under him while he writhed in pain and pushed to her feet. The stairs should be close. If she could reach them before he recovered, she stood a good chance of reaching the wood room and arming herself. How many rooms were left? Two?

Two, one. The stairs should be near. They have to be right here!

Will hit her from behind. Her arms flew out to catch herself, but instead of finding floor, they found air, then the edge of a stair tread. The impact vibrated up to her shoulder, radiating pain every inch of the way. They tumbled down three stairs, tangled together. She felt every bounce as a jolt of lightning through her joints. His effort to stop their descent caused her to roll over him. Her ribs caught the rim of a tread, then her injured foot hit the iron railing. Her scream of pain echoed around them. He skidded down behind her, grabbing at any part of her he could reach. She kicked out, catching him in the stomach. He lost his balance and fell on her, taking them down four more stairs. She punched every inch of him she could reach, scrabbled out from under him, and staggered off the last step.

And still he came after her, too fast, too strong, not injured enough to give her any hope of evasion or surprise. She sprinted across the lobby by the dim light of the fire he hadn't quite managed to completely bank. Her pounding footfalls pushed the shards of glass deeper into her flesh. Her breath rasped in and out, her lungs laboring. A wracking cough tried to slow her. She fought it back, choking as her throat itched madly. His boots slammed the floor behind her, gaining. His own breath came labored and harsh. Nearly there. And nearly caught. Any second he would grab her hair, or the neck of her shirt, or he'd tackle her.

The reception desk loomed before her, a dark straight line holding back a darker pool of shadows. She launched herself over it, rolling into a ball as she sailed over the grimy wood counter and hit the wall behind. The blunt force of her landing jarred her joints, which now shrieked as though filled with glass dust. Her hand swept the floor, seeking the machete, finding only dust and dirt and the remains of the ancient carpet.

"Looking for this?"

Aghast, she stared at the machete silhouetted against the dim light of the banked fire across the room, held aloft in a triumphant salute. Well, son-of-a-bitch. Where the hell had he squirreled that away?

He grinned the victorious grin of a conqueror. So this was how it ended, her quest for life over existence. A long, arduous journey across the wasteland of civilization, only to die at the hands of her turncoat companion.

She reached deep down for the energy to fight and found her reserve empty. Slumping to the floor in defeat, she turned her face away as he approached, his steps deliberate, his pace unhurried, her blade in his hand resting against his leg. He bent over near her feet and she flinched, but he only dragged a battery-operated camp lantern out of a cubbyhole and fired it up. She squinted against the

273

brightness. Given her druthers, she'd rather die in the gloom, but of course he would want to watch her go. Would want to gloat. It would be the crowning moment of his mission.

"I'd like to say it's nothing personal, but…it kind of is."

The itch in her throat flared, demanding attention. Her throat seized as the cough rumbled from deep in her chest. She rolled onto her side and curled up, her body wracked by her violent hacking. Seeking something, anything, to look at other than Will as he bore down on her, bringing death, her eyes fell on the cubbies under the counter, mostly empty and laced with cobwebs. Papers were stuffed in one, yellowed with age and furry with dust. A handful of unsharpened wooden pencils lay scattered in another, their rubberband tether long ago disintegrated. A glint of silver in a third. Almost idly, she reached into the cubby, more curious than hopeful.

Will stopped, a booted foot on each side of her, unconcerned with her scavenging. "You've had so many chances to get away from me. If you'd only stopped to think things through, you'd have realized why I was there. Didn't Riemer warn you about who they'd team you up with? You should have known as soon as I told you we were to be partnered. Riemer knew."

"You already made your point about my naïveté long ago, Will."

"You should have gone with Rico and his men. They wanted to go to the islands, and they wanted to take you with them."

"We left camp because of a Revenant, and then they drove off without us at the farmhouse, remember?"

"*I* pushed them to leave camp because of the Revenant. I knew it was Ren Leonard. I knew I'd have no chance to complete my mission if he were with us. I encouraged them to stop at the farmhouse, to clear it in the dark. I set them up to die, Mackenzie, because they would have been in my way." He barked out a humorless laugh and said with an unexpectedly desperate sorrow, "Why didn't you see through that? Why are you making me kill you?"

All these weeks and months together, he had protected her and watched over her, nurtured her misplaced trust, but somehow she was to blame?

"Don't act like this is all my fault. You made the choice to kill me. That's on you."

He leaned over her, his tone soft and intimate as though he

were offering secrets of love rather than confessions of betrayal. "My sweet 'Kenz, defiant to the end."

He stroked her hair. Bile rose in her throat. She gagged, which brought another bout of hacking that ripped at her throat and wrenched her ribs.

"I waited to tell you this because, even sick, you're pretty bad-ass and this battle could have ended with me dead instead of you. And if you survived, I didn't want you to know until you were too far gone to turn the blade on yourself."

He brushed her cheek with the back of his hand, a gentle caress made into a damning lie by his brutality over the last hour. "I infected you with the Revenant Virus. Pretty simple to get a cup of infected blood and add it to your evening tea. You don't have the 'flu, 'Kenz. Your cells are mutating. You proved time and again since we left the Stronghold that you're a deadly opponent, so I had to make sure that even if you won, you still lost. The Stronghold is safe from your vengeance."

He lies. He's lied about so much already; he has to be lying now. And if he wasn't…well, she could always open an artery with a shard of broken glass before the virus progressed to the point she lost her cognitive thinking. Before she became one more facet of the world's greatest problem.

Mackenzie clenched her hand around the slim, flat length of metal laying on the dusty bottom of the cubby. Icy against her skin, it grounded her, giving her a momentary clarity she would need for the next seconds.

He kissed his fingers and pressed them to her lips, then straightened and raised the machete. "Any last words, Mackenzie Bright Runner?"

"Yeah," she croaked. "You lose."

She flung herself upright, her arm flashing in a vicious arc to plant eight lethal inches of chrome into his side. He choked on his own squeal of pain as she slammed the heel of her hand on the handle of the letter opener, driving it deeper into his body. Blood surged over her fingers, hot and slick. The machete clattered to the floor, out of her reach.

Will's scream was so great his vocal cords could not voice it. His mouth gaped silently. His hands clutched at the puncture site, scrabbling over it, trying to grip the tiny bit of handle that protruded from his flesh.

He fell with a remarkable lack of grace, an awkward tumble that landed him squarely on top of her. Inches from hers, his face registered shock and fear, but his eyes accused betrayal. She collapsed under his weight. Her head knocked against the floor, exploding brilliant stars in her vision. The last of her reserves expended, she lay on the cold floor in the growing pool of Will's blood, its scent bitter and cloying. The taste of copper lay heavy on her tongue. Her exhaustion outweighed her astonishment at having bested him; she couldn't even move to brush away a spider that scurried over her hand. Dispassionately, she watched it crawl away toward her feet and when it vanished from her line of sight, she closed her eyes.

A thump and crash sounded somewhere upstairs, and then Mackenzie let go of consciousness and heard no more.

31

The world was burning, and Mackenzie was blind. Orange-yellow light boiled out of the engulfing darkness and then faded. Boiled again and faded. The forest crackled in the flames, pockets of pitch snapping in the heat. The endless heat. No matter where she turned, she couldn't escape it. The very air she breathed boiled in her lungs and scorched her lips on the exhale.

And then came the cold. Freezing cold, shivering cold, the frozen ground stubbornly hoarding its chill while the forest burned around her.

Then, for a while, there was nothing but a great, black, endless void she found oddly comforting, just the gentle sway of the universe with clean, crisp air and strange dreams of bare ground and evergreen branches peeking through drifts of snow.

At last came cognizance. The trees and snow really did exist, but the great, black void had been a fiction of her imagination, or perhaps the interpretation her subconscious assigned to her fever dreams. The universe still swayed, but that was because she was strapped to a surprisingly sturdy travois, being dragged behind person or persons unknown.

Stupidly, her first thought was that she hoped whomever had custody of her at present at least cleaned Will's blood off her before dragging her out into the snow-covered wilderness.

Or maybe it was Will dragging her behind him, and his betrayal had simply been a dream borne of fever, fear, and sorrow. Tied as she was to the travois, she couldn't turn to look. She scrunched her head back as far as she could and caught a glimpse of a figure draped in layers of winter gear, a pack strapped to his – her? – back, huddled into the hood of a heavy coat.

"Will?" Her voice came out in a phlegmy croak. She coughed to clear her throat and erupted into a fit of hacking that resulted in a sore throat and a lot of unpleasantness that she spit into the snow.

The swaying stopped; her unseen companion came to a halt.

"He's just as dead as when you last saw him." That voice –

sardonic, gravelly, the sound of great boulders shifting against one another.

"Leonard?"

"In the flesh," he confirmed and muttered, "The miserable, freezing, frostbitten flesh."

"What the hell are we doing out here?" She squinted at the forest, draped in white and blindingly lit by the sun to a wattage that was painful to her aching head. The road beneath them was a road in name only and was still covered in a significant amount of snow. Once it had been a well-traveled route; now it was barely more than a deer trail through the mountain wilderness. They'd had shelter, food, and warmth at the hotel. And, she was certain, a few more weeks would have brought company in the form of the seasonal caretakers of the hotel.

"We, my troublesome girl, are climbing off the mountain. Which was a lot fucking easier in my day," he added in another muttered aside.

"We should"—she broke into another coughing fit—"we should have stayed put." Now that she was awake, her true physical condition was becoming clear. Lungs still congested, skin flushed with fever, body lethargic. Her ribs and arms ached fiercely from her fall down the hotel stairs. If they were attacked by Revenants or some other wild thing, she would be of absolutely no help, especially while attached to a travois.

"We don't have that option."

True, perhaps. The hotel offered warmth, shelter, food – and possibly more. There was still the mysterious thump and crash she'd heard as she'd lost consciousness.

"Was the hotel compromised?"

"Compro..." Leonard broke off. "You use very militant terms for a girl coming from a supposedly peaceful settlement."

"It's a militant world. Can you come around here where I can see you while I talk to you?"

"Tone, Bright Runner. You're mighty irritable." He lowered the travois to the ground and tromped around it. Snow crunched under his boots as he hunkered down beside her and unbound her so she could sit up. "Better?"

"Yeah." Sort of. Up close, his stench was overpowering, even in the cold mountain air. He was bundled against the cold in a thick down coat, heavy winter gloves, and sunglasses that covered the eyeholes of the ski mask under his hood. His blue-ringed eyes peered out over the top rim of the glasses like twin nightmares floating in mottled, waxy flesh. She closed her eyes, the sun and his visage too much to bear.

"That bad, huh?"

"I'd kill for a pain reliever."

"I brought what appears to be the modern version of medicine, but frankly I don't want to stop long enough to fix anything. Once we've found shelter for the night, you can tell me what will work."

"Feverfew. And in a pinch, valerian. It might not stop the headache, but it will surely put me to sleep so I don't care how much my head hurts."

"I'd give my left nut for a bottle of aspirin right now," he grumbled. "We've got a few more hours of daylight, long enough to safely reach Duvall and find secure shelter before dark."

She opened her eyes. "Duvall? How the hell did we get to Duvall?" She had studied the maps in the hotel restaurant, committed as much of it to memory as she could manage. Duvall was north of the main route west, on a secondary highway. "This isn't the route I planned."

"No doubt you thought you'd waltz through Seattle proper, just trot on up I-5 without a care in the world. While it might have been priceless to see your face when you reached the tunnel in downtown Seattle, it's doubtful you'd have lived long enough to reach it."

"There's a tunnel?"

"The interstate express lanes tunnel under the northbound lanes. Surely full of Revenants, if it hasn't collapsed. It will be interesting to hear how you planned to travel alone, too. Sleep with one eye open? Fight off a pack of Revenants – or worse – all on your own?"

"What could be worse than Revenants?"

"Feral people, like the ones who tried to carve you into steaks back in the desert."

She waved a weary hand, closing her eyes again as the brightness of the day made them water. "Yeah, okay. Whatever. So we're near Duvall. Just so you know, I planned to cut off this road at Fall

City – the map didn't show very many towns on that route. How many days have I been out?"

"Three."

"Jesus." And how many of those days had she lain on the cold floor behind the check-in desk under Will's lifeless body, soaked in his blood? She wasn't sure she wanted to know.

"We've been on the road two of those days," he said, as though anticipating her question. "I've pushed as hard as I can to go as many miles as quickly as possible." He fiddled with the travois, and her restraints fell away. "Sit up for a while. We can afford to take a break. I've been trying to keep you upright as much as possible."

She raised herself slowly, alarmed at how weak she was, and blinked at him, dislodging tears from her eyes. Her head took up a nauseating beat, making her want to lie back down. She shut her eyes tight and slumped forward.

"Now is where you have to pay attention, Bright Runner." He prodded her arm until she looked at him. "It sounds like you planned to go on the 202 – few towns, skirts past most of civilization until you get to Redmond. Also very little shelter, and right now we need a town desperately. We need to get a car. Every place we come to, I try to find one that will take us the rest of the way. So far, no success. When we get to Duvall, I'm going to fix your medicine and lay out your meals, and I'm going to have to leave you to take care of yourself for a few hours while I look for a truck that runs. Because if I don't get you somewhere that has people who can take care of you, you're going to die. You have pneumonia. Or at least I'm fairly certain you do. You're not going to get any better without help. I don't have the skills necessary to help you."

Pneumonia. Even back at the Stronghold, with proper food, shelter, and lots of garlic, pneumonia was hard to beat. Even harder to beat was the Revenant Virus. The chance of her having a naturally high resistance like Ren Leonard was slim to none.

"So I guess you weren't a professor in the medical field."

"Hardly. Aircraft maintenance. It's what I did in the military. In college, I majored in history with a minor in sociology, but I found I didn't play well with others in the university arena."

"History and sociology – that explains your dim view of mankind's future. We've been on the road two days – that means you

280

found me soon after…"

"Soon after you gutted Crawford?" he said callously. "Yeah. You wouldn't have faced him alone except he got the jump on me. Gagged and strung up by my feet, sawing through a nylon rope with my fingernails for three days. Did you know he set snares in some of the rooms?"

"No, but it doesn't surprise me. I suspected he'd been busy. Let me guess – the rooms that were unlocked?"

He chuckled. "No. The rooms that were locked. He wasn't stupid, that's for sure. He must've figured you wouldn't trust an unlocked room. And it wasn't just rope snares. Thank *Christ* you didn't find one of the bear traps, though half of them sprung on their own by the time I got to the hotel." He paused. "He spent a lot of time preparing."

"I know." Bear traps. That must have been what she'd been hearing that Will shrugged off as wildlife loose in the hotel. It was his traps springing, perhaps because he'd not set them correctly.

"The point is, you *didn't* know. You didn't have a clue what he was up to until the shit hit the fan."

You've got to grow up. You can't be this naïve and expect to survive. The memory made her squirm. Had she not been so naïve, would she have seen through Will before their confrontation in the hotel? Would she have seen through him the second she saw him picking apples outside her hideout while she waited for Elijah to join her?

"No, I didn't know. I trusted him. I didn't listen to Elijah Riemer when he told me to trust no one." She risked a glance at him even though the sun on the snow behind him stabbed through her head like an ice pick. "So I guess I shouldn't be trusting you."

Leonard laughed. Mac's imagination threw up a random image of the tectonic plates scraping together to go with the sound. And then she broke out coughing, and the rattle in her chest banished all images from her mind except that of her dying alone in an unfamiliar land.

"No, you shouldn't trust me. I'm a Revenant, and I have a Revenant's temper. I also let you go off with Crawford after that debacle at the farmhouse with those idiots you met up with, even knowing he couldn't be trusted with your safety. But I was in a blood lust and didn't trust myself."

"*You* were the Revenant that jumped in the middle of the

fight?"

"What, you expected me to just let a bunch of strange men drive off with you and not follow? I've been following you since the day you left my campus. Saw when they put you out the doors. I took care of the nasties who'd have killed you before you got into your shed. Left your apples outside that maintenance shed you spent the night in. And I followed you out of the city because I saw Crawford talking to the men who were hunting you. They searched until they found you, and then the rest of them scattered while he lured you out. I didn't think you should be alone with him, so I made sure you weren't – up until the farmhouse of horrors." He shook his head. "I guess I'd better backtrack someday and see that those Wenatchee fucktards get somewhere safer. Too stupid to live by themselves."

"You should have told me about Will."

He stared at her, his blue-ringed eyes alien and discomfiting. "Well, I did tell you we were going to have to decide what to do about him. I didn't have time to tell you anything more. Then I lost you in the mountains when the snow came. Slowed me down – it was colder than a witch's tit in January."

"You should have just gone home."

"You asked for my help. I thought I offered it."

"Not to this extent." She hesitated. He deserved to know the truth – if truth was what Will had given her. The gift of honesty as the crowning jewel atop the mountain of lies he'd built to gain her trust. "Will said he infected me with the Revenant Virus. I don't have the 'flu or pneumonia, Ren. I'm mutating. And I have to lie down – my head is killing me." She eased herself back down on the travois, wanting nothing more than to curl up and sleep.

He pulled off a glove and reached for her face. She flinched back, but he only opened first one eye and then the other, examining them closely. She held her breath while he was that close. "The hell you are."

"He said—"

"He said a lot of things, Mackenzie, and most of those were lies. The rest were damned lies."

"Yeah, but—"

"You've been sick a week, but your eyes aren't changing color. You could be resistant. Or he could have been a fucking liar."

"You know as well as I do – maybe even better – that the virus can make you ill for a lot longer than a week."

He put his glove back on and leaned back. "Maybe this will put things into perspective. After I pitched Crawford's body down a ski slope and cleaned you up, I searched the town pretty thoroughly for any rope he might've missed while he was setting up the world's biggest booby-trap. I found no evidence of any Revenants in the town. Since I was the only Revenant around, and I know for damn certain he didn't take any of my blood, he was just talking out his ass again."

Without another word, he secured her to the travois again and stomped around front, lifted the poles, and started walking again. Unconvinced, Mackenzie let the subject die. Eventually the sway of the travois lulled her to sleep so she didn't have to think about the fact that Will lied, but not always.

When next she woke, she was alone in a dark house, propped up by her supply pack near the fireplace. The fire, burning low enough that she suspected Leonard had been gone for a few hours, provided the only light in the room. On the hearth beside her, still warm from the fire, was a chipped ceramic cup of some sort of tea, a Salisbury steak pouch meal, and a five-shot revolver, which made her laugh. Obviously he had no concept of her training, which involved all manner of blades but not firearms due to the limited availability of ammunition.

She lifted the gun, careful to keep her finger away from the trigger, and the heat waves from the fire fluttered the cryptic note he'd left beneath it: *Point and shoot. It's not rocket science.*

Indeed. She set the gun aside, ate her pouch meal, then added more wood to the fire from a small stack of sticks and branches beside the fireplace. The tea was feverfew, judging from its bitterness; she didn't linger over it, just downed it in several gulps, wincing at the disagreeable flavor, which she banished from her mouth by licking gravy out of the discarded pouch. She slept again, waking deep in the night and still alone but with less of a headache than she had taken into slumber. The cough, however, was worse.

The fire was burned down to embers; she added more branches and fixed more feverfew tea, adding a few pinches of dried thyme leaves for the cough, and nearly set her jacket on fire when she pulled the cup away from the flames. By the time the cup cooled enough to pick up, the tea had also cooled to an unpleasant lukewarm temperature. She drank it anyway. Although she waited up a while, Leonard didn't return, and eventually she fell back asleep.

A clatter and rattle woke her as dawn colored the sky outside and filled with grey light the barren, dusty front room of the long-abandoned house she sheltered in. Mackenzie opened her eyes, staring straight up at the ceiling. She thought she must have fallen off her pack as she slept, but when she sat up, she found Leonard rummaging through it. He tossed a food pouch her way and glanced at the hearth, where another cup of tea was heating.

"Feel any better?"

"No headache. It will probably come back later if we aren't able to make more tea while we travel. You have to wean yourself off the dosage or the headache comes back."

He looked at the mug of tea dubiously. "Maybe I should fill the canteen with tea."

"Please don't. It tastes like shit." She took the mug he handed her, tested the temperature with the tip of her tongue, then drank down the warm contents in several gulps. "Are we walking again?"

"No. I found a truck and some gas to fill the tank. We probably have enough to get us to Anacortes."

"What's in Anacortes?"

He pinned her with a look. "I thought you studied the maps."

"I did. I didn't memorize everything."

"That's where the ferry terminal is. Or used to be."

"Ferry to what?"

"The islands."

She scoffed, then broke out in a coughing fit that left her already aching ribs screaming in pain and her throat raw. "The islands — just a fairytale I wanted to believe in. Clear the islands of Revenants and you could live fairly secure. No evidence people have done it."

"No evidence they haven't."

"And if there's no one to help when I get there, Ren? Then what? I die alone on the islands from pneumonia."

"You'll die alone here from pneumonia," he pointed out. "Why not take a chance that you're not the only one who thought clearing the islands and living worry-free was a good idea? Besides, if you really are infected with the Revenant Virus and there are no inhabitants on the islands, what better place for you to mutate?"

She started to argue that if she were infected and there *were* people on the islands, everyone would be in danger, but the cough reared up again, hard enough to make her gag. When the fit passed, she opened her pouch meal and ate noodles coated in some flavor of gravy she couldn't identify; her sense of taste was dulled from illness and tainted from feverfew aftertaste. The cold gravy soothed her throat.

Leonard packed the truck while she ate, tossing even the travois into the bed. When there was nothing else to put in the truck except her, she reluctantly limped out of the house to the vehicle, the puncture wounds in her foot protesting every inch of the way. She hadn't expected much, and therefore wasn't surprised or disappointed to see that the truck was pitted with rust and the windshield cracked. But the engine was running, and Leonard seemed pleased enough with that. Mac climbed into the cab, wrapped herself in the blankets from the travois, and did her best to sleep through the jostling journey.

Full unconsciousness wasn't possible; the truck bounced and creaked and Leonard swore furiously. Sometimes the road was smooth and the truck attained speeds Mackenzie had never before experienced, leaving her both too exhilarated and too terrified to sleep. Other times the vehicle crawled over rough road, hitting ruts and potholes deep enough to bounce her off the seat and inciting violently snarled invective from Leonard.

Exhaustion and illness eventually dragged her into semi-unconsciousness, where the pain from her head and her ribs from coughing and the various aches and injuries from her fight with Will couldn't reach her. It was an emotional realm, however, where the loss of Elijah was a dagger stabbing repeatedly into her heart, where Will's betrayal was a constant, razor-sharp reminder of her stupidity, and her fear of devolving into a flesh-eating, rampaging beast robbed all hope of the future.

The truck lurched to a stop, engine sputtering. Leonard's viciously snarled expletive jolted Mac from her semi-slumber.

"Problem?"

"Truck's dead."

She pushed herself upright. Her body felt hot and itchy, her eyes grainy. The setting sun stabbed her eyeballs, the pain echoing through her head. "How far to the ferry?"

"Three miles."

"Shit."

"You're getting good at swearing."

"I'm not sure that's something I should be proud of. Do I have any water left?"

He handed her the canteen, and she drank deeply.

"I'm not sure I can walk three miles. I still have glass in my foot."

"Yes. Well, pottery, to be exact. I got most of it out, but there's one shard that's in deep. It will have to be removed by cutting your foot open. I didn't think that was a wise idea right before traveling."

"It's almost dark." The street ahead of them was bathed in the almost-orange light of sunset. Derelict homes, fallen into ruin from the harsh sea air or Revenant vandalism, hulked in the shadows of evergreens, looking ominous and threatening.

"All the better to get moving immediately. Luckily, this road runs along the coast – at the edge of the neighborhood. I'd take you along the beach to the terminal, which would be much safer, but it's high tide."

She sighed, which made her cough. Her inflamed lungs screamed as they tried to expand. *You've got to go, Mac, or you're going to die.* Her fevered brain didn't much care, but her body's instinct for survival was still strong enough to make her jam her blanket into her mostly empty pack and pop open her door.

Leonard met her in front of the truck, where he took the pack and pressed the revolver into her hands.

He said, "Point and shoot."

She said, "It's not rocket science."

He set a quick pace. Despite the stabbing pain in her foot and the one in her chest, Mac didn't ask him to slow down. Trees and houses flashed by, a surreal stream of blurred images to her fevered eyes. A stitch developed in her side after the first mile, and by the second mile her sock inside her boot felt wet and squelchy with blood. She slowed her pace as the road forked past the remains of a road sign, the reflective sheeting deteriorated by time and weather.

"Are you sure this is the right way?"

"Positive. It's been a while, but I went to the islands a lot before the Upheaval."

He didn't slow his pace at all, so she jogged to catch up, and then had to stop altogether as a racking cough doubled her over. Leonard backtracked, hovering near her and scanning the area nervously.

She caught her breath, clearing her throat to satisfy the itch. "Are there Revenants around?" she croaked.

"Yeah, pretty sure there are."

"Have they seen us?"

"Hardly matters since they certainly heard you. Let's go."

They started off again. The sun sank lower, throwing the road into shadow. Trees lined either side, providing ideal camouflage for hiding Revenants. Every whisper from the breeze became the threat of a stalking Revenant in Mac's mind. Her breath rasped in and out, impossibly loud to her ears. Her boot filled with blood; she could feel it splatter every time her heel came down and jabbed the glass into her flesh.

"Can't...keep...up," she panted.

Leonard threw a glance behind them. "Got to. We've picked up two or three nasties."

"Can't you, like, kill them or something?" She wrapped an arm over her injured ribs to ease the pain.

"What, do I look like Hercules or something? I'm not invincible. It's not far – we're almost to the terminal."

It sounded promising, in theory, but Mac hadn't failed to realize the problems the terminal itself presented. For one, it was doubtful that it was manned by anything other than sheltering Revenants. They would likely have to fight their way inside and then barricade themselves in a hopefully secure location to wait for dawn. For another, they would then have to find a way to hail anyone living on the islands to come and get her. She was fairly certain that finding a boat would be nigh impossible, not to mention the fact that she was completely unfamiliar with this area and would likely pilot a boat out to open sea, missing the islands completely.

She forced her legs to keep pumping, pounding past shadowy buildings and treacherous woods, pounding the glass farther into her heel until she was sure it was striking bone. Every step became an agony. She forced away thoughts of lying down and resting, afraid that in her fevered state, she would do just that and become a Revenant's meal. The road made an interminable curve, and around every bend she expected to run into a pack of waiting Revenants. The sound of the sea lapping the shore drowned out the scraping, stealthy sounds of the Revenants tracking them.

They broke from the trees and the harbor loomed on their right. Ahead, the sun fell on the deserted toll booths, limning them in golden light. Leonard veered off the main road and streaked past them. Mac followed, limping heavily as she tried to run on the ball of her foot, her starved lungs gasping in the cold sea air.

The waiting lanes for boarding the ferry were scattered with derelict vehicles. Leonard skirted around them. Mac followed, scraping along the side of one as she misjudged her trajectory. The door handle caught on her pants pocket, checking her flight and spinning her around, bringing her face to face with the Revenants on her heels. She spun back around and bolted after Leonard, not caring about the pain in her heel, not caring about not being able to breathe, not caring how much her ribs hurt, completely unnerved by the skittering grasp of Revenant fingers that had barely missed finding purchase in her jacket.

The terminal loomed ahead. Mac was sure her fever had spiked, for surely the sound of a motor was a hallucination spawned by her illness. Leonard pounded toward the dock. Mac pelted after him, flagging badly. Her body needed oxygen; the dark spots in her vision signaled it as surely as the futile bellowing of her lungs.

Leonard stopped on the dock, waving his arms like a lunatic, roaring, "WAIT! FOR GOD'S SAKE, WAIT!"

Mac stumbled and flailed for balance. A hand caught the back of her jacket and yanked. Unzipped, it slid off easily, catching on the revolver in her hand and jerking her around. Let go of the weapon and run – to where? – or fight over her jacket with a Revenant seemed to be her only choices. Without the gun, running would only postpone the inevitable.

She pulled, trying to free both her hand and the revolver, and succeeded in bringing the snarling Revenant within inches of her face. She fumbled through the folds of her sleeve and found the trigger. Snarling back, she pulled it. The Revenant jumped, a stain of blood spreading across its abdomen. It toppled over backward and lay twitching.

The other two howled with rage and lunged. Mackenzie was knocked off her feet from behind, shunted to the side as Leonard charged into the fray. The three Revenants erupted into a frenzy of snapping jaws and growled threats.

Mac climbed to her feet, aiming the revolver, but she couldn't tell one from the other, and she certainly wasn't skilled enough to pick the intruders off without hitting Leonard.

There was a shout behind her, and the hiss of wind by her ear. A crossbow bolt planted itself in the back of one of the Revenants and it fell to the ground, dead. Before Mac could comprehend this surreal event, a second arrow shot passed her, and the other Revenant fell.

Leonard turned, fixing Mac with a wild-eyed stare. "GO!"

A third arrow caught him in the chest. Mac's scream stuck in her throat, her labored lungs unable to voice it, as he fell backward onto the crumbling blacktop road.

Hands grappled her as she tried to run. She swung her fist wildly, beating back her aggressor. *"What have you done? He was my friend!"* She fell to her knees, sobbing. A face hovered in front of her, unfamiliar but human. Blessedly human.

The man gaped at her, disbelievingly, then laid a hand on her forehead. "Jesus, she's burning up. She must be hallucinating. Reynolds, let's get her to the boat and get the hell out of here."

Hands bore her away into the darkness. Her last glimpse of Ren Leonard was a motionless shadow sprawled on the ruined road.

32

Her fever had finally stolen her vision. It was the only explanation for the blurry haze that made her unable to focus. So Mackenzie closed her eyes again, grateful to sink back into deep sleep because being awake felt bloody awful.

When she next opened them, the blurriness was gone but something was clamped to her nose and seemed to be force-feeding her air. The air felt sterile and dry and made her sinuses ache. She reached up to remove the source and was stunned to find she could barely move her hand.

"You don't want to do that," advised an achingly familiar voice, laced with amusement. "Even if you could manage to lift your hand."

She licked her lips; dry and flaky skin had been liberally coated with something greasy with a disagreeable taste. But that wasn't the most important thing right now. That voice – it was impossible.

"Bon?" she croaked.

"The one and only." Bonfils Moreau stood up, leaning over her to reapply balm to her chapped lips. He smiled, but worry lurked in his eyes.

Now she knew where she was, and why the room was so bright. The infirmary. Something must have happened on the way back from the college campus. Her head throbbed so much she couldn't pull out a coherent memory.

Bon was beside her, alive and well. That meant everything had been a fever-dream: his execution, her banishment, Will's attempt to kill her. Elijah Riemer.

"Hey, hey! Why are you crying, Mac?" Bon grabbed a corner of her blanket, tugging it up to blot the tears spilling from her eyes.

Oh, couldn't he see that everything was going to be all right now? Sure, they were still in the Stronghold, but he was alive. Will was alive and had never tried to kill her. Elijah hadn't died trying to get to her before she fell into the clutches of a killer.

She smiled, or tried to. Everything hurt so much she couldn't tell if her muscles were obeying. All she wanted was to fall back asleep. "I feel awful."

He smiled again. "Of course you do. You've had pneumonia. They only took you out of the oxygen tent yesterday." His smile faded. "They say if we'd found you a day later, you might not have survived. You were in bad shape. Of course, the Revenants attacking you would have eaten you before anyone found you anyway."

"What happened?"

Before he could answer, movement on her other side claimed her attention. A plump young woman in a patterned shirt was wrapping something around her arm. She'd never seen a contraption like that before, and the woman wasn't a healer she remembered ever meeting. Mac tried to yank away, but she was too weak. Bon reached over her to hold her arm still. The band around her arm squeezed until it hurt.

"Ouch! Who the hell are you?"

"Let her do her job, Mac."

"I can't remember what happened. I dreamt it all, didn't it? While I was in a fever. I thought it was real. I thought *he* was real. I'm in the Stronghold infirmary, aren't I?"

"He who?" The woman asked brightly, not at all put off by Mac's resistance to her care. "And we don't call this an infirmary; we call it a hospital. Granted, our care is very limited, what with the shortage of doctors and surgeons, not to mention nurses and orderlies…"

"And supplies, and equipment, and technicians to run the equipment, and medicine…"

"And electricity."

"But at least we have plenty of oxygen tanks."

Bon and the young woman grinned at each other. Mac divided a blank look between them. Hospital? Surgeons? Orderlies? What the hell were they talking about?

"This isn't the Stronghold?"

"We call it Friday Harbor, because…well, that's what it's been called for almost three hundred years." When Mac still looked at her blankly, she clarified, "You're on San Juan Island. You made it over the mountains, Mackenzie. Barely alive, but you made it. You've been here two days. And you're still feverish, my dear – I think we need to make that clear. You're not out of the woods yet."

Mac hardly dared to breathe. "Elijah?"

Bon said, "I haven't seen him. Is he supposed to be here? Was he with you?"

Mac started crying again.

The nurse shushed whatever reply Bon was about to make. "Mackenzie, I'm Ivy. I'm a nurse here at probably the only hospital in existence. Welcome to the islands."

"What's a nurse?"

"It's like a healer, only better," Ivy said briskly. "I've heard about your settlement, and I'm not sure if I should be horrified that you had to live it, or if I should admire you for surviving it." She shook her head and directed her attention to Bon. "Ten minutes. I don't want you to exhaust her with all your inane chatter. She needs a lot of rest." She bustled off, leaving them alone.

"So, Mac, what the hell happened after I left? Who were you with? They found you alone, but you can't have come all this way by yourself."

"After you were executed," she said, distracted, and then, "You were executed!"

"Well, obviously I wasn't really executed. Just an elaborate hoax, delightfully perpetrated under the very noses of the Council of Elders. I came west with a couple of hunters who'd decided to defect a couple days before I was taken to the trees." He grinned.

"You let me think you were dead on purpose?" Anger flared inside her, dying a swift death because she didn't have enough strength to maintain it.

His expression turned hang-dog. "Yeah, well, sorry about that. Any number of things went wrong, and I came close to ending up dead for real. You were supposed to leave with me, but there was some interference in our carefully laid plans. In fact, things went so sideways that I don't think anyone knows I'm alive, even Elijah and Johanna."

"*Our* plans?"

"Mine, Riemer, Johanna. Mark from the detention room. And an unknown elder. But you're too sick for me to go into all the details right now – Ivy will be back soon to kick me out. When you're feeling a little better, I'll tell you everything, and you can tell me how you ended up here, out of your mind with fever and beat to hell and back – and alone. For now, you should go back to sleep. I'll come see you again after dinner."

He squeezed her hand. He was almost to the door when she finally screwed up her courage to tell him.

"Elijah is dead."

His smile faded. "Are you sure?"

Tears blurred her eyes again. "I was exiled. He was supposed to join me, but then Will Crawford showed up instead. And there were two teams of hunters looking for me, so we had to run—"

"Whoa!" Bon held up a hand to stop her, coming back to the bed. "Will Crawford is the last person Riemer would send in his place."

"I know that now."

"Did you see Riemer die?"

"No. Will told me. It happened before he left the Stronghold to find me. I didn't know until we reached the mountains. Will didn't tell me until Christmas."

Bon stared at her silently, intently, for so long that Mac began to feel self-conscious. She mopped up her face with the sleeve of her gown.

"When did you leave the Stronghold?"

"End of August."

He shook his head and gave a long, low whistle of admiration. "How the hell did he make you fall in love with him in four short weeks?"

"It doesn't matter," she said dully. "He's dead, so it doesn't really matter now."

Bon laid his hand against her cheek and smiled sweetly. His dark hair had grown out and was no longer spiked, but the blue eyes were the same: warm and kind. "I wouldn't believe a damn thing Will Crawford said."

"I guess." Maybe he was right. But she couldn't forget that Will hadn't lied about everything. "Ren Leonard is dead, too. I saw it happen. They shot him right in front of me on the ferry dock. He was only trying to help me, and they killed him."

He smoothed her hair off her forehead. "I'll ask around about it. You should sleep now. You're not well."

She drew in a breath, coughed it out. Phlegm rattled in her chest. "I don't think I'm going to get better, Bon. You should quarantine me."

He went very still. "Were you bitten?"

"No. Will said he infected me with the Revenant Virus. That's what is making me sick."

"Will did *what?* Why?"

"He tried to kill me. But just in case he failed, he wanted to make sure I died anyway. The essential part of me, anyway."

Dismayed, he drew away from her. "Okay. I'll talk to the hospital staff. Shit." Then he leaned closer and brushed a hand over her hair. "He could have lied, Mackenzie. He probably did. But we'll find a way to know for sure."

"And if I am? You'll…you won't let me kill anyone, right? You'll take care of it before then?"

He flinched, his fingers convulsing against her scalp and tangling into her hair. "We'll talk about it later. I'll be back after dinner. Sleep well, 'Kenz."

He was to the door again when she said, with quiet conviction, "Don't ever call me that again, Bon."

He nodded, troubled, and slipped out the door.

Mackenzie marked the passage of time by her dreams. Something about this didn't seem right, but her dream-self couldn't hold onto why. Bon leaned over her, asking how many Revenants had attacked her at the dock. Her dream-self told him twelve, but only three were visible. This made him laugh.

He came again, seemingly just seconds later, and said only three revenant corpses had been found. He couldn't confirm that Ren Leonard's was one of them. She told him Ren Leonard was at the college and was going to lie down in the sun. She was already lying there, and the summer sun was high and hot on her skin. Instead of laughing, Bon looked worried. He laid his hand on her forehead, and she tumbled into darkness.

Days later, she dreamed that Zane Allbrook sat in the chair beside her bed, a book in one hand propped on the cast that encased the other. Strange how her dreams had added the shadow of a beard along his jaw when she had never seen him anything but clean-shaven.

And then Johanna was hovering over her, her long blonde hair pulled back in a ponytail that emphasized the pallor of her face and the dark circles under her eyes. When she saw Mac's eyes open, her customary frown scrunched her forehead and she leaned closer, hissing, "You'd better get well, Mackenzie. Don't you dare break his heart."

The darkness swirled her away again. Blistering heat scorched her skin. She wanted to ask someone to get her a light blanket to shield her from the sun and a glass of water, but the field was empty. Dark and empty and blazing hot. A cool breeze washed over her face, moving down her neck and then her arms, making her shiver. The heat banished for the moment, she stared up at a starless sky. No, that was wrong. She had lain in this field beside Elijah and they had stared at the stars, millions of twinkling lights an unfathomable distance away.

But the stars weren't there. Neither was Elijah. A rattling sounded near her ear, and someone moved a feather over her face, but these were small curiosities compared to the loss of the stars. She stared hard into the darkness, willing them to appear. If they would just show their light, he would be there beside her. It must be so, because it had already happened.

Something rough and warm squeezed her hand and slid away. The rattling moved from her ear and pressed to her neck and then vanished completely. A light shined in one eye and then the other, making her flinch away in pain. The cool breeze came again, moving down her body. In the temporary respite, the world swam into focus for a brief second.

He sat slumped in a chair beside her bed, head tipped back and eyes closed, his dark blond hair ruffled against the top of the seat cushion. A thick cream-colored fisherman's sweater warded off the night chill and curled on his shoulder, tiny face tucked against his neck, a small grey kitten slept.

Mackenzie drank in the sight of him, hungry for more but happy enough with this tiniest glimpse from heaven. He shouldn't look so haggard and stressed, unless heaven was nothing like they'd believed. She could look at him forever, asleep like this, the kitten looking impossibly small and fragile on his wide, muscled shoulder. He had slain dragons and tended farms and now apparently nurtured cats.

But the darkness was seductive, while the dream hurt her head and destroyed her heart. So she let it go — let *him* go — and sank back into black oblivion.

While she slept, Elijah told her fantastic stories of betrayal and imprisonment and murder, of Johanna being socked in the eye and Catherine murdered as a traitor to the Council of Elders. They had been tied to the execution trees, but Zane Allbrook had zipped a crossbow bolt into them, and that had freed them.

Mackenzie wept at this, for now she knew how he had died: tied to the execution trees and Zane Allbrook's bolt through his heart. At least he wasn't alone; Johanna had been there with him to the last.

Roughness scraped the tears from her cheek. A whisper of a breeze caressed her face, scented with mint. "Don't cry, Mackenzie. Don't give up. Your life is precious, so fight for it."

But it was so hard, and she was so weak. Tired and weak. So she squinched her eyes closed, desperately seeking oblivion, falling into a black void that echoed with voices, quiet in volume but fierce in tone.

"If it's the Revenant Virus, we can inject her with blood from the vampire colony on Henry Island. It stops the deterioration; she won't become a Revenant."

"Don't call them vampires, Simon. They don't like that. It's just a blood disease."

"Sorry, Alia."

"She will still have some of the physical effects of mutation, though? And a life avoiding the sun and drinking liquid protein. Not what I call a winning solution, but at least she'd be alive."

And a quieter voice, a treasured voice, low in timbre and filled with awful certainty: *"She'd rather die than live that way, Bon."*

"Eli, it's our only option to save her. If we wait too long to find out if this is the Revenant Virus, it will be too late to inject her with the tainted blood. We lose her."

"Can we compare her blood to Revenant blood under the microscope? See if they have any of the same markers?"

"We're hardly scientists. There's no way to tell for sure."

"Can we at least try? Before we inject her and change her whole existence, can't we at least try to be sure?"

"There are no Revenants on the islands, Elijah. And how are you going to draw blood from one, anyway? You can't get close enough to one to stick it with a needle."

"I'll take the blood after I take its head. I need to go to the mainland. Bon, you're with me. Zane, no one touches her while I'm gone."

297

"The mainland is dangerous; there are too many Revenants to risk it. Besides, there's a storm rolling in, and you could get stuck there. You barely made it here from Orcas Island."

"When I heard about the girl they rescued who claimed a Revenant as a friend, I had to see if it was her. And now that I know it is, a storm is not going to stop me from trying to save her. No one does anything until I'm back with the blood sample. If I come back to find she's been injected with the tainted blood, I will have your heads. And I mean that literally."

The darkness sucked her down again, for a long, long time, to a place of cool air and no dreams.

33

When she opened her eyes again, it was to find a dim room with the curtains closed against the sun and a round, black face hovering over her. She recoiled. Full lips spread in a gap-toothed grin and the face retreated, allowing her to focus on the huge body the face belonged to. Built like a brick wall, this body should have produced a voice like a booming bass, but instead a high tenor laugh escaped those lips.

"Sorry about that. I didn't expect you to wake up right in the middle of the exam."

She licked her lips and found a desert landscape of cracked, flaking skin. "Ouch."

"Don't lick them. Here, I've got some balm." Remembering the oily, disgusting taste of the stuff Bon had smeared on her lips, she submitted reluctantly, pleasantly surprised when it felt more like wax than grease.

He chuckled, correctly interpreting her reluctance. "Beeswax and canola oil, not that nasty-ass stuff Ivy uses. They'll be right as rain in no time."

"Shouldn't your voice be deeper?" she asked in a deep frog-croak.

"Shouldn't yours be higher?" He winked, then reached down to the foot of the bed and dropped something on her chest, which immediately curled up and began to purr. "We believe in kitten therapy here. And puppy therapy, but you're in no condition to have a puppy romping all over you."

She stroked the grey fur. The kitten's tiny body rumbled with its purr. She had dreamed of the cat, and the cat existed. If only it were so easy where Elijah was concerned. But because Will hadn't always lied, she trusted that Eli's death was one of his truths.

"It's been a rough few days, Mackenzie, but your fever's broken, and your lungs are sounding clearer all the time." He held up a contraption that hung around his neck and ended with a flat round disk. "Ever seen one before? It's called a stethoscope. It allows me to listen to all the sounds inside you. Even the embarrassing ones."

He unhooked the prongs from around his neck and stuck them in her ears, pressing the disk again the kitten. Instantly, the purr amplified.

"Who are you?"

"I'm Simon, your nurse *du jour*. That means—"

"Of the day," she interrupted. "Yeah, they tried to teach us some French."

"Well, you lose most of it unless you use it. Except random things like *du jour* and all the curse words you ever learned." He grinned his gap-toothed grin again. "What serves as a doctor around these parts will be in shortly—"

"Did I mutate?"

Some of the laughter fled Simon's expression. "You weren't infected with the Revenant Virus, Mackenzie. It's just simple pneumonia, but we nearly lost you anyway."

"No tainted blood – vampire blood?" she persisted.

Simon frowned. "I'll let the doctor explain your state of health and just how high your fever was. High enough that you were hallucinating. We gave you so many cold baths this place was like an Alaskan swamp. And after the doc comes, you can have visitors. There's a pack of 'em waiting down the hall. Pathetic lot – they don't look like they've ate or slept in days."

Hallucinating. No injection of vampire blood. No Elijah Riemer. "I only know one person here."

"Well, then." He ruffled the kitten's fur with an impossibly large hand, sparking a furious purr and a luxurious stretch. "I'll just leave Cloudy here with you for moral support, since you're facing an empathetic mob of strangers."

"Cloudy?"

"Yeah, Cloudy with a Chance of Rain is her full name. We just call her Cloudy for short. You know – chance of rain…grey fur…grey clouds…oh, never mind. You've been sick too long to have a sense of humor."

Mac said, "Well, you know what they say about the difference between a duck with one wing and a duck with two wings."

"Oh? What's that?"

"It's just a difference of a pinion."

Simon laughed heartily all the way to the door. "I withdraw my callous opinion of your sense of humor."

True to Simon's word, the doctor arrived shortly after, a round little woman named Alia with shiny black hair and slightly slanted, exotic eyes. She pronounced Mackenzie well on the road to recovery and damn lucky to be alive.

A difference of a pinion, Mac thought, and immediately felt ashamed as she remembered Elijah's dream-words. *Your life is precious, so fight for it.*

"The vampire blood," she said as Alia scribbled notes on a clipboard. The doctor paused. "The tainted blood. Was I injected? Is that why the curtains are closed?"

"Well." Alia set aside the clipboard. "There was a scientific term for the blood disorder that comprised the healing half of the Revenant Virus, but you're right – it's commonly called the vampire virus. The other half of the virus – not a virus at all, but what they called a flesh-eating bacteria – is halted by a large amount of so-called vampire blood. You were not injected, because you were not infected with the Revenant Virus."

"But you were considering it, weren't you?"

Alia met her gaze steadily. "We *always* consider it, especially when a person who is ill is brought from the mainland. You were quarantined from the start, before you asked to be, just as a standard precautionary measure, and we discussed injecting you. That was three days ago. The day before yesterday, we got a Revenant blood sample and we were able to confirm you were not infected, so we did not need the tainted blood."

She went to the window and drew back the curtains. Sunlight flooded across the bed. Mackenzie's head felt the stab of a dozen ice picks from the wattage of the light, but her skin didn't burn. The doctor reclaimed her seat, this time not meeting Mackenzie's eyes. She looked troubled.

"As you can see, no reaction to the sunlight but a headache. Your blood is clear."

"Okay."

"I'm going to let your visitors in to see you in about an hour. I'm not going to limit their visiting time because I doubt they would listen to me anyway. If they tire you out, tell them to leave. Or I've found that falling asleep while they're in mid-sentence gets the message across pretty clearly." Alia smiled slightly as she rose again, this time going to the door, where she paused. She opened her mouth, then reconsidered her words, opting for the neutral "Try to rest until then so you're not too tired to see your guests." Still not looking at her, the doctor slipped out the door.

There was something wrong, something they didn't want to tell her. She wasn't infected with the Revenant Virus and they hadn't given her the tainted blood, but maybe her illness was worse than they were leading her to believe. Pneumonia was a tricky thing; one day you appeared to be getting better by leaps and bounds, and the next you were dead.

But worrying over her health took too much effort. Just being awake, her eyes squinched shut against the piercing beams of light pouring through the window, was too much effort in itself. She must have dozed for a while, for when she woke, the curtains were closed again, dimming the light to a tolerable level, and the chair beside the bed was occupied.

He was dozing too, leaning forward with his head resting on his folded arms on the bed, his face turned toward her. His nose and cheeks were chapped as though he'd been caught in a high wind. She wanted to touch him, just to see if you could touch a dream, but she couldn't make herself do it for fear of the vision vanishing.

Then Cloudy the kitten must have sensed she was awake, for it stretched and clambered over his head toward her. His eyes opened and blinked at her sleepily a few times before he realized she was staring back.

He said, "You're awake."

She said, "You're alive."

His mouth curved, not quite a smile. More like a grimace. "Somewhat worse for wear," he admitted. He reached out a hand, found hers, and curled their fingers together. "Nice to see you again, Mackenzie Bright Runner."

"Will told me you were dead," she whispered. The tears came then, the ones she'd held in check after Christmas night because shedding them seemed like letting go of Elijah Riemer, and she couldn't bear it.

"Hey now." He stood up, nudged her over, and claimed the space next to her on the bed, one arm snaking around her to pull her close to him, his leg hooking around hers to hold her there. "None of that. I'm not dead yet."

"Don't. Don't even joke about it." She pressed her face into his sweater, which smelled like sun and sea and mint.

"I'm sorry." He stroked her hair. His chest rose and fell beneath her cheek, a reassurance of his continued existence that she couldn't quite believe. "Mackenzie... Bon said when they found you, you were alone. Where is Will Crawford?"

Her mind flashed up an image of Will, snarling at her to get on her feet and take her machete, followed by another one of him crumpled at the bottom of a mountain ravine. She had no basis for this one, just Ren Leonard's word.

"At the bottom of a mountain."

He drew in a sharp breath and let it out slowly. "An accident?"

She laughed, a harsh bark that seemed to alarm him. He set her away from him a few inches and looked at her with concern.

"Hardly. Ren Leonard threw him there." Elijah's eyes widened. "After I planted a letter opener in what I hope was Will's kidney."

He flinched. "So it's true. Bon wasn't sure if it was a fever dream when you told him Will tried to kill you. God, I'm so sorry I wasn't there for you. I wasn't even sure you were still alive. They'd killed Catherine and came for the rest of us, so we knew they had control of you."

"How could you know that? Maybe I'd slipped away without them ever seeing me."

He smiled. "You're good but not so good you can elude twelve of the most ruthless killers I've ever seen. Or the most skilled gatherer. I knew as soon as they paired you with him that he couldn't be trusted. Remember I told you they usually make a clean sweep of a team?"

She flushed. "Yeah. And you said trust no one, but I did. I trusted him."

"Of course you did. That's who you are."

"Will said I'm naïve."

Elijah was silent for a moment, stroking her hair absently. "You want to believe the best of people. That means the council hasn't managed to squeeze out all of your compassion. Bon managed to save that part of you, which is what he and I set out to do when you were fifteen."

"Fifteen! But..."

He shushed her, and with a finger still held over her lips explained Laura's dire prediction that the council would choose her for hunting; how Bon and he had conspired to keep her from becoming as brutal and jaded as the hunters and most of the gatherers were from day after day of killing Revenants and fighting for survival; how thankful she should be that the council chose Will Crawford and not Juarez to be her new partner because Juarez would have just killed her the second he had an opportunity to make it look like an accident. Will was a seducer, and she wouldn't need to be seduced to be killed out of hand. The council had other plans for her, which bought the underground some time to counter them.

"Your wound was healing. They were going to put you back into rotation soon, which meant the council was ready to make their move on the underground. It was time for us to go so we could cross the mountains before snowfall. I swiped Ren Leonard's letter from your pack and gave it to my contact in the elders – that turned out to be Catherine, of all people. We planned your 'execution,' but Louis interfered. If all had gone according to plan, Johanna and I would have been brought to say goodbye, and we would all have been smuggled out together."

"You didn't tell me we were leaving that night."

"The fewer people who knew, the better. Especially if things went bad – which they did. Louis exiled you instead of sentencing you to die. When they killed Catherine, I thought they had captured you and that we were going to have to spring you from the detention center. Then Zane Allbrook said you might be with Will. The hunters looking for you all came back to the Stronghold, but Will was still gone. I knew then they were using you to dismantle the underground. We thought we found signs of you on the road here and there, but we couldn't be positive, and then there was nothing for a long time. When we got to the islands, I expected I'd find you on one of them before winter hit, but you never showed up."

"There were some setbacks which put us in the mountains after snowfall. We found a hotel in the mountain pass, and we holed up there. Things..." She bit her lip. How exactly did she explain what had happened with Will without revealing her gross assumptions about the depth of her relationship with Elijah? "Things got really strange after that. He wanted more than I wanted to give, and when I refused him, he decided to follow through with his mission to kill me and obliterate all signs of the underground."

His sharp gaze didn't miss the burning blush on her cheeks. Of course, being as ill as she was, the blush probably stood out like a blazing sunset.

"Hmm," he said, the corners of his mouth twitching. His hand moved up her back, cupped the back of her head, and brought her forehead-to-forehead with him. "Tell me everything," he whispered. "Every...last...detail." His smile this time was wide and wicked.

"You're a tease, Elijah Riemer."

"No, I'm a flirt."

"Yeah, you are."

"Only with you. So spill the beans. I want to hear all about you sleeping with the enemy." She pinched his side and he squirmed away. "Seriously, Mackenzie. Every last detail. Even the ones you don't want to tell me."

She swallowed over a sudden lump in her throat. "What, like how many stupid mistakes I made?"

"We all make mistakes. Tell me about your journey here, and I'll tell you how bad-ass it was when Zane Allbrook put a crossbow bolt through the guard, repelled down the wall, cut our ropes, and skewered no less than eight Revenants on our mad dash out of the city."

Her blush drained away. "You were really tied to the trees?"

"Yeah. Crawford might actually have thought he was telling you the truth when he told you I was dead; Louis probably told him they were executing me that day – a real execution this time."

"He said you asked to see him and gave him the medallion, told you to find me."

"Never happened. I think he stole Johanna's. Hers went missing just before we were arrested. And I never sent him in my place, Mackenzie. He's—"

"The last person you would send," she finished. "Yeah, I know that now."

And because that seemed as good an opening as any, she told him of seeing Will outside the house where she hid, picking the apples she planned to take, and everything after that seemed to just tumble out of her mouth, even the parts she didn't want to tell him, those gross assumptions that made her seem childish and foolishly obsessive.

When she finished, he stared at her for a long time, silent, thoughtful. Reserved. Again, Mackenzie sensed there was something very wrong. But when she pressed him to tell her, he simply smiled – a tired, troubled smile – and kissed her. She forgot about everything else and kissed him back. Which, of course, was how she found herself half-sprawled over him a half-hour later, her intimate exploration halted by his fingers wrapped around her wrist in a steel grip.

"We can't."

"I'm feeling better. All things considered."

He pressed his face into her neck, his one-armed embrace tightening to the point of discomfort, his fingers still around her wrist, keeping her in check.

"I'm old enough," she said evenly, and he laughed reluctantly. "Just in case you subscribed to Johanna's belief that 'only seventeen' is too young to be involved with you. Besides, I'm eighteen now."

He pulled away. His eyes were sad. "I didn't want to have this conversation today."

She knew it. There was definitely something wrong, something that made even the doctor avert her eyes. Maybe she escaped the Revenant Virus only to fall victim to another illness just as bad – or worse.

"I know something is wrong. What is it? Am I dying? Elijah, you'd better tell me if I'm dying. You can't keep that from me." He laid a finger across her lips again and she fell silent. He struggled for several minutes to speak.

"I feared I'd never you see again. And when you were found damn near dead, I'd have given anything to save you. Anything." He drew in a steadying breath. He removed his finger to cup her face. "As it turns out, I gave everything. But that's okay, because God knows I love you."

Mackenzie's heart rapped frantically at her ribs, shrieking alarm, her fear eclipsing the joy his admission should have given her. She couldn't force her voice above a whisper. "What are you saying?"

"Bon and I went to the mainland, hunted up a Revenant so I could get a blood sample to compare to yours. I got one, all right." He swallowed hard. Dread bloomed black and suffocating inside her. "Maybe I'm off my game. Spent too long growing cabbages and lost my edge."

Horrified, she whispered, "You were bitten."

"Sprayed with blood." Now he seemed to be having trouble breathing. His chest hitched. "In my mouth. My eyes."

With one blink of an eye, I was screwed.

"You're – you're—" The word stuck in her throat, jammed between her horror and her disbelief at this living nightmare. She walked all this way, suffered weather and hunger and thirst, battled cannibals, fought Will to the death, and crawled out of the abyss of a near-fatal illness – only to lose him anyway? "What if you're wrong? You can't know this soon."

"Alia draws blood twice a day. She confirmed it this morning. I'm infected." He held her gaze while spoke, steady and calm. How he managed it, she couldn't even fathom. She wanted to rage and scream and make God take it back. He couldn't do this to them after all they'd been through. It wasn't right.

"Then I'll be infected too from kissing you."

He shook his head. "You know better. Blood transfer only. Saliva doesn't infect. But I can't make love with you; I can't risk you becoming pregnant. God only knows what would…well."

"You could stay here, in quarantine. Maybe…maybe you'll be like Ren Leonard …and …and …"

"The odds are astronomical. And we still wouldn't be able to be together." His smile came again, sad, twisted. And then it fractured as he broke. "I'm a dead man, Mackenzie."

34

It was time to go.

Mackenzie limped to the dock, her hand gripping Elijah's so tightly she thought their flesh would meld. They climbed into the boat with Zane, Johanna, and Bon and sat huddled close together, their backs to the wind. His thumb stroked hers compulsively, as though for luck.

But they both knew they were out of luck. Any hope that Alia misinterpreted his blood samples vanished yesterday when he'd awakened with a high fever, body aches, and tiny blue flecks mixed with the green of his irises. Revenant blue.

Elijah had a plan that required cognizant thought and a gun.

Mackenzie only had two hours to talk him out of it.

But as the boat slipped into the channel between Shaw and Lopez islands, he turned in his seat, taking both her hands, and said quietly, "Let's not argue away our last two hours together." He raised her hands to his lips and kissed her fingers.

She bit back the words that hovered on her lips: "Are you sure we can't try the vampire blood?" A changed existence such as that was surely better than either the Revenant Virus or ceasing to exist. But in the tests Alia and Simon performed, his mutating blood neutralized the tainted blood; the Revenant Virus had progressed too far. They crossed it off as an option two days ago. Mackenzie spent that entire night crying.

Elijah distracted her with a memory from his childhood, drawing her into a half-hearted conversation with him and Bon about their shared experience of the Foster Parent section of the Stronghold. Zane's head was tipped back and he was watching puffy white clouds drift across the sky, absently caressing the plaster cast that encased the wrist he'd broken while fishing. Johanna was silent, her usually scowling expression absent. She looked like she had cried all night. Mackenzie let Elijah sidetrack her, because she knew deep down inside that his plan was the only viable option. The tainted blood wouldn't work on him. The Revenant Virus would turn him into a violent, conscienceless animal. Ending it before he became a danger was the only solution.

The dock came into view. Her heart thudded wildly as though sensing its impending, fatal break. His fingers tightened around hers; she couldn't tell if it was in reassurance or fear. He didn't look scared; he looked resigned, and the glances he sent her were searching and worried.

Reynolds cut the engine and turned the rudder so the boat floated up to the dock pole to which they'd attached an iron ladder. Although the largest she'd ever seen, the boat must be small compared to the old ferries, judging from how the dock dwarfed it.

Elijah drew in a deep breath and stood up. Mackenzie couldn't move. Denial paralyzed her. This couldn't be happening – they'd only been given six weeks together, total, since Bon left the Stronghold, and one week of that she had spent in fevered hallucinations. His hand tugged her upward and her body obeyed. Her feet carried her across the deck to the ladder before her mind finally shouted it back into paralysis. She stopped, her hands clutching the iron rungs that still vibrated from Bon's journey up. Elijah's hands came down on her shoulders from behind, squeezing gently. Pressed against her back, the heat of his body confirmed his fever was rising dangerously.

His lips at her ear, he whispered, "If staying on this boat would stop this virus, I would never set foot on land again so I could be with you. But we know that's just a wish, and wishing won't change what's happened."

Tears overflowed her eyes despite her attempt to stave them off. "This is my fault. If I hadn't believed Will when he said he infected me, you wouldn't have gone to the mainland."

"Oh, Mackenzie, no. No, no, no." He pried her hands off the ladder rung and turned her around, cradling her face between his hands and forcing her to look at him. "No. I went to the mainland because saving your life was more important than the risk to mine. Nobody blames you for this, least of all me."

"Johanna does."

"No, she doesn't, actually. We have to do this. I know you have the hardest part now, but I know you have the courage to make it through this. Be brave for me and climb up."

She did, because his last minutes with her shouldn't be spent witnessing her falling apart. That could come later, when she was back on the island where he couldn't see it.

Johanna was already crying when they arrived topside. She flung herself into his arms and clutched him in a death-grip, sobbing into his shirt. Elijah held her tightly, exchanging a look of desperate sorrow with Bon over her golden head. At length, he prised her off him and held her at arm's length, talking to her in a voice too soft for Mackenzie to hear what he said. Then he kissed her forehead and moved her aside to shake hands with Zane, to whom he said something that, again, Mackenzie couldn't hear. She suspected it was about her from the way Zane's gaze cut to her and then away again as though burned.

Bon handed Elijah something Mackenzie couldn't see, which he tucked into the back waistband of his pants under his shirt. They exchanged an embrace that involved a lot of thumping and pounding on each other. Ordinarily, she would have found this amusing, but she didn't think she'd ever laugh again.

At last, he turned back to her and pulled her against him. His arms were strong and warm around her. Minutes passed, filled with the sound of the surf and the cries of gulls and Johanna's quiet sobbing. He buried his face in her neck. Mackenzie held onto him, willing God to freeze them in this moment, stop time, stop everything, and just let them be here forever, together like they were supposed to be.

And then they were cheek-to-cheek, their tears mingling. And then forehead-to-forehead. He gripped her so tightly for a moment that she couldn't breathe, and then he released her by degrees. An inch between them and then two, three, six. He brushed a finger across her cheek, sweeping away the tears, and tried a smile.

Nearly strangling on her tears, she said, "I love you, Elijah, *please*. There has to be something we haven't thought of."

He shook his head. "We've gone over it and over it. There's no other way." He kissed her quick and hard, once, twice, three times. Then deeper and longer.

"Oh, I do love you, Mackenzie Bright Runner," he whispered fervently.

And then he slipped out of her grasp and she let him go, powerless to stop him, impotent in the face of fate. He took four steps backward, his eyes locked on hers, and then he turned and walked away. He didn't look back as he cut through the ferry lanes, becoming smaller and harder to see, slipping between cars and passing the tollbooths, at last merging onto Ferry Terminal Road.

And, finally, he was gone, vanishing around a curve in the road.

"Come on, Mackenzie," Bon said quietly. "Back to the boat."

"Maybe he won't...he could come back and..."

Johanna took her arm. "He's not coming back. Let's go. The deal was he let you come to the dock if you left without a fight. You promised him." She tugged Mackenzie toward the boat.

It was only that promise that allowed her feet to move, that propelled her to the ladder and down it, that anchored her body in her seat as Reynolds piloted the boat back into the strait to return to the island. Johanna put her arm around her shoulders and she closed her eyes, every nerve in her body on alert for it. It seemed an eternity passed before it came.

The gunshot echoed across the water.

Mackenzie shattered.

Walking away from them took every ounce of strength Elijah Riemer possessed. The revolver Bon Moreau had covertly passed to him pressed against the base of his spine, a malignant reminder of fate's shitty sense of justice. It was only fair, he supposed, that after taking so many Revenant lives, his would end with their curse coursing through his blood.

He felt her eyes boring into his back as he sidled between derelict cars abandoned in the ferry lanes and skirted the tollbooths, a strangely comforting sensation, as though part of her walked with him. And then he rounded a curve in the road, and she was gone. The boat motor was a distant, reassuring purr: they were leaving, as they had promised. No witnessing his last moments, no more scars to carry through their lives.

With his eyes closed, he could almost picture the scene: the boat skimming through the lapping waves. Gulls wheeling over-head, crying as though in sympathy with their loss. Johanna sob-bing. Bon manfully choking back his own tears.

Mackenzie dying inside.

He opened his eyes, pushing the image away as fast as he could manage. His heart could not linger on her or he would never be able to do this. There was no need to go any farther. From here, they wouldn't be able to see, but they would be able to hear, and they would know.

No sense in delaying. He felt like shit, feverish and achy. And heartbroken and cheated and everything in between. The pistol was heavy in his hand. He snapped the cylinder out, checked that rounds filled all the chambers, and snapped it back in. A chipmunk scurried out of the trees on his right, darted past him and into the tall grass on the other side of the road. He watched it go, bemused but hardly interested enough to see what scared it, then closed his eyes and raised the gun to his temple.

"Do you people ever do any-fucking-thing right?" An icy hand gripped his wrist and twisted the barrel away from his head.

Riemer flowed with the movement and used his momentum to turn the wrist-hold on his assailant and flip him, only to find a frigid arm around his throat in a chokehold. The gun was wrested from his grip, and he was released with a small shove that put some distance between them. He whirled around, striking a defensive posture, which made the Revenant laugh sardonically.

"Good luck."

He blinked in astonishment at the creature draped in a leather duster and scuffed engineer boots, a wide-brimmed felt hat crammed on top of his head. Sunglasses threw his reflection back at him before they were yanked off. Bloodshot eyes, dilated pupils ringed in vibrant blue, swept over him from head to foot, squinting against the bright day. "Blond hair, green eyes, muscle-bound, and tragically brokenhearted. Let me guess – you're the guy she was hell-bent on finding."

Riemer raised his chin a fraction, straightening slowly, warily, a niggling suspicion dialing back his alarm a fraction. "Who the hell are you?"

The Revenant shook his head. "And she said you were brilliant. Well, there's no truth in advertising anymore. Bright Runner," he barked, and Elijah jumped, startled. "Did she die? Is that why you're out here with a gun to your head?"

"You know Mackenzie?" It was coming together now. "You're Ren Leonard."

"Yeah, not for much longer if I don't get out of the sun," the Revenant growled. "And not for the lack of the goddamn islanders trying to kill me." He rubbed his chest. "Thank God for breastbones and lousy archers. So when did she die?"

"She didn't."

"Ah. Did she reject you and now you can't bear the pain of living without her? How poetic. She told me about you, but she failed to mention your flair for the dramatic." He spun the gun in his hand so he was holding the barrel and held it out, the grip toward Riemer. "You stick it under your chin and fire upward into your brain. Less chance of the bullet bouncing off your skull and giving you a concussion instead of nirvana."

Elijah took the gun. "Well, one thing she was right about: you're a sarcastic son-of-a-bitch."

"Yeah, one of my many character flaws. So what's the story, Romeo?"

"The name's Elijah Riemer. The only story is the same old tired tragedy: one miscalculation, a lot of blood spray, and next thing you know, your eyes are turning blue."

Leonard's eyes popped wide for a second, then squinted again. "Well, that fucking sucks."

"I'd say 'try it from my end,' but you already have."

"How long have you been sick?"

"I was infected a week and a half ago."

"And you're just now coming on feverish? Eyes just now changing?"

"Yeah."

The Revenant pinned him with an unnerving, silent stare for a long moment. "The slower the symptoms, the better the chance you end up like me."

"I don't *want* to be like you. Hence, the gun. So as soon as you move along"—he motioned with the gun, making Leonard duck—"I can get this done."

"I get it now. You're out here being noble. You won't become a ravaging animal but you won't let her see you die, either. Is she waiting for the shot?"

"Yes. I don't want her to wonder if I chickened out. She'd hesitate to kill a Revenant because she'd be wondering if it was me."

"Then fire the goddamn gun and let's get going."

Elijah laughed sourly. "Going? I'm not going anywhere. As soon as you leave, I'm putting a bullet in my brain."

Leonard chuckled. "Sure you are." Faster than Riemer believed possible, the Revenant grabbed his hand, aimed the gun skyward, and pulled the trigger. Elijah gaped at him, outraged.

"What the *hell* was that?"

"Eight years in the Marine Corps, paying off yet again. Oorah! Now that that's out of the way..." He yanked the gun away again, snapped out the cylinder and dumped the bullets into his hand. One hearty fling sent them into the trees. Another hurled the gun as good measure. "You can't shoot again or she'll think you botched the job and are out here turning yourself into the first Revenant vegetable. Let her live thinking you're a man who got things done the right way."

"I can just go find the gun and the bullets and shoot myself later."

Leonard shook his head. "Fucktards, the whole human race," he muttered. "Come with me, bright eyes. We can reach the county jail long before you go full-fledged ape-shit on me. Lock you up nice and tight until we know if you're still among the higher intelligence."

Nonplused, Riemer watched the Revenant walking away. As a last protest, he called out, "And what if I *don't* turn out like you? What if I'm like...them?"

Leonard stopped and turned back toward him. He put his sunglasses on and said evenly, "Then I'll kill you myself. But if you're like me...well. You can still protect her, just not the way you expected. I admit there are a lot of fringe benefits you'll miss out on, but that girl will keep you plenty busy otherwise. A walking magnet for danger."

Riemer couldn't deny that.

"Daylight's burning – thank Christ – and we have things to do."

"What things?" His eyes narrowed suspiciously. "Are you going back to the Stronghold?"

"Nope. But she is." Leonard pointed in the general direction of the departing boat. "She's probably in no condition to travel right now, but by next summer, maybe the summer after, she'll be on her way to bring them some justice, unless I haven't learned a fucking thing about women in my very long life. Are you coming or are you going after that gun?"

Without waiting for an answer, the Revenant spun around and

stalked off. "What do you know about solar power?" he called over his shoulder.

"Not a damn thing. Why?"

"You don't think I sat around for a century doing nothing, do you? How about biology?"

"Basic anatomy and genetics. What we could learn from the books we could find."

The Revenant shook his head resignedly. "It's a start. If you love that girl, you'd best come with me. I won't keep asking."

"*Why* you're asking is what bothers me. You could have let me kill myself. Or you could have killed me."

"Well, I couldn't very well do that, not when you belong to Mackenzie Bright Runner. She'd be pissed and she knows some pretty cool ninja moves I don't want her using on me."

Interesting. Extraordinarily interesting, but not surprising, even considering Ren Leonard was Revenant, and Revenants weren't known for forming emotional attachments. Mackenzie did have a way of drawing people to her and then, somehow, she became the center of their universe.

"What's a ninja?" And when Leonard didn't respond, he added, "If I come with you, where are we going? I mean, if I'm not…"

"First stop: Wyoming. I've got a mega shit-ton of stuff to grab there."

"And what are we gonna do with your mega shit-ton of stuff?"

Leonard grinned over his shoulder. If Riemer hadn't been so ill, he'd have been scared shitless by that nightmare smile.

"We are going to save the world, Elijah Riemer."

After a long moment of consideration, Elijah followed after him.

 **Sharon Gerlach** was in training to be a ninja, but a dismaying lack of physical grace and balance—not to mention the inability to keep her big mouth shut—ended her ninja career before it had really begun.

Now she writes. She doesn't write about ninjas because that's obviously a sore subject. But she writes about other really cool things and figures someone else will cover the ninjas. Life's really not all about ninjas, anyway.

Sharon lives on the dry side of the Pacific Northwest with her husband (who must really be fond of her as he hasn't left her yet despite her ninja failings), her three kids and two grandkids (none of whom possess ninja qualities either), and four cats. Yes, you guessed it—ninja cats!

Website: sharongerlach.com
Twitter: twitter.com/SharonGerlach
Facebook Fan Page:
http://www.facebook.com/AuthorSharonGerlach

**Turn the page for a preview of the
next book in the Revenant Chronicles**

July 2160

Mackenzie woke to the sun pounding down on her and the smell of burning flesh in her nose. She opened a cautious eye to the back of a pair of worn boots, denim pants tugged neatly over their tops.

"How many times do I have to tell you I'm perfectly safe up here with the wall guards?"

Rico Garcia grunted a response but didn't defend himself. He stood with one hand arched over his forehead, shielding the field glasses he looked through. Finding no sense in drifting back to sleep, she stood and stretched.

"What's wrong?"

"Could be nothing. You'd better get up, though. I called for Bon and Zane already."

"Let me see."

He handed over the field glasses and pointed southeast. She could see the smoke with her naked eye, though the fire looked small. Probably another Revenant caught in the sunlight. It happened occasionally, if they were injured or killed in a fight with another pack and left for dead out of reach of the shade.

The field glasses could only confirm that the fire was small, because what burned lay behind a row of derelict houses, leaning drunkenly against one another as support beams disintegrated beneath heavy roofs. Most of the city was falling apart; the Stronghold could only save what their manpower allowed.

Footsteps behind her signaled the arrival of Bon and Zane. As she handed the field glasses to Bon, she stepped backward into his shadow, finding respite from the sun. It was going to be a scorcher today, and she silently willed the field glasses to show him something she had missed that would make investigation unnecessary.

"From the position of the smoke, I'd say it's in a front yard. We'd better check it out to be sure the house isn't going to catch fire."

Damn. Mackenzie heaved a mental sigh. She reached down for her pack, which had served as a pillow. Always kept ready for her immediate departure, it traveled everywhere with her, just in case. Never again would she be outside these walls with just the clothes on her back.

"How far away, do you think?"

"Maybe a mile," Bon estimated

"We can rappel down from here and take off," Zane suggested. "Be back in time for breakfast, with any luck. It's just coming on seven-thirty."

Too damn early to be awake, Mac thought, especially for Zane. He had an eighteen-month-old daughter and a pregnant wife, which meant no one in his quarters was getting adequate sleep. Bon and Johanna had a four-year-old boy who slept in a near-comatose state, so by comparison he looked well rested and alert.

"Say goodbye to your families," Mackenzie said, quietly but firmly. "I'll meet you downstairs at the front doors."

They didn't argue. Bon simply handed the field glasses to Rico and headed back down the concrete bleachers to go inside, Zane keeping step beside him and talking in a low voice – probably about her having slept outside on the wall again. These days, people listened to Mackenzie Bright Runner when she spoke. She wasn't in charge – not of the Stronghold, nor of her team of long-distance foragers – but people tended to defer to her unofficial authority, quite possibly because of the manner in which she'd returned to the settlement and cleaned house.

Those who wish to stay under these terms may do so without prejudice or suspicion. But if you're caught trying to subvert the new government, you will be relocated to the crummiest part of the city I can find, and I may or may not allow you to keep the clothes on your back.

Some feared her, perhaps, but mostly they respected her, enough to allow without question her strange quirks and preferences. Her insistence on saying goodbye to loved ones was one of those quirks. Life outside these walls was dangerous and unpredictable, and a good day could turn into your last faster than you could blink.

With one blink of an eye, I was screwed.

The memory made her flinch. She studiously avoiding looking any farther to the southeast than the wispy trails of smoke. In an effort to move forward, unfettered by the past, she hadn't been to Ren Leonard's college campus in two years. They passed it frequently when heading out on their long scavenger hunts but never ventured onto the campus. The last time she had, it was only to assure herself that Ren's building was empty. Four Revenants on the dock, and only three corpses had been found. Six years later her foolish heart still wanted to believe Ren Leonard's was the one missing.

"Something else, Mackenzie," Rico said. He was looking through the field glasses again, this time west toward the old highway. "I don't see the island group on the highway yet."

"What time did they leave?"

"Five-thirty. Too soon yet, maybe? They had some kids with them. Sampson's leading, says he's gonna stay on the islands this time."

She didn't ask if he'd be able to see them on the highway. The field glasses were powerful. He should have been able to see them as soon as they crossed the suspension bridge and passed out of the forest.

"Could be they had an injury or something. Maybe they're coming back. That will put them a few days behind."

"Here, your eyes are better. You might be able to see them even if I can't."

Mackenzie took the field glasses obligingly. It wasn't that her vision was better; it was that her paranoia was sharper. She trusted that nothing would go right until after it had; and even then, she was wary.

She aimed toward the suspension bridge and followed the tree line to the parkway that led to the old highway. Nothing moved – wait! No, just deer, grazing in the sun. It seemed amazing that the Revenants hadn't wiped them all out, but it appeared that deer were somewhat like cockroaches: thick as fleas on a rabbit and impossible to get rid of. That boded well for the Stronghold, which relied on venison to feed their growing population.

Nothing moved out on the highway. If something moved in the forest, she couldn't tell. So she backtracked the route from the suspension bridge and into the neighborhood just south of the Stronghold, looking for signs of the party returning.

Not that block. Nor that one. Nor the next – whoa. Had that been movement between the houses?

She trained the glasses between that block and the next and waited. Several minutes passed. Rico said, "What is it?" and she shushed him. A moment later, she caught another flash of movement. There was definitely something down there, moving slowly through the neighborhood.

She pointed. "Something's there, moving along Princeton but could be cutting through yards. Might just be a deer."

They watched. Rico pointed, this time half a block closer.

"Saw something there."

Mackenzie adjusted the focus and the glasses slipped out of her sweaty hands. She caught them by the strap just before they hit the wall.

"Lucky save."

"Zane would kill me. He hacked up four Revenants single-handedly to get these."

Bringing the glasses back to her eyes, she swung back toward the neighborhood and nearly recoiled at the bloody, shambling figure that filled her vision before disappearing behind an overgrown hedge.

"Jesus! Someone's down there. Come on, come on! Get past the shrubs."

As though hearing her command, the figure stumbled out from behind the hedge and into the middle of the street, swaying on its feet, one hand reaching toward the Stronghold as though beseeching.

"Oh, God, it's Sampson!" She shoved the field glasses into Rico's hands, snatched up her pack, and grabbed the emergency rope that would let her rappel down the outside wall.

"Mackenzie, wait!"

She didn't. The rope in her hands and swinging between her knees, she climbed over the side of the wall and began a hand-under-hand descent as fast as she could go. When she was a safe distance down, Rico climbed onto the rope above her. Mackenzie dropped the last five feet to the ground, shouting for Zane and Bon even as she sprinted past Benny Jacobs' bleating goats toward Princeton Avenue. Pounding footfalls behind her assured her that at least Rico had followed.

Dust in her face, thrown up by her feet slamming bare dry dirt, then by Bon's and Rico's feet as they overtook her. A stitch in her side, reminding her to breathe right when she panicked and ran. Glass in her joints as her bones jarred and scraped together.

John Sampson fell just seconds before they reached him. Not a dramatic fall, like the theater troupe that put on plays a couple times a year in the Stronghold. Instead, he crumbled, as though the bones in his legs had collapsed in on themselves.

The men reached him first, and it was a credit to their expertise that they didn't all bark confusing questions at the same time.

"Sampson, it's me, Bon Moreau. What happened? Where's the group?"

Sampson's mouth worked to form words. His face twitched. Mackenzie panted to a stop, bending forward with a hand on her knee and the other pressed to the stitch in her side. Sampson's eyes went wide.

"K-ken...zzzie," he gasped, and she dropped to her knees beside him. His hands clutched at the air, and she caught them in hers.

"I'm here, John. I'm here. What happened? Who did this to you?"

"F-f-fah...therrr...apaaaaaahh..." Her blood ran cold as he tried again. "F-fatherrrr ... of ... apaaahclipsss."

Stricken, she raised her gaze to find Bon, Zane, and Rico staring at her. *Father of the Apocalypse*, John Sampson was trying to say.

Ren Leonard.

www.ingramcontent.com/pod-product-compliance
Lightning Source LLC
Chambersburg PA
CBHW020248200626
46816CB00001BA/185